CW00420254

the pucking coach's daughter

S. Massery

contents

To the girlies who can't pick just one book boyfriend:
Have three. You're welcome.

Special thanks to Kristy, Brittany, Maria, Alaina, Beth, Lindsey, and Maddy for your support!

---

patreon.com/smassery

introduction

Hello dear reader!

If you've read me before (especially my Hockey Gods series), you know they run quite dark.

This book contains themes common to dark romance, including bullying, blackmail, stalking, non consent and dubious consent, blood and knife play, primal/chasing, and somnophilia. This story also includes attempted sexual assault, torture (briefly described), self harm, and a sprinkle of murder.

Stay safe out there, friends, and happy reading!

xoxo,
    Sara

one
sydney

I'm not a stalker.

Yes, I'm outside of his house. And yes, I'm wearing all black, so close to the bushes of his across-the-street neighbor's that I'm practically in them.

But that's because of necessity, not *obsession*.

He has something of mine.

Okay... it's not mine. It *should* be mine, which is why I'm outside his house. The fact that he lives in an actual house in a fine neighborhood and not some shitty apartment with three other guys is appalling and unfair, although I try not to dwell on that. The listing online shows a different name, which means he splurges on what is probably rent every single month to live alone.

We're three blocks from campus. If I strain my listening, the distant music floats on the air from parties taking place closer to campus. The guy who lives in the house left—hopefully for those parties—an hour ago.

Now I'm just being paranoid.

But it's now or never, and the longer I wait, the more chance I have of him coming back and discovering me. Worst-case scenario, he's the type to shoot first and ask questions later. Best-case scenario, second to not getting caught at all, is that he doesn't believe in violence.

Which... well, let's just say that's fucking doubtful.

I look around and step out of the bushes, pulling my black scarf up over my nose and mouth. I don't run to the door, or around the side. I stroll up with my hands in my pockets like I belong there.

The fake rock with the spare key is easy enough to find, even in the dark. I saw him crouched in this spot just two nights ago, weaving a little in some drunken stupor, and hold up the key like it was cherished treasure.

I'll tell you what's cherished—the object I came to take back.

The rock houses a plain silver key, which I use to unlock the door. There are no alarms or security system, luckily. I close myself in and pause, standing in the front hallway.

Immediately in front of me are stairs leading to the second floor and a hallway that goes alongside it on its left. Another hallway to my right would take me into the living room, I'd guess. A large doorway on my right reveals a front sitting room.

The idea of a bachelor having a sitting room, hosting parties or whatever there, has me second-guessing my whole idea of this guy. For all intents and purposes, the house is *neat*. At least, from here. There's no clutter, no coats or shoes kicked off right by the door like in my house.

Even the sitting room seems proper, with the brief glance around that I give it.

Shuddering at the monstrosity of *money*, I start upstairs.

There are just two bedrooms and a bathroom between them up there. One bedroom is on the smaller side, with a daybed covered in pillows, a desk facing the front window, and a closet closed up tight.

The other bedroom finally has a hint of being lived in. There's a single pair of jeans crumpled on the floor beside the hamper, the closet doors are open, the bed is made but not well.

I hum and go to the dresser. There's a box on top, like a men's jewelry box sort of thing. I flip it open and click on my flashlight, examining the contents.

Cuff links, a necklace chain, another one with a pendant on it, a few bracelets—but not the one I need.

Great.

I close it and take stock of the room, making a beeline for the nightstands. The first one reveals packets of condoms, lube, freaking lotion. I gag and push past it, but besides a crinkled magazine, that's it. On the other side of the bed, I have worse luck.

It's empty.

Sighing, I go back to the desk in the other bedroom. I rifle through the drawers, open the guy's laptop—it's password protected, of course, but his name is right above the blinking cursor. Confirming that I am in the right house, at the very least.

Voices outside catch my attention. I rush to the window, turning off my flashlight, and watch as the guy comes up the sidewalk with another guy and two girls.

Fuck me.

At the last second, my gaze lands on the binder on the edge of the desk.

It's familiar. Not like, that exact one is familiar. But the binder style—

Whatever. I grab it and flip it open, and my breathing stops. Without thinking, I take pictures of every fucking page.

And then my time runs out because the front door opens.

I close the binder and place it exactly where I found it, backing away from the desk. It was the only thing I truly messed with, but hopefully no one will notice.

They turn on lights as they go, heading thankfully toward the back of the house. I wait a moment, their laughter drifting toward me in waves and ebbs. They don't sound particularly drunk, but I can't risk them taking their gathering to the bedrooms.

I creep down the stairs, peering over the banister. My scarf is in place, as is my black cap. My hair is tucked up into it. I don't see them from where I stand, and after waiting another long moment, I make a run for it.

A quiet run, but it doesn't really work. The floorboards creak; my breathing sounds loud in my ears.

"Hey!" a voice shouts.

I glance over my shoulder, meeting the gaze of the owner of the house.

His hazel eyes burn into me, somewhere between confused and *pissed*. He fills the hallway, my adrenaline and fear making him seem bigger than life.

He's just a guy. A regular douchebag.

When he steps toward me, I burst into motion again. I sprint out and away from that fucking house, although I will most likely return when he's not expecting it.

He has it, I just need to *find* it.

I look back more than once, but the street stays empty. The asshole decided I wasn't worth the time. Or he saw that I wasn't carrying anything...

My car is parked three blocks away. I jump in it like I'm still being chased—like I was being chased at all—and make a quick U-turn. I speed away, laughing at myself. At my stupidity.

What the fuck was that?

Why did he come back so early?

Ten minutes later, I'm back in the safety of my own town. I peel off the scarf and cap, tossing them both in my backseat, and head straight to my apartment one block up from my school's campus.

Except when I get there, my best friend and roommate is standing in the doorway waiting for me. Her hand is behind her, and she's wearing a tight, short dress. She eyes me up and down and reveals what she's holding: a matching dress.

"We're not going out," I groan.

"We are," Lettie argues. "We're going to the biggest bash of the year."

Biggest might be an exaggeration. The *biggest* is usually at the beginning of the year to kick off hockey season. This one is to celebrate the start of our hockey team's *playoff* run. Because here, hockey is absolutely everything.

If it doesn't have to do with hockey, it doesn't exist.

I sigh and hold out my hand for the glittery blue dress. She squeals in reply and kisses my cheek, ushering me to get ready faster. I forget about my unsuccessful break-in and do my makeup and hair, and within the hour we're arm in arm, strolling up to the huge house party.

Lettie, aka Scarlett Blake, comes from old money. She and I were put together freshmen year. She wasn't getting an apartment off campus immediately because she wanted to, in her words, *slum it like a real college freshman*. Like me.

I was so poor, I didn't have two nickels to rub together. I lived off of the meal plan, used the class textbooks the library had, did all my online work in the computer room, and went out if there was free liquor.

It was a miracle I had made it to college at all, but I digress.

Lettie and I got along okay at first, better once she understood I wasn't being purposefully cheap.

Now we're sophomores, about to be juniors, and that so-called *slumming it* phase is officially over. Lettie didn't give me a choice in the matter. I think she secretly covers more of the rent than I do, simply because she wanted something out of my budget.

And it's still tight.

But that's fine. I'd rather live with Lettie and scrape together rent each month than have to figure out how to navigate living with someone else.

Even if she drags me out to parties when I just want to crawl into bed and cry. It's my way of paying her back, in a way.

She takes the lead inside the house. It's packed, the music so loud I'm not sure how anyone can hear each other.

People love her, and by extension, me. It seems like we can't go more than a few steps before someone else is rushing toward us, throwing their arms first around her, then me. Their chatter is too animated, the music overwhelming.

My gaze drifts around the room. In the corner of the living room, the dance girls. They're the popular ones, like high school cheerleaders on steroids. They hold court over there. Lettie would fit in with them, and I'm not really sure why she hasn't joined them.

She dances. She showed me videos of her dance competitions, and they blew whatever these girls do out of the water.

Then there's the dance floor. It's just a space in the living room that's been shoved clear of furniture, filled with gyrating couples. I don't like looking at that kind of thing. It seems too sexual, all for the sake of an audience. I prefer to keep my affection *not* on public display.

Finally, I spot the jocks.

Hockey players rule this whole freaking county, with football coming in close second. But football season is over, our soccer team sucks, and the hockey team is going to the playoffs. It's not really surprising to see some of the team surrounded by girls.

I squeeze Lettie's arm and mumble an excuse, although I know she can't hear me until I shout in her ear. She lets me slip away.

My first stop is the kitchen, where the bar is set up. There's a freshman football player behind a folding table, an array of booze at his back. He perks up when I enter and motions behind him.

"Um..." I shrug. "Vodka. Orange juice."

"Coming right up," he replies with a shout.

He fills a cup with ice and then a heavy pour of alcohol. I wince when he tops it off with barely a splash of juice.

"Here—"

A hand intercepts the red cup.

I meet the gaze of Carter Masters and immediately scowl.

We dated for a few seconds last year, and it ended poorly. He's unfortunately attractive, with chocolate-brown hair cut short, blue eyes, a sharp jaw, and lips that... well, I don't really need to imagine how they feel.

"Try the opposite ratio," he tells the amateur bartender. "Syd doesn't like to get wasted on her first drink."

I snort.

He takes a sip, his gaze locked on my face. I studiously ignore it—*him*—and watch the new drink be made. A shot's worth of vodka, more OJ.

"Thanks," I tell the guy.

Carter hands him a twenty.

I frown.

"What? They're not free. We're raising money for the playoffs."

"Uh-huh." I narrow my eyes.

He shrugs. "Okay, maybe it's going to the guys' drinking fund when this whole thing is over."

"That's more believable." I shift and sip my drink. It's a lot better than the monstrosity Carter's drinking.

"You look good." His gaze rakes down my body and back up, ending at my face. "More than good."

Not for the first time, I allow myself to swallow the dose of regret at ending things between us. It wasn't bad—kind of the opposite, actually. Which is why we both decided to stop.

Hard and fast as freshmen in college? *No way.* Not with the knowledge that my mother barely finished college, nine months pregnant and waddling across the stage with a hand on her rounded belly. It's a miracle she graduated at all.

I'm not going to be her. Two more years, and I'll walk away from here with my bachelor's degree. So many more doors will be open for me because of it. A piece of paper that defines my worth. I won't be pregnant. I won't be caught in the web of a guy who is in constant danger of losing his teeth.

Hockey players are not for me.

"Thanks." I roll my eyes at his antics. Always flirting. Always staring too long at me.

Always watching.

I start to push past him, but he catches my wrist.

"Seriously," he says.

Carter Masters is hot enough—and unfortunately, skilled enough at hockey—that literally every girl has a crush on him. They can't help it. He's an asshole on the ice and charming off of it. The perfect combination.

"How have you been?" He tips his head in a motion toward the door.

Against my better judgment, I follow him outside. We lean against the porch railing facing each other.

I shrug. "I'm fine. Surviving."

He nods slowly. "And your mom?"

My stomach twists. "She's just being her normal self."

She's destroying both of us from afar, running through the money I saved up working through high school like there's an infinite amount. She struggles to hold a job at the best of times. But...

"I think she has a boyfriend," I tell him. The words just slip out. "She's been flakier lately, so, I guess that's not a bad thing."

It is, though.

She never brought guys home. But she left me alone plenty growing up to spend nights or weekends with her latest infatuation.

"And your dad?"

I narrow my eyes. "What about him?"

He's off-limits.

Carter lifts one shoulder. "He lives here, doesn't he? Does he know you're attending St. James?"

"Probably." I kick at the floor. One thing I didn't budge on was wearing my black ankle boots. There's no way Lettie was getting me in heels. "I mean, how could he not? He had to fill out that scholarship form."

Because he's the only parent with a full-time job. Because, even though I was on the cusp of eighteen, it didn't mean shit to the financial aid office.

But knowing that he's only a ten-minute drive away, *if that*, and he hasn't reached out... it sets my teeth on edge. He must have my phone number.

Would it really be so hard to have a relationship with me?

"Hey!" someone yells. "Cops are coming! Meet us at the beach!"

A chorus of half-cheers, half-screams travel through the house. There's a mad rush of people, and, in the distance, a wail of sirens.

I take a sip of my drink and immediately shake my head. Carter watches me, frowning a little. I have the urge to get completely smashed, so I lift the cup out of his hand and gulp down half of it.

"Whoa." He steals the cup back. "Come on, party girl. We've got to get out of here."

I roll my eyes. "I'm fine."

He nods along with my lie.

The sirens are getting louder, and more people are pouring out onto the back steps. In their arms are bottles of booze, cups.

"Let's go, then." Carter grabs my hand and drags me along with him, down the steps and out into the yard. Then farther, until we're swallowed by the trees at the back of the property.

two
sydney

There's a narrow footpath through the woods to the beach, and we race along with everyone else. By the time my feet sink into the sand at the edge of the trees, I'm laughing. I somehow managed to hold on to both my original drink, which only sloshed like half of it out, and Carter's hand. He lost more than half of his drink, although he doesn't seem to mind.

The inky water comes into view. We head farther away from the house, sticking to the shadows. The police don't really give a fuck if we party on the beach—they just don't want the neighborhood to complain about the noise.

The music starts back up, and someone lights a bonfire. I chug the remainder of my drink, crumpling the plastic cup in my hand. The vodka warms me from the inside out, and it takes a minute to hit.

I crane around, searching for my best friend. She's standing with some other girls and hockey players—Carter's teammates—a little ways from the fire.

"You okay?" Carter nudges me.

"I'm *great*." The vodka is getting to me, bleeding through my bones and melting my muscles. "I want to dance."

He laughs. "Okay."

"And I want another drink."

"Done."

I nod.

He nods.

"You're really okay?" he asks again.

"Shut up, Carter. Can't you go back to being an asshole?"

"Only if I can get you drunk enough to let me kiss you," he counters.

"Pretty sure I don't need to be drunk for that."

He goes for it, and I palm his face. I burst into laughter at his darkening expression. I trail my fingers down his cheek, jaw, throat. I grip the front of his sweatshirt and sway toward him.

Bad idea, Sydney.

"Maybe I should walk away," I murmur.

It's one of those moments that I'm not exactly sure if I want to... and the longer I look into his ocean eyes, the more I want to lean forward just a bit more...

"Maybe," he agrees.

I do.

Kissing him is not a good move.

I turn on my heel and stride right for Lettie, who won't let me make out with my ex. Maybe another hockey player—*no, Carter would run interference there*—or someone else. When she sees me, she loops her arm around my shoulders and pulls me into the conversation.

"Oh, Marcy!" She points. "You grabbed the vodka?"

The other girl, a year older than us, nods. She offers it, and I take it without thinking. I don't like the taste of alcohol, but I swig a huge gulp straight from the bottle and hand it back.

"You okay, babe?" Lettie's breath is warm in my ear. "I was about to come rescue you from Masters if you let him kiss you."

See? Always the rescuer.

I force a laugh. "I'm not that desperate."

We migrate as a group, six of us, closer to the music. Marcy grabs our hands, and we all move in some sort of dance. Not my vibe, but the vodka is getting to me. So maybe it *is* my vibe.

"Hey," someone says in Lettie's ear. On my side, which means I hear it loud and clear.

I find myself staring at the guy and try not to let my mouth drop open.

It's the asshole I just robbed. Tried to rob. The one I've been stalking for over a week...

His hazel eyes swing to mine, but his hands are on my best friend's hips. I try not to focus on that. Or any of it, really.

She glances over her shoulder, her brows furrowing for only a split second. She doesn't recognize him. Why would she? He doesn't go to our school.

Oliver Ruiz goes to the rival school—Framingham State University. He plays hockey for my father. He's the freaking captain of the team, and if my best friend knew anything about hockey, she'd know that.

She twists around and brings her hand up between them. A handshake.

"Scarlett," she introduces.

"Ruiz."

"Do you speak Spanish?" She tilts her head, going into flirt mode. "Are you a local? I don't recognize you."

His gaze slides to mine again, and he ignores her question to ask, "Who's your friend?"

She pauses and follows his line of sight. Not that she has far to go—I'm standing right next to her. Shifting my weight like a freaking madwoman because I keep sipping my drink, which has to be ninety percent vodka, and the music has taken over my limbs. The alcohol is going straight to my head, making the rest of me a bit numb. I'm not entirely in control of how I'm dancing.

If we can call it that.

"That's Syd," she says. "Great gal. Kind of a prude, if you know what I mean."

I choke. "Lettie!"

She giggles. "What? Sorry, sorry. I mean, you're not the type to make out with a stranger at a party. Right? You wouldn't even make out with your ex."

Her comment cuts, and I look away.

"Syd," he says.

I scoff.

"Is Ruiz your first or last name?" Lettie asks.

He glances at her. "Most people call me Ruiz."

"Hmm." She puts her hand on his chest.

"I think your prickly friend is trying to ignore us, Scarlett," he says to her.

She laughs. "She's not comfortable with where your hands are drifting."

"They're not drifting," he counters. "Do you think she'd dance with me?"

My friend considers him. She steps back and makes a show of looking him up and down, even reaching out and pushing his upper lip up, as if to examine his teeth. The most bizarre part is that he *lets* her.

Finally, she shrugs. "You're hot enough, Ruiz. I don't know why she'd say no. Except that you just called her prickly."

"I thought girls liked that kind of thing."

Oh, jeez. I face him. Them.

"Insults?" I plant my hands on my hips.

"Yeah." His expression is a challenge. "Dance with me, *Syd*."

"It's Sydney."

"I figured."

What I should do is run in the other direction. But instead, I motion for him to lead the way. I don't know where —really, just away from Lettie and her group of friends.

He still wears the amused expression, and he puts his hand on my back and guides me out of the circle of girls. All the way around to the other side of the fire, where he puts my hands on his shoulders and locks his arms around my back.

We're suddenly a whole hell of a lot closer than I planned.

We're fucking swaying in the sand like it's an eighth grade dance, and the DJ put on a mandatory slow song—the opposite to what's blaring through the speakers on the other side of the bonfire.

"You seem kind of familiar," he says in a low voice.

"Do I?"

From here, the flames seem to reflect back at me in his eyes. The brown in the center is almost amber colored, and all the more captivating in the flickering light. Until he lifts one hand and blocks his view of my nose and mouth.

My heart fucking stops.

"Hmm, even more familiar."

I step out of his hold, but his fingers catch in the fabric of my dress. He drags me forward, crashing into him.

"What did you steal?" he asks. "Was it a dare?"

"I didn't take anything," I lie, lifting my chin. "And you should let go of me."

He sneers.

"Sydney," he tries out. "How about you tell Masters that fucking with me won't make anything easier on them. In fact, the opposite." His gaze rakes down my body. From this angle, he probably has a perfect view down my dress. "And sending sluts to distract us is a tired trick. Time to retire that one."

I jerk out of his grip and spin on my heel. I tug down the hem of my dress. Not that he made it ride up, it's just stupidly short and annoying and I fucking hate that I'm not wearing my own clothes.

Oliver Ruiz thinks I'm a slut? That I wasn't sent to his house to steal but to seduce.

It's laughable.

Scarlett's vision of me suddenly seems right. Achingly so.

Prudish.

And Oliver's assessment: prickly.

No one sent me, but especially not the *hockey team*. Not to fuck Oliver or fuck *with* him. But now I have the strong urge to lower myself to the standards he thinks.

He's an asshole. Plain and simple.

He judged me when he doesn't know me, which makes him the worst sort of person.

I find Lettie and the girls. But by the time I glance back over my shoulder for Ruiz, scanning the crowd for him, he's gone.

He called me a slut, and he thinks I nicked *nothing* from his house.

Above all, he underestimated me.

I reach down into my left boot, where I stashed my phone. I scroll through the photos, zooming in on the plays. The little handwritten notes scrawled along the margins. Formations, patterns, lineups that have been tweaked for the playoffs. There's a handwritten date in the top corner of one of the pages from only a week ago.

"Syd?" Lettie's eyelids are drooped, her smile drunk.

My gaze moves up and over her shoulder to Carter. He's drinking and laughing with his teammates, gathered around the fucking keg while one of them goes heels over head above it.

Without thinking, I slip past her and slam to a halt in front of him. "When are you playing them?"

He slow-blinks at me.

My father is a college hockey coach.

And, like St. James University, his team is going to the playoffs.

"Who?"

"The Vipers," I spit. *Framingham State University.* "Obviously."

His gaze softens. "Is this about your dad? I'm sorry for poking a sore spot, Syd— What are you doing?"

I shake my head slightly, selecting the images and adding it to the message.

They'll never know it was me. It isn't about my father, not really. I wasn't going to send the playbook to anyone. But Oliver Ruiz pushed the right buttons. He called me a slut, and for what? Because he thinks I'm Carter's puppet? That I was sent, the whole thing was orchestrated—

I hit send.

I'd rather St. James win than Ruiz get one chance at scoring on the ice.

Carter pulls out his phone and scans the text. It takes him a minute to register what he's looking at, but once he does, his eyes grow big. He scrolls through the photos, zooming in and covering his mouth to hide his laugh.

Finally, he lowers his phone and stares at me. *Hard*.

But he doesn't ask how I got the photos.

Just like I figured.

"Keep my name out of this," I warn him.

He extends his hand.

I'm fuming, shaking with adrenaline, but sliding my hand into his is easy. His fingers wrap around mine, and he squeezes, then drags me closer.

His lips touch mine, sealing our dirty deal with a kiss.

three
sydney

Game time.

I am buzzing with nerves and anticipation, mainly because I have no idea what's going to happen. That's why I'm not really a sports person—there's so much fucking uncertainty. We could be the best team in the league and still lose in a shootout.

Or a *tie*, which seems even worse.

Secretly, I like hockey. It kind of kills me to admit it, especially since I like to pretend otherwise. My guilty pleasure is watching NHL games after they've already aired, once I know the final score. There's something calming about the outcome already being determined, but still seeing it unfold for the first time.

But that can't happen in real-life situations, so here I sit. Nervously.

The crowd around me is buzzing, too. We're all wearing our black and maroon Seawolves colors. We're in the shared arena between the two universities, but as the home team. It's kind of funny how that works—both teams use the huge arena for home games and practices, somehow coming to an amicable agreement.

As in: a schedule worked out between the schools by an outside source that everyone has to adhere by.

The place was originally built by an SJU alum, but part of the funding came from an FSU donor. And so, when it was all wrapped up, no one really knew who had the rights to it. And given its location, right in the middle of the two schools, it was determined a second one didn't need to be built.

Because of that, there are two permanent home team locker rooms—one for St. James and one for Framingham State. There's a rink coordinator who schedules practice times and when each team can be on the ice. Not super convenient, especially since they also share it for home games.

I don't want to think about the logistical nightmare it must be, but they make it work.

"You seem paler than usual," Lettie comments. "Is it because you're back with Masters and you didn't tell me?"

I flinch. "We are absolutely not back together."

"You kissed him. After dancing with that other guy." She straightens. "Ooh, did that make him jealous? You dirty ho. I don't feel so bad about letting you go with him."

I knock my shoulder into hers. "Shut up. It was just a drunken kiss."

Not our first... probably not our last.

Carter Masters is worse than a magnet.

A cheer ripples through the arena, and the lights go all dim except the crazy swinging spotlights. The players are introduced, and we all scream and clap when they take to the ice. The FSU crowd makes their displeasure known, unsurprisingly.

When the FSU team is called, we return the favor. On the opposite side of the rink are the FSU students, a big blob of purple and white.

I spot Oliver Ruiz, the royal-purple number eighteen emblazoned on his back under his last name.

Lettie nudges me, and I drag my attention away from him.

Our other friends, including the vodka supplier, Marcy, are all around us. We've got the football team a few rows back, already flicking popcorn at the hot girls to draw their attention away from the hockey stars.

After a painfully sung national anthem, the game starts.

Right from the first puck drop, it becomes apparent that the SJU Seawolves have turned into fucking mind readers. The pace starts off furiously, with the Framingham State Vipers winning the face-off. But it doesn't seem to matter, because wherever the Vipers put a player, the Seawolves are there.

The coverage is intense. My breathing catches when they slam into the boards.

Rivalries like this make the games exciting—but right now, I think I'd rather be anywhere else.

The players move into the Seawolves' offensive zone. Carter has the puck at the blue line, quarterbacking the play. Less than ten seconds later, one of his wingers scores.

Our section erupts.

Lettie and I high-five, and she hugs the girl on her other side.

The game restarts.

By the time the horn blows at the end of the first period, the score is 3-0 in our favor. As soon as that horn goes off, a fight breaks out on the ice. I lean forward in my seat, trying to figure out who's in the thick of it. One of Carter's buddies and a Vipers winger have their gloves off, sticks and helmets tossed. The refs zoom in and try to pull apart the larger pile of hockey players, but they leave those two alone.

After a few punches, they're separated.

I blow out a slow breath and follow Lettie up and out of the stands. We wait in line for concessions with a million other students. One of the football guys stays with us, seeming determined to get in Lettie's good graces.

"There's a rumor going around of a snitch," he says casually, scratching his neck.

Lettie frowns at him. "What kind of snitch?"

"From FSU. Someone leaked their playbook, that's why we're crushing it."

I scoff before I can stop myself.

"You don't believe it?" He eyes me. "Aren't you related to the FSU coach?"

"It's a common last name." I move up in line. I've had almost two full years of peace, and *now* someone makes that connection? "You think someone snuck over there and stole a playbook?"

He shrugs. "That's what my brother said. His girlfriend goes to FSU."

"So much for not crossing enemy lines," I mutter.

The guy nods along with me. "Right? That player, Ruiz—"

"Oh, shit," Lettie exclaims. "I knew his name sounded familiar."

"He was telling everyone that someone broke into his house. So it's not out of the ordinary..."

Lettie's gaze flicks to me.

I ignore her. My pulse has picked up, and a new clammy sensation breaks out across my back. If that's the rumor, then I'm fucking screwed. He already thinks I stole something—is he going to put me and *this* together? Of course he will.

Fuck.

The rest of the game is a bloodbath. The refs eventually put away their whistles. The playoffs are single elimination, which really just means higher stakes for the game. Winner moves on. Loser goes home.

What's happening now, on the ice, is purely psychological. The Seawolves have gotten into their opponents' heads, and the rest is history.

In the last minute of the game, I glance over at my father on the bench. I had carefully not looked in his direction the whole game, but now I'm just in time for him to throw his papers down. He's in a gray suit and purple tie. Unlike the last time I saw him, he sports a trimmed, salt-and-pepper goatee that he now rakes his hand over.

The hair on his head is still dark. Same shade as mine, I'd hazard to guess.

While Carter's question from the party still rankles, I understand why I haven't actually seen my father in a while. Mom lost her shit, and he got the courts involved. While she shielded me from it, I was twelve going on twenty. Forced to grow up way too fast. The trauma of it still seeped in.

It was something about custody. She would come home and shed the silk blouse and pencil skirt from her day job, wiggling into sweatpants and crawling onto the couch beside me. And she'd lie, saying everything was going fine. That my dad was just trying to get out of our once-a-month visits.

And before that, when we were actually a real family...

My father and I have the same mouth. The shape of it, the way we smile. Mom used to point it out when I was younger, tracing my lip. And then later, after Dad left, she'd whisper it almost to herself with a weird expression.

It wasn't until I was older that I realized my smile hurt her. So I stopped smiling.

Mom's eyes are brown, his blue. And mine were probably meant to be blue, but instead they're somewhere stuck between gray and colorless. We have similar hair color. He's freaking tall, I can tell even from here. And I remember it, looking up and up and up at him as a kid.

I passed Mom's height in seventh grade.

The final horn blows, the game over. The St. James crowd around me leaps to their feet, while I am slower to rise. The score is almost painful to see.

St. James had a complete fucking shutout.

6-0.

"Celebration time!" Lettie sings in my ear.

Three hours after the end of the game, I'm blissfully

drunk. The party rages around me, but I've got to the stage where I can't really feel my toes. The rest of me is solid. And Lettie, knowing that glazed glint in my eye, hands me a bottle of water on her way by.

I sip it and people-watch.

Although people have been watching me, too. It didn't bother me at first. Just a few glances. But as the night wears on, they become more... *more*. Itches on my skin in places I can't quite reach, an uncomfortable sharpness to them.

Finally, someone drops into the chair beside me. A girl in a tight little dress, kind of like the one Lettie's wearing and the one I wore to the last party. This time, I dressed fucking sensibly. Jeans. Sweater.

"You're Sydney Windsor, right?"

I tilt my head. "Do I know you?"

"Not personally." She leans in. "There's a rumor going around, I just wanted to know if it was true."

I'm beginning to hate rumors.

"Let's hear it," I say. "But it's probably not true."

"No, I think this one has some merit." She leans in closer, almost hanging off her damn chair to get closer to me. "I *heard* that you stole the FSU playbook and gave it to your boyfriend."

I stare at her.

If my brain wasn't fuzzy, I might be able to think of a response. But instead, I've got nothing. My mind blanks out.

"I thought that had some truth to it," she says in my silence. She stands, hovering over me. "This is for costing us the playoffs, bitch."

Like a bad horror movie, she overturns her drink on my head.

Cold liquid pours down my front. It misses most of my hair and face, but instead drenches my sweater.

"Secret's out." She spins on her heel.

Her act has drawn more attention, and people jump out

of her way to let her pass. Some watch her, but a majority focus on *me*.

If some random FSU girl has heard about it, then the rumor is about to solidify into fact.

I slump back in the chair, ignoring the uncomfortable wetness sliding into my pants.

The court of public opinion will now be hearing the case of Sydney Windsor...

four
sydney

Six Months Later

"You don't have to do this." I say it with no small amount of trepidation.

Beside me in the Registrar's office is my father. The man I haven't talked to in full sentences since I was fifteen and discovered he was about to remarry. At eighteen, I went full no-contact.

Now I'm twenty.

Six months ago, I had the luxury of crawling back to him for help and falling on his mercy. Him, his wife. Standing in the house I'd only been to a handful of times before I stopped going at all, pleading my case to two strangers.

Everything has changed.

While St. James *students* don't hate me for what I did, the administration had a problem with it. They pulled me into the dean's office and informed me that my scholarships were based on merit, which included ethics.

In their eyes, it was cheating.

With suddenly no extra slack in the line, I had a choice: get an off-campus job and work my tail off all summer to afford my junior year tuition, continue working through classes and

parties and whatnot, or... figure something else out. In a word
—*leave*.

By the time the school year ended, my friends had abandoned me, and then Mom disappeared.

One shit thing on top of another.

"Here you go," my new academic advisor says, standing on the other side of a long counter. She sets down a thick folder and flips it open, pointing to one side. "Your schedule is here. Your login for our portal is here. We have an online program the professors sometimes utilize for assignment turn-in, which is here. Your meal plan..."

I nod along until she finally stops talking, and I retract the folder off the counter.

Outside the administration building, across the quad, the residences are buzzing with life. Students are moving in today, and older ones who volunteered to help wear bright-purple t-shirts. They're all swarming around the cars that pull up, unloading in a fervor.

Like ants.

"Sydney..."

I glance at my father.

A lot has changed in six months, but most of all, *us*. I don't know if he took pity on me or if he heard whispers about what happened, or—

"It'll be okay," he says.

He said it then, too. Before I finally caved and asked for help.

I couldn't go out without running into an FSU student. I had more drinks and food dumped on me in two weeks than in my entire lifetime, because that seemed to be a go-to maneuver. My apartment front door was splashed in bright-red paint. Handwritten threats were shoved in the mailbox.

It was obvious they knew exactly where I lived—it was only a matter of time before things escalated.

Lettie went away. As soon as her last final was done, her

bags were packed and a driver helped load her things into a blacked-out SUV at the curb. She hugged me goodbye, but even that felt too... superficial. She said we had the apartment through the summer, that her father had taken care of rent with the landlord.

I didn't say anything to that. I couldn't, because it was very clear that my best friend would not be returning. Yet, I waved as her driver spirited her away. I waved, knowing that she was taking the easy way out. Of living here, of being my friend.

Dad called me out of the blue shortly after that, sounding raspy and a little sad. Maybe it was disappointment. But his number wasn't even in my contacts. And when the call came in, early on a Saturday, it took me a moment to place his voice.

"Sydney." He paused. *"I should've reached out sooner. But I've caught wind of what you've been going through, and just wanted to extend an olive branch. I'm not mad, honey, and no matter what—it'll be okay."*

It wasn't.

It isn't.

And while he thinks he had his finger on the pulse of what was happening, like many adults, he only gets the tip of the iceberg.

People can be vicious.

Over the summer, my mother disappeared. I thought that living in the targeted apartment was bad—it's nothing compared to walking into the trailer we used to live in together and find it...

Horrible.

Abandoned.

She had stopped responding to texts, stopped answering her phone, but it still took me a while to get back to Emerald Cove to check in on her.

Once I did, I wish I hadn't.

I spent the day at the police precinct, trying to file a

missing person's report. Except I couldn't tell them anything useful. When was the last time I talked to her? Three weeks prior. When was the last time I saw her? Winter break. To which they reminded me that it was July.

I hadn't seen my mother in seven months?

Correct, Detective.

He gave me his card, took my contact information, and said he'd look into it.

Then... nothing. Not from him, not from my mother. I moved her stuff into storage and let go of the trailer, thinking *that*, at least, would make her reach out when she returned. But she hasn't.

Once the lease on the two-bedroom SJU place came up, I moved into a new one-bedroom apartment in Framingham.

Everything is totally fine. The house—the metaphorical one—is not on fire. The sky isn't falling anymore. I can deal with whatever else comes.

"I'm sorry," I tell him again.

I do not like apologizing, but I can't seem to stop when it comes to my father.

He waves me off. "You know, your mother and I met here."

I tilt my head. "Here, where? Like... you both went to school here?"

"We were in the same year." His expression turns sad. "If you're missing her terribly, you could check the yearbook archive in the library. She was in quite a few clubs."

"Wow." I should've known that. I think I might've, even, in the back of my head.

"Come to dinner with Perri and me tonight," he continues, effectively changing the subject.

I chew on that. It's not like I'm going to any parties, even if the idea of more bonding time with Dad is a bit... uncomfortable.

St. James, the university I once considered home, simultaneously feels close enough to touch and a universe away. As soon as my dad swooped in, and word started spreading that I was transferring to FSU, my classmates turned on me.

There should be a case study on such a rivalry.

I might be the most hated person in the county.

And when I consider that...

I nod along. Perri is nice enough. She took me shopping for furniture when Dad had to work, and while it was awkward enough that I wanted to scream, it was also kind of... *fine*. She let me pick out a couch after sitting on half a dozen with me, brought along a little measuring tape to ensure everything would fit in my rooms and through the doorways, even took me out for a fancy cup of coffee afterward.

There was something in the back of my mind that knew my mother and I were dirt-poor while my father was the opposite. Mom used to mutter about old money. A trust-fund baby.

Him, not me.

Obviously.

Dad and I make it to his truck without incident, and he drops me off at my new apartment. I thank him gruffly and close the truck door, booking it up to the second floor. It's a rather small apartment building, just eight apartments in the brownstone. Two on each floor. I'm three B.

As soon as I lock myself inside, I shed my sweatshirt and slump into a chair at the kitchen table.

I am rubbed raw. Emotionally. I just can't seem to calm myself down enough to *breathe*, let alone digest what I'm doing. Tomorrow, when classes start, I anticipate the tensions around me to only get worse.

If I can get through the day without something being spilled on me, or gum in my hair, I'll count myself lucky.

My phone chimes. I groan, but it goes off again almost immediately.

Then again.

And again, so fast the sound cuts itself off to begin again.

What the...?

I check the notifications, my brows furrowing. Text after text from different unknown numbers. I get to the bottom, and my heart stops. I've been tagged in a video... of myself. Today. I have to do a double take, confirming I'm wearing the same clothes as right this very moment.

It's of me walking across campus, although it's cropped in a way that hides my father, who must've been beside me. It's very obvious where I am, though.

And the caption announces it, too:

We have a snitch amongst us, Vipers... how about we give her a warm welcome? You can reach her at 617-555-4399 or sydwindsor@xmail.com.

The page that posted it is an FSU gossip and hot-takes page. I scroll, scanning other posts. They seem intent on dragging down whoever steps out of line, spotlighting embarrassing moments and the occasional achievement from the sports teams. There are multiple posts about Oliver Ruiz's greatness, unfortunately.

More texts come in, nearly constant, and my phone lights up with a call.

I swipe to answer it, a tentative, "Hello?" barely out before the caller interrupts me.

"Go home, you fucking bitch. No one wants you here."

Click.

I don't have time to process it, because another call comes in.

"Yeah?"

"Sydney Windsor?" Gruff. Male.

I remain silent.

"Yeah, thought so. St. James didn't want you so you thought to try your luck here? Nice try, fucking slut—"

I hang up. My hands are shaking. When another call comes in, I decline it and put my phone on silent. I drop it into a drawer in my kitchen.

What the *fuck*?

five
sydney

I'm not sure if I'm bored or a masochist, but I decide to scroll through the many texts that came in overnight. Some are trying to get me to answer them, clearly baiting or goading me with inflammatory comments, while others are just straight-up mean. Those don't care if I respond—it's more about the knife wound. I don't know if I should delete them or report them, but when Dad picked me up for dinner last night, I didn't even mention it.

Once I get through as many texts as I can stomach, I go back to the video. Since it was posted from the FSU gossip account, I have zero luck. There's no indication of who might run it, and I don't know enough about the school to even attempt a guess. Not that it would help.

The court of public opinion at FSU is currently strongly against me.

Social media is a nightmare, too. The video tagged me, which seemed to open the floodgates for other people to tag me in shit, too. People I'm not friends with are tagging me in shit-talking posts, memes, edited screenshots of the video where they enlarge certain body parts. There are hideous comments on most of my posts.

I absorb it all without an outward reaction, but inside, I'm boiling. I shouldn't have come to FSU. I shouldn't have gotten caught up in trying to figure life out *here*.

What I should've done was just leave. Get a job, take classes part time, maybe get a roommate or something. Now, I'm in too deep. What am I supposed to do, tell my father—who risked his own job to get me accepted—that I changed my mind? Thanks for the nice apartment, for funding basically my entire life for the last six months, for getting me into school without loans, but I'm out?

Not a chance.

A new text comes in, and I automatically click on it. Masochist, as I said.

> **UNKNOWN**
>
> Just block them out.

That's a new one.

And before I know it, I'm responding.

> **ME**
>
> I don't know how.

> **UNKNOWN**
>
> Someone will fuck over the football team and they'll be the new spit-roasted pig over the fire.
>
> If you can last till then, you're golden.

I cover my mouth before I can *laugh*. It's not funny—but that is exactly how I feel.

Part of me doesn't want to respond and ruin it, because what if this is just a con to get me to admit something? Or... I don't know. Maybe they'll plaster screenshots everywhere as soon as something *does* happen to someone else.

Like, "Look! Sydney Windsor wanted this bad shit to happen!"

It's been less than five hours since the video was posted,

and I'm already fucking gun-shy. I haven't even been out. To the restaurant with Dad and Perri doesn't count, because we went to some nice place a town over in the opposite direction of St. James.

So, in the end, I don't respond. I get out of bed and take my time getting ready for the day. My makeup feels a bit like armor, which steadies my hand.

Day one and I'm already starting off defeated.

But I put my backpack on and walk to school, gazing around like someone's going to come out of nowhere and punch me. I make it to campus, through the coffee line—the barista seems bored, yes, but also older. They don't recognize me, and I get the impression that they wouldn't give a shit if they did.

Coffee secured, I find my first class and take a seat in the very back. It's an economics class, which I'm taking to satisfy some desire to have an understanding of our world and marketplace, and not a huge room.

But, by some miracle, no one recognizes me.

I keep my head down and take notes, and when the lecture is over, I'm the last one out. I've got another one straight away, so I head for that. English writing class. I added it on a whim because it sounded vaguely interesting.

Arriving, however, I discover that this is absolutely the wrong one for me.

It's not a traditional room with desks— there are four long tables arranged in a square, so we're all facing each other. The professor is already at one of the seats, and four more are filled. Leaving six empty.

Shit.

I pick one at random, slinking down.

Tomorrow, I'll invest in a hat.

Or camouflage.

"Good morning," the professor says. "My name is Lucy Page, your illustrious guide through this writing course. You can call me Professor Page, Professor P, or just Lucy, whichever you prefer. Just don't call me late to dinner."

Some chuckle. I'm so anxious, I can't even muster a smile.

There's a shuffle of papers, and the person to my left—the tables have now filled in while I stared at my lap—slides a stack of class syllabi in front of me. I take one and pass the rest, finally risking a glance at the professor.

"A little about me," she continues. "I'm an investigative journalist by day. I own my own company. My team and I work on longer pieces in the Greater Boston Area. I'm *here*," she drums her nails on the table, "because the professor who was supposed to run this class got hit by a car last week."

Someone gasps.

"So, here I am."

A girl raises her hand. "Um, Professor?"

"Yes. Name?"

"Andi Sharpe," she replies. "You're an investigative journalist, but the course description said creative writing?"

Professor Page smiles. She's kind of sharp-looking. Glasses, short, white-blonde hair that just barely misses brushing the tops of her shoulders. Her light eyes seem to cut straight through the student she focuses on. "Do you think journalists can't be creative?"

"No, um, I—"

"We tell stories. Storytelling is the framework of our entire society. Hell, even politicians weave stories to suit themselves. Everyone does. Investigative journalism is just as much about relaying the story as it is about facts. If it's not interesting, who's going to read it?"

Silence.

"Exactly," she finishes. "Not a damn person. Your challenge, therefore, is to write something worth reading."

"Isn't that in the eye of the beholder?" another girl asks.

The professor gestures to a guy on her right. "You don't agree."

He straightens, the eyes of ten students and our professor suddenly on him. His dark hair is thick and curly, flopping down over his forehead, and he's got a hint of shadow on his jaws. Attractive in a book smart kind of way.

"Brandon Moore," he introduces. "Society often dictates what's worth reading. Take the classics, for instance. Actually reading them nowadays, well, some of them are boring or hard to get through. Yet people insist, because they're *classics*." He pauses. "I think interesting and worth reading are two separate things."

"Is a comic book worth reading?"

He tilts his head. "Yes."

"Why?"

"Because... it's entertaining."

"Because it's worth *your* time. So maybe there's a correlation between entertainment and interest?" The girl who spoke flips her hair off her shoulder. "Miranda Summers."

"Frankenstein was interesting," I mutter before I can stop myself.

I draw gazes.

"Name?" the professor prompts.

"Sydney. And, um, I like classics. They stick around for a reason, right? Whether it's a message or how they tell the story. Like Virginia Woolfe, her stream-of-consciousness writing is sometimes hard to grasp but it was groundbreaking. And Frankenstein continues to send a message, it can be picked apart in so many different ways..."

"Of course the SJU slut is in this class," someone says under a cough.

Our professor straightens. "Excuse me?"

The first girl—Andi—leans forward. Her gaze burns into me. "She stole from our hockey team and sold us out to our rival, and then she has the nerve to transfer here? I won't be in a class with her."

"Then leave."

I stop breathing.

Our professor looks around the room, then pauses on Andi. "I mean it. Get out of my classroom if you can't be respectful." She makes a shooing motion.

Andi seems a bit in shock, and she shoots me a withering glare as she shoves her notebook in her backpack. She leaves in a flurry of movement, slamming the door closed behind her.

"Now," Professor Page says in the resulting silence. "Anyone else want to join her?"

No one moves.

"Good. Your first assignment is on the syllabus. I suggest you start working on it now... creative writing can be a tricky beast when you first start." She rises. "See you Thursday!"

She leaves.

It takes us a moment to all get our shit together, and I'm once again the last one out. Except someone waits for me in the hallway.

"Brandon," he introduces, extending his hand.

"Sydney." I shake it.

"I hope Andi didn't scare you off."

I shrug, heading down the hall. I'm done with classes for today, thankfully, and I'm looking forward to hunkering down at home.

"What year are you?" he asks.

I twitch. "Junior."

"Major?"

"Criminal Justice," I lie.

He snorts. "Oh, I didn't take you for a meathead jock."

"What's that supposed to mean?"

"You know the old adage—the only people who major in Criminal Justice are the athletes who will never use their degree."

"Maybe I want to join the FBI," I say.

"Maybe," he allows. "Do you?"

I roll my eyes. "Okay, fine, I think I'm going to major in English Writing. They're giving me the semester to decide."

There's no way he can use that against me, right?

"Care to join me for lunch?" he asks.

Not really. But I find I can't quite say no fast enough, because before I know it, we're in the dining hall surrounded by a hundred other students with the same idea. I keep my head low and stick close to him, although using a stranger as a shield isn't really a great idea.

This could be a trap.

My stomach flips, and I resist the urge to sprint away.

"You okay?"

"I, uh..."

He glances around. "I take it other people share Andi's vitriolic opinion?"

I choke on a laugh. "You could say that."

He makes a face. "Heathens."

We get food and find a table in a back corner, and I breathe a little easier once we're seated at a four-person table.

"What are you majoring in?" I ask him.

"Double majoring in sociology and education. It just so happens that I had an elective, and one of my first loves is creative writing." He glances over my shoulder and waves to someone.

They set their plate and drink down beside me, dropping into the vacant chair. Girl. She's tall, her shoulder at least a few inches above mine while seated, with long blonde hair and zero makeup. It isn't until she's fully settled that she looks to me.

Her jaw drops, and she faces Brandon. "No."

"Yes."

"Brandon Moore," she hisses.

"I can hear you," I murmur.

"She's nice," he says to her. "Sydney, this is Dylan. Dylan, Sydney. You have the y's in your names in common."

"Pleasure," I say, sticking out my hand.

She stares at me like I'm a freaking bomb about to go off. There's a *thud* under the table, and she jerks slightly. She takes my hand, squeezing tight.

"Pleasure," she echoes. "Great."

"Dylan is on the women's volleyball team," Brandon says in the wake of our awkward-as-shit introductions. "She likes to tell people she has an innate ability because she's tall and talented, but really she practices more than anyone else."

"Brandon," she snaps again.

"And Sydney has some thoughts on what makes writing interesting," he continues. "So she might have read your mom, Dyl."

I straighten. "Is your mom an author?"

Dylan blushes. "Unfortunately, yes. She writes romance books. The kind with half-naked cowboys on the cover."

I don't want to say that sounds interesting, but I am intrigued. "No hockey guys?"

She snorts. "No."

"That's a bonus. So does she write under a pen name, or..."

Brandon bursts into laughter.

"Shut up," she mutters. She offers me a small smile. "If you mention that to anyone, I'll fucking kill you."

"That's a sign of friendship," Brandon explains. "As soon as the murder talk starts, you're in."

My smile fades at the idea of murder.

What if my mom hasn't come home because she can't?

six

sydney

UNKNOWN

How many texts do you get a day?

ME

Texts, emails, phone calls…

All of them.

Well, there's a feature that lets you send unknown calls right to voicemail. So I turned that on, and now I have 150 voicemails. I think it's full, though, because they've stopped.

And I've been trying to delete the texts as they come in, but I gave up.

It's been a week.

And you're still talking to me.

You're intriguing.

I get that you think that, but I'm about as far from it as possible.

Boring people don't interest me like you.

Because you saw a photo of me online?

Because you were ballsy enough to steal a playbook and give it to their enemy.

Come back.

I'm just trying to formulate a reply to that...

Some sort of defense? An excuse?

I knew you were too nice.

I think you just don't want to take responsibility for it.

Ha. I've done nothing but pay for it.

The hockey fans at these schools have long memories.

Sounds ominous.

I thought I was supposed to be praying for someone to fuck around with the football team?

I spoke too soon. Their season has already gone to shit anyway.

Okay, well, thanks a lot.

Dylan and Brandon become my allies. Friends, maybe. I don't know if I can call them that. But after a few more shared meals, they seem to make a pact to stay close to me.

Almost as soon as I reach campus, one of them is there.

It helps that I've got two classes with Brandon—the writing class and a crime fiction class—and one with Dyl. It's her who joins me on our walk from the coffee cart up to the second floor in the student center, which has a short row of classrooms behind the school bookstore.

"Have you talked to your dad lately?"

I wince. After he helped register for classes, and then took me out to dinner with his new wife, I've been avoiding him. He sent me several messages that were easy to lose in the onslaught of spam.

Eventually, he's going to intercept me here or wait for me outside my apartment, and I'll have to deal with it.

Him.

"And your SJU friend, Lettie?"

I chuckle. "Yeah, no."

It's funny how things change. Her text thread is at the bottom of my messages, but I can't make myself delete it. Even when my phone prompts me to deal with the storage issue. But why would I get rid of her messages and keep the hate texts?

For every text I delete, another three come in. Although I've started noticing that some double or triple text, hoping to pull something out of me. Or trying new angles. Poking at different spots hoping to find a bruise.

My ending with Lettie wasn't vitriolic. Just... abrupt.

I put Lettie through too much trouble. She was a casualty in the war against Sydney Windsor, and she decided it was best to cut ties than try to weather the storm with me. I'm not mad about it—it's just the kind of friend she is.

Was.

The worst part is, I keep expecting Dyl and Brandon to abandon me, too. I wouldn't even blame them for leaving.

"Uh-oh," Dylan says under her breath.

I follow her line of sight.

Oliver Ruiz and two others, both in FSU Hockey sweatshirts, are strolling our way. Dark hair, sun-kissed tan skin, hazel eyes, perfect fucking face. I want to punch him.

One of the others, a guy with dark-blond hair that flops in

his face, has a black eye. His green eyes bore into mine from this distance, and I automatically shiver as goosebumps rise along the backs of my arms.

"You are probably familiar with Oliver Ruiz," Dyl says in my ear. "On his left is Bear."

Not the one who's eyeing me. Bear is a big fucker, a few inches taller than Oliver and the third, and packed with muscle. Dark hair, dark scruff on his jaw, a mean scowl in place. His gaze rakes over both of us but doesn't linger.

"And the third?"

"Penn Walker. Fucking crazy goalie, although he's actually pretty nice if you catch him in a good mood."

I scoff. "He doesn't look too nice right about now."

"Well, yeah..."

"Maybe we should get out of here." I tug at her arm.

"Hey, Windsor!"

The three guys are around me in an instant, subtly boxing out Dylan. Oliver Ruiz wedges between us, forcing me to drop her arm.

"Enjoying your stay at FSU so far?" he asks.

I scowl at him.

"Still trying to sabotage us?" Bear questions. He tips his head. "I bet you're fucking someone on the hockey team within a month."

"She'll try to get in my pants," Oliver says, flashing me a smile. "All the girls do."

"There's no way in hell," I sputter.

He pretends to consider that. "Your friend, Scarlett, did say you were a prude..."

"Scarlett?" The goalie with the black eye pipes up.

"Lettie Blake," Oliver tells him.

My gaze bounces around them. "What about her?"

Ruiz pulls out his phone and scrolls for a minute, then flashes it at me. It's a picture of her... naked, on her knees.

Mouth open. Her nose is practically touching his pubic bone—

Things I never wanted to see.

I snatch for his phone, but he's faster.

"Does she know you took that?" I hiss.

He laughs. "Yeah, she got all indignant about it. Kind of cute, actually. I might go back for seconds, see if I can get a few more shots... It would sell better, don't you think? A full set as opposed to just one."

My body goes cold. "You can't do that."

"No? I mean, she might've driven your getaway car for all I know." He taps my chin. "Close your mouth. Wouldn't want you to give me any ideas."

I scowl. "Just leave me the fuck alone."

"But we have a bet," the goalie calls. "You may as well settle it for us, snitch. A month. Over or under?"

"Over," I say through my teeth. "Way, *way* fucking over."

I shove past Oliver, ignoring his laugh. Dylan grabs my arm and urges me along faster, although my stomach is twisting. I need to tell Lettie that he has a photo of her. I need to warn her that he might share it, or—

"Breathe," Dylan says. "They're still watching."

"Everyone is always watching," I reply.

"So, even better reason to not fall apart."

She's got a point. I hate that I have to swallow that down. Every emotion gets shoved to the back of my head, where the tears can't find it.

We get to class, and I automatically take a seat in the far back, but as close to the door as possible. Dylan sits in front of me. After Calculus, I've got a break of time, and then an introduction to law class that gets out at five o'clock. And after, I fully plan on going home and hibernating until I have to be back for class on Monday.

When everyone is here, our professor jumps right into class.

I liked math at SJU. I was planning on minoring in Mathematics, although I hadn't quite figured out what I was going to do with the rest of it. English was something I was leaning toward, although at that point I had only done the introductory courses.

I keep my head down and do the work, occasionally glancing at the back of Dylan's head. She seems just as focused, which is good. I like problem solving, especially when there are clear-cut answers.

It's so different than analyzing a piece of literature, in which there's no true right answer. There's what the professor thinks, of course, but sometimes the table being blue has nothing to do with the state of the author's mind.

Anyway.

The skin on the back of my neck prickles halfway through class, and I glance over. A girl is glaring at me, and she slowly lifts her middle finger.

So. Fucking. Classy.

As soon as the professor dismisses us, Dylan and I hurry out.

"I need to make a call," I say, pausing outside of the dining hall. "You go in, I'll meet you."

Dylan gives me a skeptical look, but she eventually nods and swipes in. I pull out my phone and go to Lettie's number, my thumb hovering over it.

Just call her.

Too exposed in the middle of the atrium, I go down the hall where the restrooms are. Trying not to think about how poorly this conversation can go, I press it and raise the phone to my ear.

"Come on, Lettie," I murmur to myself.

It goes to voicemail. I let out a low breath, when really, it should hurt more. But maybe I'm just a fucking coward, because I don't want to hear her reaction in real time.

I clear my throat and wait for the telltale *beep*. "Hey, it's me. I just wanted to give you a heads-up that Oliver Ruiz has a compromising photo of you... And he's threatening to get more. Which I guess is fine if it's consensual, but at the very least you should know what he's saying. Okay. I hope you're doing well... Call me back."

"Aww, that was so *sweet*."

I turn slowly.

The goalie leans against the wall, arms crossed over his chest. I can't help but recognize that he's blocking my way, albeit in a subtle fashion. If I were to accuse him of it, he could double down or motion to the space between him and the far wall.

"Warning your little friend about Ollie's threats?" He tilts his head, watching me with a curious expression.

I lift my chin. "Something like that."

"Because you're such a good person."

"I'm a fine person."

He pushes off the wall and stalks closer. "Yeah? And yet, you snitched. On your dad's team, no less. That's fucking cold."

"Cold? You don't know the half of it." I don't back away. And I really wish I could recall his stupid name.

"Why, did he do something to you?"

He backs me into the wall. When I edge to the left, he slams his hand down next to my ear. A wicked thrill goes through me, and I have to seriously look *up* to see into his eyes. But he doesn't seem pissed. More curious than anything.

"Not so fast, princess." He trails his fingers down my arm. "Why do you want to bother pretty Lettie with worries? We're not going to leak her pictures... It's *you* we want photos of, don't you think?"

Yeah, right.

"Photos of you tied up, choking on our cocks, tears decorating your pale skin..." His pupils dilate, like he's fucking turned on by that. "I say under a month before you break and get naked with one of us."

"As I said, it'll be a cold day in hell when that happens."

He laughs. "Oh, I do like your bluster. But winter is coming, princess, and I'm pretty sure this is your own personal Hell."

He leans in, his lips brushing my ear. A chill shoots down my spine that I try desperately to suppress. But my heart is beating against my ribs in a way that almost hurts, and I don't know why I'm staying in this position. Why I'm letting him talk to me like this.

"But if it's not..." He pulls back just enough to meet my gaze. "Feel free to let me know, and I'll adjust the temperature."

seven
sydney

"No." I plant my hands on my hips. "Absolutely not."

Dad frowns. "It could go a long way. I consulted a public relations team—"

"For what?"

"For *you*." He sighs and pats the cushion beside me. "Sit. Please?"

I slink closer and drop onto the couch beside him. When he called and asked if he could swing by, I was tempted to lie and say I was out. At the library or wherever. But something about this weekend was already feeling lonely, so I let him up.

And now he's trying to get me to go out.

He holds out the black FSU Hockey sweatshirt. Their logo, the crossed hockey sticks with the snake intertwined, is front and center.

"Come to the game," he reiterates. "You'll sit with Perri and your two friends—"

"You know I've only made two friends?"

His smile drops off. "I'm friends with some of the professors, particularly your Calculus professor, Amy. She's had Dylan in her class before, said she mostly keeps a small circle of friends and doesn't tend to be influenced by rumors or gossip. Which is exactly what you need."

"Right..."

"You can travel with me." He smiles, then grabs my phone from the coffee table and pushes it into my hands. "Text your friends and get ready. I'll wait."

He's clearly not taking no for an answer.

I sigh, reaching for the sweatshirt and phone. I close myself in my bedroom and shut my eyes, counting to ten.

Maybe a ride with Dad to the stadium might provide some much-needed time to interrogate him. I mean, get to know him better. Or at least find out more about my mother, see if he has any information that could point me toward her...

I change, pull my long dark hair up into a high ponytail and slick on some makeup. At the last second, I snag a black headband that'll keep my hair warm, pulling out the few strands of long, outgrown curtain bangs. I don't even think I can classify them as bangs at this point.

The ride to the stadium, however, isn't what I expect.

Because he heads away from the arena, instead coasting to a stop in front of a tiny single-family home. It's white, but all the windows are dark.

A second later, the freaking goalie comes out the door on the attached garage. He tosses his hockey bag into the bed of the truck. He stops short when he sees me already in the front seat, changes directions, and climbs in the back. Right behind me.

"Have you met Penn Walker?"

I crane around and eye him. He, like my father, is wearing a suit. His is light gray with matching slacks. White shirt. Royal-purple tie. His hair is combed back, out of his face, and he offers me an award-winning smile.

"Sydney, I presume? You didn't say your daughter was coming along, Coach."

Dad rolls his eyes. "Because I don't run everything by you, Penn."

The boy at my back grins wider.

I sit forward again, gripping the seat belt across my torso. "Any more surprises?"

"Just Ruiz," Penn answers.

I stare at my father. There are a hundred things I want to blurt out, but I can't seem to make my voice work. The words get trapped in my throat.

Sure enough, we stop at a very fucking familiar house, and Oliver Ruiz strolls out. He motions to my dad, who parks and hops out without a backward glance.

"Hey, Syd," Penn says, his lips nearly on my ear. *Again*. "Did you know Ollie already has an NHL contract? That's why he lives in this nice-as-shit house. He doesn't host parties here or anything."

"Oh, yeah?" I can't turn and face him. He's too close. All I can do is stare straight ahead while Dad and Oliver do God-knows-what.

"Do you know anything about hockey?" Penn asks.

"Not as much as you," I reply.

He huffs. "You're not very fun."

"I'm a boring person."

"Hmm... maybe. Are you hoping if you're boring enough, people will stop thinking you're a snitch? I don't think it works like that."

"I don't really care what you think," I whisper.

The doors on the driver's side open, Dad hoisting himself back in and Oliver first tossing his hockey bag into the back, then seeming to float into the backseat. The truck felt like overkill when I first saw it, but now... well, if he's carting around hockey boys and all their gear, it makes more sense.

"Anyone else?" I question.

Dad chuckles. "Nope."

No one speaks on the way to the arena. I fidget, picking at my nails, until we park. Instead of climbing out, Dad cranes around to face his players.

"Go ahead inside," he tells them.

They abide by his orders without question, and we watch them cross the lot and disappear through a set of double doors.

"Are your friends coming?" he asks me.

I check my phone. Dylan has volleyball practice, and Brandon is working. In short: *no*.

And Lettie hasn't reached out either. She never returned my phone call.

"Okay. Come on." He leads me inside, through the same doors Oliver and Penn entered, and I recognize enough to know we're under the main part of the arena. This is where the players go, staff, everyone else. The hall splits, curving to the right and left.

"Stairs to get up to the seating are on the left," he says. "But come with me this way."

I follow him. I'm not really sure why, because he seems to think this problem has an easy solution. When we get to the locker room, I balk.

"They're probably naked," I hiss.

He chuckles. "Hang tight out here."

He goes in. A minute later, he opens it back up and waves me through.

This is dumb. The *last* place I want to be is in the locker room of a team that all hates my guts, and yet...

"Attention," Oliver yells as soon as he sees us.

The room goes quiet. It's a large, open space with cubbies around the outer wall. They're labeled with engraved black plaques, the guys' first initials and last names. Most are shirtless or in various states of dress.

"This is our only scrimmage before our season starts," Dad says when all eyes are on him. "There's a good turn out of students, but I will tell you right now: brush off how last season ended."

Grumbles.

"I understand being mad, but holding grudges will not be tolerated. And that includes against my daughter."

Twenty pairs of eyes swing in my direction.

I think I'd rather die. What the hell is my father thinking?

Putting me on display and saying, *BE NICE TO HER!* to a bunch of guys is absolutely not going to work. I have no doubt these guys respect their coach, but me? And what goes on behind his back? It's a little laughable.

I cross my arms across my chest and shift my weight, but I say nothing. Their expressions might be mild, but it's just a show. I remind myself of that when one stands and heads toward me. He towers over me, but he sticks out his hand into the air between us.

"No hard feelings," he says.

Dad smiles.

I shake his hand, and he squeezes hard enough to grind my bones together. I clench my jaw and refuse to show the pain, although his wicked, secret smile is enough to tell me he knows the power of his grip strength.

"Thank you," Dad says to the player. He checks his watch and claps. "Okay, finish getting ready, we've got warm-ups in fifteen. Let's put on a good show for FSU, yeah?"

He leads me out to a chorus of cheers and whoops. We go back down the hall the way we came, then past the exit and to the staircase he mentioned go up to the seats. From his pocket, he produces a paper ticket. "Here. Perri will take you home after, okay?"

"Thanks," I tell him.

But really... I might mean the opposite. Depending on how this goes.

The Vipers are playing a team from the next state over. They're in the same conference, which means they'll be facing off quite a bit this season. It's not a real game, in that the season hasn't started. But they take it seriously enough.

It also means tonight will set the tone for their next game.

Perri finds me and drops into the seat beside me. We're toward the back of the section, luckily. I'm not checking over my shoulder as much as I would be if most of the crowd was behind me.

It's kind of weird to be in this arena and not be at an SJU game. The crowd—mostly students—around us are decked out in purple. When the FSU Vipers skate out onto the ice, they're wearing all-purple sweaters with white stripes and lettering.

The snake logo is in black and white.

My gaze flicks from Penn Walker, one of the two goalies, to Oliver Ruiz. He skates like he was born on blades, and I add that to my mental list of things that irritate me about him. Also: the way he stares, the way he scowls, the way his lips form a perfect pout—

"You okay?"

Yikes.

"Just thinking," I say to Perri. "Do you like hockey?"

She wrinkles her nose. She's always properly made up, and today is no exception. Her dark hair is in a perfect bun at the base of her neck, her makeup subtle and yet seems to accent and highlight all of her good features. Not that she has any bad features.

"I come to support the boys," she allows. "But the violence turns my stomach."

I smile. "The fights are the best part."

"Interesting."

I spend the rest of the first period hoping and wishing for a fight. Mainly because hockey can be a little boring if it's a low-scoring game, or if they spend more time passing than shooting. And I can't think of a single FSU player who doesn't deserve to have their face pummeled in.

The cage helmets make things a bit more difficult, although they usually come flying off soon after the guys engage. There's no good reason to break your knuckles trying to hit *through* the cage.

The horn blows, and I let out a loud sigh. The score is 0-0.

"I'm going to see your father," Perri says. "Want to join me?"

"Nah, I'll just hang here."

Although that doesn't feel safe either. As soon as she's gone, I get up and speed to the women's restroom. I wait in line, grateful to be sandwiched by the opposing team's fans. I tap my foot as the line moves, until I'm up next. As soon as a stall is free, I lock myself in.

I sit on the toilet and check my phone, hunting for a text from the person I've been having random conversations with. I don't trust them, not entirely, but their conversation makes me feel... better.

Still, I find myself picturing a million different faces on the other side of the text thread. Boy, girl, young, old. It could be someone at SJU or FSU, or a complete stranger with a bucket of empathy.

The not knowing is going to kill me, although I've been trying to stay patient. People have a way of revealing themselves...

The restroom eventually goes quiet. It's my sign, maybe, that the game is about to start again. I finish my business and tuck my phone in my pocket, flipping the lock on the door.

Leaning against one of the far sinks is the girl from my writing class.

The one who called me a slut... Andi, I think?

Miranda Summers, another girl from the writing class, stands in the doorway with her arms crossed. Of the two, she looks decidedly uncomfortable.

"Is this an ambush?" I ask.

Andi smiles.

"I'm going to take that as a yes," I say under my breath.

eight
sydney

Andi Sharpe seems, for all intents and purposes, to be a good student. But she has a *serious* grudge against me, so much so that she showed up to class yesterday and glared daggers at me the whole time. But she didn't call me any names, which probably would've made our professor excuse her from class again.

Miranda is bright. She speaks up when she has something to say, and the two girls don't sit next to each other. Which is why I'm surprised that she's here with Andi.

"Oliver asked me to send you a message." Andi tips her head. "Ambush is what you did to *us*, snitch. This is a warning."

I hold up my hands. "I should probably wash before you do whatever you've got planned. You know, hygiene."

She glowers at me but waves me to the sink. It gives me time to try and think of a fucking solution, but... I've got nothing.

I glance over at Miranda. "Why are you here?"

"What?"

I make a face. "You're not the bullying type."

Andi's scowl deepens. "Don't talk to her."

"Uh-huh." I eye her. "What are you going to do, pour water over my head? Or beer? That shit's expensive, but you're welcome to do it if it makes you feel better." I shake the water droplets off my hands. "Or, hmm... public humiliation? Or just humiliation in general?"

Andi's gaze flicks over my shoulder. Someone grabs me from behind, manipulating my arms until my shoulders torque. Pain spikes down to my fingers, and I wince.

I didn't even have a chance to freaking struggle.

"Public humiliation sounds great," Andi murmurs.

In the mirror, I make eye contact with the person holding me. The sad part is, I don't even recognize her. Her light-brown hair is up in a severe ponytail, her eyeshadow is an interesting shade of purple, and her face is utterly ordinary.

Minus the hate in her gaze.

I squirm, trying to wiggle loose while focusing on Andi. She's clearly the one running this show. The one holding me is strong, though, and doesn't allow me any leeway.

"How long did you wait for me?" I ask.

She huffs. "Fucking forever. Oliver texted me that you were here before the game started, but you were with the coach's wife. Thank God she decided to leave you alone, right?"

Because Perri and my father don't really know the extent of bullying... or how much the entire school seems to loathe me.

Like my unknown texter said, maybe I just need to wait for someone to fuck over the football team. If only they had made it to the playoffs.

"The last thing we need is you showing up at a hockey game," Andi continues. "Miranda, do you have it?"

She pulls out a roll of duct tape from her coat pocket, coming into the bathroom and placing it in Andi's hand. She quickly retreats to the doorway, her gaze turned outward.

"Now..." Andi tilts her head. "Maybe off with the sweatshirt."

The girl behind me immediately yanks it over my head. I

throw myself backward, crashing into her, but the mountain of a girl barely stumbles. She shoves me into the counter, bending me over until my cheek is pressed to the faucet. They get the hoodie the rest of the way off, and the *rip* of duct tape comes a second later.

They bind my wrists together and hoists me upright.

The muscle turns me to face them, one hand on my upper arm.

"You seem cockier now that my hands are bound," I observe. "What's your name?"

She frowns. "You don't know?"

"I don't really care minus having someone on my mental shit list. Unless you want to be called Ogre…"

"Kate," she snaps.

"*Kate*," I repeat. "Got it. Not sure why you'd think I would know that. Do you just follow Andi here around like a little lamb?"

Andi punches me in the stomach.

The pain of it is surprising—as is my unpreparedness. I let out an unholy grunt, nearly doubling forward.

"Careful." Andi grips my hair and yanks my head back. "You're all alone here."

"Sorry," Miranda suddenly says. "There was an overflowed toilet, it's flooding… we already called maintenance."

"Have you seen Sydney Windsor?" Perri asks.

I open my mouth, and Andi lunges forward. Her palm connects with my lips, her sharp nails digging into my cheek. I stare at her. Because really, is it worth this? The anger in her eyes seems visceral, though. How far she'll go is anyone's guess.

"She hasn't come back to her seat," Perri finishes.

"No, ma'am, I'm sorry."

After a long minute, Miranda pops her head back in and gives us a thumbs-up.

Well, gives her friends the motion.

Andi rips off another few inches of tape and covers my

mouth. I shake my head, scowling at her. There will be fucking payback for this.

Kate pulls me sideways. I nearly trip over my feet as I try to follow her quick movement.

Fuck.

This.

I struggle harder, headbutting her and digging my heels into the floor. I connect with something important, because while my head hurts from the collision, it's got nothing on the way Kate yelps. She clutches at her nose with one hand, the other still death-gripping my arm.

Andi groans. It takes both of them to shove me into the stall.

While I fear they're going to dunk my head in the toilet—*they might not be above drowning*—instead, they turn me around to face them. The backs of my knees bump the toilet.

"Hold her," Andi orders.

Kate grabs my hair with her free hand, tugging hard. My head automatically goes back, trying to lessen the burning in my scalp, until I'm staring at the ceiling. My eyes water. I blink, but the pain doesn't ease.

My stomach aches, and I fight the tape around my wrists without success. The edges dig into my skin, and my fingers tingle.

Andi moves fast. She undoes the button of my jeans and pulls them all the way to my fucking ankles. My phone falls out of my pocket, and she kicks it away. It slides and scrapes across the tile, out of reach.

"Thank fuck you're wearing underwear, slut."

They shove me down, and the tape materializes back in Andi's manicured hand. I stare at her long, purple nails as she pulls a little free and slaps it on my thigh. She takes her time winding it around my legs, pressing them together.

When she goes for my ankles, I kick at her. I catch her in the side, knocking her on her ass. She comes back just as fast, slapping me across the face. She hands the tape to Kate and grabs my chin.

"This is nothing," she whispers in my ear.

They continue to secure my legs... and tape them to the toilet. My thighs are taped to the bowl, the tape securing my wrists attached to the hardware at the back. I can't go forward, there's nowhere to go backward.

When they're done, my gray shirt is barely visible beneath the layers of silver tape. My bare legs already smart from the pull and adhesive.

My cheek burns. But it's nothing compared to the helplessness that rushes through me when they both step back and I can't fucking move. I squeeze my legs together more; the *only* saving grace is that my red underwear covers enough for me to not feel *completely* naked.

A flash goes off in my face, and I jerk back as much as I can. Stars pop in front of my eyes. I blink rapidly to clear it, only slowly registering that this isn't humiliating enough— they've gone and taken a picture, too.

"This will make a great photo on your social media, Sydney," Kate sneers. "Enjoy your night."

They leave.

They leave me there.

And here I thought this shit only happened to high school nerds from the eighties.

nine
sydney

I'm not found until well after the game ends... by a janitor who shrieks her head off. She swears in Spanish and practically sprints out of the bathroom before I can get her to undo the tape.

This. Sucks.

She returns with another woman ten minutes later. The second is in a security uniform, and they both stare at me for a long moment.

"I need to make a call. Take the tape off of her mouth," the security guard tells the janitor in a low voice. "Carefully."

No one came in during the game, which I can't decide is a good or bad thing. Like, on one hand... I kept expecting someone to walk in, get a good fright, and then help me out. But the worst-case scenario would've been between the second and third period, when the restrooms are at their busiest. In that case, I think some FSU girls would probably take some enjoyment out of it.

At that point, it would become one of those things where bystanders don't fucking do anything because no one else is.

She slowly peels off the strip covering my mouth.

"Are you okay?" she asks.

I'll be honest. With my mouth free, but her just watching

instead of doing something? It's really fucking with me. My eyes fill with tears, and my chest tightens.

"Please get me out," I beg her. I twist my fingers together, although I can barely feel my pinkies. "Help me. *Please*."

The janitor puts her hand on my shoulder. "Shonda is calling the EMTs. There's a lot of tape on your skin, and we're afraid... it could cause more damage if we pull it. They can free you better."

I gulp. She goes to her cart and returns with a Styrofoam cup of water, complete with a lid and plastic straw. She puts the straw at my lips, and I suck down the ice water without question. My throat is raw, although I don't think I made much noise.

Maybe I did.

The security guard returns with two EMTs. They cut me free enough so I can stand on wobbling, half-asleep legs. They remove my jeans and sit me on the stretcher they wheeled in to get the rest off of my legs.

All the while, they pepper me with questions.

I close my eyes. Them removing the tape strips, even delicately, stings worse than anything else today. I have hives on my legs where the adhesive reacted. They advise that I might bruise, too. One looks at my cheek, checks my eyes. I figured I don't have any sort of concussion, but they confirm it.

"You're good to go," one says to me. "Shonda?"

"We need you to come to the campus security office," Shonda says.

I hop off of the stretcher and put my jeans back on carefully, my cheeks burning with shame.

She puts her arms around my shoulders. "This has been a traumatic event. We need to file a report, and it's important to get the details accurate. Come on, honey."

I open and close my mouth. My lips are raw, still sticky with a bitter taste from the glue.

I'm also really fucking tired.

I don't know where my phone ended up. I pause and mention it, and she quickly searches the bathroom. She finds it two stalls over. The screen is cracked diagonally, but other than that seems to be in working order.

It's almost midnight.

I suck in another breath, although it comes in shuddering. I should've fought harder. I basically just gave in at the end, didn't I?

Shonda leads me out of the arena through a side exit and into the campus security SUV. I lean back against the seat and touch the cheek Andi slapped. My legs are some mix of itchy and painful, every rasp of my jeans against the skin like sandpaper, but it's my cheek that seems to draw most of my focus.

We park on campus, and Shonda ushers me across the lot and into the Admin building, down a slight ramp, and through the first door on the right. The office seems quiet, with another security guard manning a desk. Although he's kicked back, his feet up on the desk beside a stack of folders, he quickly drops them and offers me a concerned gaze.

"Sit here," Shonda says.

I almost fall into the cushioned chair she gestures to. I check my phone again, having to scroll through another onslaught of blocked callers and unsaved numbers to find five texts from Perri asking where I am. Then two from Dad...

God.

I swallow around the lump in my throat.

I reply to Perri that I had a bad run-in and went home early. I thank Dad for inviting me. For trying. I find Unknown's thread, and they, too, seem to be questioning where I am. Because their last text hangs unanswered:

UNKNOWN

Savory or sweet?

Followed by, hours later:

How do they know what's like me or not? I don't reply.
Can't. It feels too personal to admit what just happened. And,
besides, I have a feeling they'll be finding out sooner rather
than later.

Did Andi send the photo to Oliver?

Or is she going to post it herself?

"Okay, here we are." Shonda sits beside me with a clipboard. There seems to be a blank form attached to it, and she
poises her pen above the first line. "Eleven twenty-seven p.m.,
janitor calls campus security at the arena. Responding officer,
Shonda McDermid," she points to herself, "finds female
student…"

"In a compromising position?" I joke.

She sighs and passes me the clipboard and pen. "Listen.
This is important, we just… we can't have this sort of thing
happening. Do you understand? Help us stop this. FSU has a
no-tolerance policy for bullying."

I bite my lower lip. "So they'd get in trouble? If it was a
student."

"It would be brought before the Dean of Students and a
decision made from there, yes."

She pats my shoulder again, leaving the clipboard held
loosely in my lap. "I'll give you some time, okay? Just write
down everything you remember."

I want to be home. I want to shower in scalding water and
wrap myself in a fluffy robe I stole from a hotel once, and then
crawl into bed and not emerge for a week.

At the very least.

I fill out the top part. Name, student ID number, date.

Location of incident. I start to write out what happens, but when I get to the part about coming *out* of the bathroom, when Andi and Miranda are waiting in plain sight, and Kate is still hidden, I freeze.

If I write down their names, I will officially, *actually* be a snitch.

That will only make things worse. Besides, do I blame Andi, who's arguably just a pawn in this scheme against me? Or do I blame Oliver Ruiz?

Or do I blame Kate, who manhandled me the most?

Or do I fucking blame myself for giving those playbook page photos to Carter?

I rise.

Shonda, who has been chatting with her colleague quietly, turns to me. Her eyebrows hike. "Done already?"

I'm shaking my head no before her question is finished. "I don't want to file a report. I'm sorry, but I can't tell you anything, and I'm not going to press charges. Everything is fine."

She takes the clipboard from me and scans what I'd filled out.

"Sydney Windsor," she says. "Why—?"

"Frank's kid," the other guard supplies. "Hockey coach."

Her lips part. "Who would do this to the coach's daughter?" She faces me. "Are you not naming names because you don't know? Was it someone from the visiting team?"

"I—*no*. I'm not saying anything. I don't want to make this into a bigger deal..."

"We're going to have to notify your father," the guy says. "Protocol."

"Fuck your protocol. It was a harmless prank, nothing more." I snatch the paper back, ripping it up and crumpling the pieces into a ball. I drop it in the trash on my way out, and I pick up a jog as soon as I'm outside.

But the jog turns into a sprint pretty damn quick, and it

seems like I make it back to my apartment in record time. It doesn't matter that my whole body is screaming at me to slow down—it isn't until I can see my building's front door, and the person sitting on the steps waiting for me, that I pause.

The goalie.

Penn Walker?

Sweat dampens the hair at the base of my neck and along my temples, but I slow my breathing in an attempt to not appear weak... or out of shape. Not that he saw me running like my hair was on fire...

Don't give them any ideas.

He looks up when I stop at the base of the stairs. He seems to unfold, getting bigger—and the added height of the steps he has on me doesn't help.

"What are you doing?" I demand.

"Sent on a mission by your father, princess." He trots down the steps and tosses a bundle at me. My jacket, complete with my keys in the pocket.

I had left it at my seat... which means he might not buy my excuse. Not if he sent Penn here. And why would he do that if... if he thought Penn might hurt me?

"He trusts you?"

"More than he trusts you," he counters. "I haven't stabbed him in the back and almost got him fired."

I tilt my head. "What?"

He rolls his eyes, slipping past me. "It's not rocket science. You're the source of the issue and you share his last name. Not only that, but you cost FSU our playoffs run. That fucking means something, especially when St. James was the one to knock us out."

I rotate. "Did you go in my apartment?"

"Yeah, I stole your panties." He scoffs. "No, Sydney. I'm not obsessed with you like everyone else."

"Sure seems like it," I say under my breath. And louder, "Weren't you just threatening me this afternoon?"

He's already heading down the sidewalk away from me, but his condescending laugh floats back. I shake my head and hurry to unlock the front door.

But not before the hairs on the back of my neck rise.

I pause just inside and stare out at the darkness. I swear I can see something...

Someone?

But the more I look, the more I convince myself I don't see anyone. That weird feeling goes away, too. I ease the door closed and head upstairs.

The good news: I have a day to myself.

The bad news: another shoe is about to fucking drop, in the form of an embarrassing photo. And maybe a story circulated by Andi or the hockey team, to boot.

Why else would she take a picture and go through the trouble of humiliating me?

ten
sydney

Savory or sweet?

Not like you to go missing like this.

Such an important question left unanswered…

U OK?

ME

Both. Salted dark chocolate is my jam.

…and I'm sorry, something came up.

I'm fine.

Something in the form of assholes, or…?

Just a few bullies.

Did they get any of their own medicine?

If you see a girl sporting a broken nose and pair of black eyes, it definitely *wasn't* me.

[laughing gif]

Noted.

You know my name, right?

Yes.

And I know virtually nothing about you.

I suppose that's a fair assessment.

I need something.

Fine, ask and I'll answer… maybe.

Name?

Right for the jugular. Call me L.

A single letter? How fashion-forward your parents were.

L.

I know. I give them shit all the time for it. The period is a package deal with the letter, by the way.

Jeez. Okay, well, since that gives me nothing—guy or girl?

Guy.

In college. That one's a freebie. I'm not some sick 60-year-old hoping to talk you into sending nudes.

Although I wouldn't turn them down either

FSU or SJU?

Pass

Why???

> I want you to think of me as a neutral party. Where I go to school doesn't matter, right? I'm kind of awesome at being a voice of reason and being on your side at the same time.

>> Uh-huh.

> Does that bother you?

>> I'd be lying if I said no.

> Tell me a lie, then.

>> I was tied up in the women's restroom during the hockey game tonight.

The photo doesn't appear online. Not on Sunday anyway. And I don't get any more disgruntled looks than usual when I head to meet Dylan before Calculus Monday morning, which makes me think the gossip hasn't fully ramped up.

Maybe since yesterday was a recovery day for the campus, following what I'm assuming was a party-filled night after FSU's win. I don't want to look a gift horse in the mouth.

But Calculus also gives Dylan her first glimpse of the bruise on my cheek that I tried to cover up. An attempt that apparently completely failed.

She touches my chin and turns my head to the side, mouth open.

"Who—what—when—*where*?"

"But not why?"

She touches my cheekbone, and I wince.

"The why is obvious." She passes me the coffee she bought before I arrived.

I really need a job. I don't like to think about how fucking *poor* I feel all the time. It only creeps up on me for the little things, like buying my own coffee. If Dad didn't secure me essentially a free ride to FSU, fund my textbooks and school supplies, *and* cover the basics, like my meal plan, housing, groceries, and utilities, I'd be shit out of luck. The coffee place uses those flex dollars attached to my meal plan, but coffee is expensive. I'd burn through those too fast if I wanted coffee every damn morning.

As it is, my bank account is down to a single digit.

When I asked Dad for help, I didn't expect *everything*. The unfortunate truth of the matter is that he made me comfortable... and that made me complacent.

"Do you know anywhere that's hiring?" I ask Dylan as we walk to class.

She hums. "I don't, but you could check with Brandon. He's got that bartending job at Briar, maybe they need more help. Have you waitressed?"

I straighten. "Yeah, I did in high school."

"The good thing is, FSU has a shit ton of bars around it because we're all alcoholics." She snorts. "I can't vouch for how well college assholes tip, but I'm pretty sure they all shifted to paying fair wages. Talk to Brandon."

"Good idea."

She nudges me. "So, what, where, when, *who*...?"

I shake my head and brush her off.

Halfway through Calculus is when it happens. There seems to be a rolling tide of attention shifting in my direction, so much so that even the professor stops teaching. Students have their phones out, some vibrating or going off silently with alerts.

Even Dylan's goes off, and she turns to show me the screen.

A photo of me from Saturday night, with the security guard's arm around my shoulders.

The caption reads, *Once a snitch, always a snitch.*

Fuck.

"Settle," the professor calls. "Now, once you've solved..."

It was posted by the FSU gossip page, the one that gave out my information. My concentration is *fucked*. My mind keeps wandering back to Saturday. And it sucks because Sunday in my apartment actually felt somewhat good. I didn't think about anything other than the show I decided to binge. I stayed in bed and hid from the world.

But now this?

It's not like it's paired with the photo Andi took, because at least that would explain why I was with security. But, no. There are already replies to the main content, people taking the photo and warping it, editing horns into my hair or making my eyes red, my brows bushy and overexaggerated.

"Class is over." Dylan closes my notebook for me. "Let's get out of here."

Agreed.

I shove my stuff in my bag and follow her to the library. We find a table in the far back, half hidden by the stacks. She shoots Brandon a text, then dumps everything from her bag onto the table.

Not school supplies.

Food...?

Granola bars, candy bars, a rather large bag of pretzels, one of those squeeze tubes of peanut butter. Her notebook from Calculus comes sliding out, too.

"Why...?"

"I have diabetes, so I'm always prepared. I need sugar if my levels drop too low." She lifts her shirt slightly, revealing the pod stuck to her stomach a few inches above the waistband of her leggings. She taps the compact black case amongst the snacks. "This has my extra insulin and supplies in case I spike, but this device usually keeps track and gives me insulin as needed."

"I had no idea."

She shrugs. "I don't advertise it. It doesn't stop me from living my life, I just have to make some adjustments."

"Okay, good."

"Trust me, I have more at my apartment. Take whatever you want."

I'm still deciding when Brandon arrives, breathless and wet-haired.

"Did you run here?" Dylan asks.

"I was on my way out anyway." He makes a face at her.

"With wet hair? Who are you, and what have you done with my best friend?"

"Shut it." He focuses on me. "I saw the post. I'm sorry, Sydney, I don't know why they *keep* targeting you."

I sigh. "Yeah, well…"

The real problem is Oliver Ruiz. He seems intent on keeping my past fresh in people's minds by any means necessary.

"This story is going to require more than snacks," I finish.

Something behind me catches Dylan's attention. And Brandon's.

"Oh, shit." She grabs my hand. "Don't turn around. They probably don't see you."

"Who?"

"Ruiz, Walker, and some others."

I close my eyes.

"We're tucked pretty far out of the way," she offers.

"I found you pretty easily," Brandon mumbles. "But—I knew you were here."

"And you don't think they look around when they get into the library?" I shake my head. "I need to get out of here. Or, I don't know—"

"Too late," Brandon interrupts.

Someone drags out the empty chair beside me and drops into it. I glance over at Oliver Ruiz. His dark hair is perfectly styled, and he raises a thick eyebrow at whatever expression is on my face.

Probably irritation.

"Sydney." He says it like he's never said my name before.

"Oliver."

"You and your friends are formally invited to our next party."

Dylan chokes.

"I've been to parties, and they don't tend to come with formal invitations attached." I scowl. "Why would I want to be surrounded by people who hate me anyway?"

He shrugs. His hazel eyes are more green than brown today. "It would go a long way to convincing your dad you're okay. Since Bear can't keep his mouth shut, and it's only a matter of time before something about the *snitch* slips out."

"It seems unlikely that he doesn't already hear rumors. Is that why he brought me into the locker room? To try and sway you guys?"

"Such a straightlaced guy, your father." He leans in. "An honest man. Makes me wonder about the other genes his daughter possesses to turn out so different?"

Every muscle in my body goes tight at his insinuation about my mother. My absent mother, who I haven't given a thought to since last week.

"Okay," Brandon interjects. "We're trying to work here. You're welcome to do a case study on nature versus nurture if you're so inclined... as long as you're not in our space."

He smiles. "Sure thing, Moore. Just remember—once someone has a history of lying, you can't trust a damn thing they say."

He strolls back to his table, and I can't help but turn and watch him go. He, along with most hockey players, Carter and Penn included, has a fantastic ass. Even in dark-wash jeans.

I meet Penn's darkening gaze at their table and quickly swivel back around.

"I, um, have to go." I grab my bag. "Thanks for trying to cheer me up with sugar. I'll see you guys later."

In reality, though, the library is the exact place I need to be. I ask the student at the front desk for past yearbooks—I shoot for nineteen to twenty-three years ago, because I can't quite remember when Mom graduated—and take the stack upstairs. There's just a narrow strip of two-person desks up here, arranged along a railing that overlooks the first floor.

The fact that my mother attended FSU continually shocks me. The more I think on it, the more I am convinced she never mentioned it.

She knew of the rivalry and didn't stop me from going to SJU. Never said a word about it even when I was enrolled at St. James. And Dad works *here*. I'd bet they met here, although I never asked. All signs should've pointed to me attending FSU from the beginning.

Once I have a table, conveniently with a line of sight on the hockey table and my friends, I dig in.

My first find comes in the second yearbook. Not from the individual portraits, but one of the clubs that are listed first. It's her face that snags my attention, and then her name in a short list at the bottom confirms it.

I suddenly can't get in enough air.

The thing is, I have a picture of my mom in my head. It's been shaped by growing up with her, loving her, and trauma in fair portions. Living with her over the summer revealed traits that I had either been blind to or ignorant of, and that kind of eye-opening is hard.

But what's worse is seeing this completely different version of her. One that's smiling easily, with her hair loose around her shoulders and her hand on a guy's arm. This one doesn't have to wear layers of makeup to hide the dark circles under her eyes. *This* one didn't scrounge enough money together for months just to buy a nice shirt and skirt for her job.

Happiness seems foreign on her.

The mother I knew was stressed and tired. She would sometimes disappear on me for a day or two, especially once I was old enough to use the microwave. It was up to me to get myself to school, to brush my hair and teeth, to put on clean clothes and pack my bag with all my homework.

But she always came back, delirious, sometimes caught in fits of giggles that seemed to seep out of her cracks. Even when, as I got older, her absences grew longer.

Her return was usually accompanied by cash. New food, the electricity bill paid. The heat turned on, if we were lucky.

New outfits.

And within a week or two of epic, sometimes nausea-inducing mania, we were back to square one.

I shake it off, until my gaze snags on the bracelet she's wearing.

My body goes clammy.

I flip through the rest of the book, scanning each page for her, although now queasiness distracts me. Mom was in the drama club—that's the first picture I found. But I don't see her again until the juniors are listed, and her maiden name in small print: *Jessica Hansen*.

There she is. *Again*. I'm going to throw up for real, but the important thing is that I'm not crazy—she was here. Now I just need to figure out if it connects to where she went.

eleven
sydney

This is my third Intro to Law class, and I'm not a hundred percent convinced it's for me. The more we discuss how law works, and the many ways it seems to *not* work, the more I'm convinced the police will never help me find my mother.

I have the Emerald Cove detective's number saved in my phone from when I reported her missing, but since then? Crickets.

My mind goes back to the yearbook photo. She was wearing the bracelet in it. If her stories are to be believed, it was handed down from her grandmother's grandmother.

And now it's somewhere in Oliver Ruiz's house, if the paper trail is to be believed.

Breaking into his house seems a little insane at this point. It's brought along no small amount of struggle. And there's that saying: *possession is nine tenths of the law*. He, or someone in his family, bought the bracelet that has been in my family for generations.

"If whatever career path you go down doesn't work, you could always become a confidential informant," a voice says in my ear.

I shudder.

Penn sinks into the seat behind me, kicking the back of my

chair. The lecture hasn't begun yet, although he's definitely late. He doesn't seem to care. His black eye seems better. Almost gone, just kind of yellowish in a ring around the socket.

"Where'd you get the black eye?" I ask.

"Bar fight. Who hit you?"

I frown.

He stares at me some more, his green eyes looking almost blue in comparison to the yellow hue around the one.

"No one hit me," I mumble.

"Uh-huh. And that girl who follows Andi Sharpe around like a Mindy doesn't have two black eyes."

"Does she? I haven't seen."

"Interesting." He reaches out and presses on the back of my head. The bruised, tender skin.

I jerk forward, biting my tongue to keep from swearing.

"Like a headbutt," he muses. "Something happen, princess? Want to report it to the authorities?"

"I had the opportunity and I didn't," I snap. "So just leave me alone."

He chuckles. "I'm not talking about the scum in-campus security. I'm talking about me."

I twist toward him fully. The professor is still unpacking his bag, for fuck's sake. Everyone around us is conversing, too. I grab on to the back of my chair, but Penn is leaning forward. He's practically in my face already.

"You're the authority? Your *bestie* is the one who issued the order."

His brows furrow.

"Maybe I'll just transfer out of this class and take art or something. Especially if you're here. You can't call yourself an authority and be this thick, Penn."

I shove my things in my bag, just as the professor calls the class to settle down. He makes a noise when I rise and head straight for the door.

"Ms. Windsor—"

I'm gone before he can finish that sentence. Instead of going to the registrar—seems like a tomorrow problem—I head home and change into running clothes. I haven't gone on an actual run in a long time, and maybe the restlessness in my muscles will finally quiet if I give it an outlet.

Hooking up my earbuds, zipping the lightweight jacket over my sports bra, I hit the road. Almost immediately, my breathing is labored. That's what I fucking get for not running in almost a month.

Everything with my mom just messed me up, I guess. Running is a healthy habit, and I may have been more interested in self-destructing.

But once I push past that painful part, it gets easier. I hit that zone where it's just my stride and breathing and the music in my ears.

I skirt campus, instead heading toward St. James. I don't know why... I just miss seeing people who don't hate me on sight. There's a more direct route, but the road is more like a highway. The sidewalks there aren't maintained well. So I take the winding road that curves through the forest and gives a decent view of the lake.

Few cars come this way, it seems. The road is quiet until a car whizzes past me. The brake lights illuminate a second later, and the vehicle swerves across the lane to stop in my path.

My stride slows.

It isn't until the driver's door opens and Carter Masters gets out that I realize I recognize his vehicle.

I put my hand on my chest, dropping into a walk and pulling out my earbuds with my other hand. "You scared me!"

"You're running out here all by yourself?" He approaches quickly, stopping just short of me. His gaze snaps to my cheek. "What the fuck happened?"

I shiver and touch the bruise I can't seem to hide. "Oh, uh..."

"Sydney."

"Some stupid drama," I mutter. "FSU's student body doesn't like me very much."

"All of them?" His blue eyes are so freaking intense. "That doesn't explain—did someone hit you?"

"I..." I don't want to lie. But literally *everyone* found out about what I did from Carter. "How did they know it was me that gave you the FSU plays?"

He blinks. "Whoa, that's quite the change in direction."

"We haven't talked about it since I was kicked out of SJU." I plant my hands on my hips. "And why are you out here—?"

"I was on my way back into town." He shifts back, sliding his hands into his pockets. "It's kind of cold out here, huh? Can I buy you some lunch? Maybe not in FSU territory."

My stomach grumbles, and I crack a smile when he raises his eyebrow.

"Okay," I allow.

I settle in his car and run my hands along my thighs. The hives from the tape have mostly gone away, but I'm covered in bruises from struggling. It's easy to hide when the weather is cool, and long-sleeve shirts or sweatshirts are acceptable. But when Carter cranks the heat...

I want to crack the window instead of take off the jacket.

"How has SJU been without me?"

He glances over. "You miss us?"

"Something like that." I roll my eyes. "I'm not sure I miss you, Carter. You didn't say how they found out it was me."

"It's shitty," he confesses. "And it snowballed."

I motion for him to continue.

"Coach wouldn't take the photos without proof that they came from someone reliable. And you... you're the most reliable source I could've asked for, Syd. You're literally the FSU coach's daughter. Estranged or not—"

"Our relationship is under construction," I interrupt.

"Okay," he allows. "But he saw your name on the message

thread, and it just kind of spiraled from there. It definitely got out of control as soon as the administration got wind of it."

The worst part is that Carter and the hockey team didn't get in trouble—not more than just a slap on the wrist anyway. They had the playoffs, they had prestige and glory to bring to the school, while I was the one jeopardizing everything by cheating.

Stealing.

Whatever they said.

"Going in front of the ethics committee was humiliating."

"I went in front of them, too. I told them it wasn't your fault, that I stole the photos from your phone, but they didn't believe me." He reaches over and puts his hand on my thigh. "How much do you hate me?"

I flinch.

He retracts quickly, lips parting. "What kind of reaction was that?"

"I just—"

"Sydney."

"I have some bruising. And places where my skin is a little fragile at the moment." I look out the window. "It's fine."

It's not a complete lie.

If Andi or Oliver aren't going to post that photo, I'm sure as shit not going to tell anyone.

"I don't understand why you went there." He pulls into the parking lot of the diner we used to frequent, in the spot he always parks in. Except today, he's out of the car and around to my door in a flash, leaning over me and gently touching the top of my thigh. "Here?"

My head falls back. "Just assume everywhere hurts."

"Fucking hell, Sydney."

I unbuckle and climb out, forcing him to move back. We stare at each other for a beat, and my face heats at the memory of our last encounter. The last kiss... The one that ruined my life as I knew it.

Finally, I shake it off and brush past him, heading for the door.

"I don't have any money, by the way," I call over my shoulder.

"Good thing it's my treat," he counters.

He practically chases me inside. We sit at the booth that Lettie and I spent many Sundays slumped in, nursing our hangovers with bottomless mimosas and sugar-dusted pancakes.

If I close my eyes, I can practically envision Lettie, Marcy, and whoever else piled into the booth, laughing over the latest scandal... not knowing that eventually, it would be me.

"FSU had their first scrimmage this weekend," he says.

I stiffen.

"Did they get new plays, or are we going to wipe the ice with their asses again?"

He's not fucking serious, is he?

I lean forward. "Did you bring me here just to try and get information out of me, Carter?"

"Nah." He settles back, hooking his arm over the back of his seat. "You know me better than that. It was a simple question."

I scoff. "Yeah, right. I changed my mind about lunch."

"Your stomach growled," he points out. "I won't ask about hockey, okay?"

"How about *I* ask *you* about hockey?" I counter. "How're the Seawolves doing? Any good prospects come in this year?"

"Some." His smile tells me he knows exactly what I'm doing.

I like hockey. I've said it before, I'll say it again. I still have vivid memories of learning to skate with my dad holding my hands as a toddler, and then later, when he put me on the ice to wander around as he coached, some of the older boys helping. Their version of it anyway.

But I haven't been on the ice in years. Not since the last

time I stayed with Dad, and I'm pretty sure I was on the cusp of eighteen. Right before we went no-contact. One final visit, even though I hated every minute of it.

The waitress comes by and takes our drink and food orders. While she repeats what we said, Carter's foot runs up the inside of my ankle. It sends a spike of heat through me, although I don't want it to—I'm supposed to be mad at him.

But how can I be mad when he's the only one who doesn't hate my guts?

My fragile new friendships don't count. I'm still wary of them exploding in my face. Not that I would admit that to anyone but myself.

I tuck my hair behind my ear. The waitress leaves, and I decide to try and unnerve him a little. Just because he's touching me like he still has a right to do so.

"Oliver Ruiz. What else do you know about him?"

Carter scowls. "He's a devil on the ice. He was drafted out of high school, although he committed to FSU for two years. This is his last year. He plays forward... Please tell me he wasn't the one who hurt you."

"Not directly. And Penn Walker?"

"Goalie."

"Obviously."

He sighs. "Did you show this much interest in me when you went to St. James, Syd?"

"Yeah, right. Your ego doesn't need inflating any more." I nudge his leg with my toe. "So, you threw me under the bus and got me kicked out, and now you're buying me lunch. Should I remind you that this doesn't usually end well for us?"

His eyes gleam. "I don't know... if by that you mean naked, then you can remind me all you want."

I roll my eyes, but my face flames. It's been too fucking long since I had sex, and now that he's insinuating, it seems like all the adrenaline drops straight to my core.

No. I'm not about to fall down that rabbit hole.

Was he the last person I had sex with? Maybe.

Does he need to know that? *Nope.*

"You know," he leans forward, "I can do that thing with my tongue that gets you to come all over my face in seconds."

Jesus. My face gets hotter.

He smirks. "Your choice."

Of course it is.

The waitress delivers our drinks and food quickly, and by the time we're done, Carter has traced every inch of the inside of my leg with his foot. Something that absolutely shouldn't turn me on, but maybe I've just been fucking starved of positive touch.

So when he drives us back to my place, I bite my lip and silently invite him up.

He follows closer than a shadow up the three floors, brushing my hair off my neck and kissing just behind my ear when I stop to unlock my apartment door.

This is bad.

We barely make it inside. He kicks the door closed and spins me in place, my back hitting the door with a soft thud. I toe off my shoes, flinging them to the side. He flips the lock, his lips crashing into mine. I rise on my toes, wrapping my arms around his neck. He knows how to make a girl feel like the sun. He unzips my jacket and shoves it off my shoulders, then goes for my leggings.

"Carter?" I gasp, tearing my lips away.

He immediately moves to my neck, sucking and nipping his way down to my collarbone.

"Just ignore the bruises, okay?"

He hums affirmation. My arms drop, and the jacket slips free. He pushes my sports bra up and palms my breast, paying my nipples attention until I whimper, then moves lower.

He does pause at the bruises on my stomach, though. He traces the fist-shaped one, then presses. The dull ache makes me squirm. He drags my leggings down and hooks my one leg over his shoulder, pressing a single kiss to my pubic bone.

And then he goes lower...

He makes good on his promise to *do that thing with his tongue*. I cry out, gripping his hair and tugging. Whether I'm trying to get him off or closer is anyone's guess, though. He chuckles against my core, and once I've stopped trembling, he surges up. I go for his jeans, pushing them down until he kicks them and his shoes off.

I take his hand and practically drag him to the couch, shoving him onto it. I straddle him, and he fists his cock, stroking once, twice while he looks me over.

"Those bruises really do fucking suck," he says. His attention drops to my thighs. "And these..."

"Ignore it," I beg. I kiss him again. My hand covers his, taking over the long, firm strokes. When his hips jack and his breathing stutters, I line him up and slowly lower myself. He stretches me, and it takes all my willpower not to chase another high immediately.

My body is singing.

He reaches up and runs his fingers through my hair, tilting my head to kiss me deeper. A quick fuck with an ex shouldn't involve so much intimacy, but it's always been our way. I feel the way he cares in how he handles me, even if he doesn't show it the best sometimes.

I hate it, too.

Hate him a bit.

There's no one to blame but myself. On a cellular level, I know this.

We fuck slowly until he can't take it anymore. In a smooth motion, he flips us. My back hits the cushions, and he draws almost all the way out of me. My pussy is clenching at just the tip of his dick, and he waits, running his hand over my breast and trailing down between my legs again.

He replaces his dick with his fingers, and I tremble when

he finds my G-spot. He pays it special attention, his gaze rapt on my face, until I find the pressure building again.

Higher.

Higher... and then it plateaus.

"You. In me. Now."

He laughs. "Yeah? You don't like this?"

"You're fucking torturing me." No matter how I move my hips, I can't get enough.

"All right," he finally accepts. "Tell me this: did you give it back to them? Whoever did this to you?"

I hesitate.

"Yeah. She's probably sporting a pair of black eyes by now."

He smiles. "Good girl. Now, let me take care of that for you."

Fingers disappear, coming back to my breasts. Both hands. Pinching and rolling my nipples, tugging my breasts, while he notches himself again.

He thrusts forward hard enough to make me scream. I arch, my eyes barely staying open. He fucks me hard and fast, chasing his own orgasm. My fingers go to my clit. I rub little circles, the pressure just how I like it, until I'm riding the edge.

He locks eyes with me, and I nod.

"Now," he groans.

I shove myself over the cliff, my orgasm somehow more intense than the first. I clench around him, and two fast pumps later, he comes, too.

Without a condom.

"Carter."

He falls forward, wrapping his arms around me. He continues jacking his hips slowly, even after finishing. I hook my legs around his hips, but my muscles are trembling.

"I'm not on birth control," I whisper.

He kisses my throat. "Okay."

"*Okay?* Not okay."

"We'll take care of it."

I push his face away. "You better not be referring to a baby."

His nose wrinkles. "I meant the morning after pill or whatever. I'll get you some."

As in, one of the more expensive birth control options. I can't afford that, and I'm sure as hell not asking my father for money to get it.

So either he's telling the truth, or I'm fucked.

twelve

carter

Sydney Windsor is an elixir I didn't know I needed.

Okay, that's a lie. Scarlett Blake shoved her into my path, and I never wanted to let her go. But that intensity, that soon... it scared her. And me, a bit. We were freshmen in college, and I was just figuring out the hockey thing.

Hockey is and always has been my life. Turning my back on it, or at least letting her distract me, seemed... detrimental to my future. Unlike Oliver, who will be playing for the Colorado Titans when he stops fucking around and deferring, I'll face the NHL draft next year. My agent is working behind the scenes, but he knows I'm committed to finishing out my last year at school. All that is to say—we'll see. I just need to be enough.

I leave Sydney's apartment and head to FSU. It's an off-limits place, but I tug my ball cap lower and keep my head down. I take a seat on a bench in the quad and watch the students pass by. A lot don't look at me twice, which is nice. Some do, but I ignore them.

I ignore a lot of the attention foisted on me nowadays, because it's the only way I can keep calm.

Someone catches my eye. A collection of girls, one of which is sporting two black eyes. Sydney's soft admission before I left was that it wasn't any of the hockey guys. Which is good, because I would go straight to her fucking father and get them all expelled.

Which leaves girls. And these girls...

Well, it would make sense that Sydney would fight back, right?

They leave the student center and part ways. I stick with the girl with the black eyes, more curious than anything. She peels off and heads for the parking garage. She doesn't notice me tagging along, sticking to the shadows. I keep my head down, peeking under the brim of my hat. The last thing I need is for her to report what I'm about to do...

And for cameras to confirm her story.

A few cars ahead of her, an SUV's lights flash. I pick up my pace and catch up just as she steps between her vehicle and the one beside it. She's tall and muscular, almost my height, but I take her by surprise.

I shove her against her car, my hand on the back of her head keeping her cheek to the glass.

"Don't look at me," I hiss. "I'll cut your fucking eyes out."

Her eyes squeeze shut.

"Tell me what happened with Sydney."

"Nothing," she cries. "Sydney? I've never—"

"Don't fucking lie to me." My knife is in my hand in an instant, the blade sliding free from the handle with a soft scrape. I press it to her throat. "Try again. Sydney Windsor."

"I don't—"

"She broke your nose, hmm?" I lean forward, until my lips are almost at her ear. I don't want to touch her, but I'm practically flattened against her. The brim of my hat touches her temple. "She got the best of you for a moment, didn't she? And now I do."

I press harder on her throat. At the first cut, the girl breaks. She's trembling so bad, I have to remove the knife or risk slitting her throat on *accident*. That would be a travesty.

I like to do things with purpose. This girl bleeding out in the FSU parking garage would only create... sympathy for her.

When Sydney deserves the school's sympathy more than anyone.

I grit my teeth and curl my fingers into her hair. I pull her head back a fraction and slam it back to the glass.

"*Talk*," I order.

"It wasn't my idea," she cries. Tears spill down her cheeks. "I just wanted to fit in with Andi's group. When she asked me, I couldn't say no."

"Ask her what?"

"T-to help her teach Sydney a lesson. We followed her into the bathroom during the game and—"

"And?" I tug on her hair.

"And when it was empty, we taped her to the toilet. Took pictures—"

My stomach flips. They fucking taped her—those bruises are from *tape*?

"How long?"

She licks her lips. Such an unattractive girl, blubbering in my hold.

"Come on," I say, switching tactics. "You tell me this, I let you go. Yeah? You can go home like none of this happened. Or you clam up, and I give you a permanent reminder of tonight."

Take that as she will.

The smell of urine rises between us.

I bite back my curse and shift back, out of the way as she loses control of her bladder.

"We closed the bathroom," she finally whispers. "I think the janitor found her after the game..."

I release her. The knife folds, tucks back in my pocket. The phone comes out.

I snap a picture of my own.

"Andi Sharpe. She was the mastermind behind your little plan?"

The girl jumps away from me. Her gaze sticks to my shoes, my earlier threat apparently still fresh in her mind. The business of cutting out her eyes turns my stomach, but she doesn't have to know that.

"Oliver texted her that Sydney was at the game," she whispers. "But I don't think he told her what to d0—"

"Where can I find her?"

"I—"

"If you lie, this picture is going straight to your FSU gossip page." I shove my phone, and the photo of her with soiled pants, under her face. "Where does she live?"

Andi Sharpe lives with one roommate. I wait until their lights go out, then wait a little more. When I'm convinced they're most likely asleep, I break into their first-floor apartment. I don't bother concealing the sounds. The cracking, falling glass is loud enough.

I climb in, my boots hitting the floor hard. I glance around the common area and grab a chair from their kitchen table. I drag it with me and shove it under the roommate's door handle. It wouldn't stop her if she tried to force it open, since it swings inward, but it'll stop the handle from turning... and that should be enough for someone who might be too scared to even try.

Following the loose instructions the black-eyed girl gave me, I head down the hallway and shove open Andi's bedroom door.

It *cracks* against the far wall, and the girl screams. She's sitting upright in bed, her phone in her hand.

"I've called nine-one-one," she cries.

I stride forward and snatch it, ending the call. I'm going to fucking hold on to her phone and get to the bottom of who decided to hurt Sydney. But not right now. Now, Andi scrambles back. Except there's nowhere for her to go. I grab her by her throat and haul her out of bed.

My face is obscured by a ski mask, but she can see my eyes. She grasps at my hands, trying to pry my fingers away. I squeeze. Her feet kick, but she's petite. At this angle, she can't reach the floor.

"Sydney is off-limits," I say. "Say yes."

Andi's face reddens. It's obvious even in the dark.

We stare at each other, until finally she lets out a croaking, "Yes!"

Good enough.

I throw her onto the bed and turn away. The sirens in the distance make me tilt my head. I look down at her.

"I'm sure you have some pretty nasty texts," I say, sliding her phone back out of my pocket. "Talking shit about people, maybe a few secrets you hold close or let slip..."

Her jaw works. She's afraid *and* defiant.

I'd be into that if I didn't already have Sydney.

"This didn't happen. A lot of embarrassing shit about you will come out if you tell anyone. Say yes if you understand."

She glowers and finally mutters, "Yes."

I turn on my heel. I slip out the way I came and move between the buildings. I peel the ski mask from my head and toss it in a bin in the alley. My gloves go in my pockets. Whether she's actually going to call the police is anyone's guess.

In a matter of minutes, I'm back outside Sydney's apartment.

She needs to be better looked after. She has no one else... no one but me.

I rotate in a small circle. Hockey seems like a lifetime away. My whole life at St. James does. The guilt of not being able to stop the avalanche that buried Sydney consumes me. It has since the summer...

But this is next level.

This street is filled with brownstones. My attention snags on a small sign in the window of one across the street. *Apartments for rent.*

A phone number.

Maybe the best way to keep Sydney safe is to be so close to her I'll practically be her shadow.

thirteen
sydney

Have you ever thought about running away?

L.

Like, out of state?

Maybe out of the country

I have not considered it. Where would you go?

I think about it often.

Where? As far as I could get.

We're approaching a month since Penn and Oliver made that stupid over-under bet. And obviously Carter doesn't count. He came through with the morning after pill, delivering it to my door the next day with a muffin and coffee. And I got my period a week later.

All's well that ends well...

Except I can't shake the feeling that I'm being watched.

Things have actually calmed the fuck down on campus. I don't seem to be in mortal danger anymore, although that's starting to create some paranoia on its own. I walk around with my shoulders inching higher and higher, waiting for that shoe to drop.

Everyone has backed off.

I spot Kate walking across the quad one day. And although it's been a few weeks since that scrimmage game where she assaulted me, her eyes are still a lovely shade of green bruising. Kind of like how Penn's were...

He's back to normal, though.

And Kate? She turns tail and practically runs away from me.

After leaving Intro to Law, I had a change of heart about transferring out of the class. I'm not going to let one asshole dictate my course of study. So I never filed the paperwork, never even met with my academic advisor.

He hasn't tried anything. He's being kind of nice, actually. It's *weird*.

Now, Penn sits beside me and automatically reaches for my hair. He plays with it during class sometimes, never tugging, but constantly twirling locks between his fingers. I tried to get him to stop once, and he just smirked.

So now I let him. Grudgingly.

But when he pulls twice, I glance over my shoulder at him.

"You didn't come to the party."

"I was never planning on it."

The party that Oliver previously invited me and my friends to was last weekend.

"Are you coming to our games? It's a double header this weekend." He leans into my space. "Against SJU."

I shake my head. "No, I like to avoid that arena at all costs."

"What if I could guarantee your safety?"

I narrow my eyes.

He smiles. It's absolutely a *gotcha* smile.

"Don't you miss hockey?" he questions. "Since you missed most of that scrimmage, you didn't get to see my kick-ass skills. Just saying."

"Hmm." I don't want to encourage him, so I go for nonchalant instead.

The lecture begins, and I face forward. There's the familiar sensation of him fiddling with my hair again, but then he tosses it over my shoulder.

A piece of paper lands on my breast, *tied in my hair*.

I scowl and carefully undo it. I hold the note in my palm, considering reading it or just throwing it back at him. Curiosity finally gets the better of me, and I open it.

Pick you up at five, princess.

Now I do crumple it, dropping it on the corner of my desk. This class gets *out* at five. I shake my head, but there's not much I can do about it.

After a long moment, he resumes playing with my hair. It's actually kind of soothing. There's nothing better than someone running their fingers through my hair, and he's getting dangerously close to that.

"Do you run?" he asks me on our way out of class.

He stuck with me as I dragged my bag closer and packed up. I purposefully moved slowly, but now we're alone in the hallway.

"I do..." I eye him. "Why do you ask?"

"You have the look."

"Lovely."

"I'll run with you."

"You *really* don't have to do that." My grip on my bag's strap tightens. "I like solitude."

"So does Ollie. It's why he lives all alone in that big house."

"You've said that before." I sigh. "What's that angle about?"

He smiles and nods at someone passing us. Takes a moment to slap hands and pat backs—the guy version of a hug—with another. I keep walking.

I'm hungry and not entirely sure I want to be dragged to the arena on a Friday night.

"I could just sit with the SJU crowd," I say when he catches up to me. "They'd be nice to me."

He considers that, subtly guiding me to a car in one of the student lots. When we reach the sleek black car, he leans on the passenger door and faces me.

"You so sure about that?"

"I..."

"Rumors have been spreading over there, too. About how you're fucking Carter Masters to get info from him. You've switched sides, so to speak."

My cheeks burn. "Excuse me?"

"Oh, hasn't he mentioned?" Penn's expression is the picture of innocence.

And I almost believe it, except for the keen sharpness in his eyes. Like when he touched the bruise on the back of my head —he doesn't care, he's just trying to expose a secret.

"He wouldn't *mention*, since he and I aren't anything."

"Oh, of course." He steps aside, yanking open the door for me. "Get in."

I balk. "No."

"Yes." His brows furrow. "Sydney. I've been nothing short of nice to you. I've got to get to the arena early for a meeting, but what you need for students to leave you alone is there."

"What I need," I repeat.

"Yeah." He lifts his shoulder. "If I had it in my car, I'd just give it to you now."

"And what is it?"

"A magic talisman." The *duh* is silent.

I wait a beat, then sigh.

Fine.

Going will make my dad happy, at any rate. He made sure I knew that I had tickets available at the box office whenever I wanted to go. And while I haven't taken him up on it, at least it'll come in handy tonight.

I slide in, and he shuts the door. I'm immediately enveloped by his cologne. It smells like some sort of sandalwood and citrus. I find myself breathing a bit deeper—until he gets in anyway.

"What are you majoring in?" he asks.

"English." It's not official, but I like it.

"You're in a writing class with Andi?"

"Um..."

"She's dating Ollie." He glances over at me. "Well, maybe dating is too constricting. They fuck sometimes."

"Lovely."

"Just in case you had any ideas about him."

I grit my teeth. "Definitely didn't. Don't."

He chuckles.

The arena really isn't that far—it's around the corner from campus, which makes the drive seem silly. We could've walked and been here in ten minutes. It was built with the idea of being just for Framingham State. It's the SJU hockey team that has to travel farther for practices. Something Carter occasionally griped about.

"Come on, I'm running late." He's out of the car in a flash, and he practically drags me out along with him. He keeps his hand locked around my wrist, going in through the metal doors and straight down the hall toward the locker room.

Most of the lights are off, like no one's here for the game yet.

Instead of leaving me outside the locker room, he keeps me with him. We get inside the darkened room, and my heart all but lurches into my throat.

He's not alone.

Oliver Ruiz stands with his hands on his hips, waiting for us.

"Girl of the hour," he drawls. "Your month is up."

My mouth dries. "That's not exactly the terms of your bet."

"We bet under." Penn leaves me standing there, drifting back to flick the lock on the door. "And we don't lose."

Oliver watches me and tilts his head. "Are you scared?"

"I just don't particularly see the need to screw one of you." I cross my arms.

"Has Scarlett called you back?" he suddenly asks.

I narrow my eyes.

Oliver motions. From the showers comes Andi and Scarlett. They've got their arms linked together, their makeup perfect... they're both looking at me like I'm an alien.

"Lettie?"

She doesn't react, minus a nostril flare that says quite a bit. About how far I've fallen in her eyes, or how disappointed she is with me.

"What are you doing here?" I ask.

"I'm wondering how you could go so far off the rails, Sydney."

She looks me up and down, and her lips press together. She's given that look to many people who don't make the cut in her eyes, too. I've just never seen it directed at *me*.

"Didn't think you'd be friends with a girl with so much mean-girl energy," Penn says in my ear.

I almost jump out of my skin. I didn't hear him approach. And he drifts to the side, sitting at his cubby.

"The tape wasn't funny, Andi," Oliver says suddenly. "You left her in bruises. I thought you were more clever than that."

Andi's mouth drops open. "I—"

"For the record, I'm against all of this," I interject.

Andi scoffs. "Right."

"I don't want to be part of this," I repeat.

I back up, but Penn catches me. He moved again. The fucker is silent, but his hands on my upper arms stop my movement.

Ice floods through me.

"Whose cock do you think she'd enjoy more, Scarlett?"

Is he asking because she's already—

"Save some of that anger for the fuck," Penn whispers to me.

A flush creeps up Scarlett's neck. And probably colors her cheeks, too, but she's so made up it's hard to tell. "I don't care. She'll choke either way."

"Unlike her." Penn continues to narrate softly, the words just for me. "She swallowed him down like a good little slut."

I wrench to the side, but he holds fast. He drags me back against him, and his erection digs into my ass. Oliver and Andi are still talking, seemingly trying to elicit an answer from my ex-best friend.

"Personally? I like a bit of crying with my face fucking." He licks at the shell of my ear. "And gagging. And choking."

I exhale.

"I'll pick," I finally voice. "As soon as they get the fuck out."

Oliver's eyes widen. I get the impression that not much surprises him, but that did. And then his expression is gone, wiped clean and replaced with smugness. "You're too late. Scarlett picked for you."

I narrow my eyes.

Andi moves fast, suddenly dragging Scarlett out past me. I want to yell at her, but Penn might actually be right. I need to hold on to my anger.

I shake Penn loose immediately after the door closes behind him, and I raise my eyebrows.

"Well?"

Oliver sneers. "Your lucky day, doll. You get Penn."

The hairs on the back of my neck rise.

"And we're on a countdown," he adds, checking his watch. "Team's arriving in fifteen."

Penn tilts his head. "We could move this to the offices."

Oliver's eyes light, and he nods once. Penn crowds behind me, moving me simply by getting too close. I follow Oliver's quick steps out of the locker room and into an elevator. We arrive on the suite floor—but there are offices here, too. Most are locked, except one.

Marked with my father's name.

"He probably just left," Penn says to me. "And hopefully he doesn't come back. Wouldn't that be awkward?"

I just shake my head.

The door swings in, and the automatic light flickers on when Oliver crosses the threshold. I look around, expecting to see some sort of familiarity.

I don't. It's as unfamiliar as his home, as this school, as the boys in front of me.

Penn locks the door and pulls the shade down. His hands are already at his jeans, popping the button. "Remember what I said?"

"Choking, gagging, crying." My voice comes out breathy. "Got it. And... what do I get out of this?"

Oliver is the one behind me now, and his laugh goes straight into me like an arrow. "Haven't you enjoyed the peace of the last few weeks? Wouldn't you want to know that's permanent?" He steps closer and lifts my shirt. "This needs to come off."

I let him drag it off and drop it on Dad's chair. He unbuttons my jeans, his hands reaching around me, and I slap at them.

Penn tsks.

I focus back on the goalie. His cock is out, and he strokes it slowly. He twists at the top, squeezing the head, before going down to the root. There are dark swirls...

"You tattooed your dick?"

He lets out a groan. "Makes it taste better. Promise."

I shake my head.

Oliver has my pants undone, so fast I hadn't realized he was back at it until cool air brushes my thighs.

"What are you waiting for?" he asks suddenly, the only voice in the silence. "On your knees."

I'm actually going to do this. It's kind of crazy to even think about, let alone let myself be in the moment for it. I let my mind take a backseat to the physical desire.

Scarlett always called me a prude... but really, I just never resonated with vanilla.

There's a thrill with Carter because he's not mine. At least, that's what I tell myself. Sex with your ex is supposed to be against the rules, right?

But these two are against the rules, too.

I drop to my knees and inch forward, until his cock is at eye level. It's bigger up close, and an unexpected dose of nerves flutters in my chest.

I look up at him. "Do you want crying beforehand or—?"

He shakes his head once and grips the back of my head. His fingers curl into my hair, and he waits only a moment for me to open my mouth.

His dick slides across my tongue and keeps going. And going. Until he's pressed against the ring of muscles at my throat. I gag, and he groans.

"Relax," he grunts.

He pushes in, blocking off my airway. I gag again, my throat working around him, but there's nothing I can do. I can't pull off him—his fingers tighten painfully in my hair, pulling at my scalp. My nose is almost to his pubic bone.

Don't fucking panic.

I claw his thighs and flick my tongue against his shaft. He seems content to suffocate me, waiting until I'm on the verge of passing out before he withdraws.

I inhale sharply, getting half a lungful before he thrusts

back in. My eyes roll. It's really his show for this, and I'm along for the ride.

Hands touch my hips from behind, and I flinch.

Penn laughs. His grip on my hair doesn't let me withdraw, although I try.

"Can't tell if she likes that or was surprised," he says.

Oliver's hands dip lower, nudging aside the hem of my panties. He reaches my core and swipes a single finger down to my slit, pressing into me.

I groan.

"Likes it," Penn says. "Make her groan again."

Oliver remains silent, but he finger-fucks me lazily, giving me the bare minimum. I clench around him, but every time I do, Penn takes my breath away.

It isn't long before the mess of sensations has the tears running down my cheeks.

He makes a noise in the back of his throat, and that's my only indication that he's going to come. He spills down my throat, and I choke on it. I try not to swallow, but it's impossible. I fall forward to my hands as soon as he withdraws.

Before I can expel it, he drops to his knees and pries open my mouth.

He spits.

I jerk again, but he clams a hand over my mouth.

"Swallow it," he orders, his green eyes boring into mine.

I can't look away.

Cold air touches my ass. Penn doesn't release my face, and then something large is sliding between my cheeks. Down lower, to my core. Bigger than a finger.

Oliver strokes his cock through my arousal, then lines up—

I stare at Penn as Oliver thrusts into me. The goalie's hand on my face keeps me from flying forward, and his lip ticks up in a shadow of a smile. Oliver's fingers dig into my hips. All I can think is—*what the fuck am I doing?*

But I'm too lost in it. Staring at Penn while his teammate drills into me is doing some weird things to my arousal.

Like increasing it by a thousand.

Penn moves to my side, keeping his hand on my face, and he reaches between my legs. His fingers skate over my clit, and I groan again.

This is dirty. We're on the floor of my father's office—their coach's office—and yet, none of us stop. Penn's fingers rub me into a frenzy, and Oliver matches his pace.

I cry out. It's muffled by his palm, but it seems to echo in the small space nonetheless. The orgasm that hits me is rough. It wrecks me, my limbs turning to jelly, and it takes me a minute to realize Oliver has finished, too.

He pulls off the condom I didn't notice him put on, wadding it in a tissue and dropping it in the otherwise empty trash.

"Guess we win the bet," he says to Penn.

The latter slowly peels his fingers off my face, tipping his head to watch me.

I finally swallow. With intention.

"Good pet."

I rock back on my heels. The regret is immediate, but the horror of my actions take longer to sink in. It isn't until the door closes, the *snick* making me raise my head, that I realize I zoned out while they packed up and left.

And my shirt is gone.

fourteen
sydney

Convincing myself that walking out in a bra and jeans is a fashion statement, I leave the office with my head held... not *high*, really. But not afraid.

I stick to the far wall and hurry to the stairwell, taking the steps a few at a time in my hurry to get down to the exit. I can't risk going to the main level, where they sell t-shirts and jerseys. One, because I'm fucking poor. And two, because I'm pretty sure the doors have already opened.

Which means I'm going to fucking run all the way home, *again*, and pray that no one encounters me.

My bag is still in Penn's car.

I make it outside without incident, shockingly, and glance around. I pause on the sidewalk, the cold air biting at my bare skin. Do I go for his car? The odds of getting all the way home without *someone* seeing seems impossibly low.

Once a thief, always a thief?

I debate it. I don't know anything about cars, but I do know that Penn Walker is every bit as arrogant as he is good at goaltending. So when I find his car, I'm not really surprised that it's unlocked.

I sit in it, debating, then pop the hood. His school bag is there, along with his FSU sweatshirt. His name and his number, twenty, are stitched on the right sleeve in purple. Well, maybe *this* is my safe passage. I pull it on and go back to the driver's seat, pulling down the visor to examine my reflection.

Hair—a mess, but manageable. I rake my fingers through it. It's my ruined mascara that really cements the mental image of a slut. Once that's fixed, as in, wiped away with a few licked fingers and scrubbing under my eyes with the sleeve of the sweatshirt, I lean back.

The real question is, does he keep his wallet on him or in the glove box?

I flick it open and laugh.

There's a banded wad of cash.

What a college kid does with that much cash is beyond me. Drug dealing, maybe? Running an illegal gambling ring? Planning on crashing a strip club after the games?

Either way.

I count all of it, my eyes widening every time I get through another hundred.

Two thousand dollars in low-denomination bills.

I take all of it, scrawling a note on the back of a forgotten receipt and leaving it in the money's place.

You want to treat me like a whore, you better pay me like one.

Okay. Too much time spent here. I put everything back the way it was, minus the money, and hurry away from the vehicle with my bag over my shoulder. I go to the box office and get the ticket my father has held for me, go through security, and splurge on a bucket of popcorn. And a soda. And maybe, later, I'll get something else.

Just because I can.

And if this is the worst they've got for me, I may as well actually enjoy the game.

The guys are on the ice warming up. Penn off to the side in his thick goalie gear, Oliver somewhere in the mess of

105

swarming FSU players. The Seawolves are in their away colors, mostly white with black and maroon accents. It doesn't take me long at all to find Carter.

Which should be a problem, right?

Because he's just a guy I used to know, and now we're on opposite sides of a rivalry.

I take my seat, crossing my legs and leaning back. I'm getting new looks now, but less so with loathing—which I'm actually expecting—but... confusion?

Someone takes the seat next to me, sees Penn's name on the sweatshirt's upper arm, and does a double take.

"You're wearing his sweatshirt?" she asks, her eyebrows nearly in her hairline.

I just smile.

She turns to the girl beside her, and I catch a few snippets of words. Sydney Windsor, Penn, sweatshirt. Naturally, it spreads like fucking wildfire after that.

But no one throws a drink on me. No one touches me, or bumps into me when we stand to let more people into the row, or coughs out ugly names under their breath.

I pull out my phone, and shoot a text to Dylan.

ME

> Does wearing a player's sweatshirt mean the same here as it does at SJU...?

Because there, it means they're exclusive. And I didn't really think about that when I put it on, but the looks... the way people are behaving...

DYL

> Like, their personal one?

> The one that has their name embroidered on it

> omg.

[BRANDON HAS BEEN ADDED TO THE CHAT]
DYLAN

She's wearing one of their personal sweatshirts.

BRANDON

???

DYL

SEND US A PICTURE.

I shake my head and lift my phone, making sure that Penn's name on my sleeve isn't legible.

ME

[IMAGE]

BRANDON

Well, there's your golden ticket.

DYL

Although, if you were ever planning on hiding under the radar…

BRANDON

Even Andi never got to wear Ruiz's.

Shit.

I glance around and slink lower.

The arena goes dark. We stand for the national anthem, sang by the a capella group.

"So, you're team Vipers now, right?" the girl beside me asks.

"Oh." My gaze flicks to my father on the bench, behind the line of players not starting. "Yeah. Yes."

She smiles. "Cool."

I don't know how to respond, so I... don't.

The puck is dropped. FSU wins the face-off, sending it back into their defensive zone. Now that I've said it out loud, I realize it's true. After everything my father has done for me, I want *him* to win.

That's more than I ever thought he'd get from me.

Oliver and an SJU d-man slam into the boards. The glass in the corner warps with the impact, and the people at the glass seem to grow more animated. They battle the puck out of their defensive zone and fly toward the Seawolves goalie.

One of the huge, burly guys—Bear, I'm ninety percent sure—muscles the puck away from the other winger on Carter's line. He sends it up the boards to Oliver, who takes it into the offensive zone on the far side.

A few passes later, everyone seeming to shuffle and grapple for position and screening, and Oliver delivers a wicked slap shot toward the goal. His teammate lifts his stick slightly and deflects it right past the goalie's glove.

I look up at the scoreboard.

Fifty-six seconds into the first period. 1-0.

A remarkable difference from their last game, that's for sure.

By the end of the first period, it's 2-0 and SJU seems *pissed*. Their playing is getting increasingly aggressive, and it's probably good that the horn blows before the players drop their gloves and go at it.

Unlike the last game, I stay in my seat until the second period starts. In fact, I'm not fucking moving until the game is over.

SJU comes out swinging.

I wince when Carter and Oliver collide on open ice. They both end up sprawled, the puck that they were chasing long gone. And then St. James scores.

The maroon-clad crowd erupts.

I watch Carter's celebration, zooming to join his teammates in the far corner. They leave the ice, switching out for a shift, and I lean forward.

The next few minutes are slow.

But when the FSU first line comes back out, the SJU fourth line joins them.

I grit my teeth. The tension ramps up, winding everyone in the arena tighter and tighter. I wouldn't be surprised if everyone was collectively holding their breath.

An SJU forward intercepts a pass and breaks away, streaking down the far side toward the FSU goal. Penn is ready for him, skating to the top of his crease. The forward tries to fake him out, but Penn doesn't fall for it—and the trick shot meant to sail into an empty net lands right in Penn's glove.

The whistle to stop play is blown.

I cheer before I can stop myself.

My lack of control only lasts a moment, and then I quickly sit back down.

"How long have you two been dating?" the girl beside me asks. "I didn't think he was the settling down type."

Huh?

Her gaze moves pointedly to my sweatshirt.

So, yeah, he's going to kill me.

I'm going to kill me.

"Oh, uh…"

"I would've thought you'd want it to be more public," she continues. "Immediately, I mean. But with the rumors about the St. James captain, I guess I understand wanting to wait." She gives me a sympathetic knee pat. "Must be nice to have so many hockey players falling over you."

I snort. "It's not all it's cracked up to be."

I only met Carter because of Scarlett. I only dated him for what feels like a brief a moment in time. And then we stopped because it was… *scary* in its intensity.

Stones drop into my belly.

Now that I'm gone, and Scarlett is clearly anti-Sydney, is she going to try and have her way with him? That would be fucked up.

Luckily, my phone goes off and saves me from replying to the girl.

L.

[LINK]

??

My heart does this weird little skip.

It's ridiculous that I react this way, when I don't even know who I'm talking to.

I click on the link. It opens to the damn FSU gossip page, and there's some write-up about me wearing a certain FSU player's sweatshirt at the game. Which means Sydney Windsor is officially *Team Viper*.

Great.

They work fast, at least.

ME

Jeez, if that's all it took to fix my image...

Wait. If *this* is the fucking magic talisman Penn joked about giving me, then it was in his damn car the whole time.

What the fuck, Penn?

Obviously it was a ruse to get me into the locker room. To get me in a compromising position...

At least, in the end, we traded. He kept my shirt. I keep this and start wicked rumors about us.

L.

Whose are you wearing?

You can't be jealous if I don't know who you are.

I'm not.

Really?

> It's coming across a little... envious.

Mere curiosity.

And I want to know how you got it.

> You wouldn't believe me if I told you.

So I don't tell him. I stash my phone and cross my arms over my chest, trying desperately not to think about how Penn's going to react to me stealing more than one thing from him.

A sweatshirt is one thing, but the cash burning a hole in my pocket?

The players restart.

FSU scores again.

3-1.

Exactly a minute later, SJU scores. It's a filthy goal, and the player who made the shot ends up slammed into the glass. He falls to the ice, and suddenly, it's like everyone just lets go of their control.

I jump up when Carter and Oliver collide. They shed their helmets and gloves, toss their sticks. Doesn't matter that they really haven't had anything to do with this most recent goal, it seems like the captains are just taking matters into their own hands.

"I can't watch this." I cover my face and peek through my fingers.

They trade blows until they both go down in a heap—but it's Oliver who ends up on top. And the crowd around me goes fucking bananas.

"He can scrap with the best of them," the girl beside me yells. "God, he's so hot."

And he was inside me only a few hours ago.

The refs give both players five-minute majors for fighting.

I don't really need to see any more. In the end, it won't matter who wins.

At least, that's what I tell myself.

fifteen
sydney

The buzzing from the front door's intercom drags me out of a dream. I wake up gasping, clutching at my breast, before I register that I'm awake.

Sunlight streams in through the windows, and I flop back down.

The buzzer goes off again, and I groan into my pillow. But only for a moment.

The intercom is by the door, and I press the button to talk. "Who is it?"

There's another button to listen.

"Penn," comes the gravely reply.

I pause, my finger still on the button to listen.

"Come on, Sydney. I could figure out another way up, but this is easier. Don't you think?"

His tone begs me to argue with him just for the challenge of it. But it would result in something worse for me, and I'm too damn tired.

I buzz him up.

He arrives at my apartment door a few minutes later, running his fingers through his blond hair. He appraises me, and I belatedly cover my chest.

"Did I wake you?"

I hum, stepping aside to let him in. He strolls in like he owns the place, his gaze skating over my things. While he does that, I rush to put on something to cover myself.

"You took something from me."

He follows me into my bedroom, all the way across to my dresser. He pushes my hand down, stopping me from putting on the sweater. His gaze seems glued to my nipples, which are tight little pebbles in the cool air and are visible through my shirt.

"Did I?"

He tips his head to the side. "Either that, or everyone is lying about you showing up to the game wearing my sweatshirt."

I pretend to suddenly remember, my mouth parting. "*Oh, that!* Thanks for letting me borrow it."

I point. It's slung over the corner of my bed, haphazardly tossed there when I peeled it off and climbed straight into bed last night.

He spots it but makes no move to grab it.

"It looks good on you," he says.

My mouth dries.

He steps in closer, fisting the front of my shirt and dragging me into him.

"No clothes is a good look, too."

"That was a one-time thing," I breathe.

"Oh, so the wad of cash was a one-off?" He sneers. "You got me off once, you get paid once?" He reaches in his pocket and produces more cash. "Or..."

"I don't want that." It comes out automatically.

He shrugs and drops it on the bed. It lands on top of the sweatshirt.

"I don't think you get a say." He uses the hand in my shirt to direct me backward, until my spine touches the wall. "You're in my head, and I'd really rather you not be."

"And fucking me is supposed to make that go away?" I let my head fall back and look at him with half-closed eyes.

There's a very real possibility that I'm still dreaming.

"Exactly. I don't fuck anyone twice."

"And head doesn't count."

He nods, totally serious. "Now you're getting it."

Well, if it gets me off his radar... I shove my sleep shorts and panties down, kicking them away. My hands go to his jeans, but I only get them far enough down to free his erection. I stroke him, trying to get a better look at the ink. But he doesn't give me a chance, instead knocking my hand aside and hiking me up into his arms.

I latch on to his shoulders. But it puts us at a perfect height.

"Guide me in," he says.

I hope I have more bruises on my legs. There are quarter-sized bruises on my hips from Oliver—I can only assume—and I want more.

This is my greedy moment. The one where I say fuck everything else, *sex* is what I want.

It's kind of liberating and scary at the same time.

I do what he says, and as soon as he's lined up, he sinks into me.

We both groan. He keeps eye contact with me, not moving in to kiss me or anything so intimate as that. But staring... it's like he's looking right through me. I lock my legs around his hips, trying to get him closer.

More.

Deeper.

But his expression—or lack thereof—is throwing me off.

I let go of his shoulder and grab his chin. "If you're going to fuck me, look me in the eye while you do it."

He starts, blinking rapidly.

"Don't fucking disassociate while you're inside me," I hiss.

"Who knew you could be so bossy?"

"If I was bossy, I'd be on top," I counter.

He pulls out and drops my legs. In an instant, he's on the bed with the cash in his hand. "Come and get it, then. Do the work and make us come."

I growl. I straddle him, taking the money and throwing it onto the floor. I take him back inside me, biting the inside of my cheek until he's buried deep.

"Maybe you're the one who likes choking and tears." I lean down. I pin his wrists to the bed, adjacent with his head. "Maybe you want to be choked until you nearly pass out, and that's the only way you can come inside a girl."

He's not wearing protection.

For fuck's sake.

"Condom?" I question.

He shakes his head slowly, his expression positively wicked. "I'd love to see you choke me, princess." He lifts his chin and exposes his throat. "Just let go when I pass out so you don't kill me."

I could do it. I could—

He doesn't stop me from putting my hand on his throat. His eyes light when I put a little pressure on it, my fingers tightening and blocking the blood flow from reaching his brain. And at the same time, my hips begin to move.

I chase my pleasure and watch him slowly start to lose consciousness. When his eyes roll back, I release him and press my palms to his chest. I fuck him harder, and he comes awake with a roar.

There's a new demon in his eyes.

I lick my lips. He lifts me off him, tossing me aside like I weigh nothing. I hit the far side of the mattress and roll onto my stomach. He's on top of me in an instant.

I'm facedown, but he doesn't care. He just slides back in like he was made to fit between my legs. He wraps his hand around my throat, but he doesn't squeeze. He just keeps it there, lightly, and fucks me fast. He doesn't hold anything

116

back, grunting and groaning swears like he wants his audio to live in my fantasies.

His pace turns into a near frenzy, and I shut my eyes at what could be about to happen. *At least you can afford some sort of birth control.*

Wait—I'm thinking like I already accepted the money he threw at me. And I haven't. I'm going to shove it right back at him as soon as he leaves—

"Fuck," he groans, and then there's the loss of him.

Warm liquid hits my ass. More on my lower back. He shoves my shirt up, crisscrossing my skin with his cum.

I want desperately to catch my breath, but I think he's broken something in me.

It isn't until he shifts lower, his exhale coasting across my center, that I flinch.

He holds me by my ass, and his tongue touches my enflamed, sensitive pussy.

"You taste so fucking sweet," he says. "You could bottle it and sell it as a love potion."

I wrinkle my nose, but my retort is lost on a gasp.

Carter is talented, but Penn—

Fuck, he knows some tricks, too. He flips me over, seeming to not care about my cum-covered back. I rise on my elbows and look down at him. We share brief eye contact, and then he sucks my clit into his mouth.

His tongue flicks at it, and then his teeth make contact. I shudder and fall back. My fingers slide across the sheets, trying for some sort of relief.

He plays with me, though, until I'm squirming to get away from him. I want to do it myself—

"I'm waiting to hear you ask for it," he says, his gaze between my legs. "Your cunt is clenching..." He inserts one finger. "You're ready, you just need to ask."

"Dick," I groan. "Make me come."

"That's not quite right." He takes another taste. "Asking

usually ends in a question mark. You're the one who's in the English classes."

"I want to—"

"No," he interrupts. A nip to my thigh.

Something in me shudders to even consider it a question. A demand, a statement—those are in my control. But since he came in here, he's held all of it and I've had none.

"Can I come?" I ask in a broken whisper.

He smiles. "Yes, princess."

Then he fulfills my wish.

Again.

And again.

And again.

Until I'm crying, and he's kissing the tears away from my cheeks, stroking my hair, and securing something around my neck. I'm delirious, I can't move.

"Wear the sweatshirt tomorrow," he says in my ear. "I want to see the look on Ollie's face when he realizes."

I think he leaves after that. A door closes in the distance, coming from a long way away. My muscles are jelly, my bones have disintegrated. I couldn't move if I wanted to. So I close my eyes and allow myself to drop into a deep sleep. Because that beats trying to figure out what the fuck just happened.

sixteen
sydney

I wake up confused. Again. I'm diagonal across my bed, smelling of sex, and it takes me a long moment to put together what just happened.

Fear flashes through me at the thought of Penn snooping around my apartment. I hop up and search the place, but there's no trace of him. There *is* a shit ton of cash scattered across my bedroom floor, though.

I'm going to be sick. I bolt for the bathroom and fall to my knees in front of the toilet, my stomach contracting and purging its contents. I cough and spit, and after a long moment clamber back to my feet.

It isn't until I catch my reflection in the mirror that I notice the necklace.

I lean in and pull it away from my throat to see it better. There's a little pendant at the end of the slender gold chain. A snake woven around a goalie mask.

What the fuck?

From cruel to possessive?

This is borderline insanity. It's also mid-afternoon. Which means I slept away most of my Saturday.

My phone goes off, and I lunge for it. I hope for L., my

mystery texter, but instead get Carter. Which wouldn't necessarily be a bad thing, if he wasn't asking to be let up.

The sound of the buzzer from the intercom punctuates it.

I accept it and text him that my door is unlocked.

He enters shortly after, stopping dead at the sight of me in the middle of my living room. He looks particularly delicious today, his hair combed back, black long-sleeve t-shirt that's tight around his biceps and chest. Jeans. The black eye and cut on his cheek from his fight with Oliver stand out.

"You have a habit of wearing minimal clothes when you let people up?" His voice is husky. "Or is this just for me?"

I bite my lip.

"Sydney."

He advances, and I put my hand out to stop him. He leans into my palm, planted on his chest, and eye-fucks me. And then his gaze trips over the necklace.

He reaches for it.

I let him.

He picks up the little gold pendant, and his fingers curl around it. For a second, I worry he might tear it from my neck.

"Rumors must be true, then," he says. "You went to the game in Walker's sweatshirt, and this fucking confirms it."

I grab his wrist to keep him here. "It's not what you think."

Carter feels like home. I don't know why. He feels safe in an exhilarating way. If that isn't the most confusing, mindfuck of a sentence, I don't know what is.

"I'm just trying to survive," I whisper.

His jaw muscle tics.

"I want to be anywhere but here." I drag him closer, reaching up and skating my thumb over his cheek. "But... I also want to know why you keep coming here like we're something. Are we?"

He kisses me.

It should answer my question, but it doesn't. Because this

120

is a preamble for sex, and while he could erase the feeling of Penn between my legs, I also... I kind of want to hold on to it.

Never mind that his cum is still on my back and smeared across my sheets.

So I let him kiss me until I'm weak in the knees, and then I push him away. "You should go."

He exhales and turns away, running a hand through his hair. "Fuck."

"I'm not—"

He heads for the door, but he pauses before leaving. "You're not getting rid of me, Syd. Tell that to your FSU fuckboys. You and me? End-fucking-game."

seventeen
carter

I sit in my new apartment across from Sydney's brownstone. I'm one level up, with a perfect view in through her front-facing windows. With the help of binoculars, I can see everything.

She's cleaning with an unmatched fervor.

But it's Monday morning, and I expect she's just delaying the inevitable trip to school. I don't have class until later, and my muscles are getting stiff from remaining in the same position for so long.

The apartment I'm in is empty except for a cot and the chair I currently occupy. The lease is paid through the end of the semester in cash, above the asking rent price, and the owner was kind enough to not put my name on a lease.

I don't think anyone would go looking into who's living across from her, but I don't want to make my intentions obvious. Especially with that fucking goalie circling...

The fact that she even transferred here is a tragedy. If I knew what the SJU administration was going to do, I never would've showed Coach those plays. Or I would've lied about where they came from. And if there was something different I could've said to the ethics board to put the blame on me instead of her, I would've done that in a heartbeat.

Her best friend, Scarlett—ex-friend, I suppose, since they haven't seen each other in quite a while—has been all over me at parties and when she catches me between classes.

Avoiding her has been a full-time job. She wears red lipstick that she might think is hot, but all I can picture is the color hiding spilled blood.

I like blood.

I like the idea of Sydney's blood.

It's one of those fucked-up fantasies that I haven't been able to find someone to act out with me. Sex with Syd is too good. And there's this undercurrent of thrill that keeps me coming back to her.

But we never got to the point where I could push her. There was just... possibility.

She's still wearing Walker's necklace, and she hesitates holding his sweatshirt. I will her not to put it on, but it's also armor. I can't blame her for wanting protection, *or* her hesitation. The double-edged sword sits heavy in her hands.

After a long moment, she tugs it over her head.

The black fabric hangs on her slim frame, the sleeves too long for her, too. She pushes them up to her elbows and tucks the necklace in, hiding it from sight. Her long dark hair is in a crown braid, and only a few strands came loose from putting it on.

I let out a sigh.

Once she's gone, striding down the street with purpose, her backpack on both shoulders and her head held high, I leave my brownstone and slip into hers. I have a copy of her key, so the semantics on whether it's *breaking* and entering—or just entering—could be debated.

A frantic call to maintenance about her stove being left on secured me entrance while she was at school one day, and I took the spare she had in her kitchen. Once it was copied, I replaced it.

She never noticed.

She hasn't noticed when I've been in here this past week either, but that's going to change. I want her to feel my presence. Not the Carter Masters she associates with currently, but the darker side of me. The one who wants to pull at her until she comes apart.

What she *has* begun to sense, however, is that I'm following her. She glances around more, double-checking over her shoulder.

It's a long, drawn-out hunt.

Poor Sydney. I feel almost bad that she thinks I'm some safety net for her. It's the last thing I can be.

It's time for my stalking to be more apparent.

I move some things around. I yank open the dresser drawers in her room, rifling through her panties. Some cotton, some lace, some thongs. Buried at the bottom is a stack of cash that gives me pause.

She has more than a poor, jobless college girl should have. Especially since she admitted that her mom is missing.

I thought the woman simply moved on. She's never been a good mother to Sydney, and the woman *should* disappear. But is my girl saving up for a private investigator or something?

Hmm.

There's an idea.

I leave her drawer open, the money exposed, and exit her apartment.

She'll be in class with her volleyball-playing friend, Dylan, and then another one with Penn Walker later. If he doesn't throw her under the bus, then she should be safe enough on campus.

And it's the one place I can't follow.

But I have a phone call to make and a plan to set in motion.

eighteen
sydney

Dylan and Brandon have found me a new friend. They arrive at my upstairs table in the library, although I'm not sure who told them to check for me up here. And with them is the girl who sat next to me at the last hockey game.

"This is Maddy," Dylan says. "She's my roommate's cousin."

"Okay..."

"We think you'd get along," Brandon says. "And Maddy said you guys sat together at the game."

"We did," I allow.

And yet, it still feels like an ambush.

Today has been weird, so I've taken to hiding. Again. I'm wearing Penn's hoodie, and it might be fucking magic. People who would've locked the door behind them now hold it open for me, their eyes wide. I haven't braved the dining hall, but Penn and I have a class later.

I can only imagine how that's going to go.

It seems like my outcast status is slowly fading, just like L. predicted. Just... not quite the *way* he predicted it.

Speaking of L., he's been absent. I sent him a text, to which he didn't reply. And it's not like I should care that much, because he's this stranger who doesn't tell me much at all. I know that he goes to college at either St. James or Framingham State, that he's honest and on my side most of the time. I know he doesn't want to run away like I do.

People who want to run away think about it.

I daydream of using the money to run as far as I can get. And when I voiced it to L., he seemed... well, maybe not confused, but just kind of blank.

My thinking is that he's upset with me about the sweatshirt thing. It would make him one of the only ones... plus Carter. I can't imagine telling Carter about Penn's sweatshirt would go over well at all. He already discovered the necklace, although he exhibited some self-control and didn't yank it off.

"Well, have fun!" Brandon's voice brings me back to the present. He taps Maddy's arm and points to the seat across from me. "See you guys later. For dinner?"

"Sure," I manage. "My last class gets out at five."

"We'll meet you in the student center," Dylan promises.

I let out a sigh, and then they're gone. It's just Maddy and me. I eye her. She's cute, with super-light blonde hair, a smattering of freckles across her cheeks and nose, and deep-blue eyes. She seems to smile easily, while mine takes longer to surface.

"Did you hate me on sight?" I blurt out. "Before you saw me wearing this?"

I pluck at the hoodie.

Her gaze drops to the table, and she makes a face. "Unfortunately, I did listen to the rumors. But you genuinely seemed cool at the game. You were cheering for Penn." She smiles softly. "I think everyone is afraid that you're just here to spy."

"Rumors are ridiculous—"

"I'm not denying that, but they're stronger when they have a kernel of truth to them. You snuck into Oliver's house to get those plays, didn't you?"

"Well... I did end up stealing them." I haven't told anyone this, and I'm not ready to admit that I'm after a family heirloom. Putting any importance on finding that bracelet will make it nearly impossible to find, simply because Oliver Ruiz hates my guts.

But he has it. I know he does, I followed the fucking path from my mother to the pawnshop to Ruiz. Not an older person, like maybe his father. Not a woman. Him.

The unwelcome truth is that he probably bought it for someone. A girl, obviously. Who else would he buy for? And I was too late.

I didn't notice it was gone from my mother's jewelry box until I went looking for it. And why did I do that?

Sentimental fucking sap.

It was Christmas break, the one time in the year I willingly go home, and something made me look for it. I was caught between being grateful that my mom was home—she was holding a steady job at the time and everything seemed normal —and longing for more family.

When I couldn't find it, I screamed at my mother. I didn't know why—I couldn't figure the anger bubbling like lava in my chest, boiling up my throat and erupting out my mouth at her. I wanted my words to fucking burn her, too. I used every jab in the book.

She finally confessed that she had sold it a month prior.

I'm convinced that's what made her leave. Not because she had some boyfriend to run to, like in the past. I know that's where she went. She would go whore out her body—

That stops me cold.

How am I any fucking better than her?

The necklace around my throat suddenly feels heavy. More like a collar than a slender chain. I got this because Penn threw money at me and fucked me.

Simple as that.

This hoodie doesn't represent any goodwill between us. It marks me as his slut.

"You okay?" Maddy asks. She's pulled out her laptop and

headphones, clearly intent on... working here with me. A phenomenon. "You just got pale."

"I'm fine," I lie.

On my phone, I click on Mom's conversation thread.

There are ten unanswered texts from me, the earliest from two weeks ago. I close out of it and switch to L.

> ME
>
> I'm having a weird weekend.
>
> Did you see the SJU/FSU game? Were you there?
>
> Where are you?

Nothing. Radio silence. My gut twisting, I type out another message. I didn't think I'd ever be the type to double text, but here I am.

> ME
>
> I'm going fucking crazy, L.

And finally, he replies:

> L.
>
> Me, too.
>
> Tell me another lie.
>
> My feelings are too big for my chest sometimes.
>
> And I want to run until I drop dead.

Maddy actually isn't bad company. We work in near silence, only pausing when we need to get up and stretch our legs. I watch her stuff while she goes to the restroom downstairs, and she returns with two sodas for us.

I think about what I said to L., about running until I drop dead. The weather is getting colder. At night, especially, it's starting to get that crispness. It'll snow soon, I bet. We're higher in elevation here, and snow tends to come hard and fast as soon as we slip into winter.

"What class do you have?"

I check my watch. "Intro to Law in twenty-five minutes."

"And you've been staring at the wall for almost fifteen." She laughs. "Do you need a break?"

"Nah, just... thinking. I have a writing assignment I need to get working on."

"What's it about?"

I pull out my folder of syllabi and flip to the writing class's. "I need to pick an event that happened more than ten years ago and write a short story like I was there."

Which should be fun. I actually was intrigued when I first skimmed it last week. Since the start of the semester, we've turned in a few short stories working on different techniques, but our professor hasn't actually got into the grit of the class: critiquing. This is the first piece that we'll be bringing enough copies for everyone, and then critiquing them over the next two classes. Andi Sharpe has since transferred out of the class, which makes it a little better. Since everyone will soon be reading what I come up with.

"The problem is, there are too many options and not enough information. Do I go abstract with it? I don't think I want to pick a tragic event." I frown. "I just can't decide."

"What about the Olympics? You could pick any event, any year, really."

"Hmm..."

Boring.

"I've got some time," I hedge. "I'll figure it out this week." She nods.

"What are you working on?" I ask.

She sighs and rubs the bridge of her nose. "My parents

thought it would be in my best interest to double major in political science and business. So I'm currently writing a mock policy proposal that I'll have to present in front of the class, who will pretend to be the United Nations."

"That sounds like the opposite of fun."

"I like it in theory, but the idea of standing up and talking, and then answering questions... some of the guys take it super seriously, like this is going to propel them toward the actual UN. They ask insane questions, and if you show any weakness —they pounce."

I can relate to waiting for the pounce moment.

"I'm sure you're gonna crush it," I offer.

She smiles. "Thank you."

"Are you joining us for dinner?"

"Only if you don't mind?"

"Not at all."

"My two friends transferred out last year," she admits. "It's been kind of lonely, and I know my cousin is getting irritated with me. She's a senior, I'm a sophomore."

"You seem cool." I narrow my eyes. "But if you're just hanging out to talk shit..."

She raises her hands. "The mean-girl stuff is over, promise. I've learned my lesson about judging a book by its cover."

I smile. "I'm going to head over there now. But I'll see you for dinner."

I gather my stuff up and finish the soda. Class is on the other side of campus, and I kind of want to catch Penn before it starts.

"See you later, then. Thanks for hanging out." I go downstairs and across the quad. Most of these buildings are old, which means my mother probably walked this same route. It's eerie.

What I need to do is ask Dad about her.

Someone falls into step with me. Out of the corner of my

eye, I catch the dark hair and olive skin. My shoulders inch up automatically, my guard slamming into place.

Oliver doesn't say anything. In fact, he seems to be waiting for me to speak.

When I get to the Admin building, he beats me to the door. He doesn't open it, though. Instead, he turns and leans against it.

"Seriously?"

He appraises me.

"I'm pretty sure you could be giving me the silent treatment from the other side of campus," I huff. "You don't have to do it in my face."

"I'm not giving you the silent treatment," he says. "I'm trying to figure out how you got Penn wrapped around your traitorous little finger."

I shrug. If Penn didn't tell him about the money, then I'm sure as fuck not going to spill the beans. No way in hell is that getting out.

"Ask him," I manage.

His brows lower. "I did."

"Great, then take whatever he says with a grain of salt and move on."

I go for the door handle, but he slides over to block me again.

"I think you're just trying to get close to him so you can screw us over again."

Maddy said that was the rumor. That I'm just here as a spy. I step in closer to him, my chest tightening. I mean—he can't honestly believe that, can he?

"Here's the thing, Ruiz." I glare up at him. "If I wanted to screw you over, I'd break into your house again."

He smirks. "Try. I'll be waiting, doll."

I bristle. "Don't call me that."

"Why? You'd look great covered in plastic and perched on my shelf. Immobile. Silent..."

I don't like that the whole immobile thing does something to me. And I don't like that my body reacts to just his words.

He seems to spot the fleeting desire, though, because he leans in. "I can do that, you know. Tie you down and spank you until you're screaming into the gag for relief that will never come."

I push my shoulders back. "Get out of the way. I'm going to be late."

He chuckles and moves aside. "Just know, the instant you step out of line, or even *hint* about giving St. James a clue, you're going to wish you were dead."

Don't I already?

Wait.

He's already striding away, back the way we came, while I puzzle out that thought. A dark, insidious thought that shouldn't have popped up in the first place.

The worry sticks with me all the way to class, where Penn waits outside the room. His expression darkens when he spots me, but it's not anger.

It's something more like lust.

"Want to skip?" he asks in a low voice. "There's a good bathroom on the fifth floor that never gets used at this time of day."

"I want to go to class."

Penn pouts. "You're no fun."

"You're trying to be a bad influence."

He follows me in. "Obviously. Also, take down your hair."

I eye him. "Excuse me?"

He motions to my head. "It's all up, and I want it down. It's our thing."

"We don't have any *thing*."

He eyes me, and I glance away. Okay, fine, maybe it has become sort of a ritual. I didn't even think about it as I put my hair up this morning. It needs a good washing, and I didn't want to deal with it. So I braided it and looped it around my head, pinning it into place.

"It'd take a while to undo," I hedge.

"You have a choice, princess. Take your hair down or I'll rip my sweatshirt off you. No matter how good it looks. And then all the nice treatment disappears, going right back to how it was before. Or maybe it'll be worse, because they'll wonder what made me take it back."

I glower at him.

But I feel strangely caught.

So I slowly pull the pins out, dropping them into his waiting hand. When the two braids hang down, Penn inches closer. We haven't even taken our seats yet, although we both stand in the aisle, by our respective desks.

He reaches for one, undoing the invisible elastic. He rakes his fingers through it, the strands wavy after being caught up in it all day, while I do the same to the other side. He brushes my hands away and runs his fingers through all of my hair, pulling it forward over my shoulders.

"Better."

"If you say so."

The professor clears his throat.

I glance around. All eyes are on us, the last remaining standing students. I drop into my seat quick as a flash, while Penn takes his time. He nods at the professor, who starts the lecture as soon as his ass is down.

Penn drums his fingers on my back.

I sigh and flip my hair back. Because apparently he has some fixation with it. But then his finger coasts across the back of my neck, and a chill shoots straight down my spine. He's touching the necklace chain, I think. It's been hidden all day, tucked under my shirt even.

He leans forward, over his desk, when the professor turns to write something on the board. "I could've taken the sweatshirt and ripped it to shreds. The necklace keeps you just as safe, princess."

I grit my teeth. He seems to have no qualms about drawing attention to himself or talking during class. He also manages to pay attention, because he speaks up and answers questions frequently.

What would Oliver think about the necklace? The sweatshirt is one thing. Stolen or gifted, it doesn't matter. But this pendant?

I tug at the chain and struggle not to frown. I don't like being pulled in two different directions—between Carter and Penn—but it's even worse when I consider Oliver.

Although I shouldn't, I can't help it. He slips into my mind when I least expect it, and sometimes he stays there.

And, of course, L.

He's quickly becoming a crutch... and a crush.

Horrible, terrible, *stupid*.

Me, that is. And my emotions.

ME

> You never said if you preferred savory or sweet.

I wait, staring at the screen, but the reply doesn't come. Not until toward the end of class.

L.

> I have an incurable sweet tooth.

> You should see a dentist about that.

> They offered to pull it, but I told them my sweet tooth is satiated whenever I talk to you.

I scoff, drawing a few side-eyes.

Oops.

Penn tugs on my hair.

I glance back and scowl at him, but he just stares at me. His green eyes are the color of sea glass in this lighting, with little flecks of gold toward the center.

The people around us move, beginning to shuffle their things together and pack up their bags.

"What?" I finally ask him.

"Nothing," he answers. "Dinner?"

"I'm meeting friends."

"Later, then."

"Is this an every night thing?"

He smirks. "Do you want it to be? I left you alone last night."

And I was lonely. For the first time in a while.

"You left me alone because you had an away game," I point out.

"Fine. See you tonight." He hooks his bag over his shoulder and leaves me sitting at my desk, still in fucking disarray.

nineteen
sydney

The health clinic on campus can prescribe birth control. I learn that from Maddy, after I try to casually ask her about it at dinner. Having none seems a little too dangerous, especially since Penn lives on the reckless side. And Carter... he brought me the morning after pill, but I can't rely on that.

I won't.

Getting pregnant young is exactly what my mother did. And since I'm already following in her footsteps in more ways than one, I can't jinx myself.

Better safe than sorry.

I head down after dinner, feigning nausea to my friends. But when I get there, I tell the nurse practitioner what I really need.

She nods without judgment. That's a small miracle all on its own.

After reviewing my options, we go with the monthly shot. She gives me one right then and there—after a pregnancy test that thankfully comes back negative—and makes me an appointment to return at the end of November.

"Halloween is next week," I gasp.

She laughs, ushering me out.

Halloween used to be fun. Like in high school, when I

would go to house parties of my classmates, but everyone was kind of on equal footing in terms of sneaking alcohol and having enough funds to actually get good costumes.

I, for one, always put my creativity to the test.

I walk home, and a chill like ice slides down my spine. I stop short on the sidewalk. It's a residential area, the university perfectly blended in with the surrounding neighborhoods in Framingham. The street is quiet, and yet...

There's no one around. No one walking or jogging. I spin in a slow circle, trying to make sure, before I shrug it off and continue.

A car turns onto the road ahead of me. Their headlights are bright, but then they flick on their high beams.

I raise my hand to block the light.

The engine revs, the car flying toward me. My body goes tense as it draws nearer, my heart skipping. I almost fall off the sidewalk into the yard beside me, but the squeal of brakes comes a second later. It stops a foot from me, and someone jumps out of the passenger side. They're wearing a mask.

Hell. No.

I backpedal, then turn and run across the lawn. The big one is on me in a second. He's huge, easily doubling my body weight, and takes me down hard. We hit the ground, the air kicked out of my lungs, but he grabs my arms and hauls me up faster than I can comprehend. The driver looms in front of me. He dodges my kick and grabs my legs while the first guy takes my upper body. I manage to get out a piercing shriek before the big one stuffs something in my mouth.

I try to spit it out, but there's too much of it. The one behind me has my arms pinned to my sides. Desperation kicks through me, and I twist harder than even I expect. I get a foot free. Without hesitation, I slam it into the driver's stomach.

He lets out an *oof*, but his grasp on my other ankle doesn't loosen. He quickly gets my other foot, and they carry me the short distance back to the car. The trunk is already open.

It's sick how time slows down. I know what's coming. They're going to put me in it, shut the door. Once I'm in, I'll be even more vulnerable.

I scream around the cloth in my mouth and throw my head back. It worked on the girl in the bathroom, but this angle sucks and I just bash it into his chest.

They toss me into the trunk without preamble. I curl, protecting my head, and the door slams down a second later. I'm encased in pitch-black, blinking rapidly as I try to adjust to the darkness.

Shit.

I lie unmoving, shock more than anything holding me hostage.

What the fuck do I do? Two doors close, and the engine revs. The car takes off, and I slide headfirst into the side of the trunk. I yank the cloth out of my mouth.

"Let me go!" I pound on the roof and yell as loud as I can.

Music starts up a second later, something awful—a thumping bass that easily disguises my attempts to signal anyone.

What the *fuck*?

I brace myself in the trunk and feel around for something —anything—I can use as a weapon or means of escape. But it's completely empty. It's no better than a freaking rental car.

My backpack didn't make it in with me, but my phone is in my pocket. I yank it out and scroll my contacts, but I don't have Penn's or Oliver's numbers. Which fucking sucks, because I'm pretty sure one of them is driving.

And I would have words for them.

I won't call my dad. This will either worry him or infuriate him, and either way, I don't want to be held responsible for his reaction. I would, too. If I told him what's going on, he would react and it would be my fault. The school would go back to hating me, with or without Penn's sweatshirt's protection.

There's only one real viable option—Carter. I can barely

scroll to his name, my hands are shaking so badly. Once I get to him, it takes a second to click.

It goes straight to voicemail.

I squeeze my eyes shut.

It feels fucking terrible to be out of options. Is this my karmic retribution? I never should've snuck into Oliver Ruiz's house. Never should've sent those pictures of the playbook to Carter.

> ME
>
> I know we don't do the whole calling thing, or face-to-face thing, but if I said I was in the trunk of a car…

L.

What?

> Two guys threw me in the back of the trunk. I don't suppose you're one of them? That would be a real laugh.
>
> Not really. Kind of traumatizing, actually…

The car stops so suddenly, I slide forward and slam into the front of the trunk. I rub my shoulder, which takes the brunt of the impact. The music cuts off. I shove my phone into the waistband of my pants, hurrying to tug my shirt and Penn's sweatshirt down over it. I don't trust them not to search for it, wherever we are. But maybe they won't feel… there.

I don't know if I can trust L., but I'm really hoping he comes through.

The trunk pops open, and a bright light sears my eyes. I squint up at the two figures, their silhouettes dark behind the light.

"*Get out of the trunk.*" The voice isn't human, though. It's robotic, like read through a computer program.

The flashlight moves away from my face, and I sit up slowly. I peek around.

We're in some sort of mechanical shop. They drove all the way into it, parked in one of the bays. To my left and right are empty bays for more cars, and a warehouse spreads out behind my abductors.

I climb out slowly. They drove for maybe twenty minutes, I think, but my limbs are stiff from tensing at every turn.

The two of them look even worse in the overhead fluorescent lighting giving their masks pits of shadows. They stand back, waiting for me to emerge. The huge guy is within grabbing distance, and the one who drove stands a few yards away with a phone in his hand. He presses another button, and the voice comes out of the phone.

"*Sit in that chair.*"

He points.

Their masks are not cool like those neon stitch ones, or even the *Scream* mask. These are grotesque, more like something you'd find at Fright Night or going through a haunted house. The driver's is a bloody, smiling skull. The other's is a creepy clown mask.

They're both wearing nondescript clothing. Black sweatshirts and pants, black boots. The masks completely hide their heads, too.

I stare at the black mesh where the driver's eyes would be. I fucking *hate* masks, and the fact that they both seem to be watching me with a keen gaze—all in my head, since I can't confirm—does nothing to calm me. If I lose control over my even breathing, I'd quickly fall into hyperventilation.

All I need to do is hide the trembling and convince them I'm not afraid.

Easy.

"Don't suppose you have a school affiliation," I ask in a low voice. "Is there a point you're trying to make here?"

He points again. More insistently.

I move past him and sit in the metal folding chair, brushing off my thighs. Isn't there something about not showing fear to bad men? I feel like Mom told me that once upon a time... a lesson in walking through the trailer park where we lived, when I had to do it alone at night.

A whispered, *Don't show fear, honey.* A kiss on the top of my head when I made it back, trembling, after someone spooked me bad enough to sprint home.

This is just like that.

My phone digs into my abdomen, but I ignore it. When my fingers shake, I squeeze my thighs.

Neither of them move.

I raise my eyebrows at them, like, *Now what?*

My phone is on silent, even the vibration turned off. I don't know if texting L. was the right idea. Maybe I should've called my dad? Or the freaking police?

Snitch.

The word rings in my ears.

The guy in charge presses a button on his phone. "*You have what we want.*"

"Am I supposed to know what that means?" I lift my chin. "My grandma's lasagna recipe, perhaps?"

They exchange a glance, although how they can interpret a nonverbal look with *masks* on is anyone's guess.

He types something, and it plays a second later. "*You're close to the FSU goalie. We want to know what you know.*"

"I don't know anything."

"*Liar.*"

"What, do you think I sleep with him and then flip through his playbook in the middle of the night? Why the fuck would I do that after everything that happened?"

Silence.

I glare at the one speaking. "You want me to give up secrets about FSU?"

"*Yes.*"

"Well that's too fucking bad, because I don't have any."

A low buzz punctuates my words. Not my phone—the driver's?

"*She's not scared enough.*" The driver tips his head to the other guy. His phone is still going off in his hand, but he swipes and it falls silent.

I swallow.

They drift a short distance away, maybe whispering or deciding what to do with me, or talking about the fucking weather. I don't know. But then the driver goes to one of those mechanic toolboxes and pulls out a coil of rope.

He throws it to the big guy.

From far behind me, toward the back of the warehouse, comes a banging noise.

The driver points at the big guy and moves off in that direction.

"Just let me go," I say to the remaining one.

He hasn't spoken either. But I'm pretty sure every single television show about a kidnapped girl suggested getting on *one* of their good sides.

His hands flex on the rope.

My gaze goes down to it automatically, drawn by the slight motion. He unravels it and approaches.

I stand, but he shoves me down just as fast. I hit the chair hard. He ties my hands in front of me, the rope tightening every second.

His mask freaks me out the most.

Clowns... *no, thank you*.

But I bite the inside of my cheek and force myself to stare at where I think his eyes are.

"I haven't done anything to you," I whisper. "Please. You don't want to know about FSU. I don't even know anything—"

"Quiet," he mutters.

"This is ridiculous. I won't press charges or anything, I swear."

He drops the rope over my head. It drapes across my shoulders.

It isn't until he slowly pulls the end, holding my wrists with his other hand, that the rope tightens slowly around my throat. My eyes widen. I lean back with the pressure, but it doesn't ease.

I jerk uselessly at my hands.

He keeps tightening until I can barely inhale—and even that hurts. My chest immediately aches for more air, but I can only manage to draw in the weakest of breaths. The rope digs into my windpipe.

And yet, there's some part of me that's convinced this is a terrible joke.

"Now that you're goddamn *quiet*," he says, "And he's distracted..."

He wraps the rest of the rope around my torso, catching my arms. Everything is attached. I move my hands; the neck rope shifts.

When he shifts back to check his handiwork, he tilts his head. The clown mask is the worst, and I fight my shudder. I don't want anything else to tighten.

"He gave you options," he says. "But I think there should be an *and* instead of an *or* to his proposition." He flicks out a knife. "First, I'm going to cut the scraps of clothes off you. Then, I'm going to fuck your ass so hard, you'll be shitting my cum for a week."

My eyes widen.

I don't recognize his voice. That's what scares me more than anything—and makes me believe him. It's not Oliver or Penn pulling some sick prank. He seems to mean every word he just said.

He steps closer, dropping to his knees in front of me. It puts us practically at eye level.

He runs his hands up my thighs, spreading them with rough hands. "I like the idea of you choking for air while I violate you."

From my thighs to my hips—

He finds my phone. He grunts and tosses it away, then drags me off the chair. The motion is shocking, the impact of hitting the floor reverberating up my spine. He rips the button on my jeans and yanks my pants down.

No.

White spots flicker in my vision, but I'm not going out like this. I kick at him and try to scream, but all that comes out is a hoarse whisper. Panic rises in me, sharp and swift. It nearly blinds me with fear.

"Yes, scream some more," he groans.

I can't scream. It's just the low whistle of air—but he seems to like it, because he pinches my thigh until I do it again. Make the pathetic noise, empty my lungs and struggle to fill them.

He dodges my kicks and kneels between my bare legs. Through the mask, it seems like his attention keeps dancing around. From my face to the rope to... *lower*.

And I'm helpless to stop him from unbuttoning his pants and palming himself. From leaning over me, the mask filling my vision.

twenty
sydney

"What the *fuck*?"

I catch sight of the driver storming in with someone else hot on his heels. Everything is blurring. But the driver doesn't just *stop*—he lunges at the clown-masked man and rips him away from me.

The rope around my neck loosens.

I suck in a deep breath immediately, my lungs filling and the burning subsiding. I inhale so hard I cough. But it soon turns into hyperventilating. I roll into a fetal position and press my forehead to the concrete.

My gasping breaths sound loud in my ears.

"Sit up." Hands grasp at me, and I'm dragged back against a warm chest. "Hang on, just try to take slow inhales and exhales. Like me."

I can't think about breathing until this rope is off my neck. He makes quick work of unwinding it from my torso and hands, finally lifting it up and over my head. My quick inhales and exhales are too shallow, and I try to calm down. The spots in my vision are back, and even Penn's steadiness at my back doesn't help much.

My attention is pulled away from me, though, to the

driver. He has the clown-masked asshole against one of the mechanic's lifts. His hand is around the bigger guy's throat, and while he's weakly clawing at his arm... he's not trying to dislodge the driver.

When he releases him and steps back, the big guy sags against the lift.

It's not enough.

He almost *raped* me.

"He wouldn't have." Penn. In my ear, like always. The little voice of fucking reason.

I shove off him and pull up my damn pants. The button is gone, but the zipper isn't.

I have always been an underdog, and I know it has a lot to do with money.

Until college, my mom and I were the definition of white trash. Someone who lives in a trailer and doesn't have a car and walks to school because the bus doesn't pick up there. And bikes? Bikes cost money. The last time I had a bike was at my dad's house, and I was seven. It had pink streamers coming from the handles.

When I outgrew it, I didn't ask for another.

To some, a lack of money means a lack of strength. It's easy to take advantage of a poor person. It's easy to dangle something impossible in front of them, just to watch them dance.

And how many times has Mom disappeared with boyfriends for the promise of money? How long did it take me to decide to use some of my savings for a car to get to college?

So maybe people look at me and they see where I came from, but I know I'm worth more.

I'm worth more than *this*.

Oliver is the driver. His mask is on, but Penn is here... And where would Penn go that Oliver wouldn't?

Oliver is the one who orchestrated me to be grabbed off the sidewalk and shoved in a trunk.

Oliver is the one who wanted to scare me.

Oliver left me alone with this monster.

Before either can stop me, I march forward and grip the top of the clown mask. My skin crawls being this close to him, but I have to fucking know. I rip it off.

Bear.

I should've guessed. He seems to have hated me from day one, right? Even when Oliver was appraising and Penn curious...

He looks at me with such loathing, even now, that I have no doubt he would've done it. He might've apologized for it later—to Oliver, not to me—but he enjoyed the quick moments of torture.

Oliver slides in front of me, blocking my view of Bear. He's still wearing the bloody, grinning skull mask. Maybe he even thinks the ruse is still going.

"I believe in karma." My throat burns with every word, but I keep forcing them out. "I believe you're going to get what's coming to you, Oliver Ruiz. Your NHL team will see you for who you are. And when your life starts spiraling, I'm going to be there. I'll fucking *delight* in your fall."

He jerks, the words hitting their target.

After a long moment, he removes the mask from his head. His gaze is hot enough to set me on fire. He seems to catalog my neck, face, and lower. Like he can still see me flat on my back with my pants around my ankles and Bear between them.

"Ollie." Penn stops beside me, his fingers finding my hip. "This is where you fight. This isn't where you intimidate girls."

Fight?

I glance from Oliver to Penn and try to resist the urge to lean into Penn's hand. To sidle even closer and let him comfort me. It's an insane thought, because we're not on that level.

We're on the level of using each other. Nothing more.

"You are all insane," I breathe. "You, Oliver, for thinking I'd make the same mistake as last year."

His eyes flash. "Once a snitch, always a snitch."

I knock Penn's hand around. "And you? Why did you show up out of the blue?"

Penn goes around Oliver and shoves his other teammate. "Get the fuck out of here, Bear. And if you ever so much as look at Sydney wrong, I'll fucking cut your balls off."

The huge man glares at the goalie as he picks himself up. He absently rubs at his throat, and I scowl. He looks like he's twenty-seven, not college aged. That's creepier than his mask, and not to mention questionable. He tosses the mask into the car. While he climbs in, Penn opens the garage door for him.

Bear backs it out, and we all wait in silence until he's turned onto the street and out of view. Penn yanks the garage door back down and slides the bolt to lock it.

He returns to us and meets my gaze. "I showed up here because I saw someone grab you, and no one was fucking returning my calls."

Oliver scowls.

"And you decided to recruit Bear. He was really bringing down the mood." I aim for something more lighthearted, although it doesn't quite hit. Everything hurts, and I'm sure I'm a snotty, tear-soaked mess, but I can fake it with the best of them.

Penn scoffs.

I grab my phone from the floor where Bear threw it and face Oliver. The crack from the taping incident was luckily just to the screen protector, and it was good as new as soon as I replaced it. Not that I need another reminder of Oliver's cruelty. Indirect or otherwise.

"Did I pass your test?"

His expression is stoic. Like talking to a fucking brick wall.

So I'm going to take that as a *yes*, and he just doesn't want to admit it.

To Penn, I ask, "You still going to break into my apartment tonight?"

The goalie forces a grin. His brows stay lowered, though. Concerned. "Why would I do that when I have you now?"

"Because right now I want to throttle both of you. Mainly him, though." I wait a beat. "I'm glad you stopped him." I can't quite muster a thank you, though.

Oliver nods once, but a flush creeps up his neck. He turns away from us abruptly and strides over to the shelving on the wall, swiping his arms across the surface. Tools and items go crashing to the floor.

Penn threads his fingers through mine, and I really want to hate him.

Except... I don't think I do.

"He put me in the trunk." I touch my throat. "You knew that, though. You said you saw it."

His gaze hardens. "Yeah, princess. I got here as fast as I could."

"And I want to know more about this fighting thing," I add. Since I seem to be pushing my luck getting any sort of admission from them, I may as well ask about this, too.

"No," Oliver barks.

Penn considers it.

I keep eye contact with him, sucking my lower lip between my teeth. I didn't bother putting my hair up after class, and he reaches for a lock automatically. He twirls it in his fingers, thinking something through.

"Is that where you got that black eye from before? No goalie gets a black eye in a game unless they're asking for it. And even then..."

"Walker," Oliver warns.

"Yes," Penn says. "We do fight nights after a home game

149

loss. Everyone knows to come here." He steps into my personal space, his chest and mine nearly brushing.

"Everyone," I repeat. I have to tip my head back to meet his gaze.

"Everyone who matters."

"Everyone who pays," Oliver corrects. "No snitches allowed."

"First rule of fight club, don't talk about fight club," I say.

"Exactly." Penn snaps his fingers. "But since you now know both the where and the when, you're welcome to come. In fact, you should be here to root me on."

"How are you so—*normal*?" Oliver interrupts. "What the fuck is going on in your head, doll? Anything but air?"

"Of course you're going to be nasty after your teammate tries to strangle and rape me," I snap. My voice cracks, though, which kind of ruins my anger. Besides, the best way to get over something is to pretend it didn't happen.

Penn touches my neck, and I cringe.

"You didn't feel it," he says to Oliver. "It was really fucking tight."

They glare at each other.

I blink back tears, trying to keep to my *pretend this didn't just happen* mantra. But it's really hard when my throat hurts, and my body is still zipping with adrenaline, and I have the urge to break something.

"She's going to bruise," Penn adds.

I lean into his side, suddenly done with tonight. He steers me out the door they came through and puts me in his car. He disappears back inside, presumably to get Oliver's version of events. But it's pretty cut and dry—they grabbed me. They threatened me.

Then Bear took it further.

My skin crawls. He *touched* me, and I couldn't do anything about it.

I check my phone and stare at the texts from L.

L.

Who is it?? Where are they taking you?

Damn it, Sydney. Where are you?

Penn returns, setting my backpack in the footwell behind his chair and sliding into the driver's seat. He looks at me, his brows furrowing.

"What's wrong?"

A tear rolls down my cheek before I realize I'm at that point. My vision goes blurry. I blink rapidly, swiping at my face. I don't want to keep crying or reliving the last hour of my life. I just want to keep pretending that I'm fucking *fine*.

"I'm fine."

I just thought L. would be able to help me. But how on earth would he do that?

My phone lights up with Carter's name. I glance over at Penn, who's still watching me—not my phone. But his gaze does drop to it, and he scowls.

He snatches my phone and answers the call.

"You're too late," he says.

I can't make out Carter's words from here. I reach, but Penn dodges my hands.

"You had the chance to rescue the princess, asshole, but apparently you screen your calls." Penn gazes at me, listening. Then, "She's fine now. Don't worry—I plan on comforting her all night long."

I look away.

He tosses my phone in the cup holder.

I wipe at another fucking tear. Crying is *stupid*. It's all stupid.

"Talk to me."

I just—

I unbuckle and get out of the car. I'm too hot. I have too much energy. It's all pent up and useless, and I fucking hate it.

"I've got just the thing," Oliver says. He leans in the

doorway of the mechanic's warehouse, the light behind him silhouetting his body and hiding his expression. "If you can stomach me for an hour or so."

"What is it?"

He lifts one shoulder. "Come find out. But I can guarantee you I'm not going to baby you. Not now, not ever."

"Okay," I agree. I hold out my arms. "Lead the way."

twenty-one
sydney

Oliver Ruiz has a motorcycle.

He passes me a helmet and watches passively as I struggle to get it buckled under my chin. He got his on in record time, and he straddles the seat with a comfortability that is, quite frankly, shocking.

I'm already regretting choosing his option instead of Penn's.

"Sometime tonight, Sydney."

My eyebrows hike up. "I think that's the first time you've said my name."

"At least this month," he allows. "I'm sure I've used it before."

"Okay, it's the first time you've said it without looking like you're chewing glass."

He snickers, but it only lasts a few seconds. "Get on."

I carefully swing my leg over. I don't want to touch him. But he glances back and shakes his head. He grips my legs, fingers catching the backs of my knees, and drags me forward. I collide with his back, my helmet bouncing off his.

But he's not done rearranging me. He points to where I should put my feet, then takes my wrists and wraps them around him.

Yeah, not exactly the best idea.

I clench my jaw.

His whole body moves when he kick-starts the bike, the engine roaring beneath us.

I admit; I momentarily forget who's in front of me and squeeze him, alarm shooting up my spine. I feel more than hear his laugh, and everything in me tenses when we bolt forward.

The first five minutes are pure terror. My eyes are screwed shut, my fingers immediately go numb from the cold air whipping at us. He leans with each turn, forcing me to either lean with him or separate.

"Open your eyes," he calls.

I do.

We're heading for the bridge. It's ahead of us, lit in warm lights. The dark water sparkles on either side of the road. His body radiates heat, which is directly at odds with the wind chill.

Fifteen minutes later, and a whole county over from Framingham, and Oliver turns down a quaint main street strip. The buildings that line it are close enough to touch. Cafés, clothing shops, a pet supply store. Three-quarters down, we slow to a coast and park in front of a blacked-out storefront.

The sign above it says: *Ruiz Rage.*

My brows furrow.

Oliver taps my thigh, and I climb off. My legs wobble, knees weak, and I stumble away from the evil bike—and the devil who rides it. I fumble with the clasp on the helmet. He undoes his and watches me for a moment. He seems to decide that a moment is all it's worth, because he approaches and knocks away my hands.

He undoes the helmet's buckle and lifts it off my head. I shake out my hair, finger-combing through the snarls.

Since Penn isn't here, I pull it over my shoulder and braid it.

While Oliver just… stares.

"Maybe you should take a picture," I say. "It'll last longer."

He smiles. "I have a picture."

My expression drops.

"Let's go." He heads for the building.

We enter, a bell above the door announcing our entrance. We're in a waiting room of sorts. It seems warm and cozy, the walls a rustic orange and covered in framed photos, the rug patterned in oranges, reds, and bright blues. There's a counter straight ahead, and the door off to the left of it opens.

An older woman comes out.

"Gabriel!" she exclaims. "*Hace tanto tiempo que no te veo, mi niño.*"

When she cups his face, he bends for her to kiss both cheeks.

"Hi, *Abuelita*. This is my friend, Sydney." He glances at me, and there's a very clear warning there. "Sydney, this is my abuela, Juana Ruiz."

Her black hair has streaks of gray in it, but her face is nearly wrinkle-free. Except when she smiles—she smiles with her whole face. Unfortunately, she doesn't smile at me. Her gaze turns more to worry.

"You're bringing a girl here, Gabriel? This isn't date material." Her Spanish accent is very thick, and she eyes me like I might attack *her*. But I don't even know what we're doing, so I keep my mouth shut.

He lifts one shoulder. "I think she could benefit from it."

His abuela tsks. "If you insist. Room three. I have paperwork to complete. Come see me before you leave."

"Why does she call you Gabriel?" I ask him once she's gone.

He smiles. A nice one. It's directed at his abuela, obviously, not me. I'll be damned if he ever smiles at me like that. Seems to be a similar sentiment between them, although he doesn't act bothered by her cold demeanor.

"It's my middle name," he says. "Mom is white. Dad is first generation Mexican American. My parents agreed to name me Oliver because it was her father's name, so he chose my middle name. My dad's side of the family mostly calls me Gabriel, but Abue set the tone for it early."

"Got it."

Oliver Gabriel Ruiz. There's no L there, unless we count the two in his first and middle names. I don't think that's enough to entirely clear him of being L., but... Stop thinking about him.

He leads the way through the door his abuela came through. The hallway is wide, and there's a long row of shelving on the right. He goes to it and plucks items from cubbies, handing me first a hard hat, then a pair of safety goggles. He moves farther down, taking an apron made of thicker rubber off a rack. He hooks one over his neck, then passes me the other.

"I don't really understand what's going on." I tie the apron at the small of my back.

We go to the third door on the left. It has a white light on over it, unlike the others. Their lights are off. One is red.

He opens the door and ushers me in, his hand briefly touching my back.

I scoot in quick.

The room is... a kitchen? Minus the sink and appliances. The cabinets have no doors, but there are stacks of plates and glassware on every shelf. There's also miscellaneous stuff: picture frames lining the counter, a collection of vases filled with water and flowers.

Oliver taps me on the shoulder.

I turn.

He didn't touch me with his hand—there's a baseball bat in his grip, and he offers me the handle.

I take it with a silent question on my face.

"Rage rooms." He takes a glass from one of the cabinets and throws it on the floor.

It smashes. I do my best not to flinch at the sudden noise, but I don't think I succeed. Glass goes everywhere, and he kicks one of the larger chunks toward the wall.

"How did you feel when you realized it was me?" Oliver goads.

"Angry."

"And when Penn said some bullshit about treating you nice?"

"Like I was going to crawl out of my skin."

"Because it was so fucking easy to pick you up off the street and get you in the trunk," he says. "Right? Because you didn't know how to stop Bear from grabbing you, you didn't react quick enough, you didn't scream loud enough. You weren't enough."

"Stop it."

He holds out a plate. "How does that make you feel, doll?"

"Frustrated."

"*Helpless*," he corrects, his tone biting. "You're so fucking helpless. That's why you're a doll. You run a mile or two every other day and call yourself athletic, but you have no muscles. Andi fucking Sharpe taped you down to a toilet with the help of one other person."

He comes closer and squeezes my biceps with his free hand. To prove a point.

I knock him away and grip the bat tighter. "Stop."

"Bear almost raped you tonight." His gaze presses in on me. It hurts worse than a bruise. "Did you sit there like a good little girl while he tied your hands? Did you want him to fuck you?"

"Shut up."

He holds out a plate. Taunting, offering...

"*Make me.*"

I swing the bat.

It knocks the plate out of his hand, sending it crashing against the wall. I stare at it, shocked at myself. I could've broken his damn fingers. But he nods encouragingly, giving me a 'come on' hand motion.

"More," he demands.

I smash the vases first. Flowers and water mix with the glass, the water immediately dripping down the bare counters.

He picks up a crowbar and drives it into the stack of plates closest to him. The crash is satisfying. I grin. I attack the picture frames next. They just have stock photos in them, which reminds me of home. The way everything was so superficial.

You didn't tell anyone I took a little trip, did you, baby? It's only for a few days; if they knew they might take you away.

You don't want to go live with your father, right?

It was a guilt trip.

I drop the bat and pick out a plate, throwing it against the wall. Oliver hands me another one. And another.

Why do I even want to find my mother?

Your father is getting remarried, baby, she said to me when I was fifteen. *I told him he couldn't replace us. But if he's more distant...*

Why am I thinking about her?

Why am I only thinking about the bad stuff?

I was mad at Oliver for tossing me in a fucking trunk and trying to get me to admit something I know nothing about. He's testing loyalty I don't have or want. But somehow, that anger has been consumed by the stuff I've been battling to keep buried.

Maybe I'm the most upset at myself for letting all of this happen. For every moment in my life where I had a choice, and I took the wrong option.

We move on to glasses. He joins me, cracking a few. Ceramic mugs. A light fixture sitting on the table, coasters I sweep off the counter and smash with the curved end of a crowbar until it's practically dust. I bring it down on the bottom of the upper cabinets, cracking the wood. Over and over again until my muscles tremble.

I don't realize I'm crying until there's nothing left to break but myself.

"Good," he says.

I drop the crowbar. It clatters against the glass and ceramic that litter the floor. He helps me pick a path to the door. At the shelving in the hall, I take off the hat and glasses, untie the apron, and hang it on the hook.

I run my hands through my hair and down my face.

"I'm going to say goodbye," he says quietly. "You can go out into the lobby, just wait for me there."

I walk out without a backward glance. Standing in the center of the room, which is so warm and alive compared to the cold, sterile rage room we were in.

The hollow sensation in my chest is new. New and strange. I rub at my sternum. When Oliver doesn't immediately appear, I drift toward the far wall.

There are groups of smiling people in the middle of different rage rooms. Some are bigger, some small and simple like the one we were in. There's a huge room that a large party stands in the center of that even has a few cars parked in the open space.

Why do they seem happy, though?

I keep moving along the wall, taking in the smiles and finding myself slipping into numbness.

"Sydney?" Oliver stops beside me. "Ready?"

"Yeah." Ready for something, I don't know what. "I thought that would make me feel better."

He eyes me. "But?"

"I just feel empty."

"Ah."

We go outside. This time, he puts the helmet on my head and buckles it under my chin, his knuckles brushing my skin. I shiver, but it's definitely the cold air and not his touch that does it.

Back on the bike, arms cinched around his abdomen, I rather expect him to take me straight home.

Nope.

He pulls into the driveway of *his* house.

I don't have a reaction, though. I don't really know why we're here unless he's going to be mean again. I just follow him up the walkway and into the house.

It's all familiar. It shouldn't be, but... I know where everything is because I scouted it out and I was merciless about it. He toes off his shoes and disappears down the hall into the kitchen. I stand in the doorway for a long moment, then ultimately do the same and follow.

He sets a small pot of milk on the stove and leans against the counter beside it.

"From threatening to return me to Penn all bloody and bruised to... what are you making? Mac 'n cheese?"

"I was going for hot chocolate."

"Whatever you're making is fine," I murmur. "What a weird fucking day."

"Yeah?"

"Obviously."

He doesn't have a reply to that.

I take a seat at the table. Penn still has my phone, so there's no distractions. The clock on the wall ticks loudly in the quiet. There's just our breathing and the slight crackle of the flame under the pot.

I open and close my mouth, but any thought on what to actually say to him has evaporated.

Trusting Ruiz is a bad idea. Such a fucking bad idea.

"My playbook is upstairs if you want to go sneak more pictures," he says.

See?

I push back from the table and go upstairs. Not that I have

my phone. Or anything, for that matter. Not that he seems to know any differently. I head straight upstairs to that room that had it last time. It's in a drawer this time, but it takes me no time at all to find it.

I cradle it to my chest and go back downstairs.

"Hey," I bark.

He turns.

I chuck his playbook at him. He catches it—*of course he fucking does*—and squints at me.

"You were an ass."

He doesn't reply.

"You were an ass," I say, louder. "That night on the beach? I don't know why I took pictures of the playbook, but I did. I wasn't going to share them, though, until you suggested Carter used me for them. 'Sending sluts to distract us is a tired trick.'"

He turns back to the small pot on the stove, turning off the burner.

"You could've just left it alone," I continue, "and those photos would've rotted on my phone."

He sets the playbook aside and lifts the pot from the stove. "You can tell yourself that."

"What?"

"You say that's what you're going to do. But what if something else happened? What if Masters sweet talked you, or kissed you, or you remembered that you have more loyalty—"

"You took care of any loyalty issues," I shoot back.

"Did I?"

He pours the water into two mugs and stirs while I stand here like a fucking idiot. My face flames, and I can't...

I don't know what to say to that. Didn't I just prove myself to him? In the face of torture or whatever they were threatening. Violence. Pain. I said nothing.

There was nothing to say.

He brings the mugs to the table and sits across from my chosen seat.

I slowly inch back into the kitchen and join him. I wrap my hands around the warm, dark-green mug. He does the same to his baby blue one.

"Why were you in my house, then?" He eyes me. "I caught you. There aren't many excuses—"

"It's because you have a family heirloom of mine," I blurt out. I press my lips together and turn away. I shouldn't have fucking said that. I didn't mean to say it. "Not that I expect you to do anything about it *now*, but I was searching for it that night."

Admitting to him why I was here seems foolhardy. He can use this against me in any way he sees fit.

"Sydney, look at me."

I cannot and will not subject myself to that.

He waits.

Finally, I glance his way.

"Explain."

"No."

His gaze hardens. "Then I'll just have to assume it's some elaborate lie."

I plant my hands on the table, suddenly mad again. So much for being numb.

"Okay, fine," I snap. "Cards on the table. If you use this against me, I will make sure you never play professional hockey."

He inclines his chin.

"It's a vintage gold bracelet inset with engravings and pearls. On the inside it has a quote."

"And how did I end up with it?"

"My mother likes money more than family history." That hurts to admit. "I got out of her where she sold it and went to the pawnshop. I pleaded with the owner until he gave me *your* name."

"My name. She sold it here?"

I frown. "She said it was when she came up to visit for Thanksgiving last year. Apparently, she was going to give it to me and then decided to sell it instead. He said he sold it to Oliver Ruiz. And since you said earlier that you're named after your grandfather on your mom's side, I have to think you're the only one local."

"I did buy a bracelet like that," he says.

I open my mouth, but he keeps going.

"I gave it to my mother for her fiftieth birthday."

I don't... I don't know what to do with that.

My expression must be a mixture of shock and hurt, but I can't seem to wrestle my feelings back under control. While my mother has been rather frivolous with our family history, only managing to hold on to that piece because I was in love with it and the history attached to it, I crave it.

I need to know everything about where I came from in order to figure out myself. Right? That's how it works. Because otherwise, I have no idea who I am.

"Sydney," he whispers. "I'm—"

I shake my head. "I can't talk about this anymore."

I sip the cocoa. It's spiced with flavors I've never tasted in it before, but it's good. It seems to warm me from the inside out, and for once, that's not an effect of alcohol.

"Do you like it?"

"Yes."

His expression falls. "Finish it and I'll take you home."

twenty-two
oliver

We ride back to her brownstone building. She seemed to feel a little better after the hot cocoa—my abuelita's recipe, which she always made for us to cheer us up. But now, as I sit on the bike with the extra helmet in my lap, I have the strangest urge to follow her.

"Sydney," I call.

She stops mid-step, but she doesn't turn around.

"What's the quote?"

"'It's better to have loved and lost than never loved at all.'"

My heart skips.

After a second, she continues up the steps. She pulls keys from her pocket and unlocks the front door. Even with her stuff still in Penn's car, which is pretty lucky. I wait until the light turns on in her third-floor apartment. Only then do I rev the engine loud enough for her to hear. Like some fucked-up goodbye.

I speed toward my family home on the other side of the lake. It's late, but they won't mind. Abue lives with my parents and two younger siblings, both of whom are still in high school.

My brother plays soccer, while my baby sister is a master at the violin.

As soon as I enter the familiar neighborhood, my home-sickness kicks up in full gear. I flip the kickstand down and hang my helmet on the handle of my bike, then head up the worn concrete walkway.

"I'm home," I call out.

The first to greet me is the damn dog. She jumps on me, her tongue flicking out to lap at my face. I lean down to accommodate her, rubbing her silky brown fur. Abue comes around the corner next, her expression warm... if not a little concerned.

Her greeting to Sydney wasn't exactly what I expected either.

"Twice in one day," she observes. "I hope things aren't serious with that girl, Gabriel, because rage is an ugly emotion for one to display so young. You look skinny. Let me fix you a plate."

I shake my head and follow her deeper into the house. My mom shrieks when she sees me, jumping from the table where her and my father play cards every night, without fail.

She throws her arms around my neck and smothers my face in kisses.

"We saw your game," she says, touching the bruise on my cheek. "Do you have to fight?"

I extract myself. "It's part of the sport."

She sighs. "You getting hurt hurts *me*, Ollie."

"I know, Mama." I kiss the top of her head. "I have to ask you something."

"So this isn't a visit just to see us?" Her eyes always have a twinkle in them. Some all-knowing, amused sparkling.

I used to think that was normal. That most women—especially mothers—were always happy. Not only that, but *joyful*. But I think it's just her. She sees the positive in absolutely everything.

"That bracelet I gave you for your birthday..."

She grins and pushes up the sleeve of her sweater. "I wear it every day."

I knew it would be exactly as Sydney described, but... "Can I see the engraving on the underside?"

She unclasps it and passes it to me.

In faint cursive, worn away by time, is the quote: *It's better to have loved and lost than never loved at all.*

I don't know if I wanted it to be something completely different or not, but my gut twists. I hand it back to her and kiss her cheek.

"Everything all right?" she asks, a line forming between her brows.

I nod and head to the table to greet my father. We'll sit and talk, and my abuela will tell me all the ways Sydney isn't right to join the family. Maybe it was stupid bringing her to Ruiz Rage, but she had a look in her eye. I get that look, too, when I'm so mad I can barely breathe.

I'm lucky, though. I have hockey. The sport is brutal even without the fighting.

Voicing any of that will get me nowhere. So I lie.

"Everything is perfect."

twenty-three
sydney

The last time I went skating was with my father.

Seems fitting that the first time I go skating since then would be with him, too. I'm not sure what spurs it, but he called me early on a Saturday and asked if I was free. I looked down at myself, my sports bra damp with sweat and the little hairs on my neck stuck to my skin.

The run was invigorating, but something is off with me.

I didn't care about the pain. And it probably doesn't have anything to do with the bruises that showed up on my throat, wrapping all the way around my neck like a collar.

It certainly doesn't have to do with the nightmares or emptiness that has bloomed in the wake of zero emotional support.

L. never texted me, Oliver seemed to pull a disappearing act this week. Penn skipped all three of our classes. And Carter... out of sight, out of mind? I don't know if Penn scared him off or what. But I haven't talked to him.

My phone and bag were both waiting for me on my bed when I got home from my adventure with Oliver. There was a bottle of cold water and ibuprofen on my nightstand, which was considerate of him. At least I know Penn can break into my apartment like he threatened.

Dylan's first volleyball game is in two weeks. She made sure to let us know that Brandon, Maddy, and I are all expected to be there under penalty of death. But that just translates to longer, harder practices.

Maddy's presentation is coming up.

Brandon has been working more.

No one has asked me about the scarves I've been wearing all week, and I'm just *tired*.

But maybe hanging out with my father is what I need, so I agreed.

He picks me up an hour later and drives me to the public ice rink. It's already crowded with people who skate counter-clockwise around the oval. We park and stare at it, and I let out a little laugh.

"You probably could've gotten us into the arena," I point out.

He chuckles, too, running his hand down his salt-and-pepper goatee. "Yeah, but this has a hot chocolate stand. And I sort of expected it to be quieter."

In the last week, temperatures have plummeted. The rink, which is hosted and maintained by the mayor's office, is situated in the park across from City Hall. It was just installed earlier this week, I think.

"I brought Perri's skates, but I also got you a pair to take home... in case you want to break them in and do this again."

I glance at him. A black beanie covers his hair and the tips of his ears. Black jacket. We match, him and I. I've got a black headband warming my ears and a black winter jacket zipped up to my throat. A thick scarf is wrapped over it just in case.

He goes to the back to get the skates. I open my door and swing my legs out, breathing in the cold air.

Which is how I hear someone call, "Hey, Coach!"

Dad turns, frowning at Oliver and Penn. They have their hockey skates slung over their shoulders, and they come up to him from the other side of the vehicle.

Which means they don't see me until Oliver peeks into the bag in the trunk and sees two sets.

Or maybe three, since Dad mentioned buying me a pair.

Oliver rounds the back bumper and stops short. His face looks worse after a week of healing, all that damage from his fight with Carter. Or maybe it's from their fight ring. Even though they haven't lost at home, that could've been a lie.

I don't really think I can trust anything they tell me.

"You two are supposed to be resting," Dad says to them. "We have a game tomorrow."

"We just wanted to check out the new rink," Penn says. "If we knew you were going to be here, we would've skipped it."

His last words are for me, his gaze finding mine through the glass.

Ouch.

"Those yours?" Oliver points to the bag.

I can't see them, so I shrug.

"They're Perri's," Dad says. "We're going to try them out, although they might be too small."

Oliver wrinkles his nose. "Figure skates, though? Really?"

I make the same face.

"Okay, Syd." Dad laughs. "I guessed you might react like that. Which is why I got you these."

He produces hockey skates. Oliver, still in the space between our truck and the car beside us and blocking Dad from reaching me, takes them from him.

I meet his gaze. He doesn't seem angry with me... I actually don't know how to read the expression covering his face. And I certainly don't know how to react when he puts his knee down on the truck's running board and picks up my foot.

He unlaces my boot and tugs it off.

I'm having a Cinderella moment, and it's really fucking weird.

True to the fairy tale, the shoe—err, *skate*—is a perfect fit. In that it's the right size anyway. They're brand-new, which means it's going to suck skating on them today. I have no doubt everyone knows it, but it's just one of those things.

You deal with it, and then the skates get better.

He puts on the other one and does up the laces. I'm having flashbacks to my father in the same position, easing any worries about the kids he coaches in a low voice while he tugs at my skates.

"Good?" Dad asks.

Oliver rises, and I nod.

"They're perfect. Thank you."

"One problem." Oliver glances around. "You'll ruin the blade walking across the lot."

Dad frowns.

"Yeah, that's—I'll just take them off and put them back on by the ice—"

"Nah, I've got it." Oliver steps into my space and slides his arm under the crooks of my knees. The other goes across my lower back, and he easily lifts me out of the truck.

I glare at him.

Dad does, too.

"Ruiz," Dad warns.

"I've got her, sir." He heads up the path toward the skating rink. It does seem to be thinning out a little. "Have you skated before?"

I don't answer.

"Silent treatment?" He sighs. "I just want you to know that we're dealing with him."

Whatever they did to Bear isn't enough.

"His actions aren't going unpunished," he repeats from earlier.

We get to the section where everyone puts on their skates. The ground is covered in rubber mats. He sets me down.

"Go walk around for a few minutes and come back. Get warm. It'll help mold the skates to your feet."

I wave him off, but I do as he says. While Dad, Oliver, and

Penn all skate up, I pace in circles around them. Finally, I drop down onto the bench next to my father.

"You could've grabbed something secondhand," I say to him. "Or I could've rented a pair..."

He pats my knee. "You kidding me? Now you can come skate during practice like the good old days. You were pretty good, you know."

"Good at what?"

"Everything. Hell, I'd bet you still are."

Gosh. My throat closes, and my eyes burn. A change in subject would be grand, but I can't seem to get any words out. When's the last time anyone said I was *good* at something?

Never.

"Sydney..."

I swipe under my eyes. "I'm fine. You should go warm up, old man. I'll join you once I've properly baked these suckers."

"Okay, Syd." He pats my knee and rises, jostling Oliver in a way that feels like they've known each other a long time—and they *like* each other.

I don't really see the appeal.

The two head for the rink, and Penn takes Dad's spot next to me. He stares after them, his brow furrowing. We sit in silence for a long moment.

I'm not going to be the one to break it. He's been avoiding me, skipping the one class we have together. Well, they've all been avoiding me. And it's made people like Andi start throwing daggered looks in my direction again.

Not that *that's* why I want him to talk to me.

Maybe life will get easier if I don't have the two menaces trying to ruin me.

"Do you like Ollie?" he asks me.

Oh. "Um, not particularly."

"Why did you go with him instead of me?"

He's hurt. I reach for his hand and squeeze his fingers.

"I didn't want comfort," I say in a low voice. "I just

wanted... an outlet. I'm sorry. I don't know what we are, but... I didn't think you'd care."

Penn meets my gaze. "I don't *care*, I'm just fucking jealous."

I smile.

After a second, he smiles, too.

"You snuck into my apartment as promised."

"You were sleeping. Didn't feel right to wake you." He leans in and tugs at the scarf at my throat. He swipes his finger across the mottled bruise that the soft fabric hides. "This hurts?"

"Yeah. But... you could sneak in when I'm awake, you know." My face immediately heats.

He sits up with interest. "I hear some kink hidden in there. Tell me more, princess. Do you have fantasies about being ravished by dirty, dirty pirates?"

I snort. "Maybe not pirates. But goalies..."

His gaze darkens.

That's my cue to rejoin society.

I stand and leave him sitting there. The skates still do not feel great, but I can't imagine we'll be on the ice for long. It's not like I have to go out and play a game.

I wait for a break in the crowd and step out onto the ice. It's the first time in a while, and I wobble rather dramatically.

Hands grab my hips.

I glance back at Penn.

He winks, then propels me forward. "Don't even *think* about holding on to the wall."

"I wouldn't dream of it," I deadpan.

But there are a fair amount of people doing that, and the stability seems nice. Still. Penn lets me regain my balance, although he somehow skates close enough behind me without actually impeding my movement.

Until it all comes back to me.

Oliver and Dad catch up to us. I automatically hook my arm through Dad's.

The smile that overtakes his face is infectious.

"Race you," Penn yells at Oliver. "First back to Syd and Coach wins."

He shoves Oliver to the ice, then takes off at a near sprint. Oliver's laugh bursts out of him, and he climbs to his feet slowly—seeming to let Penn have a decent head start before he gives chase.

"Racing in goalie skates," Dad laughs. "Now I've seen it all."

"Don't you bag skate them?"

As in, coaches making their players skate until their legs fall off.

"Only when they deserve it," he replies.

We track their progress. Oliver, predictably, catches up with Penn easily.

When they're halfway across, I tug Dad's arm. "Let's make it a little longer for them."

He agrees, and we skate across the center ice. We do it twice more before they catch on—and catch *up*. They're both breathing hard, their faces flushed.

I can't stop giggling.

"Not fair," Penn gasps. "I'm fit but I'm not that fucking fit."

"Penance for skating when you should be resting," my father says.

Oliver snickers, but his forearms are on his knees. He and Penn skate out ahead of us. It's actually nice. Being here with not just my father, but the guys, too. Especially since they seem to be on their best behavior.

"Your old man's going to take a hot chocolate break," Dad says in my ear. "You okay with them, or do you want to come with me?"

"I'm okay for now. But I do want a hot chocolate later."

"Deal."

He ducks out when we pass the opening in the boards, and I navigate my way between Oliver and Penn. They were just ahead of us, discussing something while they caught their breath, but now they both straighten.

Things have obviously been shifting between us. I want to understand it more, but I also don't want to jinx it.

"What were you discussing?"

They exchange a glance over my head.

"Oh, come on."

"We were debating if you liked what went down in your dad's office," Penn finally says. "Minus the coercion. Or..."

"You're thinking about sex?" Jesus. "Well, my preference is to avoid an audience of the bitch who hates me and my ex-best friend."

They both smirk.

"The rest was cool?" Penn clarifies.

"It wasn't cool," I mutter. "Neither of you are getting in my pants for a long, *long* time."

Oliver bumps my shoulder. "Don't make promises you can't keep, doll."

I groan. "You two are trouble."

"Double the trouble?" Penn asks.

"Double the fun," Oliver finishes.

Yeah, I'm so fucking screwed.

twenty-four
carter

I let myself into Sydney's apartment.

There's something extra exciting about sneaking around while she sleeps. The knowledge that any little noise could wake her.

I've got her schedule memorized. Her classes. I could navigate her apartment blindfolded—which I may as well be doing now, since she drew the shades in the living room before she went to bed.

Not her usual style, which makes me wonder if she's subconsciously trying to hide...

There's a single cup by the sink. She eats most of her meals on campus, which means her fridge and pantry are startlingly bare. Just cans of soda, coffee creamer, some cheap ramen.

If this is what she buys when she's on her own...

I've *seen* her kitchen when she lived with Scarlett, though. The pantry and fridge was always stuffed. Maybe that was more Scarlett than Sydney... It must've been.

I move past the kitchen and toward her bedroom. My heart hammers in anticipation at what I'll find.

I don't expect to see her having sex, though.

My fingers pause on the door, which is only open a crack.

Her blinds are open, and the street light comes in enough for me to see through...

A shadowed figure moves over her, but the longer I watch, the more I realize she's not awake.

My dick suddenly twitches. I inch forward more, holding my breath while I get a fucking erection like I'm watching amateur porn.

The blond hair—it's Penn.

I know it instantly.

He's got the blankets pooled at the bottom of the bed, her shirt pushed up and breasts exposed...

Fuck.

He barely moves her as he pushes into her. Her legs are open, and he seems to only keep one point of contact—where he's fucking her. His hands are braced on either side of her, under her arms.

It's erotic in ways it shouldn't be. I stand at the door and watch, and eventually palm myself through my jeans. It doesn't do much to alleviate the ache at watching Penn take her...

And he comes, stilling inside her and emitting the lowest of grunts. Barely audible. He makes quick work of pulling out and sliding her panties back into place. The bastard didn't even remove them... which makes me think he doesn't want her to know quite yet.

Hmm.

How deep does my dream girl sleep?

I step back into the shadows before he can spot me. I don't think I want to reveal my hand quite yet. And I was so preoccupied with Sydney, I didn't even think to watch for another intruder.

My mistake.

The sound of the window scraping open is unmistakable, and I inch forward in time to see Penn climb out onto the fire escape. He pulls the window down behind him and vanishes from sight.

I wait another long moment. It would be like him to have seen me and set a trap. He'd probably be just as curious... but I'm not running out of night just yet.

Plenty of time to continue my exploration, with the added bonus of a hard-on at what I just witnessed.

I knew the goalie had to be a kinky fucker, but this is next level.

Finally, I step into the room.

Sydney is still asleep. She's covered back up, her shirt down and her blankets up to her ribcage. Her lips are parted, and she looks too fucking serene like this.

Like she didn't just get fucked...

A necklace glitters in the low light. I lean forward to inspect it. The gold goalie mask with a snake. I ball my fists and force myself not to touch it. Not now.

It would be easy to make it disappear. Penn Walker's asinine declaration of... *possession*.

That's all it is.

I draw the fucking blinds and flip the lock on the window, just in case he decides to do something stupid. I don't want witnesses. When I return to her, now in the much darker room, I drop to my knees next to her bed and slide my hand under the blankets. I go by feel, a lot fucking less confident than Penn seemed to be.

Would she orgasm while she's asleep?

Would I want her to?

The answer comes swiftly: only if she's thinking of me.

My fingers find the edge of her panties, and then I'm touching her clit. She's slick with arousal and Penn's cum, and I stroke her slowly. I wait for any flutter of waking, but she stays asleep.

Did he drug her?

I thrust a finger inside her, then go back to her clit. I lean forward and kiss the swell of her breast through her thin shirt. She stirs ever so slightly, and I pause. I can practically feel her pulse through her clit.

After a minute, I continue.

It's decided.

I want her to come.

And I think I need to force-feed her birth control, unless she's already taken care of that... There's no fucking way Penn Walker is putting a baby in her before I do.

Then—it happens. She shudders, a full-body shiver, and she shifts. Her fingers twist in the sheets, her mouth opening wider as the pleasure moves through her.

I smile.

I pull my hand out and lick my fingers. The taste of her cum mixed with Penn's... it actually does my head in. I sit back on my heels and fumble with my jeans, shoving them down enough to free my cock. It's already red, with a bead of precum seeping from the slit.

I return my hand to between her legs, gathering more wetness, and coat my length in it. I jerk myself off with quick movements, and at the last moment I go for her hamper. I find dirty panties, the strip that sits against her pussy still slightly damp from earlier arousal—the naughty girl—and groan through my teeth as my orgasm takes over.

I jerk my hips, thrusting my length into my hand, and let the panties catch what spills out.

Electricity zips up my spine.

Riding along the razor's edge of right and wrong—or maybe wrong and *barely acceptable*—makes it even better. I want to do unspeakable things to her. I want to whisper them into her ear and watch the pretty blush creep across her cheeks.

I want to leave her sore and aching and desperate for *me*. Not Penn. Not fucking Oliver Ruiz.

Me.

I think she could go dark with me. I think she could match my interests with some curious ones of her own...

Fuck.

I ball up the panties and bury them deeper in her hamper, leaving a little surprise for later. I make sure she's all right, and for all intents and purposes she is. I smooth back her hair and kiss her forehead, silently promising to do even better, more wicked things to her when I can see her eyes.

Another piece of the puzzle of the guys around her slots into place. It's ammunition, that's all. And I'm one step closer to rooting them out of her life for good.

twenty-five
sydney

My alarm goes off bright and early Sunday.

I smack at it, cursing the light behind my closed blinds. It takes me a second to pull back into reality. I stayed up late last night, curled in bed with my eye on the window that opens onto the fire escape. With the blinds... *open*.

Because that must be how Penn got in to return my backpack, right?

But he didn't come, and I eventually fell asleep.

My back cracks when I stretch, and there's a new ache in my muscles.

The figure skating, obviously. My arm is sore, too, but that's probably from the birth control shot. I shuffle out of bed and straight to the bathroom. But on the toilet, I pause.

There's a thick white substance on my panties.

I wipe, collecting more from between my legs. It's not normal by any means. I don't like to actively think about it, but ovulation discharge is a thing... except not that much. Not for me anyway. My brows furrowed, I brush it off. Bodies change, right?

I shed my clothes to shower. There's a game this afternoon, which I may as well go to. I seem to be in good standing with the hockey team.

I eventually took a break from skating yesterday to sit with my dad and sip hot chocolate. We didn't talk about anything super important, but it was really nice. Some hints of the old him came out. The gruffness in his voice when he mentions things that matter to him. The way he sees a lot. Not just in *me*, but everything around him.

The intercom buzzer goes off when I'm nearly dressed. I finish hopping into my jeans and head for the door.

"Who is it?" I ask.

I hit the button to hear them.

"Your favorite hockey player," comes the reply.

Well, that solves nothing. So I unlock the door for him and wait.

It's Carter. He looks around the apartment and frowns.

Then does a double take.

I belatedly realize my neck is bare, and I haven't had a chance to explain... I raise my hand, but he beats me to it and bats it away.

"What's this?"

"Um..." I swallow. "Just a little misunderstanding."

His scowl deepens. "Do I need to beat the shit out of Ruiz? Someone else?"

I shrug lightly and step out of his reach. "I'm pretty sure Ruiz did the beating. It's fine. Why are you here?"

He glowers at me. "Really?"

"What's wrong?"

"What's wrong is that you should lock your windows," he says. "Anyone could break in and hurt you, Sydney."

I stare at him, but this change of subject makes no sense. If anything, I thought I'd be getting a lecture about carrying pepper spray or something.

"What do you know?"

He shakes his head, but he goes straight for my bedroom and flips the two locks on the windows with the fire escape. Again.

"Carter."

"Stop," he orders. "Stop being careless. Stop thinking that anyone at FSU gives a shit about you. They're going to use you—"

"Fuck off! Like you're not using me for something?"

"The only thing I want to use is your mouth," he snaps.

I straighten.

The thought of Carter Masters fucking my mouth does something to me. Something hot and wonderful and surprising. And it's probably because we've only ever done vanilla things, right?

"If you want it, take it." The words are out before my brain can stop them.

His gaze darkens. "Don't ask if you don't—"

"Carter." I appraise him. "You scared of hurting me?"

"Hardly."

He approaches me like I'm a wild animal. He winds his hand around the back of my neck. His frozen fingers raise goosebumps down my spine and the backs of my arms. I don't even care that his fingers dig into the bruise. In fact, it grounds me.

"I just don't want to scare you."

I grip his wrist. "Be honest with me about something."

He raises his eyebrow. "I will."

"Did you only date me because Scarlett told you to?"

"No. She may have highlighted you, but it was my decision where we went from there."

"And now..."

"She's not my type, if that's what you're asking." His gaze darkens. "You're my type."

Am I that insecure? There are three guys who seem to want to be in my orbit, and I just don't see the appeal.

"My tastes run darker than we've ever gone." His thumb moves under my ear. "There's something in me that wants you to break, Sydney. That wants you to bleed for me."

Desire pulses between my legs.

"Okay."

He closes his eyes. "Fuck."

"That's the idea." I squeeze his wrist. "Fuck me."

He pulls away. "Not like this."

"Not when I ask for it?"

"Not when you see me coming."

He steps back, his gaze dark enough to make me want to drop to my knees right now.

Fuck is right. Because now I'm a hot mess. He turns on his heel and leaves me standing in the middle of my apartment. I lock the door behind him and make a beeline for my room, rifling through my bottom drawer for my vibrator.

And I spend the next hour making myself come.

Brandon picks me up. Dylan and Maddy are already in the car, decked out in purple FSU gear. I'm wearing the hockey sweatshirt my dad got for me, although I lifted Penn's necklace to hang on the outside.

His sweatshirt is in the wash. While I was loath to toss it in with my load, his scent was starting to fade. And it really needed to be cleaned.

Which leaves me with this.

There's also the matter of Carter's confession. Who knew, hidden under that sexy exterior, lurked someone... kinkier?

He has a green light as far as I'm concerned. My phone goes off, and I glance at the incoming text.

L.

Things seem better for you.

Annoyance flares through me. Things are most certainly *not* better. Superficially, maybe. But absolutely not under the surface. He would know that if he bothered to have an actual conversation with me.

I stuff my phone in my purse and tune back in to the conversation in the car. Dylan and Maddy are debating which is harder, hockey or volleyball. Brandon is laughing at them.

I smile, too, because Maddy has no skin in the game. Her smirk says she's just ribbing Dylan, who can't seem to see that through the argument.

"They're on little death blades on *ice*," Maddy says.

"The coordination it takes, the communication to get the ball over the net—"

"That same coordination argument can be used for hockey. They have to use a stick to get a slim puck past a huge goalie."

"It's different," Dylan huffs.

"I went to the public rink yesterday," I volunteer. "With my dad."

They all go quiet. They know of my brief, sordid history with my father. How we're on tentative, shaky ground because I essentially had to go plead for his help over the summer.

Finally, Brandon asks, "How did that go?"

I smile. "It was actually really nice. Oliver and Penn were there, but—"

"Wait." Maddy swivels to face me. "Penn is Team Sydney, but Oliver has been against you since the beginning. And you're smiling as you say *both* of their names. Did something change? Or are you still Team Penn?"

I shift, considering meeting his abuela, the rage room, telling him about the bracelet. It was a lot of honesty all at once, and he didn't *entirely* run away. Besides spending a week avoiding me.

"I think we've come to an understanding," I say. "Which came about after he tossed me in a trunk and threatened to beat me up."

They gape at me. Brandon almost swerves off the road.

Dylan launches for the steering wheel at the last minute, getting us back on track, and I force another, wider smile.

"It ended up fine," I add.

"More," Brandon sputters. "More details."

"I was walking home... a car turned onto the street and came at me with high beams on, two masked guys jumped out and got me into the trunk. They brought me to some warehouse and wanted me to rat on the FSU team. Like tell them anything I knew..."

"And you didn't," Maddy confirms.

"Of course not. They said they were going to return me to Penn all bloody and bruised and basically surge the rivalry between the two schools, implying it would be my fault."

"And it was Oliver and Penn?"

"Oliver and Bear." I scowl. "Penn showed up afterward... put a stop to it."

I can't say what actually happened. How Oliver stopped *Bear* from doing something truly horrible.

"Good," Dylan echoes. "I told you he could be nice sometimes."

"Right." I do recall her saying that about Penn.

"So then what?" Maddy prompts. "There must be more to that."

"I was pissed. Penn wanted to comfort me. I didn't grow up with like... hugs, you know? It just felt wrong. So Oliver took me to a place where I could destroy a room." I obviously leave out that it's his family's business. Admitting that feels too personal. Like the fact that his abuela was there.

Meeting his family was not on my bingo card.

We park in the garage under the arena. It doesn't connect to it, with all exits leading to the street, which is why the players and staff don't use it. But it's great right now, since we have to go out to the front and scan to get in.

I check my phone out of habit, only to find another text.

L: I'll tell you a lie, if you want

Me: Why are you doing this to me?
L: I would run away with you if I could.

What the fuck does that mean?

ME

> Not good enough.

> I'm starting to think this is some sick prank.

L.

> It's not.

> If I call you right now, will you answer?

No response.

And then—it goes off.

It rings.

The call comes through, the screen illuminated with *L.* at the top. The green *accept* button is right under my thumb, but my heart stops.

"You guys go on ahead," I say to my friends. My voice wobbles. "I've got to take this."

Brandon squints at me, but I hold up the phone to indicate a phone call. And I pray that they don't ask more about it, because... he's actually calling me? I'm about to hear L.'s voice?

I was half joking. I really, *really* want to hear his voice, I want to know who he is—I want to know everything. I'm insatiable in that regard.

"Okay," Brandon agrees. "See you inside."

I answer the call with a soft, "Hello?"

I can't believe this is happening—and it could still be a sick joke. Scarlett or Andi could be on the other end of the line, ready to laugh at me.

"I thought about it," a low, raspy voice says. Male. Vaguely familiar, but at the pitch he's speaking, I can't place it. "I wouldn't run away. But I would follow you if you did."

186

Doesn't help that my heart picks up its pace, sprinting in my chest. I grip the phone tighter, turning away from the direction my friends went. A million questions bubble up my throat, but then it hits me.

"I don't know how you can say that when I know nothing about you." Not sure accusatory is the best route to go, but how long can L. string me along?

"You know more than you think."

He hangs up just as the light over my head flickers and goes out.

The whole row does.

I stare at my phone in shock. I know more than I think? I know more about him than he's let on? That all but confirms he knows who I am in real life—and it still leaves me in the dark.

Both metaphorically, and now, literally.

There's still light coming from my left, where the ramp comes down from the next level up. I hurry in that direction, heading up the incline toward the glowing red exit sign.

Someone steps out from between two cars ahead of me.

I stop short. It isn't that I'm surprised to see someone else. It's that they're not moving toward the exit like me. They stop in the middle of the aisle facing me. They're wearing all black, shadows clinging to them in the darkness. Their hood is up, hiding their face.

They slowly remove a hand from their pocket, and with a flick of their wrist, a blade appears in their hand. It catches the faint light from the other level.

Clear threat.

Nope.

I turn and run.

twenty-six
sydney

I rush away from the armed stranger, back down the way I came with my friends. I swing around the corner, into the lit section.

His footsteps are right behind me.

I make it down another straight section before he catches me. He grabs the back of my hoodie and slows me down, then swings me sideways into the back of a car. I catch myself, gasping in shock, and twist sharply.

His hold—they're a him for sure—is ripped away, but I only make it three more steps before he's on me again.

This time we go down in a tumble. He lands on top of me, his knees on either side of my hips. He drags my head up by my hair, and the cool edge of the blade presses to my throat. He climbs off of me and gets me up, first to my knees and then standing.

He directs me back up into the shadowed part, pushing me between cars.

I don't breathe.

"Such a valiant fight," he whispers in my ear.

Carter.

The knife blade pricks at my skin. He drags his free hand

through my hair, tossing it over my shoulder, and his lips touch the crook of my neck a second later.

Doesn't matter that he's still got the knife against my throat, that he could cut me at any second.

"Undo your jeans," he orders.

I inhale.

"Now."

I do it. My fingers tremble on the button, but I get it free and drag the zipper down. He keeps kissing my neck, moving up higher to just behind my ear.

"Sweatshirt off."

He backs up long enough for me to tear it off and drop it on the hood of the car next to us.

"Turn around."

I do. Carter's expression is different. Hotter, darker. He drinks me in, his gaze roving from my unbuttoned jeans to my V-neck t-shirt. It exposes too much cleavage, but he doesn't seem to mind.

"Now get on your knees."

I meet his gaze. His blue eyes burn, and I reach up and push the hood off his head. His blade flicks out and nicks my collarbone. I gasp at the tiny cut. It doesn't hurt so much as it's surprising, and we both look down at the blood that wells up.

"You wanted to know this," he says. "Now fucking kneel."

I don't know why I'm listening to him. Maybe there's already the slightest bit of trust there, but—

He unbuttons his jeans and shoves them down enough to free his erection. I lick my lips in anticipation.

"Suck," he says softly. He runs the blade down the side of my face.

I try not to flinch, but when I inch away from the tip, he grips my hair with his other hand. I open my mouth and take him in, sucking and licking around the head. Getting my bearings, then bobbing deeper. He groans above me, both hands now on my head. The metal handle of his knife touches my scalp.

Lust flares through me. I reach up and use my hand to aid my mouth, twisting around the base of his shaft and slipping to his balls when I push him deeper. Almost to my throat.

He pulls out suddenly, yanking me up and turning me around. He bends me over the hood of the car beside us and drags my pants down. I shiver with anticipation. He doesn't make me wait long, shifting behind me and pressing close.

His dick slips through my arousal, and he lines up at my entrance.

I gasp when he thrusts inside. He moves fast, and a prick of pain on my ass distracts me. I cry out and slap my hand over my mouth.

"Shameful girl." He pulls my hand away from my mouth. "Don't hide your beautiful voice from me."

He changes angles. But there's this pain that accompanies each thrust that my muddled mind can't seem to figure out.

He leans over me, covering my back with his torso, and cups my breasts through my shirt and bra. The knife clatters on the hood above my head, and I focus for a minute on the blade.

There's blood on the tip.

I make a noise low in my throat as he plays with my breasts and fucks me. Every thrust sends my hips into the car. The whole thing rocks with the force.

My hand creeps down between my legs, and I rub my clit.

"Fuck, you feel good like this."

Car headlights swing across the garage.

I freeze, but he doesn't stop. He fucks me with just as much vigor—maybe more—while the car gets closer and closer. It's driving down, searching for a parking spot.

Before it reaches us, it turns into one.

I let out a breath—but then their voices drift toward us.

They're out of the car. Of course they are, they have to get out of the parking garage. My mind is so focused on them, I barely notice that Carter's pulled out. He spins me around and sits me on the hood, immediately sinking back in.

He stretches me so deliciously, my core clenches around the invasion automatically. I'm going to leave a wet spot on the hood of the car, but that's just a fleeting thought.

Pleasure has me in its grip.

He leans in and bites the top of my breast. I cry out again, doing nothing to smother the sound. He bites and sucks at my chest, finally taking one of my sensitive nipples into his mouth. His fingers land on my clit and rub.

Harder than he has before.

Harder than I do.

But I'm panting, and it's all I can do not to fall over. I hold on to the back of his neck. My fingernails bite into him, leaving crescent-moon-shaped indents.

Without warning, I come.

And I scream.

He catches my mouth, cutting off the sound with his tongue. He tastes my lips, every inch of me, while his hands both move to my ass. His fingers dig in, lifting me with every thrust until I'm seeing stars again.

My orgasm seems drawn out, a never-ending spiral.

And when he comes, he bites my lower lip. Blood fills my mouth. He keeps kissing me, sharing that metallic flavor.

Finally, we both go still.

He pulls out of me, meeting my gaze.

His blue eyes seem almost black.

"Too much?" he asks.

I shake my head wordlessly.

"If this doesn't confirm you're my dream girl, I don't know what would." His voice is tinted with awe.

He helps me off the hood of the car and turns me around. There's a flash of his camera—I nearly jump out of my skin—but he just shows me the screen.

191

My ass. My bleeding ass cheek.

He carved his name into it.

He smirks at me, waiting for my reaction.

I…

I crane around to get a better look. A drop of blood on the T rolls down my cheek, but other than that the cuts are light and almost artistic.

"Are you still drawing?"

I whip back around. He pulls my panties and jeans back up, making quick work of buttoning me back together.

"Are you?"

"I haven't since I transferred," I admit. "I didn't even run for a while. It just felt like a lot."

"But you're writing."

"Not in the sense you're thinking," I hedge.

Because I used to write poetry and draw little charcoal images to accompany them, and that journal hasn't left the bottom drawer of my desk since I first moved in and threw it there.

"Could help you." He leans down and kisses me again.

I go up on my toes, willing him to kiss me more. Deeper. I wrap my arms around his neck and press myself into him. His arms come around the small of my back. His tongue strokes along the seam of my lips, willing me to open for him.

My body is tingling by the time we break apart.

He reaches around me and snags my sweatshirt, pushing it into my chest. "You might want to keep that on until you get a new shirt."

I look at my t-shirt.

There's a bloody handprint over my breast.

I scowl, but I can't even stay mad.

I can think of two guys who might be pissed the next time they see me…

"How is this so easy?" I ask him.

He flicks my gold necklace. The gift from Penn.

"Nothing about this is easy. Doesn't mean I'm going to give up on it, though." He lifts his chin. "Game time. No doubt you'll be missed if you're not there for the puck drop."

My chest tightens.

But he's right. I just hate that I'm being pulled in two different directions.

twenty-seven
sydney

We lose.

The FSU fans file out of the arena with a weird energy. Some are dejected, but others seem restless.

Home game loss.

Fight night.

The game started at three, but it's nearly eight o'clock by the time we get back to Brandon's car. I take the front seat this time, flipping the music to a pop channel that's all static while we're underground. My ass has been burning through the whole game, the cuts refusing to be quiet. Reminding me of Carter, even as I watched Penn and Oliver.

"So... anyone want a taste of more violence?" I glance first at Brandon, then Dylan and Maddy in the back.

Brandon shakes his head. "I'll pass."

"Is this a tonight thing? Because I have an early morning run scheduled with some of my teammates," Dylan says.

My lips flatten. I have no idea how long these fights would go.

"I'm in," Maddy says. "If you're good with just us going."

I smile at her.

"Bran, can you drop us off at my car, please?" she asks.

"You got it."

Ten minutes later, Maddy and I are on our way to the warehouse. I'm not entirely thrilled about going back to the place I was almost-raped and nearly asphyxiated. But with Maddy at my side, and the guys probably going, it should be fine.

Right?

Right.

One notable thing about the game—Bear didn't play. He wasn't even on the bench. His absence wasn't commented on by anyone who would know, so I brushed it off. Maybe he's sick. Or Oliver told him to miss the next game.

Either way, I didn't have to look at him across the arena. For that, I'm grateful.

We're not the only car on our way from Framingham. We follow a small line of cars that bump along the gravel, pothole-ridden road and park behind the warehouse. We climb out, and I shake out my hair and pull it up. It's getting a little out of hand with how long it is, but I'd rather have this than short hair.

PENN

I see you.

I don't see him, though. Not immediately. I scout around and finally pick him out of the crowd. He's standing off to the side of the huge garage door that's admitting people by the swarm. His gaze is on me.

When I get up next to him, he fists the front of my sweatshirt and drags me into him. His lips slam into mine. Our kiss turns open-mouthed and hungry in an instant. It might be the first time he's kissed me.

His kiss reminds me of a wildfire, and I gladly lean into the flames. He nibbles on my lips, thoroughly explores my mouth with his tongue, sucks on mine.

I stare up at him when he straightens. His wrist rests on

my shoulder, my hair threaded between his fingers. He smirks at me, and it's fucking devastating.

He could have any girl he wanted.

Easy.

"Wow." Maddy fans herself beside me. "I need to find myself someone who kisses me like that."

My face flames. "Sorry."

Penn focuses on me. "Stay in the warehouse. Don't go wandering. And take this."

He pulls a slender cylinder from his pocket and slips it into mine. His fingers dip into my jeans, and it should not be sensual that his knuckles brush my upper thigh.

But it is.

"By the way..." He tugs the lock of hair caught in his fingers. The next words are said directly into my ear. "You smell like sex, princess."

I lean away.

His jaw tics when I don't refute it, and he moves seamlessly into the crowd. I try to keep an eye on him, the top of his head, but in a matter of seconds, he's gone.

Guess there's no such thing as a secret with him.

"What did he give you?" Maddy asks.

I pull out the tube, unsurprised to find pepper spray in my palm. I shake my head and shove it back into my pocket. "He worries."

I don't want to elaborate. I didn't really tell them about Bear, although they obviously got the rest of the story. My scarf and jacket have been doing a fine job when I have to be outside, and I've been getting better at the makeup component, too. I practiced a lot last night, and I woke up feeling off again.

Whatever.

If I lose a little sleep because of what happened, it'll just make me stronger. In theory. Because it doesn't kill me, right?

We head inside, and Maddy takes the lead. For a petite girl, she has a surprisingly bold way of moving through crowds. Or rather, plowing through them. She takes my hand, and I simply follow in her wake, all the way to the front.

A chalk ring has been drawn on the concrete.

A guy I've never seen before stands in the center, explaining something. I catch only the end about not leaving the circle. If they do, the crowd has the right to shove them back in.

Fights end with a knockout or if one person taps out.

First up is one of the d-men on the hockey team. He's shirtless and fucking ripped, his muscles bulging on his arms and abdomen. He makes a circle, bouncing on his feet and trying to hype up the crowd. They oblige, and he stops beside the emcee.

The crowd parts again to let out his opponent, another player whose name I don't know.

Both the fighters' fists are wrapped. They wear shorts and are barefoot. Nothing else.

"How do they not get caught?" I ask in Maddy's ear.

There aren't that many people, but it's still enough that something like this should leak. It would be expected. People shift around me, the energy spiking. The emcee has left the circle, and the two fighters barely wait a moment before crashing.

"I don't get it," I say, more to myself than her. "How are they a team if they fight each other?"

"It's accountability," Maddy yells in my ear. "Right? If you know you're going to get your ass beat by your teammate after a loss, you give a hundred and ten percent every time."

I nod.

The fight lasts minutes. Someone hands us a bottle of vodka, and I take a swig before considering the dangers. Pepper spray won't really be helpful if I'm doped up. Maddy passes it along without taking a drink.

I end up swigging from two more bottles that seem to just

find their way around, and I'm swaying by the time Penn emerges as the next fighter.

Forget that other guy being ripped. Penn has a lean, corded body. He flexes, and the crowd immediately reacts.

He's fighting another guy I don't recognize.

Figures.

"The other goalie," Maddy says in my ear.

"I didn't know you followed all of this so closely."

She blushes.

I eye her with renewed interest, but then the fight starts. I step forward, toeing the line, as Penn and the other goalie come together in the center. Penn moves like lightning, dodging and striking back with hits to his opponent's torso. He gets in a few quick hits, pummeling and then slipping out of reach.

Over and over.

The other goalie gets in a hit to Penn's face, and his head whips to the side.

He spits blood and goes right back into it. This time, they seem content to stop fucking around and just trade blows to the face, until Penn gets in an uppercut that snaps his opponent's head back.

The guy falls hard.

Penn's chest is heaving, and I don't know whether to run and check on him or cheer along with everyone else.

He disappears the way he came, swallowed by the crowd.

We watch the next three fights while I grow increasingly anxious. Penn doesn't come back. I check my phone. I text him. But nothing.

"Final fight," the emcee calls.

The crowd parts, and Oliver strides out. He's shirtless, his muscles rippling. There's a nasty bruise in the center of his stomach, and I vividly recall kicking him before they tossed me in the trunk.

He walks right up to me and appraises me.

I stare back. My heart thunders against my ribcage.

Did Penn say something?

Is he about to drag *me* into the ring?

There's a few gasps behind us, but he shifts his body to block what's happening behind him. There's something in his expression... I don't know, but I want to fall into his eyes. I reach out and touch the bruise on his stomach, and he catches my fingers.

Squeezes gently.

Finally, he moves enough so I can see—

Bear.

He's covered in bruises, his face swollen so bad, his eyes are forced almost completely shut. He walks in a shuffle, his left leg dragging. I'm not sure how he's even standing, let alone entering the ring on his own. Every bruise reminds me of my own, until my chest has tightened so much, I might as well be wrapped up by a boa constrictor.

"Eyes," Oliver demands.

I shift my attention to his face.

"You walked away from him."

Yes, I did.

"He's not going to do the same."

What?

He moves away from me, circling Bear and stopping next to the emcee. There's no brief introduction, no cheering. No one seems to know what to do with this, because the huge hockey player—who towers over Oliver, for the record—seems to already be on the cusp of a knockout.

This is the sort of public humiliation I wouldn't have dreamed up in my worst nightmares.

The emcee leaves.

Oliver attacks.

It's a bloodbath that Bear can't escape. He dodges, raises his arms, but no matter what he does, Oliver targets somewhere else. Compared to the giant, Oliver is quick. He uses bursts of speed to get out of range when Bear tries to strike back, then darts in and delivers two, three powerful blows.

I watch through my fingers. The marks around my throat seem to pulse with every hit delivered to Bear. Maddy's arm is pressed tight to mine, and she seems to wince with every connection, too.

The last blow comes when Bear staggers toward him, yelling incoherent gibberish. A final hail Mary to end it, maybe.

Oliver steps aside and kicks out. His foot connects with the side of his knee, and there's a sickening *crack* that goes straight through me.

Bear screams, falling and clutching at his leg. The sound just goes on and on and on, and no one fucking moves.

He doesn't tap out.

Oliver leans over him, that analytical expression on his face belying nothing. His attention sweeps lower, to the knee that's bent at an awkward angle. Bear holds it with both hands, quickly dissolving into a blubbering mess.

"Get up or tap out," Oliver says.

I have no idea how Bear hears him, or even registers that he's giving him an order. Maybe it's just ingrained after a year and a half of playing hockey together. But he manages to get on his good knee and then hop up.

His injured leg holds none of his weight. He stares at Oliver, his lips still moving. The words have stopped, though. He could be praying.

The final hit comes fast, finally putting him out of his misery. A blow to the temple that he doesn't even attempt to block.

When he falls, I feel nothing.

And I'm pretty sure it just confirms I'm more broken than I originally thought.

twenty-eight
penn

Someone follows Sydney.

Someone who breaks into her house the same way I do, who rifles through her belongings—particularly her underwear drawer. Someone who counted the cash she took from me but left it exactly where it was.

It's easy to be obsessed with her.

Oliver told me about the break-in and the girl with the strange, silver eyes, and I couldn't grasp how someone from SJU could be so bold and so fucking stupid. But then, later, he finds her at a party. He sees her full face. He learns her name.

Sydney, sure. But *Windsor*.

Frank Windsor has been in our lives for years. Since Ollie was first learning how to skate, anyway, and then when I came along a few years later.

Even thinking back, though, I couldn't remember him having a daughter. I have vague memories of a young girl on the ice with us, but she always did her own thing. And at that age, ten or eleven, girls were gross.

Hockey was cool.

Her father is who put me in the crease for the very first time. Goaltending isn't for the faint-hearted, and my father did everything he could to discourage my interest in the position. I still remember how he planted me in the net and sent the puck at me as hard as he could.

It didn't dissuade me. In fact, I stopped more than half of his shots.

And when I got to practice the next day, I was fired up and Coach was ready to direct my energy.

Moral of the story: I owe him. It's why I chose FSU, why I worked my ass off in high school to excel and get a scholarship. I don't really care about professional hockey, but I do want to find kids like me and help them excel.

All that to say, Sydney Windsor should've been off-limits. And in a way, she definitely is. If Coach were to find out the extent of my interest in her...

And Oliver's, I allow. The asshole doesn't want to admit it, but he finds her every bit as fascinating as I do.

But most recent nights, when I slip into her apartment and find things rearranged, I'm concerned. I put things back the way they should be, closing her drawer and straightening things that just feel off. I don't want her to worry.

I'll handle worrying.

I climb the fire escape, and the feeling of being watched hits me. Ironic, since I like to be the watcher. I pause in the shadows and scan the road below me.

Empty.

After the fight, and our final show with Bear, she left with Maddy. She didn't seem particularly intent on talking to either of us, and I can't really say I blame her.

I didn't want to see her either.

She smelled like sex. Her hair had been messed with. Her glorious, thick, dark hair. Even after sitting through a hockey game and traveling to the warehouse, the scent clung to her like perfume.

I have a suspect in mind.

The window slides open easily. I thought it might be locked, but there's a little paper taped to the sill. It flutters as the breeze catches the edge of it, and I use my phone's screen light to make out her loopy handwriting.

Does he visit?

I smirk at that, because I do visit.

I have been visiting.

My feet touch down on her carpet noiselessly, and I slowly lower the window behind me. It's cold outside. The chill might wake her up, even if fucking her doesn't.

She's buried under blankets, her hair fanned out on her pillow. I toe off my shoes and cross the bedroom to her. It's lit by the moon and a streetlight that shines in a warm yellow light, although the blinds on the window closest to the road are mostly shut.

My dick wakes up at the sight of her. I peel the blankets off her slowly, careful not to disturb her. She sleeps in panties and an oversized shirt most nights, and today is no different.

I'm obsessed with her.

I can't get enough of her.

It almost doesn't matter that Oliver saw her first.

I leave my jeans in a pile at the edge of the bed and climb over her. I want to touch her, so I fucking touch her. I push her shirt up to get a look at her full breasts. She's got some curves—more than some, less than a lot—but I love the feel of her.

The bruising stands out in sharp relief, and it makes me sick all over again.

The extent of the trauma didn't become clear until I arrived at the warehouse. They wanted to lock me out. Oliver came to confront me, to get me to leave.

Bullshit.

"I'm doing this because of you," he said at the time.

So kind of him.

We've always gotten along well. He's more family than my blood relatives, that's for sure, and it only took spending one holiday alone—Thanksgiving last year—for his family to invite me along.

Honorary Ruiz.

Still, I was tempted to deck him.

He wanted Sydney to give up secrets to them—he wanted to prove she was untrustworthy.

I know she's the opposite.

When he finally gave up and agreed for me to come in and get her, we found... Bear. Her skin was almost blue in the face, her eyes wild. I'll never forget the way she looked, and the visceral panic that claimed her as soon as I got the knot undone.

His dick wasn't out.

That, I think, is the only reason Oliver didn't murder him. Not that either of us have committed murder. But for her? I'm leaning toward that being a viable fucking option.

She shifts onto her back, her head rolling to the side. There's a new little nick on her neck, a scabbed-over cut...

I hover over her, and regardless of what's been done to her, my cock is already fucking dripping for her. I tug her panties aside and stroke her clit until she squirms.

I push inside slow enough that my muscles tremble. This is an exercise in patience. Once I'm fully seated inside her, I exhale. My body aches from the fight, but I put it out of my mind and lower myself down.

My weight settles on hers. I've been experimenting with how much she can take without waking, and the answer is—a lot. My girl is a deep fucking sleeper. Before, I was hesitant to touch her more than necessary. But now, I know I can settle my hips against hers and lower myself so we're chest to chest.

She moves less when I fuck her like this.

Eventually, we'll do this when she's awake. I shift my hips, my movements miniscule. It sends little zaps of pleasure up my cock and along the base of my spine. My lips touch her bruised throat, but her breathing remains even.

The first time I did this, I couldn't believe she stayed asleep. I kept expecting her to wake up halfway through, for her eyes to open confused and switch to fear or surprise.

I've never met anyone who sleeps this deeply. And unlike when she's awake, her face is free of worry or stress. I didn't realize how much tension she holds in her face until I saw her without it.

Unconscious.

I move faster, my forearms braced on either side of her head, until the racing pleasure shoots down my spine and down my dick. I close my eyes and clench my teeth. I stay inside her for a moment, moving to feel more. To plug her up for just one more minute.

When my cock softens, I pull out. I adjust her panties back into place and lower her shirt. I touch the pendant around her neck, smiling to myself. This part is more of a ritual than anything. I cover her with the blankets, clean my cock on something in her hamper. Put my clothes back on.

Sometimes I check her apartment. Other times, I just leave the way I came.

And when I get home, I sleep like a fucking baby.

Tonight, I decide to do a walk-through.

Tonight I slip out of her room and come face-to-face with her stalker.

He stands in the center of the living room with his hands in his pockets, his expression carefully blank. It must be work for him to keep it that way and not show me his cards. Ollie gets like that sometimes, too. He strives to be a closed book and ends up looking constipated.

"What a surprise." I mirror his stance. "Carter Masters. I didn't hear you come in."

He clenches his jaw. "I have a key."

"A stolen key?"

He doesn't answer. He seems to be considering something. Me, more than likely. But I've played against him enough to know some of his tells. That's the hazard of rival schools so close together.

We play each other a lot. And this feels a lot like a shootout, staring down the opposing player and wondering who's going to give in and move first.

Anything I know about him can also be applied to what he knows of me.

"Did you see my handiwork?" he asks.

I narrow my eyes.

"I'll take that as a no." He smirks. "How about this: you stop sneaking in here like a fucking creep, and I won't call the cops."

"Did you peek into the bedroom when you got here?"

His smirk fades while mine grows.

"Carter Masters, her ex-boyfriend stalker and peeping Tom. That's not much of a stretch." I cross to the living room windows, looking out at the street. "You must have a good hiding place out there. I didn't see you."

He grunts.

My gaze lifts to the building across the street. "Did Masters rent himself an apartment in Framingham to spy on her?" I muse to myself. "If I were him—"

"Fine."

I glance over my shoulder. "So our nighttime activities will remain off her radar?"

He nods once, his jaw muscle popping.

Lovely.

"Nice doing business with you, Masters." I pass him and head for the door. No use climbing down the fire escape if he's just going to lock the door behind me. "If you wake her up, make sure she knows the cum between her legs isn't yours."

twenty-nine
sydney

Penn joins me for my run. I'm not sure how he knows exactly when I leave my house, but he joins me a street over dressed in warm running gear. He seems to be in a mood, elbowing me and cajoling me into going faster and faster.

Because I'm a glutton for punishment, I let him.

Soon enough, we're sprinting down a path through the woods. There's snow on either side of it, and the lake is up ahead. It's all frozen over now, and everything looks a little different than the summer. But it isn't the same path Carter and I came down from the house party. I'm pretty sure we're at least two miles from there.

Penn catches my hand before we break free of the woods, and he uses my momentum to swing me around. He backs me against a tree, quick as a whip.

When his lips touch mine, I fucking melt. I let him come to me, let him devour me, until he tugs down my leggings and picks me up. My thighs straddle his hips, but my leggings keep me from wrapping my legs fully around him.

His kiss deepens. He nips at my lip, opening the cut Carter left.

I'm going out of my mind.

He slides a finger inside me. My hips buck at the sensation, but my head is a mess. I just keep kissing him so I don't have to figure out what to ask for.

I do dirty things with Carter.

I make eyes at Oliver.

I'm public with Penn. Public in a way that doesn't even cause problems anymore. People seem to have gotten used to the fact that he claimed me. No one gives me shit for it. He reels me in and kisses me when he sees me. He tries to get me to sneak away from class to fuck.

After the first time he threw cash at me and left, he hasn't repeated that. But I do find my little stockpile growing, and I can't figure out when. Or who.

Or why, since I haven't fucked him in what feels like a while. Since before Oliver's twisted loyalty test.

I'm going crazy, and the run was supposed to clear my head. Instead, I just... I'm all twisted up inside, and I'm kissing Penn while he finger-fucks me, and it's like gravity has spun one-eighty on me.

I pull away and drop my head back against the tree.

"I have a confession," I say in a low voice. "And this is the most inopportune time to bring it up."

"Wait." He removes his finger and replaces it with something... well, larger. Stiffer.

I groan when he pushes inside me.

"Okay, now it's the most inopportune time."

His eyes gleam, mischief written all over his face. He has some scruff on his cheeks now. His hair is hidden by a black beanie, and the tip of his nose is red with cold.

"Carter and I..."

"Have sex." He nods. "Yeah, figured that one out."

"And Oliver—"

"Is a bag of dicks," he finishes.

I narrow my eyes. He's not *wrong*, exactly. But then I remember something else. Something that slipped my mind because of how I woke up—which was sore between my legs and so turned on I could barely catch my breath.

"You took the note from my windowsill."

He waits.

It's not a denial.

"Which means you..."

He chooses then to move his hips. His dick slides deeper into me, and I grit my teeth against a wave of pleasure. Unlike my initial wake-up, I didn't get myself off this morning. I forced myself out of bed and into the shower.

I cleaned the cuts on my ass.

I washed the strange discharge from between my legs.

I pretended I didn't know exactly what was happening.

"Say it," he breathes.

He fucks me harder, wrapping his hand around my throat. Not hard. Not squeezing. But his finger and thumb on my chin make sure I can't turn away from him. My body jolts and reacts to every little move.

"You sneak into my apartment when I sleep," I gasp.

"It's not my fault you're already asleep."

"You fuck me."

He smiles. "It's not my fault you don't wake up for it."

I'm not crazy.

"I've been going out of my mind," I confess.

"Good." He leans in. Instead of kissing me, he bites my lower lip and tugs. "I like you out of your mind. I like the idea of you unraveling. Like when you come on my cock, but *more*. All the time."

I shudder and try to process what he's saying.

That he wants me to break?

That he—

"Carter has a key," he says softly. "But he doesn't like to climb on top of you while you sleep and fuck you like I do. He says he marked you, and I want to know where it is."

"Stop." I grip his shoulder, but he doesn't. "Stop moving, just—I need to think."

"I need to see this mark," he growls.

"No, you don't."

He pulls out and drops my legs. In an instant, my hands are on the tree and my face is nearly pressed to it, too. His hands cup my ass cheeks, and the sudden *rip* of the bandage shatters me.

I close my eyes.

He whistles under his breath.

"Penn?" I glance behind me. "I—"

His gaze crashes into mine, and it's a whole new level of terrifying.

"Hold on to that tree, princess. I'm going to turn your ass black and blue before you get to come on my cock."

He seems to be waiting for something. A rush of adrenaline hits me, and I nod. I don't *want* it, but some dark part of me is intrigued.

He nods back.

I grip the tree, my nails digging into the bark. He rubs my ass cheek, the one with Carter's name, and then loses contact.

His palm connects in a sharp *smack*. Shock chills my skin, but the pain blooms in its wake is hot. His other hand braces my hip, and he spanks me again.

I keep mental count.

Two.

Three.

Four.

When he switches cheeks, I cry out. I close my eyes and lean into the pain, bracing my forehead on my arm. My legs are trembling, but every touch seems to heighten my arousal.

Six, seven, eight.

His fingers move down and thrust into my pussy, twisting and scissoring inside me. I bite my lip and draw blood again.

210

He brings me right to the edge so fucking easily, it's like he read the manual on my body.

When he withdraws, I'm hollow.

Nine.

I cry out. It's harder than the others, directly over the cuts. And, strangely, I'm right on the fucking cusp of something insane.

Coming from pain instead of—

Ten—

My mouth opens, a silent scream, and he thrusts inside me so hard, I almost hit my face on the tree. My orgasm smashes through me, every part of me on fire. He keeps fucking me, his hips slapping my sore ass with every move. The friction of it is delicious, *deserved* agony.

By the time I come down, he's got his arms around my waist. He's more holding me up than my legs, and I blink. I will my brain to work again, but all that's there is fuzz.

He fucked my brain out. His pace is frantic. Waves of residual pleasure linger between my legs, and I push back against him weakly.

His teeth bury in my shoulder, right through my jacket and sports bra. He bites *hard*, and I whimper under him. He's holding me in place with arms and teeth and cock, and it just feels *right*.

He stills, his groan vibrating through his chest and teeth, where he's still locked on my shoulder. It's animalistic in nature.

And when he slowly releases me, first his teeth and then his bear-hug, and then his cock slipping free, I sink to my knees in the snow.

He kneels behind me, hugging me from behind. His hands wander my front, one sliding into my jacket and cupping my breast. His other goes to my throat. I touch his wrist and arm, leaning back against him.

With him, there's no trauma of being choked. I don't get

the panic that rises like nausea. Just this weird trust between us.

"You wear my necklace when he fucks you," he says in my ear. "If you ever take it off, I'm going to solder it on."

My head falls back on his shoulder. "That's fine," I sigh. "Better to be sure the clasp won't break."

Pause.

His lips touch my cheek. "You're fucking insane, princess. I think I might love it."

You know what's not fun?

Finishing a run with cum between my legs and a sore, bruised ass. Penn smirks the whole way back, running so close our arms occasionally brush. Never mind that the path back isn't really built for two. He seems content to avoid the branches and foliage and snow on the edges of the trail.

But even when we get to the road, and there's space to separate, he sticks close.

At the top of my street, I slow to a walk.

"How did you know Carter sneaks in?"

I had to replay our conversation or else my mind would be turned to mush by the pain and tingling pleasure between my legs. I had to focus on *something*, and I want to know how he knows.

"Because I fucked you while you slept last night." Now that we're walking, he snags my hand and threads our fingers together. "And when I came out, the psycho was standing in your living room waiting for me."

My mouth drops open.

Penn's gaze slides to mine. "I told him I wouldn't tell you, but since you now know I have a somnophilia kink, you may as well know he rented an apartment across from your brownstone to spy."

I stop moving. "What?"

"Carter Masters." His brows furrow. "What part is confusing?"

"The apartment."

"Oh." He resumes walking, pulling me along. "I'll show you. I don't think he's there right now."

"Why?"

"Because I watched him leave for class."

I don't have one stalker—I have two.

"When I feel like someone's watching me, is that you or him?"

He lifts one shoulder. "Probably him. I know where you're going to be, I don't usually follow you. You have two classes on Mondays, Wednesdays, and Fridays. One with your friend and one with me. You have three classes on Tuesdays and Thursdays. Your first class is the only one where you fly solo."

I stop again.

"How...?"

"I pay attention, princess. First it was to fuck with you. There were opportunities to exploit. Andi being in one of your classes was something Ollie was particularly fascinated by. I think he was going to get his hands on your writing, but then she transferred out. Something about the professor being prejudiced against her."

I roll my eyes.

"But there's that cute little notebook in your desk..."

I narrow my eyes. "That's private."

He meets my gaze. "Is it?"

"Of course it is!"

"They're pretty good. The poems. I like the one about you being swallowed by the sun."

I gape at him, my face slowly getting hotter and hotter. Being swallowed by the sun right *now* would be less painful than listening to this conversation.

He shrugs. "The drawings are good, too. Dark. You've got some demons. Carter's well aware of that, too, obviously."

I scowl.

He tugs me along again.

We reach the front steps of the brownstone, and he points to another across the street. "I'd guess one of the higher ones. Third or fourth floor at most."

"And you're not going to retaliate?"

He appraises me. "Are you going to pick me?"

"What?"

"If I just wait it out, you'll get sick of him," he reasons.

My mouth opens and closes. He smirks and taps my nose. He doesn't come up with me, but he stays there until I get inside.

Only then do I blow out a long, slow breath.

Because what if I don't want to choose?

What if I can't?

thirty
sydney

Beautiful, fragile thing
And the monsters that sing
In the dead of night.
Inevitably, the two clash
An explosive, glittering flash.
Fragility only survives with spite.

I drop my pen. My case of charcoal pencils are open in front of me, and I reach for them automatically. I don't know if it's any good, but I have the urge to draw a monster lurking behind the words. Maybe a light monster will be on the other side, like a good-and-evil battle.

The scary monster comes first, all dark shadows swirling around a human-like figure. Then another.

Then a third.

They lurk on the edges of the page, encroaching on the poem.

Poetry is not what I *should* be writing, but an itch to open the notebook and try again began soon after Penn mentioned reading it.

I give one a sadistic smile with my eraser. One doesn't have a mouth. The third just a straight across line, no hint of teeth or bravado or joy. It feels done enough, so I turn the page.

I draw a phone with a text bubble. In thinner pencil, I write: *Where did you go?*

L. has all but vanished. The last time we spoke was on the phone, his voice too low to decipher. The mystery of it is driving me *mad*. There are little to no details to focus on or exploit, which leaves me at worse than a dead end. I don't even have a beginning.

It's worse than the bruises on my ass, which remind me of the run in the woods every time I sit or put on pants or lean over. The cuts have scabbed over. There's another bruise on my shoulder from where he bit me.

I touch them sometimes. It's more about remembering— that I want to remember—than the one around my neck. Thankfully, that's starting to heal and fade. It's moving through the ugly phases, but every shade lighter it gets, the less time I have to spend blending concealer around it.

The writing class has shifted from entertainment to fiction. We each picked dates to turn our stories in. Since they're longer, more like ten pages than the shorter ones we've been writing, we'll be analyzing and critiquing two stories at a time.

In essence, I don't need to hand mine in until three weeks from now.

So it's on the back burner, although I have a few to read.

My gaze drops to the smudged outline of a phone, and I have to steel myself not to reach for my actual phone and send him that message.

And in the end, I fucking do anyway.

Here's a lie:

I miss talking to you.

I got attached to you.

I'm afraid of who you are.

L.

That was more than one.

I'm afraid for you to find out who I am.

I miss talking to you.

When I heard your voice on the phone, I immediately regretted not recording it so I could listen over and over again.

What made you text me in the first place?

Curiosity.

What made you reply?

You were different. It's weird, but the fact that you were telling me to ignore everyone else made me feel a little better.

Were you bullied when you were a kid?

I was called white trash, had my book bag regularly dumped in the hallway. Once, it was outright stolen from my locker. We didn't have the money to replace it, so when that happened I ended up carrying everything in a plastic grocery bag.

And then it turned up in lost and found a week later.

That sucks. But your dad…?

He's got money, right? Didn't he help out?

We had our scheduled visits on the weekends, but I don't think he knew how we were living.

Barely functioning.

Mom wanted it that way.

Jeez. Mood killer. How did you grow up?

Shitty dad. My mom bends over backward for him. They probably used to be in love, but it kind of fizzled... One sister who refused to get into sports.

Are you? In sports?

Yeah.

Hockey?

Sydney...

I'm going to assume hockey, because that limits my options of who you could be. Two rosters versus two undergrad populations.

Do you still see your parents? Are you close to them, even if they're shitty?

No.

I don't see my mom either.

She's missing...

For real?

I'm afraid to leave town because this is the last place she knew me to be. Her phone is off, her house—well, trailer—is gone. She used to leave a lot when I was a kid, and she always came back.

Something might be wrong.

I put the phone down and close my eyes. That felt too real to admit, but I typed and sent it without even thinking.

Something might be wrong.

She always comes back, and it's been almost three months.

When I peek at my phone, there's a reply waiting for me.

L.

No matter what happens, you'll be okay.

You're more of a survivor than you think.

Am I, though?

I rub at my eyes and shove away from the desk. I've written many poems inspired by my home life. Like the one about being swallowed by the sun. The one Penn mentioned. I go back and grab the notebook, flipping to that page.

I scan it while I pace, too restless to even stay sitting. It's not so much a poem as flash fiction. Shorter than a short story.

And I can't bear to think up a response to L.'s latest text.

I love in the same way Icarus must've yearned for the sun. So desperate to be close, to climb in someone else's skin. To be fully seen and understood and accepted. It wasn't that he wanted to escape— or maybe he did. Maybe he wanted to be engulfed by that feeling and forget reality. To leave behind the earth entirely.

If the sun loved me, I wouldn't hesitate to strap on wings and fly all the way across the universe. I'd open my arms and welcome the burn.

It's better than the alternative: cold, alone, empty.

To the sun: Burn me up. Love me. Swallow me whole.

I'm not going to judge my writing from almost a year ago. I still remember scribbling this all in one go. Poetry and flash fiction both satisfy something deep inside me. For this one, I was curled up in the floor of the bathroom. Mom was gone, and I was that alternative. So fucking empty.

There was a storm outside. The thunder boomed and echoed in the trailer, and the rain pelting down on the metal roof made everything louder.

It was the first time I remember feeling afraid in my own home.

We had recently sold our television, so there was nothing to drown out the sounds. At least in the bathroom, there were no windows. I stared at the crack under the door and watched it periodically flash as lightning hit.

My mind, back then, turned to my mother. Where she was, who she was with. It was the summer before my first semester at St. James University, and she was gone *again*. I hated the choking fear that accompanied thoughts of leaving her.

Just six months prior, she had been fired from her job. It left us even tighter on money, even when I got a waitressing gig at the local bar. I wasn't old enough to bartend—young for an upcoming college freshman at seventeen—and I couldn't deliver alcohol to the tables. It meant I had to share my tips with the waitresses who could deliver liquor.

But it was money coming in. Money that went to rent and utilities and food and clothes. That job was how I eventually afforded my first crappy car.

Without me, I didn't know how she could survive.

So I arranged an on-campus job in the financial aid office and sent home almost all of my paychecks to her. Because even while I was here, she was there, and no better off than when I lived with her.

I rub my eyes again, dragging myself out of memories.

This is why I need to find her. Because she can't function on her own. She could be in a homeless shelter or the hospital. What if she got hit by a car and is in a coma?

What if the hospital couldn't get through to me because my fucking voicemail is constantly full of vulgar messages from blocked numbers, and I stopped answering calls from people outside of my contacts? What if they have no way to ID her, so she's just an unknown Jane Doe in their system? Forever?

I'm spiraling.

I don't answer L. and I throw my notebook back in the drawer. My case of charcoal follows it. I kick it shut and stride away. It's better to leave my feelings on the page, in the dark, than relive them.

thirty-one
sydney

Bright and early on Thursday, the day before Halloween, I join my father on the ice at the arena. We skate around the perimeter with to-go coffee cups in our hands. He somehow remembered exactly how I take my coffee. I've drunk it with cream and two sugars since I was in high school.

"I wanted to talk to you about your plans for the future," he says. "And it's a tough conversation, naturally, so..."

"Doing it while skating," I agree. Because sometimes it's easier to focus on what your body is doing than where your mind is going.

"My future. Do you mean next year?" I'll be a senior if Dad allows me to stay at FSU. "I was hoping to continue here..."

He side-eyes me. "Uh-huh."

"What?"

"Don't kid me, Syd. It's hard to miss how students treat you. Or talk about you." He sighs. "I thought my name might give you some protection, but it's just made you stand out more. I apologize for that."

I grab his arm and stop. "Dad, I'm the one who owes you an apology." Shame colors my cheeks, but it's time for the truth. "I broke into Oliver Ruiz's house right before playoffs last year. And it wasn't originally to steal those plays, but..."

His eyes widen. "You did what? Sydney, *why*?"

I can't let go of his arm. My eyes burn, and my vision goes blurry. "Because Mom sold Grandma's bracelet to a pawn-shop. I bribed the owner to tell me who bought it, and he gave me Oliver's name. But then I couldn't find it in his house."

A sob builds its way up my throat.

"I took pictures of his playbook because I was stupid and angry. And my roommate and I went to a party after—he was there, he recognized me. H-he said some things and I just got even more mad. So I sent them to Carter."

I can't look at Dad, even though I'm latched on to him for dear life.

"I'm so sorry." I sniffle and wipe at my nose with my sleeve. I don't have hands—one to keep Dad from leaving, another on my cup.

Dad sighs. He takes the coffee from my hand and sets it on the ice. His, too. And then he pulls me into a hug that might as well be tight enough to draw me into his skin.

And all at once, the tension leaves my body.

"It's okay." He strokes my hair. "You don't apologize to me. I've done a lot of things wrong in regards to you."

He offers me a tissue from his pocket. I curl my fingers around it and dab at my eyes, then blow my nose. So lovely and ladylike.

After a long moment, I put some distance between us. He picks up our coffees and puts them on the bench, returning with a handful of pucks and two sticks.

I take one from him.

"You remember skating around my practices as a kid?" he asks.

I nod. I still feel raw, but an invisible wall between us that I didn't realize was there seems to have crumbled.

"I'd give you a stick and a puck, and sometimes you'd

occupy yourself going around the outside. Other times, you'd get more daring and weave between players doing drills." He laughs. "I was more in danger of being fired for bringing my six-year-old back then than I was after this last season. So ignore rumors that my job was on the line."

He meets my gaze.

I nod, he nods.

He passes me the puck, a quick flick of his wrist. The puck slaps into my stick's blade, cradling it so it doesn't go rebounding off is almost second nature. I pass it back, and we both put more distance between us.

And then he ruins it by saying, "We should discuss your mother."

Ugh.

"She's never *not* come back," I tell him. "But when I went to check on her, it was clear she hadn't been around in a while. So the house is gone..."

House is a stretch.

He sends a pass farther up the boards, making me skate for it. When I pass it back, he's watching me.

"Part of the reason my job might be a bit more secure than other coaches is because I'm an alumni. The Board is a little more lenient," he says.

My parents were together until I was five, and then the shared custody happened. At twelve, Dad took her to court for something. Fifteen, he got remarried. Eighteen, I stopped talking to him.

The thing is, though, that nothing bad ever happened at Dad's house. The three years between him getting remarried and me cutting off contact were good. If I actually think back on those shared moments, I can't pick out any truly scary or negative moments. I had three hot meals, affection, respect.

Going home was the problem. Telling my mother everything about my weekend and having her pick it apart was the problem.

I'm going to fucking start crying again at the realization.

"She wasn't a good mom." I face him again. "I don't know why I want to find her, because she sucked as a mother. And I think if I wasn't living with her seventy-five percent of the time, if she wasn't constantly in my ear, I would've kept up a better relationship with you."

He winces.

"You never talked badly about her," I add. Accuse. "Never tried to get me to see that side of her, even though you probably knew what she was doing."

"No, Syd." He puts his hands on the top of his stick. "No, I wasn't going to do that to you or her."

Then... "Where did her resentment come from? Why did you take her to court when I was a kid?"

Dad comes close again, forgetting the pucks and our passing game. "I didn't take her to court. She wanted more money from me and less visitation. I was fighting it." His gaze softens. "I don't know where her feelings came from, kiddo. I wish I did."

"Coach?"

He glances over his shoulder. Our positioning hides the other person from view—and probably hides me, too. Which is why Oliver Ruiz stops dead on his way toward us when Dad shifts enough to clear our lines of sight.

"What are you doing here?" he blurts out. He looks around. "It's..."

"Skating with my daughter, Ruiz," Dad snaps. "Do you have a problem with that?"

His hockey captain straightens. "No, sir."

"Good." He checks his watch, then glances at me. There's a lot conveyed in that glance, but compassion is at the forefront. "Come to dinner Saturday night, Syd."

I nod.

He motions to the pucks around us. "You up for a passing game, Ruiz? I've got some work to do before my nine o'clock meeting." He pushes the stick into Oliver's grasp on his way by. "Oh, and you're invited to dinner, too."

Great.

We stare at each other a beat. I haven't seen him since he beat Bear at the fight, and he doesn't seem particularly worse for wear.

"Penn talks about you," he finally says. He skates closer. Who knows why he even laced up—and on his own, no less. "It's driving me absolutely insane."

"Why?"

"Are you exclusive?"

I shake my head. No, we're definitely not.

"Do you want to be?" The muscle in his jaw jumps.

"He thinks he can convince me to pick him." I don't say the other part: that I don't know how I'm going to choose at all.

"Who's his competition?" Oliver demands.

I laugh. It startles out of me, and I have to move away from him. I can't just have a staring competition with the man, or else my thoughts will turn wicked. And I certainly can't have that with my father in the building.

"Sydney," he calls.

I snag a puck and move it to the far side of the rink. I take a snap shot toward the boards, the *boom* of it hitting and rebounding back to me satisfying.

"Sydney, who's his competition?" He skates up beside me and pauses again. "Are you dating someone else?"

"More like I have two stalkers." I flip my hair off my shoulder. "They know what they want and are going after it."

Unlike you, I don't say.

His gaze darkens.

"What are you going to do about it, Oliver?"

I head for the door, and he follows. I've admitted some pretty painful truths to him and got nothing in return.

Nothing except where my bracelet ended up, which I guess is on his mother's wrist. If she even wears it.

My stomach flips at the idea of it sitting in a box somewhere, in the dark. That's how my mother kept it, too. Hidden out of sight. But from that photo in the yearbook I found, it wasn't always like that. She wore it at school.

I want to wear it.

I met his abuela, and now his family has a piece of mine's history.

My grandmother died when I was eight. She got terribly sick and spent almost four months in and out of the hospital, then with home aid. Her husband had died before I was born. At that point, Mom already had the bracelet. Although I have no idea if she wore it at that time. Maybe she took it off when she got pregnant. Or only after her mom passed.

But Grandma used to tell me stories as I perched at the foot of the hospital bed in her living room, about her fantastic love story. Her grandmother's bracelet broke only a week after she died, and it was the one thing she passed along to her only granddaughter. The others were boys, they didn't care about jewelry.

Devastated, she took it to a jeweler to have it repaired.

And she ended up with a date. A date that turned into several over the course of a week, and before she knew it, they were madly in love.

"I want love like that," I used to say, my hand on my chin.

She smiled at me and patted my leg. There were no words of comfort or reassurance. Her smile said she knew something I didn't. Something I wouldn't figure out until I was much older.

I rub my wrist.

I never wore it before I lost it.

In the back of my mind, it occurs to me that it should've been mine. From grandmother to granddaughter, isn't that how it went?

Selfish thought. Selfish to take that piece of our family history away from my mother.

And selfish of her to sell it like it meant nothing.

Oliver follows me into the locker room, where I sit at Penn's cubby and unlace my skates. Oliver sits directly next to me and mirrors my actions, his movements faster and more practiced than mine. He finishes first and puts on his street shoes. When he's done, he leans back, watching my profile.

What are you going to do about it?

"Why are you here?" I question. "Why can't you just be honest with me?"

His brow lowers. "Honest? You want honesty, Sydney?"

"Yes," I hiss.

"You're an intrigue that never should've caught my attention." He rises.

I stand, too, vulnerable in just my socked feet. Not that he's childish enough to stomp on my toes. *Maybe.*

"I can't stop thinking about you." He inches closer.

"Good," I whisper. This feels like the opposite of the rage room, but I give him the same 'come on' motion. "More."

"You're so fucking bright." His eyes glitter. "It's like you suck up the sunshine and emit it from your skin, even in the dark, and I've just been stumbling around blind without you."

I inhale sharply.

He lifts his hand, his fingers grazing my neck. I'm a professional with the concealer by this point, although the bruising is healing nicely. It'll be gone in another week and a half. He doesn't stop at where the bruises are, though. His fingers ghost backward, into my hair, and he draws me forward.

I go.

"I'd like to think I'm Penn's competition." His lips are so close to mine, his breath feathers across my mouth.

"You are." *One of them anyway.*

Lord help me. I want him to kiss me. I want to burn in his gaze until I combust.

When his lips touch mine, electric zaps flood through me. I may as well be holding a hot wire or hit with a taser. I can't help but compare his kiss to Carter and Penn. Penn is an inferno. He stokes a fire inside me, and his kiss consumes me like flames do. Carter walks the razor's edge between pain and comfort. Sweet and controlling.

Oliver is hungry. He kisses me like I'm the first drops of rain after a drought. He cradles the back of my neck while his tongue strokes mine. He tastes me, he groans at what he discovers.

I feel seen.

It's the kind of kiss that may as well suck out my soul in the process. I want the same from him, though, and when I surge up on my toes and kiss him back, harder, he gives me everything. He tastes like mint toothpaste. His scent is citrus and musk, something that buries in my lungs and refuses to let go.

I trace his chest with my hands and move upward, to the back of his neck, into his hair. His hair. It's as silky as it looks. He makes another noise in his throat when I tug, so I do it again. His hips shift forward, his erection pressing into my belly.

The locker room door opens, and we break apart in an instant. He runs his hand down his face, while I return to my seat. I duck my head, letting my hair fall in front of my face like a curtain. My lips feel puffy.

"You left pucks," Dad says. "Ruiz."

"Yes, sir." Oliver turns around, somehow a thousand percent more composed than me. He hurries past Dad, back to the rink.

I bury my face in my hands.

Dad clears his throat, and I peek through my fingers.

"No funny business in my arena." He points at me, frowning slightly. But then he shakes his head and follows Ruiz out.

Well, *fuck*.

thirty-two
sydney

Maddy has inadvertently become my confidante.

It's not that I don't trust Brandon and Dylan. I love our friendship and actually quite appreciate their discretion, but Maddy and I just seem to hang out more. Especially since bonding after the fight.

We're holed up in my apartment on Halloween night watching scary movies. There was a party—I was invited to it, actually, and so were my three friends—but the idea of being surrounded by people in masks scared me.

I've been having more nightmares lately. I'm not sure if I was having them before and simply not remembering, but this week I've been waking up in a blind panic, covered in sweat while my heart tried to escape my chest.

Anyway. I finally admitted to Maddy the rest of the story from the warehouse. About Bear. She already knew something was up from Oliver's behavior at the fight. And Penn's. But she didn't question me about it at the time.

Now that she's all filled in, she heartily agrees that a Halloween party would be traumatic. Even the scary movies are a little hard to stomach.

"Where do you think your mom went?" She returns to the couch with a giant bowl of popcorn, handing it to me while she cocoons herself in blankets. "Did you ever find out where she'd go when you were a kid?"

I lift one shoulder. "Best guess is somewhere like Atlantic City. She'd come back with cash... I feel like that's where you go when you want to do that kind of thing."

Whore herself out.

Gamble.

Maybe some combination of the two.

"Maybe she's there. Stuck like Percy Jackson in that Lotus Flower hotel."

Another thing about Maddy? She's secretly into stuff that probably wouldn't win brownie points with the cool kids. *Star Wars*, *Lord of the Rings*, Greek mythology, *Harry Potter*... she holds on to knowledge like a sponge, but with the strange ability to spit out random trivia.

It only came out after we'd been hanging out for a while, but it's definitely gotten more frequent. And don't get me wrong—I love it. I love the references that I don't always understand because it means she trusts me to be herself.

And that seems like the greatest compliment after living with someone like Scarlett, who has never been real a day in her life.

Thinking of Scarlett reminds me that she slept with Oliver. Maybe Penn, too. That gives me the major ick. Also, she witnessed some form of my supreme humiliation and did nothing to save me. Which should put her at the bottom of my list of people I'd save in a fire.

Maybe right above Bear and Andi, but definitely below Miranda and Kate.

Not that I want to think about fires.

Or Bear, Andi, Miranda, or Kate.

Talk about a mood killer.

I restart the movie once she's settled. We only have one lamp on in the corner, adding to the scary effect. I keep flinching, spilling popcorn across my lap, which causes Maddy to cackle.

I'm not a good horror flick person.

"We're watching *Halloweentown* next." I grab my phone and head to the bathroom, although the movie keeps playing. I do not need to see the girl running from the scary chainsaw guy get caught. The faster this one is over, the better.

There's a text from my mystery guy.

L.

Bedroom.

What?

ME

What do you mean?

The one thing that wasn't doxed by that stupid fucking gossip page was my address.

I wait for him to reply, but there's nothing. I finish in the bathroom, peek into the living room to make sure Maddy is still enthralled in the movie—she is—and head back to my bedroom. The door is mostly shut.

I push it open and tiptoe in, half expecting someone to be lounging on my bed. Because that would totally make sense, right? *Wrong*.

Should've known better.

Someone grabs me from behind, their hand around the lower part of my face, keeping my jaw shut and muffling the sound that squeaks out. He's wearing thick leather gloves. He wraps a blindfold around my eyes, only releasing my mouth long enough to tie it in quick jerks. I'm walked toward my desk, until my thighs touch the edge. He folds me over, my cheek touching the surface. One hand stays on my spine.

My pants come down.

My heart is beating out of control, and I grip the edge of the desk.

He doesn't fuck me. Instead, I feel him lower himself down, his breath warming my bruised ass cheeks. He seems to inspect it, cupping the one with Carter's name and mauling it in his gloved hand. Then the glove disappears, and his bare fingers dig into the bruises.

I let out a whimper.

His other hand is already bare, and he parts my cheeks. My mouth opens, but I don't let any sound come out. Not with Maddy—

His tongue rims my asshole without warning. I jerk away from him, but there's nowhere to go. He dances around it, then thrusts in. My fingers tighten on the desk until my nails threaten to break. His fingers go lower, slipping down my center.

I'm fucking wet. It's embarrassing.

It's not how I wanted to meet him.

He inserts two fingers inside me, seeming to almost experiment with how I react. Waiting for me to turn my face into the desk, for my body to shudder. He brings me right to the edge, when my muscles just start to clench and pulse, and he withdraws.

I groan.

His mouth moves across my ass cheek. Something lightweight but hard hits the desk. It sounds like a plastic cap. Then another sensation brushes my skin.

Pen?

Marker?

I shiver as he seems to write. A message for me or someone else—

He rises, and I let out a slow breath. I'm strung tighter than a wire, everything in me screaming to peek at him, to beg to come. To say something—anything.

But is this it? He's just going to bring me to the edge and go?

There's another noise, one that doesn't make sense until

cold liquid drips down the crack of my ass. His finger follows the same path his tongue did, around and around my asshole, then pushing inside. My muscles grip at him, but he works his finger in and out until I groan.

I know what's next.

And in a moment of supreme clarity, I am one hundred percent sure I could straighten and tear off the blindfold and he wouldn't put up a fight.

Or maybe he would.

His finger is replaced by something larger. It pushes against my ring of muscles and just keeps going, finally gaining entry—but it seems never-ending. It hurts, the pain unexpected, and then suddenly gives way to something else.

I want to cry out, but all my sounds are bottled up in my throat.

After a long moment, his hips touch my ass.

He releases a slow breath—the only sound he's made so far.

"Sydney?" Maddy calls. "Are you okay?"

We go still, and I clear my throat. "J-just changing my clothes." I can't remember if I closed my bedroom door. I don't know if L. did in the case that I didn't. "The butter left a stain..."

"Okay!" Her voice is cheery, not at all suspicious.

He moves. Withdrawing and thrusting back in, his one hand now splayed across my back and the other on my wrist in front of my face. Maybe ensuring that I won't surprise him and tear it off.

His fingers dig into my skin as he fucks me harder. My ass aches, pain collecting in my nerve endings, sparking and mixing with pleasure. Like being spanked in the woods.

Why do I like pain?

My mouth is open, my breath coming in sharp pants. I won't come like this—I'm pretty sure I won't. With him not touching my clit, this is just another form of torture, and it seems to roll on and on and on.

Until he finishes inside my ass without a word. Just a quiet grunt, a quivering of his thighs against the backs of my legs, as he pumps slower and milks out the last of it.

He pulls out, but his hand on my back keeps me down. Not that I'm in any danger of moving. My legs are jelly, and my core is pulsing. I strain my ears for any hint of what he's doing, but it just sounds like fabric rustling. Then something cold touches my asshole.

It slides in, helped along by his cum, and my sphincter closes around an indent.

Butt plug, my mind supplies.

He leaves me like that, the window sliding up, the little scuff of his shoes and rattle of metal as he hops onto the fire escape.

I open my eyes, then tear off the blindfold. My phone is right in front of my face.

L.

> Leave it for one of your guys to find.

Jesus.

It feels... I've never had anything in my ass like this. I lift myself up off the desk and quickly drag my clothes back into place.

It's there, persistent, for every move I make.

Notice me, notice me, notice me.

I almost go back out into the living room, but I change my shirt at the last moment. There's writing on my ass cheek, too. But that will have to wait for later.

Maddy eyes me when I return. "You okay?"

"Yeah, sorry, Dad was texting me."

Her attention flicks back to the movie, which seems to be winding up for some grand finale. "Your relationship with him is doing better, isn't it?"

"Yeah, actually." I sit. Almost wince, but manage to hold off.

The movie ends. We watch another one—not Halloween-town, because apparently the scary one has a sequel we need to watch—but halfway through, Maddy yawns. Stretches. Yawns again. I don't say anything until the credits roll.

"I'm going to head home," she says. "Thanks for inviting me over. Rain check on *Halloweentown*?"

"Anytime." I follow her to the door. "I appreciate you spending it with me instead of..." I motion toward the window.

"Parties stress me out," she confesses. "This was a godsend. We can repeat it next year, if you want."

We share a smile, and she promises to text me when she gets back to her dorm room. As a sophomore, she can still live on campus. Next year will be a different story for her, but she mentioned moving in with Dylan. So that will be good, at any rate.

I turn on all the lights in my apartment and go straight for the bathroom. I spin in the mirror and pull down my leggings, trying to decipher the scratchy handwriting. It's bled and smudged a bit, but I think it says, *You may have had her first, but her ass virginity belongs to me.*

I groan.

Is it true? Yes.

Did I tell anyone that? No. Why the fuck would I go around advertising it?

Actually... I think back to my quick fling with Carter the previous year at SJU. Did we ever talk about it?

Is he L.? It's possible, I guess. He had my number, but he could've easily lied and said he got it from that post. I have Oliver's and Penn's numbers both saved in my phone now, too. L.'s doesn't match any of them.

There are workarounds to that, of course.

But I should also consider that it's someone else entirely.

L.

You okay?

That was…

Too much?

No.

Everything.

How's the plug?

Driving me nuts. I didn't finish, by the way.

Obviously not. Don't worry, Sydney, if I want a girl to orgasm, I know how to make it happen.

"a girl"?

You. If I want *you* to orgasm, I know how. Pinky promise.

Maybe you should get back here and help out with that.

You could stay awake for Penn. Isn't he your nightly visitor?

Or do we think Carter will be so bold tonight?

Oliver will only break into your house if you steal something important from him.

Are you saying that because you're him?

One of the three? Or do you have a specific guess?

I don't want to guess and be wrong. But you know an awful lot about them…

> Oliver doesn't know about Carter. That rules him out, I guess.

Doesn't he?

Doubt floods through me. I don't know if Penn would say anything. Their relationship confuses me. Best friends, sure, but do they share those secrets? They shared me, once upon a time...

I squeeze my eyes shut and drag my blankets higher up my body.

He seems to think someone's going to sneak into my house. That I should wait up for them just in case. My hand slips down between my legs just as another text comes through.

L.

Don't touch yourself.

Groaning, I drag my hand back up. The few strokes only took me higher. It seems to be the only fucking thing I can think about, and it's worse when the plug shifts inside me.

ME

> I hate you.

> I'm not sure why I'm even listening to you.

L.

Because you like the game.

I'm on the street. Your savior is coming now. Do me a favor and pretend to be sleeping on your stomach.

> To showcase your note?

Well, it wouldn't be much fun if they don't see it.

I sigh and slowly turn onto my stomach. I cup my breast, rolling my nipple between my fingers. I was going to sleep in panties and a t-shirt, like usual, but I couldn't even bear that much fabric touching me.

Under the blanket, I'm completely naked.

I pinch and tug, my knee hiked up to the side and my face pressed to the pillow. I don't even care if I fucking suffocate like this. My hips move, slow circles that give me no relief.

The window slides up, but I can't stop. I'm desperate with it now.

"Princess." Penn strokes my hair. "What a sight for sore eyes."

I don't respond besides a whimper so he knows I'm awake.

He pulls the blankets from my body, and goosebumps rise on my arms. He goes still when the blankets fall to the floor, staring at me for so long, I peek up at him.

His expression is rabid, and he touches the writing. Parts my cheeks and sucks in a breath at the plug. I don't know what it looks like, only what it feels like.

"Oh, princess," he breathes. "Carter plug you up and leave you high and dry?"

I shake my head. "Not him. Please, Penn."

He rolls me over. I stare up at him, my hips still moving.

"Reduced to dry humping the air." He goes to the window for a moment, then returns.

I got dark Penn tonight.

He drops his jeans, and his erection tents his boxers. He loses those and his shirt, his shoes and socks already off. And he fists his length, slowly stroking himself harder while his gaze devours me in the low light.

"Touch me," I beg. Both hands are on my breasts, still, impossibly following L.'s instructions. Maybe he is right, and I like the game. I know in the back of my head that this is one that can end at any moment anyway.

He grabs my legs and drags me around, until my ass is on

the edge of the bed. He keeps hold of my legs and goes to his knees, putting them on his shoulders. He kisses the inside of my thigh, trailing higher.

"You're killing me, Penn."

"Wonder if we're going to have company," he says, more to himself than me. "We'll give him a minute, princess. See if your ex wants to play with us."

Carter.

He means Carter.

His lips track a slow path closer to my pussy, but he draws It takes him forever to get to the crease of my inner thigh. He sucks one of my outer lips into his mouth. One digit slides inside me.

I gasp and buck, silently urging him for more. He presses down. The butt plug shifts.

"Oh, no," I cry. "No, no."

He pulls at the plug. Not enough to withdraw it, but he takes out the widest part, then pushes it back in. He does that a few times with his finger inside me.

I fist my sheets. Sweat dots my brow, and I look down my body at him.

"Why?" I pant. "Just fuck—"

My front door opens and closes.

"Oh God," I groan. "You assholes."

Carter arrives in the doorway. His expression is fucking murderous.

Penn pulls out and releases the butt plug. It slides back into place while he puts my legs back on the bed. I curl away from them and try to calm myself. I need to be rational and reasonable if they're going to fight—

"What the fuck are you doing?" Carter asks Penn. "Did you mean to point a fucking laser at my window? I thought she was in trouble."

"I wanted to get your attention," he says.

"You're naked."

"You probably will be, too. Look at her."

Footsteps approach. Cool hands touch my ass, then, like Penn did, Carter gets a peek at the plug.

"Wow." He traces his name. "This will scar nicely."

I shudder. My hands have crept up to my chest again, cupping my breasts, using pain to try and stave off the ache.

Bad system.

Zero out of ten, do not recommend.

My gaze sticks on Penn's face. "Why are you watching me like that?"

"Because you're fucking perfect."

Ugh. "I'd be more perfect with a dick in me."

Penn hums. "But you taste so good, and I was just getting started."

Carter glances at him, his expression darkening. It's not the wild chase side of him I saw before, but he seems curious enough to not leave. Or throw a punch.

"Please," I whisper.

Penn moves for me. He crawls between my legs and places a kiss on my pubic bone, then trails his lips down. He licks everywhere except my clit. His tongue slides into my pussy, which squeezes at him, and he finger-fucks me while he teases all around.

"Please," I beg louder. "Please touch my clit. Oh my God, Penn, I can't stand it. I need to come."

"The thing is, princess, you've been naughty." Penn looks up at me.

I stare down at him in disbelief.

He licks his lips and crawls over me, stealing a kiss from my lips. He's gone before I can even kiss him back.

"You let someone fuck you," he says, his voice grave. "Who?"

I gulp. "I don't know."

"Was it consensual?" Carter asks.

I manage to nod.

242

"Do your breasts give you relief, dream girl?"

I pause, then nod again. Slower.

They exchange a glance. One fully dressed, the other naked and not giving a shit. They move simultaneously, grabbing my wrists and hauling them up. I yelp and fight them, alarm fluttering in my chest. I struggle, but Carter ends up straddling my stomach and holding both while Penn hunts for a restraint.

He comes back with the blindfold left on my desk.

"He really wanted to make sure, hmm?" He drags the end of the blindfold over my face. He undoes the knot and ties my hands together, securing both to the headboard.

Fingers slip along my thigh and push into me. Three, stretching me gloriously. I stare at Carter, who's reaching behind where he straddles me to finger-fuck me. Three fingers. My hips start bucking again, the greedy need all I can think about.

Thinking—no, there's no thinking.

It's all primal.

He removes a finger, using just two. Pumping and coaxing at my G-spot, twisting inside me. His knuckles bump along my lips, but it's still not on the bundle of nerves that need pressure and friction to explode.

He takes away another finger, and then he stops entirely. I clench and groan, gripping at his finger, while he chuckles softly.

Penn returns. He shows Carter something on his phone.

"What?" I gasp.

Carter climbs off me, but he doesn't go far. He leans over and claims my lips, kissing me hard. I bite his lower lip, trying to incite something, but he just nips back. Then his finger is replacing his lips, smearing my arousal across my mouth.

"I'll see you later," he promises. "I'll pick up your pieces after they break you."

I shiver. I have no idea what he's talking about, and I can't mask the ripple of excited fear that slips down my spine. It pebbles my already sensitive nipples. Goosebumps rise all over.

"This should be fun," Penn says, stopping beside me.

"What is it?"

"A little experiment." He crouches and traces one of my ribs. "Oliver goes to extremes for you, you know? But he thinks because you wear my necklace and sweatshirt and kiss me in public that he can't have you. Even though we've both tasted you. Right?"

My body trembles for a whole new reason. "Is he...?"

"On his way over? Yes. Not great on the timing. I was hoping Carter and I would get to play with you."

"Didn't think the goaltender would be the one trying to share." I tug at my wrists again. "Didn't you say you were going to make me pick?"

A shadow crosses his expression. "Of course. We're endgame, you and me. But that doesn't mean I want you to question if someone would've been better."

"What are you going to do about the person who left me like this for you?"

"Kiss him on the mouth?" Penn's eyes narrow. "Or put him six feet under. We'll see."

We'll see.

"Oh, one more thing." He pulls out a strip of fabric and covers my eyes. He ties it gently around my head, running his fingers through my hair. "Don't worry, princess. I'll leave the door open for Ollie. Maybe he'll put you out of your misery."

A second later, noise canceling headphones slide over my ears, and the world outside myself fades away.

thirty-three
oliver

PENN

You remember where Syd lives?

?

Get there asap.

By 'ASAP' I assumed he meant an emergency. As soon as possible. 9-1-1. But I jog up to her brownstone, and the lights on her third-floor apartment are off.

And my teammate is sitting on the steps out front.

He tosses me something, clicking his tongue.

I catch the keys.

Sydney's keys. God knows she's fumbled with them enough in front of me. I stare passively at Penn, waiting for the punchline.

The last time I saw her was in the locker room, after the gut-wrenching kiss that made me question how I ever kissed any girl before her. Ever. I've had a low opinion of kissing since high school—too wet, too eager, too much tongue—and no one had been able to dissuade me from that line of thinking. No one but her.

Because god-fucking-damn, her lips are perfect. The first

time I saw her, it was her silver eyes that burned into my brain. It made recognizing her at that SJU party too easy. But now her lips are the first thing that come to mind when I think of her.

Eyes are a close second.

Body follows.

"Three B," Penn says. "Better hurry."

"This isn't an emergency you can help with?"

He shakes his head. "Nah. She was asking for you."

I huff. He moves past me, heading for his car. I was at a party earlier tonight for like half a second, but it was lame. It was too superficial, with girls in the skimpiest costumes, twirling their hair or sticking out their assets. Some of my teammates soak that shit up. Others avoid the ragers.

While sometimes I go in search of a warm cunt to sink into, most times it's a waste. I don't want a drunk girl who can barely stand. I want...

Something else.

Something worse.

My cravings scare me sometimes. I've caught myself looking up proper ways to subdue a woman, to tie them in intricate knots that give them pleasure as much as it restricts them. I even went to a fucking class three towns over using a fake name.

It was interesting.

I definitely banked some knowledge and mental imagery to get me through the lonely weeks of summer when Framingham all but empties of college students.

One more year. Only one semester left, really. And then, against all the fucking odds, I'll head to the NHL. Being drafted out of high school was a dream come true. Choosing to attend FSU for two years—mainly because of Walker and Coach Windsor—was one of the best decisions I could've made.

In that time, I've packed on muscle and learned to play

against a higher caliber of teams. Another step that shapes the way I attack the game. And Coach, well, I'm not sure how I'd ever repay him for all he's taught me.

Finally on the third floor, I push open the door to three B.

"Sydney?" I call.

It's dark. I drop her keys on the counter and continue in, scanning the apartment. She doesn't answer, and my concern spikes. I head straight for her bedroom, my phone already in my hand.

I don't expect to find her naked.

Tied.

My heart stops.

Her heels slide against her sheets. The blankets are in a heap on the floor, kicked off by her or torn off by someone else. She's writhing, seeming to not hear or see me. There's a tie over her eyes, headphones on her ears. I'm not sure if it's playing music or just canceling out the noise.

She's trying to get friction, I think. She twists, rolling onto her stomach. Her hips move, her muscles flexing as she humps her bed. She seems desperate with it—and then the little spark of something extra between her ass cheeks catches my attention.

Fuck.

Who the fuck put a plug—

There's writing on her ass.

And more.

I go back to the door and flip on the light switch, and she *flinches*. Guess the light makes its way under the tie blindfold.

"Hello?" Her voice is breathy.

I don't answer. She shifts onto her side, keeping her ass to the wall, and brings her legs up to her stomach. Like she's suddenly shy, even though she knows it's me.

Now's not the time to hide.

Do I touch her? Does she *actually* know it's me? Or is this some sick prank by Penn? I swear to God, if she says his name—

"I know you're there."

Her arms are stretched out above her and connected to the headboard. I start there, running my finger just under it along the underside of her wrist. Where her skin is probably most sensitive, judging by how she keeps intermittently pulling and releasing.

She shudders.

My fingers drag down her arm, light enough to tickle. She has goosebumps. Down her arm, armpit, side. Along the outer edge of her breast, the bumps of her ribcage. Her breathing comes fast and shallow when I reach her waist, then her hip. I press, and she gives with the pressure. She rolls on her stomach, burying her face in her arm.

Carter is cut into her skin. It's scabbed over, but the lines all look smooth cut and shallow. It might scar, but it was done with a sharp blade. One that didn't rip and pull at her skin as he dragged it across.

I clench my jaw. When we discussed competition, she never mentioned Carter.

She mentioned *me*.

So it is the three of us, then?

There's writing in marker on her other cheek, but it's smudged to shit. I can only make out *ass virginity*. Judging by the plug, it's now gone.

My fingers continue their exploration. I tap the top of the plug, and she groans. Her thighs are pressed so tightly together, her legs shake with the effort.

I move from her bruised ass back to her hip, to the outside of her thigh. Knee. Calf. Ankle. Foot.

She jerks away when I skim the sole of her foot.

I can see her tied up in *my* ropes. The special ones that I don't think she discovered when she broke into my house. But there's time for that later. If there is a next time.

248

Now, I want to open her up.

My trek north comes along the inside of her leg. She lets out a breath and rolls onto her back, her legs falling open.

Her cunt is wet and red. I've never seen one so flushed and swollen, her clit looking like it's been teased mercilessly until now. When I get to her inner thigh, higher and higher, the noise starts. A little whine that she can't seem to stop—maybe she can't hear it. She digs her heels into the bed again, her hips jerking.

Chasing pleasure no one has given her.

But there's Carter. Penn. Maybe someone else?

Not exclusive. That's what she said.

So do I throw my hat in the ring or do I walk away?

"Oliver," she whimpers. "Please keep touching me."

I go still.

She knows it's me.

Well, that changes everything, doesn't it?

"Oliver." Her voice is stronger. "Oliver."

She says it like a chanting prayer.

I glance around the room, noting the desk along the far wall, a chair tucked under it. Clothes in her hamper and not on the floor. She's tidy. Everything with its place. Although there isn't much here in terms of personality. The walls are white. There's no artwork, no personal touches besides the rug and colorful blanket.

My house was always such a riot of colors growing up, this feels clinical.

I palm my dick. It stiffened the moment I walked into the room, but now it's hard as steel. Her saying my name...

I drop my pants, kick them off with my shoes. I shed my shirt, needing to be skin-to-skin with her.

What I don't want to do is torture her.

I put a knee on the bed, and she freezes. Her legs fall apart without shame, and I use both hands to run up the insides of her thighs. I drag her body in my direction, keeping hold of her legs. Keeping her ankles together and on one shoulder.

The position lifts her ass off the bed. Most of her weight is on her shoulder blades, but she doesn't seem uncomfortable. She's trembling.

Anticipation?

I notch myself at her slit. It's hot and slick, her muscles already grabbing at me. Trying to pull me deeper. I reach down and tear the headphones off, tossing them away. I tug her blindfold down, too.

She blinks up at me, her pupils dilating.

"I knew it was you," she gasps. "I'm going crazy, Oliver."

"I know, *mi nena*." The nickname just slips out.

Covering for my lapse, I push into her. She feels different with the plug. Tighter. She cries out, her hands twisting and holding on to the restraint. I bury myself in her, giving her a second.

"I need you." Her gaze is pleading.

"You have me," I growl.

I pull out and slam back into her, banding my arm around her calves. The way her legs are together creates a new feeling of intensity. She squeezes at my cock, her hips lifting like she can meet every thrust. I keep one knee on the mattress, leveraging her against me. I bend forward slightly and run my free hand down her leg.

When my fingers land on her clit, her body bows off the bed.

Someone wound her too tight.

Tears slide down her cheeks, and I thrum the little bud in time with my thrusts. It doesn't take long for her to break, her orgasm tensing everything. *Every damn muscle*. I grit my teeth and hold on to my control, fucking her slowly through it.

I don't stop, though.

Stopping seems out of the question.

She comes down from the high, her expression near delirium. Until I pull out and spread her legs. I slide back into her. She's a slick mess, but she doesn't seem to be with it at the moment. Not when I reach down and palm her breast, flicking her nipple.

Her gaze comes back to me.

"Your clit is the only way you come?"

She lets out a breath and nods. My hand returns there, and I work her up faster than before. Her hair is sticking to her face and neck, fanned out around her head. Her silver eyes drag me into her orbit. Even deeper.

I want to be deeper.

It's strange to be *in* her and not have it be enough.

I bend forward and take her untouched nipple in my mouth. Her chest rises and falls more as she tries to control her breathing. I suck and lap at her nipple, then take more of her breast into my mouth. I bite and suck harder, determined to leave her with a hickey of my own.

I want to pierce her nipples and claim them as mine. I want to tattoo her whole body, warning off anyone and everyone else.

My hand is still at her clit, the stroking soft and slow. Teasing until she's ready to beg again, until she squirms and nearly bursts out of her skin with the need to come. The other one is on the breast I haven't marked.

"Fuck, that feels good," she groans. "You're being nice even though—"

I drag my mouth up her sternum, to the hollow of her throat. Along the side of her neck. To her jaw. I don't know where I'm going, I just want to map her body with my mouth. I want to memorize it so I can replay this later, when I'm alone in my own bed.

"Even though..." She inhales sharply. "Oliver, I—"

I kiss her.

I don't want to hear someone else's name come out of her mouth, I don't want her to take away from what I'm giving to her. Every moment I'm inside her hardens the glue between us.

It's dangerous.

She's dangerous and seductive and most definitely off-fucking-limits.

At the moment, though? None of that matters.

She opens for me. I kiss her deeply, my weight pressing down on her. Our chests crush together; the only space left between us is where I still touch her clit.

I move faster. My balls are heavy, slapping against her with every push into her. The need to orgasm is crawling up on me, but I want one more from her first.

She gives it to me. She cries into my mouth, letting me suck up her noises of pleasure, and she tries desperately to twist away from my fingers when I keep up the pressure.

I lied.

Two more.

I tear my lips from her mouth, putting them to her ear. "Let me hear you."

"I think I'm going to pass out," she says, sniffling. "You're breaking me. I can't c-come anymore, Oliver, please."

I nip her neck. Just a snap of my teeth on her flesh, and her hips move in response. I lick at the area and do it again, my teeth digging in, burrowing in her flesh, but not hard enough to make her bleed. I suck the same spot until she screams a third climax, her thighs squeezing my hips. It rolls through her.

She goes limp.

Raising my head, I check that her eyes are still open.

They are.

They shift to meet my gaze, and she licks her lips. They're puffy and red from our kiss.

I move lower.

"Oh, Oliver, no—"

I stand. My dick is wet, soaked with her arousal and cum,

pointing straight at her. I adjust her again, flipping her onto her stomach, pulling her hips up until her knees are under her. Her arms are still flat out, her head turned to the side and pressed to the mattress.

She looks like a beautiful mess.

"One more for me, *mi nena*," I say.

I pull the plug from her ass in one tug. It joins the headphones on the floor, and cum immediately seeps out. The circumstances haunt me, but I ignore my million questions and instead line up with the tight rosebud.

She bites her lower lip when I push in. It's a tighter fit than her cunt, and I groan at the new pressure. I give her another second. Her nostrils flare with every inhale, her pretty, swollen lips parted.

I'm not going to last long.

I fuck her ass hard. My hips strike the bruises and cuts on her cheeks every time I bottom out in her, and her fingers curl around the restraints again. She white-knuckles them, shuddering and gasping.

At this angle, I lean forward and reach under her. I tug at her nipples, imagining little rings in them. One hand stays braced on her abdomen while the other goes to her clit again. I alternate between dipping into her cunt and massaging the bundle of nerves.

She writhes and twitches, like she wants to escape the sensation but can't figure out where to go. I don't have her nearly as immobile as I want, but it's a good taste of the sensation for her.

To see if she'd go farther with me.

Pleasure dances down my spine. I groan and work her harder, my movements getting jerkier. I chase our pleasure— hers with my fingers, mine in a frenzy of motion. It hits me first, and I bow forward. My forehead touches her back as I come hard, my fingers still pushing her to join me.

I'm still fucking coming when she falls into her orgasm.

Her ass spasms around my cock, and I get another crushing wave of pleasure.

We collapse to the bed in a heap. I pull out of her and roll to her side, stretching up and undoing the tied restraint. My fingers are clumsy, but I get it loose and help guide her wrists out.

She faces me, her arms tucked into her chest. Her teary gaze finds me.

I wipe them from her cheeks carefully, my thumbs collecting the liquid under her eyes.

"That was intense." Her voice is hoarse. "I should..."

I shake my head and slip my arm under her neck. I shift closer, my other arm wrapping around her back. She fits perfectly against me, her head nested under my chin.

"You should stay right here."

Until my sanity comes back to me, I don't plan on moving.

thirty-four
sydney

I'm half-asleep in Oliver's arms when Penn returns. He lifts me out of bed, cradling me in his arms, and carries me to the bathroom. The water is already running in the tub, and he settles me into the warmth.

My head lolls against his arm, which he keeps around my shoulders for a moment. He moves a little, taking his arm away and gathering my hair. He ties it up on top of my head, then returns to my side at the edge of the tub.

"What time is it?" I lick my lips.

He supplies a glass of cold water, holding it to my mouth and tipping it for me.

I swallow eagerly. It soothes my throat and wakes me up a bit, but my eyes still feel heavy.

"It's a little after four," Penn replies.

"PM?"

He chuckles. "Morning."

I groan.

"I know." He shuts off the tap when the water reaches mid-upper arm. He dips a cloth into the water, then squirts soap on it. With slow, firm strokes, he cleans my skin. Starting at the back of my neck and working his way down, he operates in near silence. I hold the edges, my head leaned back on the lip as soon as he finishes with my back.

When it moves between my legs, I moan.

"How many times did you come?"

I sigh. "Four? Fourth felt more like a hallucination."

"Good." He continues cleaning. Stroking.

Teasing.

I crack one eye open. "I know what you're doing."

He smirks. "Yeah?"

"I hurt."

"You like pain."

That's true.

His gaze goes to my wrists, which are a little red. Nothing crazy, but they might bruise in a few days.

"We're going away next weekend," he says in a low voice. "We have two games out of state."

I nod carefully. "I looked at the schedule. Dylan's first volleyball match is that weekend."

His gaze travels across my face. "You'll be okay?"

"I don't have anyone to worry about, do I?" I squint at him. "Oliver took care of Bear, your necklace solves my bullying problem. The only ones who still torture me are you two, and I like it."

"You did like it?" Oliver stands in the doorway. He tugged on his boxers, but his cock is very obviously at half-mast.

My cheeks heat, and I nod.

"Which part?"

The part where he came in, or before? Is that what he's asking?

Carefully, I say, "I don't know if I *like* not knowing who L. is, but I liked what he did tonight."

It's the first time I've said his name—initial—out loud. First time I've admitted that he exists. Not even Maddy, bona fide confidante, knows about him.

"The butt plug is a fun toy." I draw up my legs and lean

forward, wrapping my arms around my knees. "The waiting was torture." My gaze goes to Penn. "The torture was torturous."

He smirks.

I look to Oliver. "There's something in me that trusts you, and I have no idea why. But I feel safe even when I'm tied up. And I..."

"Say it," Oliver demands.

It's easier when he orders it.

"I like the pain and fear that comes with pleasure. That's why Carter fits. He scratches that... craving. He's more brutal with me."

Penn grimaces. "Guy's a dick."

"He probably thinks the same of you two," I point out. I grip the edge of the tub and hoist myself up. Water rushes down my body, and I crane around. I touch his name on my ass. "He didn't ask me about this. Penn didn't *ask* to spank me for it."

Oliver and I lock into a staring contest, and he finally nods. "Variety is the spice of life."

"Right. Now you both need to get out while I use the toilet."

I dry myself off and take care of business, brushing my teeth and wrapping myself in a towel. When I emerge, neither of them are in the hall. They're in my bedroom...

Making my bed?

"We should probably tell her," Oliver is saying. "Especially since we're leaving."

Penn makes a strangled noise. "Well, I was trying—"

"Tell me what?"

They whip around.

I raise my eyebrows and move to the desk, perching on top of it. Funny, since less than ten hours ago I was bent *over* it, kicking off this insane series of events.

It just leads me to question, once again, who L. is.

My main suspects are standing in front of me.

"Tell me," I say.

Oliver glances at Penn, then leaves him with the sheets and comes toward me. His expression is... sympathetic.

"Bear's real name is Henry Bernstein," he says. "Obviously we call him Bear for more reasons than one. His last name has something to do with it."

"Great." My stomach flips. "Why are we talking about him?"

"While I thought he'd go home, it seems he lied about a lot."

"That doesn't sound good," I mutter.

"It's not." He reaches for me, steadying me with a hand at my waist. "His dad is in jail for murdering his mother. His brother is a drug dealer."

I wait for more.

"And the brother has a record." He winces. "Of sexual assault."

There it is.

Penn joins us. "Nothing is going to happen to you," he promises. "In *fact*, we don't know anything will happen at all. It's just stuff that my private investigator found out."

My lips part. "Private investigator?"

"Yeah, well, someone needs to keep track of stuff." Penn lifts one shoulder. "He's also my uncle."

Oliver snorts.

"*So*," Penn continues, "while Bear and his asshole brother live one town over, there's been no hint of retaliation against you or Oliver. Or me."

"Great."

"You said that already," he points out.

Oliver elbows him. His gaze is warm. Not hot or smoldering, just... warm. "You should go to bed," he advises. "And we're going to leave you to rest."

"But—" I grab at him. "No."

"No?" He steps closer.

There's something about these guys getting into my space that gives my heart an extra pep in its step. I look up at him and shake my head.

"Finish what you started."

As in, *please don't leave me*. That's what I mean, even if I can't say the words out loud.

There's no way in hell I can process the night I just had, and I won't process it as long as one of them is here. Penn left me hanging—on purpose, clearly. But his brows furrow watching the two of us, and I wish I could smooth it away.

There's no way this is going to end well.

"I will." The words are husky leaving Oliver's mouth. "But only if you ask your dad about joining us next weekend."

I stop.

Dylan made the three of us *promise* that we would be there to cheer her on. If I go with them—their games are Friday and Sunday—then I will absolutely miss her Saturday game.

I like these guys, but I'm quickly learning to put in the work when it comes to treasuring my friendships. They're the ones who surrounded me when everyone at FSU hated me. They're the ones who didn't shy away from me or join the crowd in throwing stones.

"I can't." My gaze falls to the floor. "I can't miss Dylan's game."

He's not going to stay. Simple as that, right?

"That's the thing with ultimatums." I slip between them. "You don't set them if you're not ready for the wrong outcome."

I drop the towel and snatch my sleep shirt from the floor. I put it on and ignore the way my hair raises on my neck. How they're probably both staring at me like a lunatic. I climb into the freshly made bed, with clean sheets, and curl up facing the wall.

"Get the light on your way out," I say. Loud enough for them to hear that my tone is normal and I am perfectly fine.

The light goes out.

Footsteps walk away.

My throat closes, and the backs of my eyes burn. It doesn't matter that I shut them as tight as I can—a tear slips loose anyway. It rolls down my temple.

I can't think of a time when intimacy hasn't ended right after sex. And as much as I hoped that it would be different with these two... they're going to walk out of my room any second. The loneliness strikes hard, crackling in my chest.

The bed leans as new weight is added. Cool air brushes my naked legs, the blankets lifted, and a body slots in behind mine.

"Fuck ultimatums," Oliver whispers in my ear. "I didn't mean to make it sound like that."

The tears don't stop. My breath comes in ragged inhales. He doesn't say anything, just loops his arm over my hips and pulls me snug into his body. He buries his face in my neck, kissing it softly.

My mind is fucked. He seems to sense that, because he stays still and solid behind me, his breathing even while I work through the mess in my head.

So much for not processing until I'm alone.

thirty-five
sydney

"We have to go to dinner."

I stare blankly at Oliver. My mind has *not* been with it. I woke up and he was gone, but there was a note on my desk from him about needing to meet teammates for a morning skate.

Acceptable...ish.

But staying in my apartment just reminded me of all the things I didn't want to think about, so I washed my hair, scrubbed my body, picked at the scabs on Carter's name, and finally ventured out to the library.

I brought my journal and charcoal with me, and I have the writing project deadline looming over my head. Otherwise, I *also* have a law paper, a crime fiction paper, and an econ presentation. Those have taken priority, as their due dates are coming up fast, too.

He drops into the chair across from me. "Your dad invited both of us to dinner."

"Right. I remembered."

He texted me, too, although the message is still unread on my phone. He invited us both when I skated with him on Thursday, and then he kind of walked in on us kissing. It's unclear if he saw anything concrete, but he *did* warn be about funny business in his arena.

So basically, this is going to be an awkward fucking dinner.

"When?" I ask.

He glances at his watch, then me. "Um, like now."

"Oops."

My table is chaotic. I jump to my feet and flip notebooks closed, piling them together. I've got two books to return to the librarian. Plus my computer and a thousand pens.

Why the fuck do I have so many pens?

I spot my journal and charcoal case at the same time as Oliver, who started stacking textbooks for me. My fingers graze the spine just as he lifts the two, and I lunge.

"Whoa." He dances back. "What's this? Some super-secret diary?"

I scowl. "No."

Penn already looked through it. I don't need another hockey asshole doing the same. I open my mouth to tell him just that, but then he opens it, and the words die. He flips the pages to get to the last one, scanning the drawing and the words.

Watching him read it is a form of intimacy I never would've expected.

It's like he *is* reading my diary, or my deepest darkest secrets.

He mouths some of the words. Then touches the page. I know exactly which one he's analyzing.

> *Ice princess in a court so cold—what will she do when the prince who claims her is made of fire?*

My brows are furrowed by the time he closes it and looks up, and there's fucking *awe* in his expression.

"What?" I snap.

"You're creative. Talented." He holds it out.

"That's it?" I snatch the journal and hug it to my chest.

"I could go on, but you seem like you want to bite my head off. And we're still late."

Ugh. I shove it and the notebooks into my bag, and he takes the borrowed books. I follow him downstairs, still zipping my bag closed. He gives the books back, and we jog outside, and I suppress my groan at the motorcycle.

His lips tip into a smile. I'm still not used to him actually smiling, especially in my direction, but I'll take it.

"Sore?" He tugs on the shoulder strap of my backpack.

I hum.

He uses it to reel me in and kisses me.

He kisses me in broad daylight.

I don't even care, I want more.

Our mouths part, and he takes his taste of me. Too soon, though, he's pulling away and removing my bag from my shoulder.

An old flash of fear that he's going to be a dick and throw it comes over me, but he just hooks it over his shoulder and continues toward the bike. Giving me no choice that this is our destination.

I put on my helmet while he stows my bag under the seat. I climb on behind him, sliding close and wrapping my arms around him. It doesn't feel weird to do it this time, and he reaches back and squeezes my thigh.

The bike rumbles to life, sending vibrations straight up through my core. I don't think I'd normally feel it, but after last night, it verges on pain.

That goes out the window when the engine revs. I dig my fingers into his abdomen, and we shoot off down the street.

He parks on the curb in front of my dad's house.

I don't know why I'm suddenly nervous. I hop off the bike at lightning speed, unbuckling the helmet and shoving it back at him.

Is it because we had sex?

Mind-blowing, chemistry-altering sex?

Do not think about sex in front of Dad.

"You okay?" Oliver smirks at me. "You're... flushed."

"I'm not." I turn and stalk up the walkway before he can say anything else.

Perri meets us at the front door. Her expression is way too knowing, and she pulls me into a hug as soon as we're all inside.

"Frank has been grilling," she says.

"I brought this," Oliver says. He extends a bottle of wine to her. "I'm not old enough to drink, and neither is Sydney, of course. But my mom gave it to me for you."

"This is perfect, thank you, Oliver." She winks at us. "We can have a taste at dinner."

We shed our jackets, kick off snowy boots, and follow her into the house. Sure enough, the patio off of the kitchen is clear of snow, the grill at the edge creating a haze of heat just above the closed lid.

"Sounds good, Mrs. Windsor."

She frowns. "Please call me Perri, Oliver."

He dips his head.

Dad comes around the corner and immediately glares at his captain. Oliver straightens his spine and frowns back.

"Hey, Dad," I interrupt.

Oliver looks away first. Dad hugs me, smacking a loud kiss to my cheek.

"Thanks for coming," he says in my ear. Then he focuses back on Oliver. "Ruiz, we're going to talk about how you handle girls breaking into your house."

Oh, shit. My eyes go wide, and I start to shake my head—

"I didn't handle it the best, sir," Oliver admits. "I've already apologized to Sydney."

I have a feeling my apology came last night...

"He did," I blurt out. "He apologized."

Dad grunts.

Perri's laugh fills the kitchen, and she touches Oliver's arm. They head for the fridge to get drinks for everyone, and I glower at my father.

"I don't really need backup for something that happened months ago," I say quietly.

"Men on my hockey team need to learn how to treat women before they're set loose on the world," he replies.

My heart gives a weird little thump at that. The thought of Oliver somewhere, playing professional hockey, living a life that doesn't include us. Me.

"When do you guys leave for those away games next week?"

We move to the bar stools at the island. He leans on one, while I sit.

"Mid-afternoon flight on Friday, but it's a quick one. An hour up and down. The team will have their morning skate at our arena, and then we fly back directly after the Sunday game." His attention wanders to his wife. "Perri is coming with me this time. If you feel like you want to get out of your apartment, you're welcome to stay here."

"Oh. Thank you."

He smiles. "We'll get you a spare key before you leave."

"The team can miss Friday classes?"

"They get excused as long as their grades don't slip. They're required to keep a two-point-five grade point average, so making up work is essential." He lifts one shoulder. "Not exactly my idea of putting education first, but I don't make that rule."

I guess I can count on taking notes for Penn in our Intro to Law class.

Oliver returns with a beer for my dad and soda in a glass for me.

"You're not dating, right?" Dad asks him.

I choke on my drink.

Dad doesn't look away from Oliver, but he reaches over and pats my back.

"Unclear, sir," Oliver mutters. A flush creeps up his neck. "We haven't really discussed it. But your daughter has grown on me."

I'm going to die.

"Since the beginning of the semester." Dad sighs. "Keep your head on straight, Oliver. You have your whole life ahead of you to date girls. And not *this* girl."

"Okay," I mumble. "I'm going to..."

I motion toward where Perri is pulling something out of the oven. I mean, we have one heart-to-heart and now he's going to try and forbid Oliver and I from seeing each other?

"You're scowling." She hands me plates for the table.

"Yeah, well..." I shake my head and go set the table.

Did Mom ever care who I was dating? She had passing interest in it when I was in college... she eyed Carter like he could be my salvation. Because he comes from a wealthy family and will most likely be headed to the NHL after college.

In high school, though, I never brought any guys home. I messed around with some in their cars, parked away from prying eyes. They didn't bring me to their house either. It was transactional more than anything. Kissing and blow jobs and fucking, but that was it. No emotional value.

I glance across at Oliver.

Are we transactional?

He meets my gaze over Dad's shoulder. Just for a second, I *feel* something. Something I really don't want to feel.

A skip in my chest, a fluttering of affection.

Bad heart.

Dad goes to attend to the protein on the grill, and Oliver doesn't seem too bothered to be made to stand out in the cold in just a t-shirt and jeans, his hands in his pockets. But they return in short order. Perri hands Dad a sharp knife while Oliver and I transfer everything to the table.

It's a fantastic spread and probably too much food for just the four of us. Grilled chicken, roasted brussels sprouts and bacon, a salad, halved baked potatoes and toppings.

"This looks amazing," I tell her.

We take our seats, Perri and Dad at the heads, Oliver and I on the long sides across from each other. The next few minutes are full of quiet shuffling and passing of plates, until we're all loaded up and my mouth is watering.

"Thank you for inviting me," Oliver tells her and my father. His foot touches mine under the table.

"Do you get home-cooked meals very often?" Perri asks.

"Only when I visit my family. Which isn't enough if you ask them, but plenty for me." He tells her where they live, which seems to be only a few blocks away from their business. "Sometimes my abuela sends my siblings with food to make sure I'm not starving."

He cracks a smile at that thought.

"They come to the games," Dad says to Perri. "Very supportive family, although your grandmother is one to be reckoned with."

"She's hard to please." He rubs the back of his neck. "Actually, Sydney met her a few weeks ago..."

Right. She definitely didn't like me, if *hard to please* reminded him of our introduction.

Dad's eyebrows are in his hairline. He sets down his fork and clears his throat. "So, Sydney, you're meeting his family?"

"Oh, uh, no—"

"So it is serious," he concludes. His attention fixes on Oliver. "You're dating. You're introducing her to your grandmother. Is that what you're saying?"

"Yes," I blurt out.

Oliver pauses and looks at me.

I didn't mean to just say it. And I'm not sure how to frame Penn in this scenario, let alone Carter. That's not any of Dad's business, though. And they're not here getting grilled by him.

"That's wonderful!" Perri exclaims. "That's great, honey, right? You always say that Oliver is a great man."

"Boy," Dad corrects. "He's barely twenty."

I mean... yeah. Me, too. I scowl at Dad, who's laying on the protective act a little thick. He raises his hands in surrender, but I highly doubt the matter is dropped.

That would be asking for too much.

We finish dinner. Oliver and I clean up the kitchen to the tune of Dad and Perri's mutual protesting, but we send them out into the front room.

"Sorry." I pass him a wet dish.

"For what?" He's on drying duty, and his movements are quick and efficient.

"For saying we're together."

"Oh." He glances at me. "No takebacks, though."

I blink. "Huh?"

"You can't unsay it."

I set down my sponge and face him. "I can't unsay it?"

"You can't unring a bell, *mi nena*."

I don't know what that word means, and I really don't want to admit that I like it. But I like the way the word rolls off his tongue. I like the way he looks at me and talks to me and—

"We're dating." He smirks. "Penn can deal."

"And Carter," I automatically add. I quickly resume washing. "I'm not leaving him out of my life. Don't ask me to."

"Penn says he's a fucking stalker," Oliver says under his breath. "I could get rid of him for you."

"Like you got rid of Bear?"

Henry Bernstein. A problem that's apparently not gone, although he's the last person I want to think about.

He winces. "Even your father doesn't know. His brother's records were sealed because he was seventeen when the sexual assault happened. His dad's the only one that we would know about, and I don't think he ever told us. If your dad knows, he didn't mention it."

"Then how did Penn's uncle find out?"

His lips quirk. "He probably bribed someone."

Oh.

"That's one way of getting stuff done," I reply. "But please don't get rid of Carter."

He grunts.

The rest of the evening is nice. We drink coffee, and Perri pulls out some fancy chocolates. We keep things light and somewhat casual, minus a few cutting glares from my father in Oliver's direction. It's like he doesn't actually know his hockey captain... which is ridiculous.

When we've said our goodbyes and Oliver is already outside, I pull Dad aside and say as much. That he's known Oliver longer than me, if you look at it a certain way.

He gives me a *don't be stupid* look. "I only wiped one of your asses, sweetheart."

He kisses the top of my head and waits for me to get down to the curb. Oliver puts the helmet on for me, buckling it under my chin.

"Well, he didn't kill you." I smile. "That's a start."

"Let's hope he never sees the hickeys," he replies.

thirty-six
sydney

The thing about Penn's kink...

I don't usually wake up while he's fucking me.

Several times this week, I've woken to cum between my legs and a new hickey somewhere on my body. Breast, collar-bone... *lower*.

But now, with sunlight streaming in through my windows, there's a distinct movement behind me. An arm slung over my waist, the hand cupping my breast. And the heat of arousal is impossible to deny.

"Good morning," Penn breathes, kissing my neck.

He's fucking me gently from behind, his hips rolling forward and sliding his dick deeper into me. He pinches at my breast, tugging my nipple, and I let out a long sigh. My hips automatically move to meet him, to help the angle...

To take him deeper.

"This is new," I manage.

"This is round two." He kisses higher, up behind my earlobe. "I wanted to wake up with you."

Something stirs inside me, and I find myself smiling. "Oh. Good."

Good.

I'm not starting the day off alone. Isn't that something?

He rolls me onto my stomach, nudging my legs open wider. He never loses contact with my core, even when he grabs something from the floor and shoves it under my hips.

A fallen pillow?

"Don't freak out," he says in my ear. His weight presses down on me.

"About?"

"You started your period."

My stomach twists, and I immediately try to rise. He grabs my wrists, pinning me to the bed.

"I said not to freak out."

"You're—"

"You feel good like this," he argues, a sharp thrust punctuating his words.

Now that he says it, I *feel* it. The difference. The dull ache in my breasts that I just assumed was from them. But, no. Fucking hormones.

I close my eyes. His hand slides under me, and his fingers go straight to my clit. He seems to be an expert in how to work me up, twisting my insides and sculpting me like fucking clay.

"Carter will probably eat you out later if you ask him nicely," Penn groans. "He likes blood, doesn't he, princess?"

"Y-yeah." I press my forehead to the bed. "Don't stop."

"Hmm."

He does keep going. Thankfully. He fucks me and rubs my clit until my body is tense enough to shatter, and only once I'm riding my orgasm does he chase his own. Faster and harder. My headboard bangs against the wall, and my cheeks heat.

Until he jerks to a stop and comes.

He kisses my shoulder. "Perfect way to start the day."

Bloody... and perfect.

FSU DAILY NEWS

FROM SNITCH TO SLUT

Big news today, Vipers! Our very own Hester Prynne (if you don't understand that reference, ask the nearest English major), Sydney Windsor, was spotted yesterday looking cozy with hockey god and captain, Oliver Ruiz.

Some say the two kissed in the parking lot.

But isn't Sydney dating Penn Walker? After all, she wears his sweatshirt and necklace. The two are frequently seen on campus together.

Sydney's infamy, for those who are unaware, stems from her past as a snitch. She sold out FSU to St. James, costing our hockey team the glory and honor of competing in the playoffs.

Her unfortunate timing transferring to FSU notwithstanding, one must ask: is she opening her legs to stave off the indomitable loathing and vitriol of the Vipers?

After all, our bite is mighty, but our venom will kill.

And now it appears she's transitioning from snitch to slut, moving up the ranks. From goalie to captain. Who's next, the coach?

Oh, wait. That's her father.

Talk about daddy issues!

Chime in with your thoughts, Vipers. How far will this girl go?

I. Am. Mortified.

There are *pictures*. Photos of Oliver and I on the back of his bike, of me and Penn walking together through campus. More of him and I running together—although luckily none from *that* day. There are shots of me on the front steps of my brownstone. A sneakily snapped pic of me in class, with Penn playing with my hair.

I hate it.

I hate everything.

Who the *fuck* has been taking creepy pictures of me?

I'm currently holed up in the library, seated at one of my regular desks on the second floor. There aren't many people here mid-morning. I imagine the dining hall, by comparison, is packed with brunchers.

The guys have a game this afternoon, and when I emerged from my shower, I found Penn's away jersey slung over my desk chair. He'd also gone to the trouble of changing my sheets, seeing as how there was a nice little blood smear on the ones we slept on.

My body aches, my breasts are sensitive, and the intermittent cramps are driving me crazy.

Sitting around doing nothing... Not today. It spurred me to head to the library instead. Fresh air is supposed to help. Exercise.

But now I wish I had just stayed in bed.

Is my father going to see that post? It's written like a damn newspaper column, and it's already getting attention. Likes and comments... shares. The more shares, the more viral it goes.

I trace the chain of Penn's necklace. I don't take it off, even to shower. I like to pretend that he went through with his threat of soldering the clasp. Since it hasn't turned my skin green or tarnished in the slightest, I've come to the horrifying realization that this is real gold.

Which means it's valuable.

It's probably the most expensive thing I own.

My phone lights up, and I snatch it because I'm a glutton for punishment.

CARTER

FSU library?

Second floor.

I'm not sure why I'm telling him where I am. Especially since he can't just stroll onto campus... I drop my phone and bury my face in my hands. That gossip page gets a lot of traction, especially when it comes to me. Every post they make with my tag—yes, I have a personal hashtag—gets hundreds of comments and thousands of likes.

Blocking it out, I open my laptop again and get back to work.

I try to anyway. I'm still staring at the same paragraph ten minutes later when Carter drops into the chair next to me. His black cap is pulled low, and he has a black hoodie on under a thin jacket. There's a dusting of snow on his shoulders and the brim of the hat.

He slowly closes my laptop.

I lean back in my chair and blow out a breath.

"What would they say if they knew we had sex before the FSU game?" he asks.

My lips flatten.

"What would they *do* to you?" He shakes his head. "They'd say everything, Syd, but they wouldn't *do* anything."

"Easy for you to say," I snap. "You watch from afar. I was taped to a toilet at the first FSU game I tried to go to. I was there with my stepmom, the coach's wife, and that did *nothing*."

That humiliation still rattles me.

He stares at me in shock. "Are you fucking kidding me?"

"It was Oliver's..." It wasn't really *his* idea. I can't say that. "He told the girl who orchestrated it that I was at the game."

He stands. "I'm going to break his pretty face and you're going to fucking watch me."

My stomach flips.

"Sydney. *Now*." His tone is dark.

I jump up and shove my stuff into my bag, following him out. He doesn't so much as glance at the student worker behind the desk or the librarian shuffling papers behind him.

We get outside, and he grabs my hand, dragging me down a shortcut to get off campus property.

"I thought you knew. I told you about the girl with the black eyes—" I'm in shape, but he's moving *fast*. And I have too much stuff in my bag to be rushing.

He pauses, seeming to register it, and takes the backpack from me. His fingers thread through mine, and although we move at a slightly slower pace, his long strides eat up the sidewalk.

"You didn't say anything about being *taped to a toilet*. That's where those bruises came from?" He eyes me. "Fucking hell, Sydney. Why didn't you say anything?"

I don't have an answer except one: supreme embarrassment. Why would I ever admit something so... *bad*?

"Did you play this weekend?" I ask, trying to divert attention away from me and my lingering humiliation.

He smirks. "Friday night, dream girl. We won."

"Naturally."

We arrive at the arena. Of course he'd know they would be here. And he doesn't hesitate to go through the doors he'd enter through if it was SJU's time on the ice.

I'm ninety-seven percent sure Oliver and Penn are on the ice right now. They must be. Or in the locker room with the rest of the team.

And Carter is about to make a spectacle.

Or should I say *we're* about to, since he has a death grip on my hand.

Sure enough, he makes a beeline for the ice. We stop at the double doors where the Zamboni drives in, although they're closed and secured from the outside—our side—while practice is in progress.

Penn is in the crease working with a coach I haven't seen before. The other goalie stands by, watching.

Everyone else seems to be working through specific plays with my father on the other end of the rink.

Oliver spots us and does a double take. His brows hike behind his helmet cage, and his mouth guard pops out. He chews on the end of it, seeming to consider us.

Carter undoes the metal arm holding the doors shut and yanks it open. He storms out onto the ice, his gaze locked on Oliver. He makes walking across the ice seem easy. Easier than easy. And there's a furious intent swirling around him.

The good news is that he let go of my hand to go confront Oliver. It leaves me as a bystander out in the open. I could back away, if I wanted, and pretend I was never here. Minus Oliver seeing me.

The bad news is that I can't hang Carter out to dry like this.

I step out onto the ice carefully, picking my way across much slower.

"Sydney?" my dad calls.

A whistle blows.

Carter is almost to Oliver. And damn it, he's going to be fucking jumped—

It seems like the whole FSU team draws closer, surrounding Carter as he reaches Oliver. The latter removes his helmet, a strange gleam in his eye. Confused but seriously fucking ready to be hit. Which makes *no* sense.

College hockey players have to play in helmets with cages over their faces. It certainly adds an interesting dynamic when there's a fight, because the helmet has to come off. But if Oliver's removing it before Carter even reaches him...

The first punch is solid. Carter puts his whole body behind it, like he knows he's only going to get the one hit. Which is true, because two of Oliver's teammates grab him and haul him back before he can do damage.

More damage.

I reach the circle of guys. Chaos breaks out. Their backs are to me. I shove at them, but on their skates, they're too tall. More resembling trees than men. My dad is on skates, too, although I've lost sight of him. I can't see anything beyond the rows of shoulders.

"Stop," I yell, *finally* squeaking between two players and making it into the tight circle they've created.

Oliver's gaze flicks over me, seeming to check if I'm okay, then zeroes back in on Carter. His lip curls, and he makes a show of taking stock of Carter, too. He wipes at his bloody lip with the back of his hand.

"You got your one hit," he says in a low voice, skating close enough to Carter that it could seem like a conversation just between them. Like his voice isn't carrying to all of us right now.

Their height difference... if they were both on skates, or both off, Oliver would still have an inch or two on Carter. But the disproportion makes Oliver tower over both Carter and me.

"Let's leave it at that." Oliver spits onto the ice. It's red-tinged.

"OUT OF THE WAY."

I flinch. I've never heard Dad yell like that, his voice booming. But his players react immediately, the tight circle I had to struggle to break through dissipating.

Dad glares at the two still holding Carter's arms. As soon as they release him, Carter shakes out his arms and balls his fists.

"Name," Dad demands of Carter.

He remains silent, his jaw working.

"Carter Masters," I say when Dad's gaze flicks to me. "Captain of the Seawolves."

"I'm familiar." He looks at Oliver. "Ruiz, get her out of here."

"Yes, sir." Oliver skates to me and picks me up without warning. Not cradling, not kind—he tosses me over his shoulder like a bag of grain.

"You're in so much fucking trouble," he says under his breath.

That should worry me, but it turns me on instead. And *that* worries me.

He sets me on my feet at the door we stormed through, touching my chin. Lifting my face so I have to look at him. For only a second. A quick check that he's not bleeding—he's not, although his jaw is red—and then my gaze slides away again.

"You're going to go into the stands and sit there until we're done," he says in a soft voice. "Alone. I want to feel your eyes on me the whole time, do you understand me?"

Chills break out across my body. I nod.

"Aloud."

"I understand."

"Good girl." His hand drops, and he skates backward. "Go."

Carter and my father are still in an intense discussion on the ice, although I have no idea what they could be saying. Either way, I don't want to find out. I take the stairs up to the main level and pick a row with a good view of the whole rink. By the time I'm there, the doors are closed and Carter is gone.

I sit and glance toward Penn, who's staring at me with his helmet off, a water bottle in his hand.

I wave.

He shakes his head, seeming to fight off a smile, and shoves his helmet back on. Dad and Oliver are now speaking by the bench, and Oliver seems pissed. Even from here. After a long moment, Dad makes a shooing motion. He blows his whistle and gathers the team, briefing them on whatever they'll be doing next.

They break in half, going toward Penn in one goal and the second goalie in the other.

Oliver is on Penn's side. My side. Which is good, because I want to keep an eye on both of them. Even though I have strict instructions otherwise. I sit there and watch, and it's almost as bad as squirming with a butt plug.

Almost.

The anticipation climbs through me, and eventually... eventually, their practice ends. Dad skates out first, and I get the sense I'm going to have to deal with a phone call from him.

I wait and wait and wait. The lights go out, only the emergency lighting remaining. I'm shroud in semi-darkness, and it takes a long moment for my eyes to adjust.

Movement in my peripheral catches my attention, and I track it.

Someone stops at the end of my row, a mere ten feet away, if that. Wearing all black, it's no wonder I didn't immediately spot them. Their hood is pulled up over their head, but it's the face that peeks out from the shadows that startles me.

They're wearing the bloody clown mask.

thirty-seven
sydney

I don't think—I just run.

I'm so glad I shed my jacket while watching them play, because it would just slow me down. Same with my bag, left on the seat beside me. It can be found later, if at all. If I'm still breathing.

It doesn't matter.

What matters is moving faster. I scramble up and over one of the rows, then another, putting some distance between me and the masked man.

Bear took his mask with him.

Bear knows how to get in here.

Of course Oliver would put me in this position. He told me to wait, but he's probably showering or taking his sweet time getting dressed. If Bear was watching any of us, he would've seen me enter.

I reach the end of a section and rush up the stairs, taking them two at a time, then three. At the top, I risk a quick glance behind me.

He's coming, but not as fast. Like he's content to terrify me first.

My chest is so tight, I can't get in a good inhale. My lungs burn. I nearly fall as soon as my feet touch the polished floors outside the ramp to the section. All the concession stands are dark, their metal grates pulled down across the fronts. It leaves me nowhere to hide.

I sprint.

A laugh floats after me, and fear slides down my spine. I reach the exit doors. There are three sets of double doors, all metal, and I slam into the first one, compressing the metal bar. My whole body rattles with the impact as the door doesn't even *budge*.

"No, no, no." I go to the next with the same result. The third set is the same. That's not even fucking *legal*.

Which means it's a setup.

Footsteps squeak on the linoleum, and I spin around.

He's coming at me almost lazily, his hands in his pockets. There's no part of his skin that's visible, but my mind can't seem to comprehend anything other than the mask.

I know what it feels like close up. The hot breath that comes out of that smile.

I keep running, this time looking for the door back down to the locker rooms. But the glass doors that go down there are locked, too. I only spend a minute trying to get them open before I move on.

Run faster.

I push myself and fly around a corner, coming up on the main entrance. There's no way these doors are locked.

I slam into someone.

Hands grab at me, and I look up into the fucking bloody clown mask.

I scream and launch myself backward, falling on my ass. I scuttle away and hop back to my feet. Tears burn the backs of my eyes at how *stupid* this is. That I can't seem to find my way out of a paper bag, that everything has been set like a perfect trap to close me in.

Footsteps again, following me at a steady pace that grinds in my ears. It's a message. I'm the prey, and there's no way out.

My capture is inevitable.

I veer up a section's ramp and take the stairs down, darting through a row and stopping.

At least here, I can *see*. My stomach rolls, threatening to heave, and I force myself to take long, slow breaths. I brush my hair out of my face.

He appears at the top of my section and comes down the steps.

Those tears that were burning before prick at my eyes. My vision blurs, and I furiously blink them away. I turn to run and fucking *slip*.

I go down hard, my forearms catching me before my face slams into the concrete steps. My shoelace is undone. I roll on my back and grip the seat, but it's too late.

He's on me.

I scream when he grabs my ankle. He drags me into him, kneeling and pinning my leg between the back of a seat—the next row down's seat—and forces my other up. I'm wearing leggings. Comfortable leggings that suddenly seem like a terrible idea, because there's nothing. No protection, no dulling of sensation.

I'm on my period. I want to yell it at him, but I can't.

Every touch, his fingers digging into my legs, the way he positions me and bats away my hands with his gloved ones, sends spikes of terror through me.

My voice doesn't work.

The last time I pleaded, he wrapped a rope around my neck and laughed as I barely clung to consciousness. I push at his hands, try to slap and strike him, but he doesn't even react besides to dodge the ones that could hurt him. He lets the blows to his arms and legs mean nothing, but when I sit up and reach for his mask, he grips my throat with surprising speed.

He shoves me flat, leaning over me.

The eyes on the mask are black and soulless. I can't look at them. This mask has had a starring role in my nightmares, and I'm petrified into sudden stillness.

He undoes his pants with one hand.

I can't watch. My gaze floats to the ceiling.

He didn't get this far last time.

No words will come out. It's like he stole my voice, and as much as I try to scream or speak—there's nothing but a vague whistling exhale.

My throat aches from the inside out, reminding me of the trauma. At the bruises that are finally fading, leaving just a few easy-to-hide splotches behind.

Will I fight him after?

When his guard drops?

I miss him pull a knife.

There's a bite of pain at the inside of my thigh, and I cry out. The *rip* that follows—

Oh God, he didn't even try to pull the leggings down. He just made himself an entrance. Something cold and sharp touches my pussy. I flinch, but he doesn't rip the crotch of my panties. No—he tugs at the string of my tampon, though. He huffs when it slides out, dropping it beside his knee.

He knows. He knows and he doesn't care.

My eyes won't fucking close, but I refuse to look at him. I refuse to give him that satisfaction. Instead, I count the pipes twisting along the ceiling, the wires that go to the screens over the ice.

He puts himself at my entrance, his fingers spreading my lips. He grunts again when he lines up, and his fingers on my throat tighten.

When he leans over me, blocking my view of the ceiling, I focus on the underside of the chairs. At my hand next to my face, which doesn't even twitch. My fingers aren't curled into a fist. They're limp.

Am I already dead?

He drags his mask along my jaw, and it may as well be a dagger flaying me open.

I sink down into myself, willing myself to make a quick retreat. To pull back the feeling between my legs, to ball my emotions up in a tight ball. I used to do this while afraid and alone, crying in the dead of night for my mother to return. When I knew that there was no way I could go to school with a puffy, tearstained face and bloodshot eyes.

He moves. Sinks a little into me. Just as he calls, "Where'd your fight go, doll?"

My concentration breaks, thrusting me right back into the present. My skin erupts in chills at the name. And the voice. And the fucking recognition.

Oliver.

His name releases some of the fear. I reach for his mask again, but his fingers tighten around my throat. I hadn't even realized he was still holding it. But with my breath cut off, my eyes go wide.

His cock withdraws, then slides back in.

The period blood makes it easier.

His dark chuckle rumbles through his chest, and his fingers tighten more. I forget reaching for the mask and grip his wrist with both hands.

He has his other braced on the floor next to my head. All leverage. He pulls out and slams into me. My groan is cut off at my throat. I'm desperate for air, but he seems content to fuck me like this. His hips move, slapping against mine with every quick punch.

The lack of air becomes too much.

My eyes roll back.

Immediately, his fingers loosen. I surge back into awareness, and he rolls his hips.

He made me think I was going to get raped.

I still can't look at the mask. I don't know where his attention is, but he makes little noises every time he slides into me.

His movements get jerkier the closer he gets to climax. He picks up speed and suddenly stops. His hips move slower, his body tensing.

After a long moment, he sits back on his heels. His hands go to his thighs, and the lack of touch allows me to breathe again.

I rise on my elbows and look at the damage to my leggings. There's no fucking way I'm walking out of here like this. The hole is the size of a fucking dinner plate, and my panties— without the tampon, there's nothing stopping the blood from spotting the thin strip of fabric. Soon enough, it'll soak through.

The roller coaster of emotions that I just went through fucks with my head. I drop back down and cover my face with my hands. I will the heels of my palms to catch the sudden flood of tears. *They don't.*

He's still wearing the mask, and I... I go back to that numb place.

He runs a finger from my entrance up to my clit.

I ignore it. *Him.* My voice is still absent. I don't trust myself to speak, because I'm barely holding on as it is. I can't tell him to stop with my words.

Aren't my actions enough?

The way he's kneeling, my legs are still pinned open. The breath I draw in is shaky, as is the one I blow out. Everything inside me is quaking, my axis shifting and trying to orient with a new truth.

Not Bear.

Oliver.

He dips his fingers in me and then goes back to my clit, over and over until he finally stays where I would need it. If I was going to come, which I'm not.

I'm not turned on, I'm not going to orgasm.

I can't even fucking *look* at him. Or anything. I won't remove my hands until it's safe, and there's no safety here.

The hardest pill to swallow is that it's my fault. I told Carter what had happened, yeah, but I also told him Oliver was to blame. Do *I* blame Oliver? To a degree. Do I think he told Andi to do it? Not so much. But Carter doesn't see shades of gray—he sees right and wrong.

And that was *wrong*.

He's still touching me.

It needs to stop.

I shift, trying to escape his fingers, but his other hand presses down on my abdomen. He doesn't let me escape until I'm squirming for another reason.

"Don't." I thought my voice had abandoned me for good, but it comes out as a rasp now. "Just stop…"

He doesn't.

Listening doesn't seem to be his fucking strong suit today.

He drags it out of me slowly, the pulse of pleasure ugly as it winds through me. My back arches, trying to escape his touch, but he keeps me still. A finger goes inside me, and my muscles clench at it.

Everything hurts. I let out a low whine through my teeth.

The orgasm finally releases me, and I sag to the floor. He inches backward.

I lower my hands from my face.

Oliver's mask is pushed up, revealing his face. His fucking blank expression. My anger is a simple flutter in my chest. I can't summon more than a whisper of it.

Disbelief, maybe.

Horror that he's so… he doesn't *care*.

When he shifts back farther, allowing me to close my legs, I lash out. My foot slams into his chest, knocking him away.

I scramble backward until I hit something else.

"Easy, princess." Hands catch me under my arms. Penn doesn't lift me or make me stand. It's more to steady me and stop my backward movement. "You got him."

Oliver coughs.

"Don't touch me." I slap at Penn until he lets go, and I stand on wobbling legs. I whip around to face him and pale.

He has a mask on top of his head, too, and reality clicks into place.

"You stopped me from leaving through the main doors," I accuse.

Betrayal.

I shove past him and rush up the stairs, saying a small prayer that this place is still empty. I get back to the section where I left my stuff. I shrug on my coat, which thankfully hits me at mid-thigh. Even though it covers me completely, I may as well be fucking naked from the waist down.

The drip of blood and cum out of me, smearing my upper thighs with every step, turns my stomach.

"I'm following you," Penn announces when I'm back in the public hallway.

I walk briskly back to the main entrances, and I barely spare him a glance. Or rather, a look of utter disgust. Stopping just shy of the glass doors, I wheel around and jab my finger at him. "If either of you shows your face at my apartment, I'm going to cut off your balls and feed them to stray cats."

"That's oddly specific."

I slam out the door without seeing another glimpse of Oliver.

Which is good, because I have a feeling he's going to be starring in my nightmares next.

thirty-eight
sydney

Carter is waiting for me on my couch, his brows pinched with concern.

He wasn't in on it.

He didn't partake in my trauma.

That's what makes him safe now. Not that he's really to blame, that his hotheadedness caused this. It's squarely on *my* shoulders, because I told him and didn't stop him from being an idiot.

Doesn't matter.

I kick off my shoes, barely hanging on to a blank face, but he understands something is wrong. He meets me halfway, opening his arms to me.

I fall into them, and the fucking dam breaks.

He eases me back to the couch, putting me on his lap before I can protest, and slowly unzips my coat. He doesn't attempt to shush me or get me to stop crying, even though I instantly buried my face in his neck.

I don't want to come out.

As soon as the coat is open, though, he freezes. "Please tell me this is your period and you didn't get fucking brutalized."

I lick my lips, tasting the salt from my tears. "I did, but it's also my period."

"Tell me," he demands.

He strokes my hair, and it makes me cry harder. Because it fucking reminds me of Penn, and right now he's no better than Oliver.

They were there.

"O-one of their t-teammates tried to rape me," I say in a rush. "They stopped it, but they were wearing masks. H-he was wearing a clown mask."

Carter's fingers tighten on me. "Keep going."

I sit up and sniff, shifting on his lap. "I need to change. I'm going to bleed—"

"Get comfortable," he says. "I don't give a shit about a little blood."

He grips my hips and adjusts me so I straddle him. Our faces are at an even height like this. His hands slide to my thighs, his palms sinking heat into my chilled skin through the thin leggings.

"Oliver told me to stay and watch their practice, then wait for them. He..." My gaze drops to Carter's chest. "He came after me wearing that same mask, pretty much dressed exactly as..."

"The teammate." His jaw tics.

"I ran for my life," I whisper. "I tried to escape and then I tried to fight, and neither were good enough."

If you asked me six months ago how well I'd fair against an attacker, I would've said something like, *I'm quick, so probably decently*. Now, my opinion has changed. I'm fucking easy prey, no good at saving myself whatsoever.

I'm the girl who goes into the basement when she hears a creepy noise in the middle of the night.

I'm the girl who runs upstairs when there's an intruder in the house instead of going *out*.

I'm the one who tries to outrun the train instead of moving aside.

The first one to die in a horror movie.

Stupid.

Fucking.

Idiot.

"I'll teach you," Carter promises. "Okay?"

He wipes away my tears. Uses his sleeve to dab under my nose. Truly heroic behavior. If I didn't know how dark he runs under the surface, I'd call him a white knight.

He clears his throat, then slowly reaches between my legs. I don't stop him, but my chin wobbles when he runs his finger down and back up, coming away with Oliver's cum and streaks of dark blood. It looks... erotic. And a little horrifying.

"He fucked you," Carter says.

"He had me pinned. He told me who he was, but he didn't take off the mask."

His eyes darken—his pupils dilate. He drags me closer and leans in, planting a kiss on my throat. Right at the center, over my windpipe.

"You're going to bruise there," he says softly. His tongue flicks out, tasting my skin.

I lift my chin.

"Let me erase the memory of what he did to you."

I huff. "How?"

"How, indeed..."

He puts me on my feet in front of him and drags my destroyed leggings and panties down. He helps me kick them off, then pushes my coat off my arms. It falls to the floor behind me. My shirt is next, and I strip out of it on my own.

"I'm on my period."

His blue eyes meet mine, searching for what I'm not saying. When he finds whatever he's looking for, he smiles. "I like a little blood, dream girl, remember? I don't care if it's fucked up, I just want to erase what they did to you."

I need that, too. It doesn't matter that it might be considered wrong. I need to feel something other than the skin-crawling sensations Oliver left me with.

He motions for me to turn around. The couch creaks slightly with his movement, and something wet touches my ass cheek.

His tongue. He runs his fingers along the scabbing letters. They're still covered in a smattering of healing bruises.

"Hands on the coffee table."

I bend over, my nerves taking over. He nudges my legs wider and pulls at my hips. I open my mouth to question him when his mouth lands on my pussy.

"Oh, shit," I groan. "You shouldn't—"

He laps at my clit just enough to tease me, then moves to my entrance. His tongue plunges into me, and I almost jump forward. This is so twisted, but his hands on my hips keep me against him. He groans, too. His teeth nip at my flesh, followed by his tongue. He goes back to my clit, playing with it. Flicking the tip of his tongue. He pushes two fingers into me.

"Fuck."

He pulls away slightly, kissing the crease where my ass and thigh meet.

"All gone." He smacks my ass. "Now come sit on my cock."

I rise, glancing back at him. He runs his thumb across his lower lip, catching a spot of blood there, and then he reaches up and undoes my bra with nimble fingers. I let the straps fall down my arms and turn back around. His jeans are open, his cock hard against his stomach. After a moment, he shifts and slides them completely down.

He smirks when I straddle him again. I fist his cock between us, stroking slowly. Around and up, twisting and squeezing. He leans in and sucks my nipple into his mouth. The one that Oliver bruised. He leaves his own mark on me, while his fingers wander up my back, to the top of my spine.

Something slips down my chest, between my breasts.

The necklace.

I touch my throat with my free hand, trying to catch it, but he's faster. He tosses it onto the coffee table and meets my eyes with a smug look of his own.

"You're mine. No doubt about it, babe."

His hand covers mine, slowing my strokes. I rise on my knees, and he helps line himself up. When I drop, I keep my attention on his eyes. My lips part at the stretch, the way it feels good and sore at the same time.

"Does this do it for you?" I say, stilling when he's fully seated inside me. "If there's no adrenaline?"

He chuckles. His response is to grab my face with both hands, slamming his lips to mine. His hips move under me, and the micromovements almost undo me. I hold on to both wrists, willing him to keep his hands on my face.

It's grounding.

I was sinking in the arena, I'm spiraling now.

Carter catches me.

He pulls away just enough to speak. "Just because I sometimes need that doesn't mean I don't also enjoy this."

I lick my lips. "But the knife?"

"Pocket."

I release one wrist and drop my hand to the waistband of his jeans, following a wandering path until I find it. It's a silver folded knife. He takes it from me and opens it, then offers me the handle.

I take it. The weight of it... I think if Carter cut all the clothes from my body, I'd be more than turned on for every cut.

But Oliver took the excitement out, leaving only fear. Even if he was turned on by it, I wasn't. My body was not on board. Even realizing it was him. Even though he made me come.

That's confusing, too.

I press my thumb to the point. It cuts immediately, sinking into the pad without resistance. A drop of blood wells up, and I bring it to my mouth. There's something in his eyes, though...

Instead of sucking the blood away, I smear it across my lower lip.

"Oh, fuck, baby." Carter's hips flex again. "More."

More blood wells up on my thumb, and I lean back slowly. I drag my thumb from my the hollow of my throat down the center of my chest. Between my breasts.

He holds out his hand. I offer him the knife. He takes it carefully.

"You trust me," he says.

I nod.

His free hand presses to my back between my shoulder blades, holding me steady. He drags the tip of the knife, light as a feather, from the hollow of my throat down between my breasts.

"Don't move," he warns. "Don't even breathe."

My lungs lock up on command. He traces an invisible pattern around my breast, spiraling toward my nipple.

Every scrape of the tip, every almost-cut, puts me on edge. Not fear, exactly, but something similar. I don't know what it is.

I almost don't notice the way his hand shifts. The blade bites my skin, but it's so sharp the pain doesn't register until two seconds later, when the blood beads up in its path.

He leans forward and kisses the cut on top of my breast. Kisses it and then sinks his teeth into it until I groan.

He gets harder. If that's even fucking possible. He thickens inside me, and my head falls back.

"Vampire," I tease.

"I need you to move," he orders. "Ride me, dream girl."

I like it when he calls me that. I like when he bosses me around.

He mauls my breasts and keeps me pressed to him while I take what I need. My hand goes between my legs, and I rub myself to an orgasm that *I* control. This is all me, even as my breathing gets shallower and a ball of pleasure pulses in my core.

I shudder. "I'm going to come."

He lifts his head and watches my face. I keep going, my tits bouncing now that he's not attached to them. I rub my clit harder, and I cry out sharply. He lets out a low breath, too, and nudges my fingers away.

He takes over stroking me, urging me to keep moving. My muscles tremble, and I lift off him. He growls at the loss of contact—the loss of *me*—but I slide to my knees between his legs and take him in my mouth. I taste myself on him, and I smear my palm across the droplets of blood on my chest. I wrap that hand around the base of his shaft, letting him see the glint of blood mixing with my saliva.

His fingers thread in my hair. I don't think about my blood mixed with arousal. I try not to think about anything except making him feel good.

I bob faster, urging him deeper. My gag reflex kicks in, but I keep pushing.

He helps me. His hips thrust, and he leans back and watches me through lidded eyes. The blood tastes coppery, but mixed with *him*, it's right. I suck hard, my cheeks hollowing, and his dick twitches.

"That," he mutters. "Do that."

I do. I take him deep and suck hard as I come up, stealing a sip of oxygen through my nose. Then down. I lap my tongue at the underside of his head until he hisses. With my other hand, I cup his balls, lightly stroking between the two sacs.

"I'm close," he warns.

Good.

I keep taking him, forcing him deeper. The ring of muscles at the top of my throat constrict around his head, and I gag.

That does it.

His balls seem to lift, and suddenly his cum fills my mouth.

I swallow around his head, then pull back. His last spurts coat my tongue.

I climb up him and kiss him hard. He doesn't fucking object when my lips part. He opens for me, and my tongue slips into his mouth. Mine tangles with his for a moment, the taste between our mouths rich and distinct.

Not bad, just... different?

When we break apart, I push off of him. Suddenly embarrassed at how forward I was. He's still fully clothed, only his jeans and boxers around his thighs, and I'm... *so naked it stings*.

"Don't retreat," he says softly. "Don't hide after I hurt you."

I tip my head toward the bathroom. "Clean me up then, dream boy."

He grins and bounds after me.

thirty-nine
penn

We fucked up.

I know it as soon as Sydney rights herself and hurries out the door, a haunted look in her eyes. We had a fragile amount of trust, and Oliver single-handedly shattered it.

No. I can't blame just him.

It was pure terror in her eyes when she crashed into me, trying to escape, and instead of letting her breeze past, I stopped her. Turned her around in Oliver's direction, put her on a path that messed with her in ways I don't think I can fully fathom.

I hate that even now, hours later.

My roommate—a football player who I roomed with freshman year—is out. I'm on the couch, trying to shake the unnerved feeling of what we did this afternoon. We had a game and lost spectacularly. I have a bruise on my forearm from taking a direct hit. The angle was all wrong and came in just over the top of my glove.

Fucking stupid. My fingers went numb for a good few minutes, although it was shortly after that incident that Coach pulled me. I haven't been able to look Oliver in the eye either.

He went to fight, as is typical after a hometown loss.

I came back here.

A bang on my door rouses me from my sulking. Whoever it is doesn't give me a chance to get to the door, though. It swings inward, and suddenly Carter Masters fills the hall.

I glare at him. "Get out of my house."

He laughs. "That's the game you want to play right now?"

Well... "I don't know," I answer. "Want a drink?"

He shrugs.

I pivot and head to the kitchen. He trails after me, only pausing to kick off his shoes. At least he's got that going for him. The galley kitchen doesn't really fit two full-grown men in it, so he leans on the doorjamb and crosses his arms.

I busy myself digging in the fridge, pulling out two beers. He takes one. I take the other. We stare at each other a beat, and then he holds out his hand.

"What's that?"

When I don't make a move, he throws it at me. A quick jerk of his arm, his fingers uncurling to release the object.

It hits me in the chest, and I barely catch it.

The necklace.

Heat crawls up the back of my neck, attacking my ears. "You saw her?"

"Saw her?" Carter repeats. "I fucking tried to put her back together after what you did to her."

I grit my teeth. "Yeah."

"Yeah?" He steps into my space and shoves me with one hand. "*Yeah?*"

I go backward. I'm sure as fuck not going to protest or object to this treatment. I deserve it. I know that—and he does, too.

"I'd say sorry, but I don't owe you that." I grimace. "Is she okay?"

Carter lifts his chin. "No."

I nod. "I should go to her—"

"You think that's smart?" He rolls his eyes. "Give me *one*

reason not to beat you black and blue and drag you to her apartment."

I straighten. "That's not a bad idea."

Carter snorts. "Fuck off. You're not getting any extra, undeserved sympathy from her."

Fair.

"Okay," I say slowly. "Then I'm going to hear her out. She should be listened to. I already fucked that up."

"I'm going to be waiting outside the apartment," Carter warns. "And if she so much as yelps, I'll come in and make good on my threat."

I extend my hand. "Fine."

He points to the necklace dangling from my fingers. "And you don't give that back to her. Not now."

My stomach flips. He thinks I shouldn't give it back to her? I was planning on connecting it around her throat without giving her a choice... but that seems to be my problem. Oliver's, too. We didn't give her an option.

I roughly nod, then push past him. I leave the necklace in my room and meet him at the front door.

"Should we talk about Oliver?" he asks.

I sigh. "One thing at a time."

First, I've got to beg for forgiveness.

forty
sydney

My window slides open.

I lie still and keep my breathing regular, but on the inside I'm fuming.

Carter and I conveniently missed the hockey game. FSU, much to our surprise, lost. Dylan texted me about it. Apparently the volleyball team all went as a bonding trip. But she said that Oliver wasn't on his game, and Penn let in too many pucks. He was swapped out for the other goalie halfway through the second period.

He didn't want to leave me. Carter, that is. But at the notification of the loss, a new fear kicked up that they'd be stupid enough to go to the warehouse and fight again.

We watched a movie and fooled around, and then he presented me with a gift. Something he'd had for a while but wasn't sure how open I'd be.

A knife of my own.

It's a slim folding knife, half the size of his.

He spent time showing me how to open it one-handed, which is a useful skill for a variety of reasons. And then he showed me—in great detail—everywhere I could keep it.

Please note: ass is definitely not one of those places.

All other holes are fair game, as long as there's no stripping, squatting, and coughing involved.

The handle is baby blue, the blade is extra sharp. He stopped me from pricking my finger on it, insisting that the first blood draw should be someone other than its owner.

I didn't want to cut him, though.

The person sneaking into my room, I'm assuming Penn, toes off their shoes and shuts the window again. He creeps forward and stands over me. Waiting.

I'm a great faker. I hope.

Eventually, he moves again. He slowly peels the blanket down, off me entirely, and rolls me over with gentle pressure on my hip bone. It's either roll onto my back or resist him, and I can't give up the ruse. Not when the folded knife is tucked in my palm, my fingers curled over to conceal it. It's in position to flip open with my thumb.

My head lolls to the side, and he exhales.

Oops. Pretty sure Carter left a mark there earlier.

"Sydney," Penn whispers.

When I don't respond, he nudges my legs apart and climbs over me. To give him credit, the bed barely tilts. I'm not sure how he has the ninja abilities of a freaking cat.

Must be that same skill that helps him excel in the crease.

Anyway.

He's hovering over me, his tops of his thighs brushing the insides of mine.

Naked, then.

The worst part is keeping my eyes closed and my body relaxed, because I really just want to fucking stab him. Not *really*, but... you know.

He pushes my shirt up.

Goosebumps cover my skin, the room chilled from the brief time the window was open. My nipples tighten, but he doesn't go far enough to expose the cut.

He shifts my panties aside. It seems he still doesn't give a shit about my period, although he makes no move to pull out my tampon.

There's one more thing Carter taught me.

He made me practice it on him until I could do it smoothly. And while he allowed that if he's expecting it, he can resist the motion, I will hopefully take Penn by surprise.

I recall exactly how Carter positioned my hands, the way I need to thrust up with my hips and drag my leg to knock him off-balance. I mentally arrange my limbs, plan out exactly where everything needs to be placed.

One-two-three-GO.

I grab Penn in a flurry of motion and manage to roll us— right off the bed. My surprise is only overshadowed by his.

We land hard on our sides, and I keep the momentum going. He lands on his back, and before he can twist us again, I flip the knife open and press it to his throat. Just under his chin. The bob of his Adam's apple as he swallows forces his skin into the blade.

It cuts him. A drop of blood rolls down.

"Stop moving," I snap. "I told you I'd cut your balls off if I saw you tonight."

He just looks at me. And looks and looks and *looks.*

"Say something."

"I'm waiting for you to make good on that." He leans up, and the blade sinks into his skin more. He lets out a hiss of pain, but he doesn't back away. "Hmm, princess? A little lower, though."

"You deserve this." I push up off his chest and stride to the door, slamming my hand on the light switch. The overhead light flickers on with blinding power.

He just lies there, although he pushes himself up on his elbows.

"You were just about to fuck me while I slept." I flex my grip on the knife. "After what I just went through? Really?"

He rolls his eyes. "You don't sleep with your mouth shut."

Oh, what the fuck?

I glare at him. Belatedly, I notice his boxer briefs.

Asshole took off his jeans but not his underwear?

"You're cute when you pretend, though. And that was a cool move." His gaze, practically upside down now with where I'm standing, slides to my hand. "And knife."

"Carter," I say.

He makes a noncommittal noise. Sometimes he seems cool with the guy, other times, not so much. And Oliver is definitely *not* okay with Carter.

Nope. It's too weird of an hour for this. What I need is liquid courage. Tequila or vodka. But as a twenty-year-old with no connections, I've got... instant coffee.

I yank on sweatpants, slipping the blade into my pocket. I hit all the lights in the apartment on the way into the kitchen. There's a modicum of comfort that comes with banishing the shadows.

He stalks after me, but he's not as up in my business as usual. I put the kitchen counter between us and click on the coffee machine.

He sits.

I stay standing.

"You understand why I'm pissed at you?" I question. "You *saw* what was happening to me. I had bruises around my fucking neck."

"We give you bruises," he reasons.

"I like *those*," I hiss. "What I don't like is thinking I'm about to be raped by some stranger. I know you. On some level, I fucking trusted you. What I don't trust right now is that you or Oliver have my best interests at heart."

His gaze drops to the counter.

"What hurts the most is that you knew. You held me right after Bear... Hell, you tried to put me back together. And you still watched Oliver bring it all back up to the surface." I focus

302

on the coffee, putting things in a clinical order in my head. Mug, coffee pod, water. Press the button.

"Sydney…"

"I can't do any excuses tonight. I just want you to know that for however long that took, I was living in a very real nightmare. And it didn't stop when Oliver made it clear it was him behind the mask. I still had to look at it. How fucking confusing to see the mask worn by my attacker and—"

I cut myself off.

I don't know what Oliver is. I don't have a fancy label for him. For once, I don't even have the right words to describe how I feel about him.

He hurts like a bruise I can't stop touching.

Penn's gaze lifts. The coffee is done, and I busy myself with sugar and cream. I mix it and hop up onto the counter. There's a good distance between us—the kitchen plus the island. Eight feet? But the way he looks at me…

He may as well be right in front of me, his breath on my lips.

"You're absolutely right," he says. "You're right. Of course you are. Now that you say it—" He hops off the stool and paces along the island's length. "He pulled out the masks, and I fucking went along with it. I stood in front of that door and I thought your panic was all part of the game."

"It wasn't a game." I glance away. "Chasing me is one thing. Capturing me and… cutting off my leggings, *whatever*, is fine. Making me believe the person who might actually kill me has me pinned down is another."

"I'm sorry," he whispers.

The lock in my door slides back, drawing both of our attention.

Carter comes in, already tucking his stolen key back in his pocket. His gaze goes to me, and his brows lower. "You good?"

I jerk my head in some semblance of a nod.

Carter closes the door and makes a beeline for me. He

seems content to ignore Penn until he gets to my side, leaning against the counter with his hip touching my thigh.

"Oh, you got him." He smirks and touches his throat. "You've got a little blood just here."

Penn grunts.

"He didn't think I was asleep." I sigh. "But the rest worked."

Carter glances at me. "Was your mouth open?"

I scowl.

Penn cracks a smile.

"So what are we going to do about Oliver?" Carter asks.

Penn's smile slips away as easily as it appeared. "What are we going to *do* about him?"

"Oh, I'm sorry." Carter pushes off the counter and strides around the island. "We talked about this."

My brows furrow.

"I—"

"You didn't," Carter repeats. "After all the shit she's endured in the past six months? You think terrifying her is *worth it*?"

"Carter—"

"You're worth fucking more than that, dream girl." His gaze cuts to mine, flashing from angry to soft. "You hear me?"

I hear him, I just don't necessarily believe him.

He faces Penn again. "If he's going to go to extremes to traumatize her for his own pleasure, I won't have it. And you shouldn't either."

I miss Carter's expression, but Penn winces.

I can't do this.

The *last* person I want to think about is Oliver Ruiz. The last *thing* I want to think about is how he deserves some sort of punishment for tormenting me. Penn has tormented me, too, hasn't he?

They're both complicit, and I am *tired*. I'm so fucking tired of this. Every muscle hurts, reliving that fight. The fear that held my body hostage. I ache, and my head pounds, and I don't want to scheme anymore.

"Both of you just... get out."

I set the mug down and head for my bedroom. They can let themselves out, but they won't let themselves in here.

I grab my desk chair—it doesn't have wheels, which is usually a pain but now convenient—and shove it under the handle of the door. I lock all my windows, fix my blankets. I long for the sort of oblivion that will ease the stabbing pain behind my eyes.

My chest is heaving by the time I crawl into bed, dragging the covers over my head.

Sleep doesn't come for a long time, yet. But when it claims me, I go with all my lights blazing.

forty-one
sydney

The landlord comes by with the maintenance man and changes my locks on Monday. He also brings me a stick to fit in the window with the fire escape, which is meant to stop it from being opened.

Kind of him.

He doesn't mention that I'm still in my pajamas, thick sweatpants, fuzzy socks and an oversized hoodie. Not Penn's, but one that Carter must've left at some point. It smells like him, and I can't help but occasionally draw up the collar over my nose and inhale deeply.

After the landlord and maintenance guy leaves, I crawl into bed. I'm not interested in television, but I put a podcast on my phone and let it play from my nightstand.

Sleep seems easier than existing, so that's what I do.

The only time I leave my bedroom is to go to the bathroom or refill my water bottle.

My appetite is nonexistent. Monday slips into Tuesday, which in turn seems to melt into Wednesday.

I don't feel bad.

I'm not worried about the missing days.

I just... don't really care.

forty-two
sydney

I ignore my phone and lie in bed, alternating between sleep and half-fevered reality. I scribble in my journal when I'm able, when I need to get thoughts out of my head. The hurried words all blend together, and I'm not sure if I'm actually *writing* or just letting words bleed onto the page.

At some point, I move from my bed to the floor. I consider inching *under* the bed.

I flick the knife Carter gave me open and closed. I press the tip into my finger, then the underside of my wrist. I almost always wear a watch there... it's nothing to drag the blade down and slice into my skin.

The pain is refreshing. With it comes feeling in my limbs, a spark of electricity that seems to wake me up.

But only for a moment.

I slip out to the bathroom and run my wrist under the water. My eyelids are heavy. It takes effort to keep them open and watch the pink swirl down the drain. A Band-Aid and my watch in place, I drift back into my bedroom.

My phone sits facedown on my desk. It died yesterday, I think. It went quiet in the middle of a podcast about farming. I had to turn it upside down to hide how much it was lighting up. Notifications, maybe tags from that stupid gossip page. Texts from my friends, from Penn and Carter.

I don't know if Oliver texted or called, but thinking about him makes the numbness return. It's a blanket I draw around my shoulders to protect myself. It tightens around my limbs, slips up my spine.

That's okay.

I crawl to my nest of blankets on the floor and curl into a ball, and I will everything away.

forty-three
penn

When I can't get Sydney's window open, I call for backup.

Carter arrives in short order, meeting me outside the tall brownstone with keys in hand. He scowls at me, but I ignore it and motion for him to take the lead. Up three flights of stairs, with me breathing down his back, until we get to her door.

"You couldn't get her window open?" he asks in a tone that says, *Are you new?*

I sigh. "No, it's blocked."

"Blocked, how?" He sticks the key in the lock, but it doesn't turn. "Huh."

I raise my eyebrows. "You can't get her door open?" I mock his tone.

He rolls his eyes. "It's just stuck."

"Uh-huh."

He tries again, then goes to his knee and fiddles with it at eye level. I put my hands on my hips and wait him out, although he sure seems to be taking his time for someone who should know what they're doing.

But underneath it is the horrible feeling that something's going wrong. That Sydney is barricading herself in there to do something drastic.

"This isn't good," I say to him. "She changed her locks? Made it so I couldn't get in through the window?"

I reach around him and knock.

Carter shoves my arm away. "It's midnight, you asshole."

"And what if she's suffering?" I counter.

My mind goes straight to a friend in high school who was secretly dealing with too much. How many messages have I left Sydney? How many did I leave that friend—only for their parents to find them with slit wrists in the bathtub?

"She probably wants some distance from you," Carter reasons. "But we'll call her dad in the morning, okay?"

Coach would know what to do. He's helped us out of jams—of the emotional or mental distress variety, in some cases—and we've all come out better on the other side.

Plus, this is his daughter.

I finally nod, accepting Carter's proposition. Because it's either that or break down her door, and he's right. We can't violate her space—or her trust—any further.

Carter eyes me on the way out. "How's Ruiz behaving?"

I grunt. "Like an idiot."

"How's that?"

"He doesn't yet realize how traumatic that day was for her. I smashed my mask to shit, but I think he held on to his."

"Fucker."

We reach the street.

I glance across, toward the brownstone I pegged as one he'd choose to stay in to spy on her. "You actually living there, or are you paying rent in two places for the hell of it?"

He snorts. "My other place has roommates. I stay with them when I have to, but otherwise I try to be here."

"You could've just said yes to having two freaking apartments," I mutter. "Mr. Moneybags."

"First of all, the one with roommates? My parents pay for that. Part of our agreement that I go to college before I go out for the NHL draft. So..." He shrugs. "They don't technically know about the second one. I paid for the semester in cash."

Jesus.

It's not like we're poor... I just don't think I'd ever be so frivolous.

"Well?" I raise my eyebrows. "Do you keep it stocked with beer?"

He pauses, then grins. "Obviously. Come on."

Maybe we can test out some of his spying equipment while we're at it. And then, when the sun rises, we'll call Sydney's dad.

forty-four
sydney

Banging wakes me up.

I lift my head, sleep trying to drag me back down. The banging is distant. Disorienting. It doesn't stop, even when I smother my head under another pillow.

It just goes on and on and on, until I climb to my feet.

I creep toward my apartment door, check the peephole, and undo the lock. Pull it open. Come face-to-face with my father.

"Are you sick?" The worry in his voice is too much.

The emotion wells up in my throat, and before I can stop it, I start crying.

The first sob that wracks through me, surprisingly strong, unsteadies me.

He hugs me, then seems to just... take charge. I don't even need to tell him that I haven't been out of my room, haven't eaten anything of substance, haven't taken care of myself in days. He might know from the smell alone. Or the condition of my hair, slicked up in a bun on top of my head.

Once my tears abate, he urges me to the bathroom with an order to shower.

Going through the motions is exhausting. I sit after I wash my hair. I stay sitting for the conditioner, leaning forward and rinsing my hair upside down under the spray. And I consider staying there longer, but the water turns cold.

I wrap myself in a towel and sit on the floor instead.

There's a knock, and then the door cracks open.

When I don't say anything, it swings inward wide enough for Perri to stick her head in. She seems to consider something.

The door closes.

When she returns, she has clothes in her arms. She sets them aside and perches on the closed toilet lid. She picks up a lock of my wet hair and combs through it. Without saying anything, she first combs my whole head, squeezes out the excess water, then brushes through it again.

My eyes close sometime during it.

When the hair dryer starts, I flinch. Her cool fingers touch my bare shoulder for a second, as if to steady me, then she continues. She pats the clothes and moves the pile closer to me, and she leaves me alone again.

Slowly, I unfold. I touch my dry, warm, *clean* hair. I pull on the shirt, underwear, jeans. A sweatshirt over the top. Tall, thick socks. The bra she picked tends to itch at my spine, and I don't really care enough for one. That's the only thing I leave behind.

"There she is," Perri says.

I shuffle out into the open, curling my arms around my stomach. I clear my throat and will my voice to work.

"What day is it?" I ask.

Her expression stays smooth. "Thursday."

Oh.

I don't bother to tell her I thought it was Wednesday.

Somehow I lost a day?

"Do you..." Perri frowns. "You know what we need?"

I shake my head.

"Ice cream."

Oh.

"Yes?"

"Yeah," I whisper. "Where did Dad go?"

"He was taking out the trash. His stress response is to start cleaning. But we can intercept him on the way down." She pulls out boots for me and a coat. The coat I wore—

"Not that one," I croak.

She glances down at it, her brow furrowing. But she puts it away without question and finds another one from the closet. I shrug it on, followed by the boots. Everything still feels... rote. I'm doing this all through muscle memory, while my brain sluggishly tries to catch up.

We catch Dad on the second floor, and he smiles at me. Without complaint, he turns around, and we all go downstairs together. His truck is parked just a little ways down the street. I climb into the back, buckling in and drawing my legs up again.

The drive to the ice cream shop is short, and I hop out on Perri's side. I pat my pockets, suddenly realizing I don't have money, but she just loops her arm through mine and pulls me onto the sidewalk.

"Our treat," she says.

I stare at the menu for too long. I don't know what I order, if I even open my mouth or make a decision. It seems like I blink and I'm seated at a small table with a cup of mint ice cream in front of me. I take a bite, anticipating the burst of flavor.

It more tastes like ash than anything.

My stomach churns. Perri and Dad don't say anything about it. They're conversing about the upcoming storm that's supposed to dump a few inches of snow on Framingham. I file that away for later just in case.

I eat half of the cup, forcing down mouthfuls until I can't anymore, and slide the cup away.

"We can bring the rest back to your apartment," Dad says. "I'll get a lid."

We return to the apartment. I shuffle to the freezer and

put the cup inside. My apartment is clean. I didn't realize it before, but the counters are clear and wiped, there are no dishes in the sink. It smells vaguely of cleaning products.

"Thank you," I say.

"We're worried about you," Dad replies. "I think you should come with us this weekend."

"To...?"

"We're playing Michigan," he says. "Two games. One tomorrow, one Sunday."

There was a reason I couldn't go, but it has slipped away. All of it has. I nod because it's the answer he's looking for, and Perri squeezes my shoulders.

"We bought you a plane ticket," Perri admits. "I was hoping you would say yes and I got ahead of myself."

I force a smile. "Thank you."

"I'll pick you up at noon," she says. She kisses my cheek.

I hug Dad.

When they leave, I lock the door behind them and slink back to my room. My clean room. All the extra blankets from the floor are folded on my desk chair. The main one is on my bed, which has fresh sheets.

I pick up the knife from my dresser and sit on the edge of the bed.

My watch stayed on in the shower—thankfully water-proof—and it kept the Band-Aid underneath dry, too. Now, I push the watch band higher and peel off the bandage.

The one cut has multiplied.

I run my finger over them. They ache a little. Itch, too, as the original has scabbed over.

I'm going to Michigan with Dad, Perri, and the whole hockey team.

I missed a week of class.

I'm not just slowly losing my mind—I think I've actually lost it.

The knife balances on my knee. I flip it open, and the

anticipation is a heady rush. I can't afford to lose my mind. Not now. Not when tomorrow, I'll be thrown to the Vipers.

I drag the blade across my wrist and groan.

Why do I feel relief instead of pain? Why do I welcome the blood that doesn't just well up in beads but runs down the curve of my wrist?

I cup my hand under it before it can drip onto the rug and stain. I watch it, breathing in hard through my nose and out through my mouth. A cord loosens in my chest. The noose around my throat slackens.

This is like meditation, but I can't look away. I smear the blood toward my hand, examining the cut. It's a little deeper than the rest.

Maybe.

It could be worse.

If I wanted to kill myself, I would go up. I'd split the vein wide open and the flow would be unstoppable. Cut arteries bleed so much worse than the few veins I slashed.

This is pain management. As in, I'm managing with pain.

When the bite of the cut dims to a dull, pulsing ache, I clean it up. Replace the bandage, then my watch band. It hurts worse with both covering it.

But I can breathe.

I just have to keep breathing.

forty-five
sydney

I can't keep using my wrist.

Standing naked in front of my mirror, I silently contemplate my body.

I've lost weight.

A lot of weight. It's been a week? The cut from Carter on my breast is almost gone, just a few flakes of scabs that I pick at with my nail. The bruises have faded. The one from Bear on my neck is gone entirely.

I thought the physical remnant finally healing would make me feel better now that there's not a constant reminder of it. I couldn't have been more wrong. Now, it all sits inside my chest.

My bag is packed. I just need to pick out an outfit for the plane... preferably something I can just wear to the game. And maybe sleep in. If Dad and Perri hadn't already seen me in these sweatpants, I would keep them on.

I don't know if they have plans for Saturday, but I hope I can just hide in my room. I'll be under parental supervision, so it's not like I can do anything. I don't even want to do anything.

All this time, my phone has stayed off. I found it on the charger after my dad and Perri left, but I turned it off without unlocking it. The last thing I need is for all those negative messages to cut me open more.

Speaking of that...

I shift my weight. Considering.

It's wrong to self-harm. It's so fucking wrong, but I can't stop. I've become addicted to the release that comes along with it. Sometimes, I'm so out of it, I don't realize my mind is gone until I'm sitting in the tub dripping blood.

That alone should scare me, but it doesn't.

Once I'm dressed, I sit on the floor with a roll of paper towels beside me. I fold up the cuff of my leggings. I sit cross-legged and look at the inner ankle of my right leg. The skin is nearly translucent.

This is right.

The first prick of the blade is unexpectedly vivid. I bow forward, my face scrunched. I paint another stroke, slicing into my skin.

Earlier, I decided on three.

The third is the deepest and highest. It bleeds the most, and I unroll a handful of paper towels to put beneath my leg.

I can breathe again.

I'd hate myself if I didn't desperately need oxygen.

Eventually, I blot at the cuts and put a thicker bandage over them. I pull the cuff of my leggings down, then add socks.

Easy.

I leave the knife on my dresser and grab my bag. I force a smile a few times just to prove that I can, although none touch my eyes. I try one more time, my grin wide enough to split my face, then let out a sigh.

It doesn't matter, does it?

At noon, I meet Perri outside. I hoist my suitcase into her trunk, and we drive the twenty minutes to the airport. The rest is a blur: going through security, getting a coffee and water bottle—both for her, although she gets me one of each, too—

and finding our gate. We sit off to the side, facing the huge windows.

She reads on her phone while I watch the planes.

"Sydney?"

I glance at her.

"I'm not sure what triggered this," she says carefully. "But if you need to talk through anything, I'd gladly listen."

"Thanks."

That doesn't seem to appease her. She continues, "If I'm too close—or, I don't know, if being your stepmom makes things weird—then we can find a therapist."

I nod. "I... I don't know what I'd say."

She considers that. "Maybe it's not what you would say, but what they would ask."

"Oh." I hesitate.

Spilling secrets to a stranger is something my mother always warned against. But I'm pretty sure every negative thought about my dad and how he would act after he married Perri—a gold-digging whore, according to Mom—was wrong.

Which means maybe she was wrong against talking to someone about mental health.

Of course, she didn't call it that. She called them "issues" and expected people to be able to sort out their shit without help.

"Yeah," I finally say. "I'll try it."

She reaches over and gently squeezes my arm. "I'll find someone. And if they're not good, we'll try someone else. Until we meet someone you like."

That in and of itself sounds daunting, but I make a noise of assent anyway. I don't want to disappoint her so quickly after agreeing, although I can just picture my energy being sucked down out of my feet.

She glances at her phone. "Oh good, your father's here."

"What?"

"Your father," she repeats. "They just got through security."

No.

No, no, no.

My breath comes short and fast, and I bolt to my feet. Why did I think I could come with them and not see the team?

Why didn't I think of that?

The oxygen in the room is instantly sucked away. My heart leaps into a sprint, and my throat closes.

I slide from my seat to the floor. My name floats toward me, like someone's calling it. Calling me. But I can't quite hear through the rushing noise in my ears. I bury my face in my arms, tucking myself into as small a ball as possible.

I pinch the insides of my biceps as hard as I can, twisting the skin. I release and do it again and again, in rapid succession. I need it to filter out some of the noise, but the panic is nowhere near done with me.

Perri is talking. Not to me. Her words are directed overhead. "I don't know—"

"We can call paramedics," a stranger suggests.

My lungs scream for air. I barely resist the urge to claw at the rope tightening around my throat, instead pinching my arm again. I dig my nails in and finally get the right hit of pain.

Panic attack, my brain supplies. Not all panic attacks are created equal. This one has me up against a wall in my mind, flickering evil sensations at me. The rope. Hands. Blade. Choking.

Helplessness.

"You're okay," Perri soothes. She rubs my back. "They want to call the paramedics, but we just need to get you breathing. Can you look at me?"

I turn my head slightly. One eye takes her in.

"Like this, okay? Follow me." She exaggerates her breathing. A long inhale, an even longer exhale.

I watch her chest rising and falling and feel my lungs respond, subconsciously mimicking her. The rope around my throat loosens inch by inch, and I finally uncurl. I lean back against the seat and wipe my eyes, then the rest of my face.

"Something happened," she guesses. "With someone on the team?"

I hesitate, then nod.

"Who?"

My lips press together. That's one thing I can't admit to her. If she knows everything that happened with Penn and Oliver, Dad would punish them. Maybe even kick them off the team. And everyone would blame me.

I won't be a snitch again. *I can't.*

I don't think I could survive the school turning against me for a second time.

forty-six
sydney

I am more or less back to normal by the time Dad arrives at the gate. He's accompanied by some guys on the team, but neither Penn or Oliver are with him.

He kisses Perri, then hugs me and plants a kiss on the top of my head.

"Glad you two are with us," he says.

Perri gives him a look.

The *we need to talk* look.

My face heats. "I'm going to use the restroom."

I move away before either of them can stop me, weaving through the rows of seats. I think I spot some hockey players coming from my right, so I head in the opposite direction.

It takes some time to find a restroom. I lock myself in a stall and plant my foot on the edge of the seat, carefully peeling down my sock and up the legging. The bandage is next, although I'm more gentle with it. I have some extras in my suitcase, but none on me.

The three lines are still very new. The skin around them is bright and angry, and there's some dried blood smeared across them. They're not going to truly scab over for another day, maybe.

For a very brief moment, I let myself consider Oliver. The

322

fact that I'm going to see him today. I'm going to come face-to-face with him at least once this weekend—it now seems inevitable. I shudder, my stomach twisting. Before I can touch the cuts, my mouth waters.

It's the only warning my body usually gives before I vomit.

I take my foot down and fall forward over the toilet just in time to throw up. It's all yellow bile and water, and it burns in my mouth. I spit, then flush and put my foot up. Back to business, the only thing my mind can focus on. Because my body is clearly revolted at the thought of Oliver.

I dig my nail into the deeper one, nearly gagging again as pain flickers out from the spot. Unlike other pain, it doesn't travel up my leg. It's so localized, it's easy to focus on my ankle instead of my brain. I add another nail and press harder, imagining this pain as a river that sweeps him away.

After a long minute, I stop. My fingernails are coated in blood, and I close the bandage over the cuts. I put everything back to normal and use the toilet, wash my hands, and eye myself in the mirror. My hair is piled on top of my head, I'm not wearing a speck of makeup. My face is sickly pale, minus the dark half-moon circles under my eyes.

The selfish part of me wants to run away. Leave the airport, catch a taxi home, hole up again.

I leave the restroom, and of course I can't take the easy way out.

Penn waits for me. He's across the hallway, leaning against a pillar with his feet crossed. He wears a backward ball cap paired with his suit.

His gaze drinks me in, from my toes upward. It finally reaches my face. My eyes.

He winces. I understand that. I, too, have been perpetually disgusted with my image.

I head back to the gate. He follows like a shadow. He doesn't say anything—why would he? Shadows don't talk—

and keeps some space between us. But his attention sticks on me, and for the first time in a week, I'm too hot for my skin.

Penn is not the feature in my nightmares.

I make it to the gate without running into anyone else. Perri and Dad are in the same spot, but now they're surrounded by the FSU hockey team. I stop short, and Penn pauses beside me.

"Have you been checking your phone?" he asks in a low voice.

Don't look at him. Don't look at him. Don't—

My eyes automatically move sideways, taking in the sight of him without turning my head. I don't want to see the little details, like that he's freshly clean shaven, and his tie is the tiniest bit crooked.

"No." I jerk my head toward our crowd. "It's in my bag."

"I meant—"

"I know what you meant." I cross my arms over my stomach. "I'm well aware of your intentions."

Almost without meaning to, I pick Oliver out. He's slouched in a far seat, head down, scrolling on his phone.

"Does he know I'm here?"

"No."

"Really?"

"I saw the back of your head when we were coming up to the gate, but he's been—"

"I don't care how he's been," I interrupt.

He stays silent.

"If you care at all about me, you won't let him near me." I face him fully. "Don't make me beg, Penn."

Green eyes meet mine, and a sad smile curves his lips. His expression is so fucking apologetic. I graze the inside of my ankle with my opposite heel. If I was alone, my face would scrunch up. I'd let out a sharp exhale. But since he's here, I bottle that up and save it for later.

Not willing to see if he'll actually do it, I lift my chin and head back to my father and stepmom. I keep my expression so blank, I could be mistaken for an ice rink. They smile at me, and I drop into the seat between them.

"Sorry," I whisper to Perri.

She just shakes her head. "Are you feeling okay?"

"Better," I lie.

"Our flight is boarding soon," Dad says.

Penn takes a seat in the row of chairs facing us, diagonally to me. He's between where I think Oliver sits in relation to us.

Dad stands.

"Guys," he calls.

They all slowly stop what they're doing and focus on him.

"You know the rules. No drinking on the flight. We're going straight from the airport to the rink. Your bags will be transferred to the hotel. Any questions?"

No one speaks. Dad nods and grabs his bag just as the announcements for boarding start. Perri and I rise quickly and follow him, while the rest of the team trails.

At the gate, Dad steps aside. Perri and I are the first of our large group to get on, and I check my seat number. 9A, which is luckily a window seat. Although it's a fast flight, only an hour and a half, I'd like the option to curl up and sleep.

We get on the plane, and I balk. It's not that I don't like flying or am afraid of it... this is just a really small plane.

Two seats on either side of the aisle.

While I stop at row nine, though, Perri keeps going.

"Where are you sitting?" I ask her.

She turns and frowns, coming back to look at my ticket. "You're supposed to be with us in seventeen. I'm sorry, Sydney. I'm not sure how that happened. Sit there for now, and hopefully we can get someone to switch."

Great.

I take my seat and watch as the hockey players start to come down the aisle. They have to bend slightly so they don't knock their heads, which would be comical if I suddenly didn't feel like throwing up again.

The other goalie boards, quickly followed by Penn. He spots me immediately.

Oliver is next.

I sink lower.

The other goalie stops at my row, glancing from his ticket to the little placard above the seats. And he starts to unfold, but Penn's hand on his arm stops him.

"Switch with me," he says. He shoves his ticket at the other goalie and ushers him along, dropping into the seat beside me.

Oliver's gaze lifts, his brow furrowed.

Until he sees me.

He opens his mouth, but that's all I see. Penn is suddenly standing, facing Oliver. They have a silent conversation. Oliver flashes his ticket at Penn, just the flutter of paper makes me cringe.

He's sitting right behind me.

It's like he's breathing in my ear. As soon as he takes his seat, I can't lean back. I sit straight as an arrow, my shoulder against the curved wall of the plane.

"Switch with me," he says as soon as another player sits beside Oliver.

I nod. We swap, and he flips off Oliver through the space between the seats.

Great. Now he can see me.

I pull my hood up, buckle my seat belt, and slide lower.

"I hate seeing you like this," Penn whispers. "But I don't know how to fix it."

That's the problem, isn't it? Neither do I.

forty-seven
carter

PENN

She's with us.

ME

...where?

PENN

On the plane headed to Michigan.

She's terrified of him.

No fucking shit.

Any chance of you getting here?

Why, so I can watch him fuck up some more?

This is the first time he's seen her since then. He absolutely wasn't prepared for her to be so spooked.

I've been running defense for her, but I can only do so much if he's determined.

Is he?

Determined?

> I don't know. He said it was a form of punishment...

> He should know what it feels like.

> Being punished?

> Helplessness.

> Give Sydney back some control.

> I'll be there Saturday morning, but I can only stay twenty-four hours.

> Oh, and by the way...

> Prepare yourself before you see her.

I call Sydney, and it goes straight to voicemail. It's been going to fucking voicemail all week. After Penn called me about not being able to get into her apartment, and I tried my key...

We called her dad. We did the right thing. But she still hasn't been answering her phone or the times I've knocked on her door.

Not going to lie, I've been going out of my fucking mind.

And through it all, I've been showing up to hockey practice, learning new plays, studying up on the team we're facing this weekend. We've got a double header at home. The team is finally playing better six weeks into our season. There was a lot of fresh blood who had to learn the ropes, sure, but we were also all disconnected.

Cheating fractures you a bit.

> ME
>
> Where is her phone?

I call him. I don't know if he's with her, but after his last ominous message, it's not so much a *want* to talk to her as a fucking *need*.

"Hey," he answers. "I'm assuming you're not calling to hear my deep baritone."

I roll my eyes. "Just give her the phone, asshole."

He chuckles.

There's a slight intake of breath, and my heart goes into double-time.

"Hello?"

"Hey, dream girl," I say.

"You're calling Penn now?"

"I needed to hear your voice." I grip the phone tighter. "How are you holding up?"

She sighs. "I don't know. I'm going to their game tonight. We're in the hotel right now."

"Do you have your own room?"

"Yeah. It's on the same floor as Dad's. The players are down a floor, but Penn snuck up here."

She sounds raspy. Has she been screaming? Or not talking at all?

"You have a game tonight?" she asks.

"I do," I confirm. "Sunday, too, but they're both home games. Is there anything I can do from here? Besides tell you that I've missed having you in my arms every second of this week?"

If I could, I would get on a plane right this second. Obligation holds me back. I've got the C on my chest. That means something to my teammates. They look to me for leadership, and if I fail them...

"I wish you were here." She sighs.

"Can you do me a favor?"

She waits.

"Can you turn your phone on tonight? After the game, when you're back in your hotel room…" I pause. "I want to talk to you. But not with Walker staring at you."

She laughs, and I smile. I'm sitting in my car in front of the arena, and I have to go inside any minute. I'm a fucking idiot for her. If she wanted me to crawl to her…

"Penn wants to talk to you," she says, her soft voice caressing me through the phone. "Thanks for calling, Carter."

"I—"

"Hey," Penn interrupts. "It's me, so shut up." More muffled, he says, "I'll be right back, princess."

I wait, gaze on the doors I'll soon be going through. Doors I stormed through with Sydney, on my way to punch Oliver in the face. Teammates are arriving, everyone dressed in their game day attire.

It's my fucking fault he traumatized her. If I had held in my anger better, he wouldn't have retaliated against her. Not me. He didn't even so much as hit me, although from the look in his eye, I was absolutely expecting it.

Instead, he just sneered. Fucking asshole.

I adjust my collar in the mirror.

"Okay," he finally says. "I stepped out into the hall."

"Okay," I repeat. "And?"

"I don't think she's laughed since…" His end of his sentence hangs in the air.

Since *before*.

"Oh. I was just insulting you," I tell him.

He snorts. "Great. Let me know when you get here."

"About that." I hesitate. "I've got an idea that I don't think she'll go for."

"Something to do with punishment?"

I make a face. "Yeah. Punishment and helplessness."

When I lay out my idea, he makes a choking noise.

"Too much?"

"Maybe." He seems to be considering. "Bring the stuff. We'll let her decide."

"After, though."

"Yeah. Of course." He hangs up without saying goodbye. Or anything at all. One minute he's there, the next, the line goes dead.

But that's okay. I've got a course of action and a plan to go along with it. Time to shelve all those details and focus on the game.

Once that's done, I can get back to worrying about my girl.

forty-eight
sydney

I am in bed, awake for some reason, when he comes.

It starts with an easy knock. A one-two-three tap that has me setting my book aside and sitting up straighter. When I don't move, the knock comes again. Harder.

My throat tightens. I creep out of bed—as if the door is transparent—and inch toward it. The knocking stops, and I exhale. I look through the peephole, only to find Oliver standing right there.

I jump back, and he pounds on the door. The sound seems to vibrate in my chest. He can't get in, though. I have the safety lock on the door plus the deadbolt under the handle. I check again. He has a bottle of something in his hand. He drags his hand through his hair, leaning a forearm on the door.

"Open up..." he calls. He tries the handle. It jiggles but doesn't turn. "Come on, Sydney, open the door."

Abso-fucking-lutely not.

I rush back to my bag and search for my phone. I power it up, staring at the logo that glows on the dark screen. It takes precious seconds while Oliver's knocking gets more intense. Carter wanted me to turn it on for him, but I couldn't.

As soon as the home screen comes alive, I unlock it and dial Penn's number.

He answers on the first ring. "Sydney?"

"Oliver is outside my room," I say in a rush. "Trying to get in."

"Shit."

"He looks drunk, Penn." I pinch the bridge of my nose. "You have two minutes, and then I'm calling my father."

"Stay on the line with me. I'm on my way up from the lobby."

A door crashes on his side of the line. I stand in the doorway of the bathroom, just in case Oliver tries to... I don't know, use the peephole in reverse. If that's even a thing. So I stick to the shadows and clutch the phone to my ear, counting down the seconds.

"Almost there." Penn's voice has a slightly echoing quality to it. "I'm in the stairwell."

They won their game tonight. I went for the first period, but I couldn't stay. I couldn't keep watching Oliver on the ice —he made sure of that. I begged off. The arena and hotel are connected by a skywalk, so I didn't even have to go outside.

I got upstairs and ordered room service. Dad and Perri stopped by to check on me, both a bit worried but also, impossibly, willing to give me space. They filled me in on the game, then they bid me goodnight and retired to their room down the hall.

"Oliver." Penn's voice comes both from my phone and outside the door. "What are you doing, man?"

"She won't open the door." Another thump.

"Yeah, well, you should take a hint. She doesn't want to see you. She doesn't want you sitting behind her. She doesn't want you lurking and scaring her even more."

"I—"

"Shut the fuck up," Penn snaps. "What is this? No wonder you're up here. You get fucked on tequila."

Oliver mutters something I can't make out.

"Fuck off," Penn answers. "Let's go."

"No."

"No? Okay, fine. Sydney, you may as well call your dad now. Oliver will get kicked off the team for underage drinking, probably, and his career will be ruined. Which is not your fault but his, because he's the stupid bag of dicks who decided to drink tequila from the bottle."

I shake my head. I know neither of them can see me, and I... I should want to call my dad. But a part of me, deep down, knows that was a hollow threat.

"She's calling," he tells Oliver.

I look through the peephole just in time to see Oliver shove off the door. He staggers away under Penn's watchful gaze. Then, like Penn knows I'm at the door, he glances my way.

"Goodnight, princess."

The next knock comes way too early. I stumble out of bed and shove open the heavy drapes, shocked when sunlight streams in.

When no more angry knocks follow, I hurry back to the door. It had better be my father, because I've had enough adrenaline for one lifetime.

Instead, I find Carter and Penn.

I open the door without thinking.

Carter's smile falls.

I look down at myself, then back at him. Long-sleeve shirt, leggings. For once, I'm appropriately dressed to answer the door. Minus a bra, because no one in their right mind sleeps in those.

Penn prods him forward.

I step back to let them in, glancing quickly down the hall

for a second. There's no sign of Oliver. And no sign of my father either. So I close and latch the door, slowly facing them.

Carter holds up a white paper bag and cup of coffee. Penn holds the other two.

"Breakfast," Carter says. "Have you eaten?"

I lick my lips. "I, um, just woke up." I inch toward the bathroom. "Give me a second."

I brush my teeth and hair in record time. Check the bandages. I bled through the bandage and into my sock on the plane yesterday, but I don't think anyone noticed. No one said anything. But now I double-check everything is hidden before I step back out.

They gave me a room with two beds. Penn sits on the made-up one, his shoes off and feet up. Carter stands in the middle of the room, his hands in his pockets.

"Hi," he says. "Penn?"

"Yeah?"

Carter doesn't take his eyes off me, but his words are for Penn. "Get the fuck out for a minute."

I smile.

Penn grumbles and grabs my keycard. "Just in case you get carried away. And only because you smiled, princess." He kisses my cheek on the way past.

The door closes with a soft *snick* behind him, and Carter strolls toward me. Lazily, almost, but his gaze gets hotter by the second.

"You shut me out," he says.

"I shut everyone out."

"That's over."

"Maybe," I allow. I mean, I don't really know if it is or not. Is that up to me? Do I get to just decide to be in a funk or out of one?

Is this a funk? Or is it depression?

Or... something worse?

Shit. What if it's something worse?

335

What's worse than depression?

"Hey."

I blink up at him.

"I'm going to kiss you," he informs me.

I nod. He cups my jaw and leans down, slowly touching his lips to mine.

When he pulls away, I try to follow.

"More?"

"Please."

He tilts his head. "Did you kiss Penn? Last night?"

"No," I breathe.

I reach for him, suddenly anxious. If I stop being valuable —if I don't want to do the dark stuff he likes, for example— will he still want me? Or what if I can't leave my apartment for months? Or what if he goes somewhere and I become emotionally reliant on him and have a panic attack the second he's out of sight?

"Sydney."

I freeze. I've been trying to drag him closer. He hasn't budged, though. He just examines me with those ocean-blue eyes that see *everything*.

"When did I break?" I ask him. "God, I can't even kiss you without losing it."

"You're not losing it."

"I am," I assure him.

I release my hold on his jeans and step back. I bump into the wall and lean against it, closing my eyes. Normal seems very fucking far away from where I am.

"I'll tell you who I blame: the guy who tried to rape you."

I stare at him.

"And then Oliver."

When I cringe, he clicks his tongue.

"I'm going to make an observation," he says. "And you can tell me if I'm wrong."

"Okay..."

"You were grabbed by two masked men and thrown into a trunk. Driven to an unknown location. Promised pain and violence. You didn't know who they were when one put the rope around your neck and tried to rape you. You only knew it was Oliver and Penn who stopped it."

My throat closes.

He reaches for my hand, and I let him take it. But it's me who ends up clinging to his fingers.

"You were dealing with that, and then you saw him again. The same mask. It brought you back to that warehouse. You relived your first trauma as you experienced the second."

"Yeah," I agree. "But—"

"But then you found out who was actually touching you in the arena, and he didn't stop. No one was there to save you from him." His gaze darkens. "You inserted Oliver behind the mask for the previous event because it was him the second time. Someone you trusted for saving you became the villain, and your memory has blended the two."

My vision blurs. As soon as I blink, tears spill down my cheeks. I can't stop fucking crying, and I hate it with every fiber of my being.

"In my dreams, the clown-masked guy succeeds in raping me. And when he takes it off, right as I'm on the verge of passing out, it's Oliver." I dash at my cheeks. "I know it wasn't him the first time."

"You know it when logic is in control," he agrees. "But then your emotions take over. Similar emotions for both events, would you agree?"

"Yes."

He sits on the bed and pulls me down with him. My knees go on either side of his hips. I like being face-to-face with him like this. It puts us on an equal level in other ways. Mentally, maybe.

"So how do I fix it?"

He lifts one shoulder. "I don't know. But I do have an idea for helping you regain control. If you want it."

I suck in a long, slow breath. With Carter's hands on my waist, the cords that bind around my chest don't seem so tight. I lean forward and press my forehead to his, closing my eyes.

Do I want control?

Did I ever have it? I guess it doesn't matter, because my answer to the first question overrides everything else.

"I want it."

forty-nine
oliver

I am going fucking insane.

We win our first game on Friday night, no thanks to me. My head is all over the place. Drinking last night absolutely did not help, because I wake up with the biggest fucking headache.

Hangover, I mentally correct.

But the first thing I do when I wake up, aside from popping pain meds and draining a bottle of water, is check my phone for messages from Sydney. Our conversation thread is one-sided enough to make me sick.

From the past week:

ME

I went overboard.

Do you forgive me?

I was pissed. I want to talk about it... apologize to you.

Sydney.

Are you skipping class?

Penn won't fucking talk to me about you. Are you home?

> I buzzed the intercom a few times, but you didn't respond. Did you go to your dad's house?
>
> The mask was over the line. I know that.
>
> Fuck, Sydney, just TALK to me.

I swipe away and toss my phone. I'm disgusted with myself, and I have been disgusted, but seeing her reaction to me on the plane...

I may as well have been Bear and carrying a chainsaw. This wasn't fear like I'd ever seen it before—she had a biological response to the sight of me. Until Penn blocked her view of me anyway. Except when I sat down behind her, she got so rigid.

My big plan was to lean over the seat and apologize. My charm has carried me through a lot in life, but this is... not quite how I thought any of it would turn out. Even Penn is being shady.

Wait.

A vague memory comes back... I groan. Did I seriously go to her room last night? Pounded on the door? She must've called Penn, because he came to retrieve me. If I remember the look on his face correctly, I'm pretty sure I'm lucky he didn't deck me.

My phone buzzes. I reach for it, my hopes lifting when I see Sydney's name.

SYDNEY
> I'll talk to you.

I type a response and delete it. I try again, but it's not quite right. Gritting my teeth, I try a third time for something that's like, appreciative of her effort but also kind of nonchalant. Not overeager.

Nailed it.

SYDNEY

Tomorrow before the game. Hotel lobby.

I blow out a breath. What's she doing today that she can't talk to me now? Fuck it, if she's not going to meet me today, I need to burn off the hangover another way.

I change into gym clothes and head to the fitness room. I've got my phone in the cupholder, music blasting in my ears, while I do two miles on the treadmill. Weights next should get me sufficiently tired. I slip into the running mindset, my thoughts drifting.

Maybe that's why I don't notice the two guys until they're practically on top of me. They grab my arms and haul me backward off the treadmill. As soon as I lose my forward momentum, it spits my feet off.

Something pinches my arm, and they shove me to my knees. I surge right back up, breaking free of their hold and lunging at one. They're both wearing ski masks and sunglasses. I swing, but they dodge backward.

The room goes out of focus.

The other one hits me between the shoulder blades, and I stumble forward. I catch myself on an exercise machine, but one is immediately in front of me. I swing at him and miss.

Why am I missing?

"Stop moving," I spit. "Fight me like a..."

I shake my head abruptly.

A tap on my shoulder has me spinning around. The room spins with me. One becomes two. They simultaneously hold up a syringe.

I roar and charge, intending to just tackle one and start

hitting him. Except there's two, and I pick the wrong one. I'm shoved from behind, and I hit the wall hard.

Mirrored wall.

Two masked men grab my wrists and wrap tape around them. I swear and curse them out, both in English and Spanish. The words run together until even I don't understand what I'm saying.

They spin me around and put tape over my mouth. Exchanging a glance, one pulls something from his pocket. A dark canvas sack. He shakes it out and shoves it over my head, and my world goes dark. It tightens around my throat, and I jerk.

The tape on my wrists holds fast.

What the fuck is happening?

They each take an arm and haul me out of the fitness room. My phone is left behind, the treadmill still whirring in motion. The door closes. They drag me outside and toss me into something. I smack my head against the floor, and stars burst in front of my closed eyelids.

I can't feel my fingers.

Whatever they injected me with is making me loopy. I can't seem to grasp reality, never mind where we're going. All I know is the rumble of an engine under me.

I doze, but I don't fall asleep or pass out. I keep pinching the tops of my knuckles to bring myself back into awareness. Eventually, the vehicle stops. I'm dragged out. Into an elevator, maybe, which rises swiftly enough to make my stomach drop.

There might be two of them still, there might be more. Either way, I can't see out of the canvas at all. And the way it hugs my throat, I'm conscious of it every time I swallow.

Suddenly, fingers close around my nose.

I jerk against it, but the second person grips my head with both hands.

I fight in vain, but with my mouth taped, I can't do anything. I resist until my muscles tremble, but my lungs are screaming.

In the end, it's not really a choice.

I feel my body drop, and my mind follows a second later.

fifty
sydney

"Are you ready?" Penn practically bounces on his heels.

I let out a low sigh, but I nod. When Perri and Dad asked if I'd get lunch with them, both guys shooed me out the door. While hiding out of sight, of course. My father would probably murder both of them if he caught them in my room.

But Carter's insights were... helpful.

I understand what he said, but there was no way I'm facing that reality on my own. Although, hearing him speak it out loud, it's easier to accept it. My brain is confusing my consent with Oliver—and, admittedly, the time in the arena is sketchy at best—with my fear of Bear's rape, and also blending the two incidents. Where one was not successful and the other... happened.

I still don't know if I can call what Oliver did in the arena consensual or not. The mask and heightened emotions fucked everything up.

But Penn and Carter think there's a way to help me. And at this point, I'm willing to try whatever it takes. While they haven't laid out exactly what their plan is, I figure it has something to do with talking to Oliver.

That thought alone twists my stomach, but I'm trying to be strong.

"I'm ready," I confirm. "You're going with me...?"

"Yes," Carter says. He shoots Penn a look.

Penn shrugs.

We're standing outside Carter's hotel room. He got a room on a different floor but luckily managed to get the same hotel.

They both seem curious, which is not a great sign.

Carter pulls his key card out and swipes it. The door clicks as it unlocks, and I grip the handle. I'm not sure what awaits me, but I need to find out.

There's a short little hallway with a bathroom on the right, and it opens into a room with two double beds. It's pretty much a carbon copy of mine.

Except tied down to one of the beds is Oliver Ruiz.

I suck in a breath and stumble back. Carter is right there, catching me around the waist. He runs his nose up my neck behind my ear.

"He can't hear us," he whispers. "He can't see us. And he can't move."

I glance over my shoulder at them. "Did you... *kidnap* him? Or did he agree to this?"

Carter smirks, and my belly tightens.

"He doesn't know where he is," Penn says quietly. "He doesn't know who took him."

Carter directs my attention to the towel laid out on the desk. Well, not so much the towel as the supplies on it.

A ball gag, a dildo with straps coming off of it, a riding crop, lube, a small rubber ring.

"You don't expect me to use those..."

Carter shrugs. He goes through each one. The rubber ring is a cock ring, which will make an erection harder. It's tight, so it restricts blood flow.

I squirm.

He gets to the strap-on dildo and moves the lube next to it. *Pass.*

"Okay," I finally say on an exhale. "Got it. You two can go."

They exchange a look.

"Are you sure?" Penn asks.

I frown.

"Maybe we'll just wait over here... out of sight," Carter suggests. "We won't peek, but if you need us we'll literally be right here."

That actually doesn't sound like a bad idea. A thrill goes through me.

"Am I a bad person for wanting this?"

They both shake their heads. They both seem... excited? Nah. That's got to be my imagination.

Once they're out of sight, I shed my coat and toss it on the other bed. Neither have been slept in, although they didn't even give Oliver pillows. He lies spread-eagle on the stripped bed, naked except for his boxers. Each wrist and ankle are tied separately. There's a black fabric bag over his head, and a thick pair of headphones on his ears over it.

I pick up the riding crop, running my finger over the folded leather tip.

He's been completely still. I don't know if he knows what's coming, if he's put together this much, or if he's unconscious. Or maybe he doesn't know that anyone has joined him in the room, and he's still waiting.

I use the crop on his stomach.

His abdomen ripples, and his whole body reacts to the pain. He makes a muffled noise, somewhere between a curse and a groan.

I aim lower this time, just at the edge of his boxer's waistband. The smack is satisfying, but his reaction is better. I'm taken back to Penn and me in the woods, and my cheeks heat. I move up the bed and run the tip of the crop along his skin. From his abdomen up his chest, to his hidden throat. Over his mouth, nose, eyes, forehead, then back down to his shoulder. Along his arm, to the fingers that are curled into fists.

I set it aside and go back to the bathroom. Penn and Carter are leaning on opposite sides, but both straighten when I appear in the doorway.

"Do you have your knife?" I ask Carter.

He pulls it from his pocket without hesitation.

I return to Oliver and cut away his boxers. I nick the skin at his hip purposefully, wanting him to know exactly what's happening. He swears in Spanish, struggling worse against the ties.

He doesn't want to be taken by a stranger either.

But physiology is basic. As soon as the scraps of fabric are gone, I lean over and touch his flaccid dick. I stroke it with one finger, up and down like I'm tickling him. It twitches and lifts a little. I spit in my hand and wrap my fingers around it.

I jerk him to hardness, and then I roll the cock ring down his shaft. His hips buck. He growls at his own response, I think.

"It doesn't feel so good when someone knows how to turn you on, does it?"

My question is met with silence.

His cock is still twitching. The ring looks tight, but it seems to just be making things, well, more strained.

Before I toss the knife, I carve my initials into his hip. He swears again. I think.

With the knife safely on the other bed, I take a deep breath and pull off my leggings. I put my knee on the mattress and swing my other leg over his hips. I straddle him, his cock right in front of me, and settle on his thighs. Slowly, I lean forward. I grip the bottom of the hood and loosen the strap. I push the hem up to his nose and rip off the tape.

I want him to talk his way out of this.

The hood comes back down, and I cinch it tight enough

to dig lightly into his throat. He can still fucking breathe—that's the important part.

"Get the fuck off of me," he growls. He slips into Spanish. Then back to English. "You fucking psychopath. This is—"

I grip his cock, and his words die. I stroke him slowly, from the ring at his base to the tip and back. Precum leaks onto my fingers.

When I lean forward again, his dick is pressed between my abdomen and his.

I rip the headphones off, then resume stroking him.

As soon as I speak, he'll know it's me.

"Please don't," he finally breathes. "Don't touch me."

Something in me cracks open. I crawl up his chest and undo the hood, shoving it up past his eyes. Eyes that blink and squint, adjusting to the light, before coming to me.

He understands a little.

Not all of it. Not the nightmares that won't let me go.

"Sydney." His voice cracks. "Oh God, I'm so fucking sorry."

I slide down his body again. There's no foreplay—I notch him at my slit and push down, taking him inside me in one movement.

His arms yank on the restraints. His eyes burn into my body. I touch his chest, the red marks left by the crop, the six-pack of abs.

"I took it too far. I deserve this."

Yes, you do.

I lift off him then slowly lower, taking him deeper inside me. I remove my hands from his body and keep them on my thighs. I'm not here for him, to make him feel better.

This is for me.

So I take my pleasure from his body. I touch myself in front of him, cupping my breasts through my shirt and bra, pinching my nipples. I get myself off using him like a fuck toy. I rub my clit hard, using him to nudge my G-spot with every downward slam. When I come, my eyes flutter shut and my core tenses around him.

I groan. I try to enjoy it.

I haven't felt anything in just over a week.

"That was hot," Penn says.

I jump. Oliver glowers at him but otherwise remains silent. It's only when Carter comes down the hall that Oliver swears in Spanish again.

"Ball gag," I say.

He's still inside me. I don't really feel inclined to move. But Carter's expression lights up, and he retrieves it. He seems to take a little too much joy wrestling it into Oliver's mouth. He pinches his nose shut until Oliver can't take it anymore, and the hard rubber fits between his teeth. Carter straps it around his head and returns to me. He pulls me toward him and kisses me.

Hard.

I moan. My hips automatically move, and Oliver's cock slides against my sensitive flesh.

"I want your ass," Carter says in my ear.

My face heats. Only Oliver and L. have gone there.

I've been ignoring my mystery texter, too. I haven't cared enough to check my phone for any texts, let alone the *where are you*s and *are you okay*s that come from loved ones.

Penn moves to the other bed and sits toward the top, even with Oliver's head. "By all means," he says. "I want her pussy. I'll wait."

Oliver groans.

Carter has no fucking problem climbing on the bed behind us. He brushes my hair over my shoulder and kisses my neck.

A chill sweeps down my back, but I tip my head to give him more room. He leans me forward more, and the cold drip of lube slips between my ass cheeks. His finger chases it, circling my asshole. When he pushes the finger in, I groan.

Oliver's gaze is fastened to my face.

Carter finger-fucks me for a minute, then withdraws.

When his dick touches me, I automatically tense. I fold lower, putting my forearms on Oliver's chest. I splay my fingers out across his pecs.

When Carter pushes in, the fullness of *both* of them registers.

"Holy shit," I moan. It hurts until it doesn't, and Carter hasn't even started to thrust in earnest yet.

"Look at me," Penn suddenly orders. He has his cock out. He fists it slowly, the tip already red and oozing.

"Ready?" Carter asks me.

I nod.

He starts off slow. Every inch rattles me with pleasure, and he seems to sink deeper with each thrust. His hips finally slap my ass, my whole body jerking forward.

Oliver slides. He seems to have enough movement to thrust his hips, too, and I gasp.

"Oh, fuck," Carter groans. "He can't say it, so I will."

"Did you feel it, too?" Penn asks him.

"Yep." He leans over my shoulder. "Do it again, Ruiz."

If looks could kill—

He does it again.

My eyes roll back. I lose track of who's doing what, but the next thing I know, there are fingers on my clit and another tugging at my nipple through my sports bra, then slipping under it to get contact with my bare skin.

"Stay with us."

I sink down on Oliver. Dig my nails into his chest. The flutter is back—a good one this time that builds between my legs. The sensation of both of them, plus Carter's wandering hands, is overwhelming.

My body can't figure out what to focus on, so I end up watching Oliver.

His hazel eyes are so dark green, his pupils dilated. I reach for him. My fingers trail across the bands of the gag. He lifts his head a little, and I undo the buckle.

He turns his head and spits it out.

"Kiss me," he whispers. "Please."

I do. Hard. He strains against the binds, his muscles tensing under me. Our lips slide, parting and opening. I catch his lower lip between my teeth and bite.

He groans.

"This is fucking hot," Penn comments. "Hurry up, C."

Carter hurries. I taste blood on my tongue and release Oliver's lip. Carter's fingers force an orgasm from my body. I cry out at the sharp burst of pleasure. I clench around them and bow forward, burying my face in his chest.

Carter lets out a groan and stills suddenly. Oliver jacks his hips up again, and Carter hisses. After a long moment, he pulls out.

"Come here, princess." Penn's voice is dark.

I rise. Oliver's cock slides out of me, and I slip away from him. His eyes track me, although he doesn't protest. He's still hard, impressively so. The veins along his shaft stand out, the head a dark red.

But I move toward Penn anyway. He grabs me and flips me onto the mattress under him, sliding into me with ease. He kisses me softly, completely at odds with how hard he drives into me.

I wind my arms around his neck, keeping him pressed against my chest.

He drags his lips across my jaw.

"Not gonna last long," he says in my ear.

I wind my legs around him and pretend not to be broken. Pretend I didn't go radio silent for a week. Pretend I don't have a serious problem. Pretend, pretend, pretend.

He, too, spills inside me. I close my eyes as he kisses my neck, sucking and biting at a spot that's sure to be visible.

It doesn't matter.

Slowly, as if air is being released from a balloon, I drain out. I relax into the mattress until he lifts up and examines my face. He brushes my hair back, tucks it behind my ear. When he sits up, he takes me with him.

I swing my legs over and look at Oliver.

Carter half sits on the desk, fully dressed and watching me.

It takes too much effort to put my clothes back on. Leggings. Jacket. Shoes. The whole time, the room is silent.

And when I walk out, no one stops me.

fifty-one
sydney

Carter shows up at my room an hour later. He's in fresh clothes, his hair damp and finger-combed back. He inspects my space and drops onto the unused bed, watching me expectantly.

"What?"

"I'm hungry," he says. "So maybe we should go to dinner."

I sit on my bed and bring my legs up. The room service menu is within reach, so I grab it and toss it at him.

He catches it and puts it aside.

"I meant out," he clarifies.

"I'm tired." I was in bed when he knocked. I wasn't sleeping, but I was pretty close. Maybe lifeless is a better description. Eyes open but dead on the inside.

"Did you shower?"

I shrug. The real answer is no, but I don't want to admit that out loud. I'm gross. I just had sex with not one but three guys, technically. Two if we're only counting finishers.

"Okay." Carter stands. He takes my wrists and pulls me to my feet. Before I know it, he's got my shirt and sports bra off.

I cover my chest.

"Since when do you do that with me?"

I look away, but I don't drop my hands.

He pulls down my leggings and panties. He goes to his knee and helps get each foot out, and his fingers wrap around my calf.

My heart is sluggish, but it gives an extra-loud thud against my ribs.

"What's this?" He traces the bandage. "It's bleeding through it."

He rips it off without warning. Sudden fear ignites in my chest. My secret can't get out—it's the only thing keeping me sane. I step away from him fast, leaving him standing with the bandage in his hand. Even from this angle, this distance, the blood is obvious. A wide patch of it, dark brown and dried at the edges, bright red in the center.

"You want me to shower?" I snap. "Fine."

I scurry into the bathroom. I slam the door, but he catches it with his shoulder. He forces his way in, and the bathroom seems to shrink around us.

"Stop." He reaches for me. "Stop running from me."

There's nowhere else to go, so he gets his wish. He grips my hips and pivots us, putting my ass on the counter next to the sink. When I try to hop down, he raises his head and glares at me.

I freeze. All I can feel is my heart pounding through my whole body.

"Please, Sydney."

His attention returns to my leg. The cuts are more like gashes now, and one still seeps blood. He lifts my ankle and inspects them, running his finger just above the top one.

When his gaze hits mine, his expression is *devastated*.

"You did this to yourself?"

"I—" I stop myself and swallow. "Don't tell anyone."

He laughs, almost to himself, and turns away. He paces the bathroom, his hands going to his hair. He yanks at the strands, then leaves his hands on the back of his neck. When he faces me again, he has a new expression.

Determination.

"Where else?" he asks.

My mouth dries. "What?"

"Where else are there cuts?"

I must hold on to my secrets. I shake my head at him, saying nothing.

He pulls his phone and types, then shoves it back in his pocket. He doesn't reply, just seems to be waiting for something. I desperately want to curl in on myself, but I don't move.

His behavior sets my teeth on edge. The unpredictability of Carter Masters, a trait that was once alluring, now gives me pause.

Almost five minutes later, a knock comes. He goes and opens the door, and Penn walks in.

Oliver follows.

"No. No, no, no—"

"He's part of this," Carter says. "You fix it with him or not at all."

Carter grabs Oliver and drags him into the bathroom with me. I curl up, too aware of my nakedness. Their gazes both drop to the floor, and I peek over the edge, too.

Blood droplets.

I bury my face in my knees.

"I'm fine," I lie to them. "I'm so fine."

"You skipped all your classes this week," Penn says.

I hadn't realized he came in, too. Fingers touch my leg. Something cold covers the cuts.

"You and you—*talk*," Carter orders. "While Penn and I search every inch of this place for things she can hurt herself with."

I jerk my head up.

It's not Penn standing in front of me but Oliver. He doesn't meet my eyes, and the other two leave us alone.

"I went too far." His voice is dark and gritty, and it

scratches some part of my soul that I don't want to remember. "I knew I was crossing a line and I did it anyway."

"Why did you even have those masks?" The question slips out before I can stop it.

He wets a washcloth, coming closer and pressing it to my ankle.

"Before we grabbed you, Bear and I bought matching ones. But then I thought it might be better to be different—I don't know, it was fucking dumb. But we had both bought the same clown mask." His other hand touches my knee.

It's to steady my leg, I know, but a shiver rushes down my spine all the same. I just don't know if it's a good or bad one, and my brain is too muddled to figure it out.

"After the fight, one of the other guys brought Bear home. His mask was still in his car, so I took it." He frowns. "I should've just left it alone."

"Yeah."

"And then Carter punched me in the face and I saw *you*." His fingers draw a pattern on my knee. "I knew you told him something about us. Or me. Maybe even my family."

Well, I did.

"I deserved today," he says. "I deserved everything I got—every way you made me feel. I understand—"

"You understand only a fraction." I push him back and hop off the counter. "You do not know what it feels like to be a woman. You worry about stupid shit, while we always worry about rape. Always looking over our shoulders. Always afraid. I live in fear, Oliver. Every woman knows exactly how vulnerable we are. Throwing it in my face not once but twice..."

He runs his hands down his face. "*Puta madre*. You're right. How can I say sorry enough for you to believe me?" He steps away from me. "I'm going to walk out that door, and I swear, I'll never bother you again. And hopefully that can ease your conscience a little. Help you heal."

I follow him to the doorway of the bathroom, but he

keeps going. I don't know what to say, but I'm not sure I want him to go. Not after what happened in Carter's room. Not after that apology...

My mouth opens and closes, but no words come out.

He yanks open the door and strides into the hallway.

The door shuts behind him.

I move farther into the room, my emotions swinging wildly from fear to anguish. The dark of nothingness, of numbness, is so tempting. But when Penn cups my cheeks, lifting my head so I have to meet his gaze, I realize I don't want to go back there.

Not yet.

I grip his wrists, and tears flood my eyes. "Please don't leave me."

"Never," he promises.

"You mean that?" Carter asks from behind him. "That you're never going to leave her?"

Penn glances back. "I'm confident that after she's had her fill of you, she'll choose me."

Carter scoffs.

"Stop." I move around Penn, standing between them. "What if I can't choose?"

They pause.

"What if I can't? What if I want both of you, or..." I shake my head. "I don't know."

I was going to say something crazy—like, what if I want all *three* of you? But that's now impossible since Oliver just walked out without a backward glance.

"Stay with me," I implore them.

They both nod.

And I don't know how that kind of relationship would work, but this is a start.

"Where did he go?" Carter asks.

"Away. I don't know."

I climb into bed, so done with today. Penn crawls over me, taking the far side, and Carter lies on his side facing me.

"We're calling room service, okay? I won't make you go out in public tonight." He touches my lower lip, swiping his thumb across it. "I have an early flight tomorrow, dream girl. You can come back with me if you want."

I lift one shoulder.

Penn's arm hooks around my waist. He kisses my shoulder.

The only thing I can focus on is that this, with them, feels *right*.

fifty-two
sydney

"It's time." Penn sits cross-legged on my bed, mirroring me. He holds out my phone. "You've got a thousand messages from people who care about you. I screened the asshole ones, of which there were only a small amount."

Carter, true to his word, left almost before the sun was up. It was a quick trip for him, but he made it for *me*. He came because Penn told him to, and there was no hesitation on his part.

After letting me lie down for almost twenty minutes, Carter dragged me up and put me in the shower. He stayed in the bathroom with me, sitting on the floor outside the tub, while I slowly scrubbed myself clean.

When we came out, Penn had ordered room service.

So we ate, and they kept conversation superficial, discussing the teams they're playing tomorrow and what classes they're taking. They didn't try to loop me into it too much, although Penn and I complained about the people in our Intro to Law class for a solid five minutes.

I can't keep my head in the sand, so I take the phone.

The missed calls are overwhelming. I skim the names: Dad, Perri, Carter, Penn, Maddy, Brandon, Dylan. Even Oliver. *Twice*. And L. five times.

He called me five times?

A lump forms in my throat. I don't even know him, and he realized my absence.

There are voicemails from most of them, too. Not L., although I would've been curious to hear what he had to say.

Text messages. Dad's go from normal to worried over the span of a few days. Perri's, too, finally concluding that they're going to swing by my apartment to check on me.

L. wondering where I am.

Maddy asking if I'm okay, then asking where I am. If I'm sick or in the hospital.

Brandon...

I cover my mouth at his last text from yesterday evening.

BRANDON

> Dyl is counting on us to be at her first home v-ball game, Sydney. You can't just up and vanish on us. All week, sure, whatever. But tonight? After you promised to be there for her? What the fuck?

Penn takes it and scans the message, then mutters something about not screening messages from my supposed *friend*.

The next thing I know, he's calling Brandon on speaker phone.

"About time," Brandon snaps. "Now that the game is over. They lost, by the way. Dylan was crushed."

"As sweet as it is that you care so deeply for your bestie," Penn drawls, "you might want to consider why Sydney went radio silent."

Brandon pauses. "Who is this?"

"Penn Walker."

"Where is she?"

"She's sitting across from me, wondering why the fuck I'm calling you. This is the first time she's had her phone on since

Monday, by the way. What a swell fucking message to read when your supposed friend is not doing well."

"What happened?" Brandon clears his throat. "Seriously."

"I'm not telling a shitty friend like you anything," he growls. He reaches over and snags my hand, squeezing tight. "Take it from me—there are more important things in life than sports."

He jabs the end button and wrinkles his nose.

"Thanks," I mutter.

"Nah, that jackass had it coming." He smiles. "I've got to get to morning skate. You want to come along?"

Surprisingly... I do.

Sometime last night, he and Carter moved their bags into my room. He pulls on sweatpants and a sweatshirt and waits for me to get dressed, too.

I text Dad that I'm coming with Penn to practice.

He responds with a yellow heart emoji.

At the rink, Penn brings me down to the bench then heads to the locker room. Dad stands with papers on a clipboard, and he seems to be marking down notes. I sit beside him, leaning against the plexiglass at our backs. The team emerges from the locker room and takes to the ice, and Dad glances my way.

"Glad to see you out and about," he comments. "With Penn..."

I smile.

"Uh-huh. I don't like that look on your face."

My eyes widen. "What?"

"Happiness." He leans over and kisses the top of my head. "A goalie making you happy, sweetheart? We've got to work on your taste."

I laugh.

When Oliver takes the ice, my heart skips. He glances our way, then does a fucking double take.

His practice, it's almost needless to say, goes terribly.

"I don't suppose I need to castrate my captain," Dad says casually, sitting beside me.

I choke.

"Because it seemed like you were dating. And then you shut down. And now you're smiling at Penn Walker." He pats my back.

"Yeah." I wave him off. "Well, I don't know. No, don't hurt Oliver. He didn't... it's fine."

He sighs.

"Dad?"

He tips his head in my direction.

"Do you think Mom is selfish enough to never come back?"

That gets his attention. He puts his hand on my knee, shaking his head slowly. "I've considered that. I've contemplated a lot of reasons for her to leave you. But the main theory I've reached is that she realized you are an adult, fully capable of living the life you want without her. You mentioned you were sending money home to cover rent? It's possible your responsibility scared her."

"So it's my fault," I murmur.

"That's not at all what I'm saying, Sydney. It's her problem whether she can cope with realistic situations. Such as a twenty-year-old woman flourishing in her own space."

My cheeks heat.

Our attention goes back to the players, and Dad stands up. He steps down and blows the whistle, calling them all to him. I tip my head back and close my eyes, wanting to absorb what he's saying but not deal with the stares.

Or see Oliver trying to avoid my gaze.

Dad's coaching voice is the same, even after all these years. It triggers memories of being on the ice with him as a kid. Those are the ones that often come back whenever I think about my childhood with him.

"Ruiz. A moment."

My eyes snap open.

Oliver and Dad remain at the bench.

"Do you remember what I told you at my house?" Dad asks.

Oliver blanches. He clears his throat and says, "That I have my whole life ahead of me to date girls. But not this girl."

"And yet..."

"And yet," Oliver repeats. His expression blanks. "Are you going to kick me off the team, Coach?"

"No. I *am* going to make the whole fucking team skate until their legs fall off as soon as we get back to Framingham." Dad smiles. "So you have that to look forward to. I'm sure your teammates will thank you. Now get back out there."

He skates away.

I groan. "Jeez, thanks."

"What?" Dad shakes his head. "I'm just protecting my baby girl."

fifty-three
penn

Exercise clears my mind.

Sort of.

Normal exercise, like playing hockey, doesn't. I'm focused, sure, but my mind whirls at the next level above genius. I am one with the puck. I am a body language reader, predictor of shots and angles. My cat-like reflexes are unmatched.

We won our second game in Michigan. The plane ride home was energized to everyone except Ollie, who seems to be growing more distant by the second.

And now that we're experiencing true pain through exercise, I've turned to scheming.

Coach blows the whistle, and there's a collective groan as we go again. My skates aren't built for speed, my pads too cumbersome. It's fucking irritating to come in nearly last every time we have to go down and back—but then, there's a shift. And I start coming in second to last, then third to last.

We go again.

Guys puke on the ice.

We go again.

There's a way to fix Oliver and Sydney. I just need to think of it. And while my brain is wiped clean, like a glossy, freshly cleaned ice rink, a solution has yet to manifest. Other than locking them in a room together...

We go again.

We already tried locking them in together, and it didn't *exactly* work. Maybe it made him understand, but it sure didn't put any fight in him. I get back to the goal line and struggle to catch my breath. My mouth is dry, my lungs are screaming.

I run for fun. But these sprints are way, *way* past fun.

RIP to the ice maintenance guys who'll have to deal with the vomit on the ice. Although from this angle, there's not much substance to it.

I glance at Coach, who stands on the bench with the whistle in his mouth and his arms crossed. There's a point to this, I'm sure there is, but I haven't put much thought into that.

Not until I catch Ollie's guilty expression.

We go again, and I aim to end up beside my best friend.

"What's this about?"

He grunts. "Messing with Sydney."

"Like messing with her, or *messing* with her?"

"Is there a dif—"

Whistle.

My muscles are slowly turning to jelly, and my stomach clenches as soon as we cross the goal line. I swallow a few times, sharply, to keep from joining the pansies who've already thrown up.

My captain seems in worse shape than me, his elbows on his knees. Sweat drips off his nose, and he spits.

"Sorry, what were you saying?" I ask, forcing cheer into my tone.

He glares at me. "He warned me that I had my whole life ahead of me to date girls. But not that one."

I roll my eyes. "You're not *dating* her."

"Coach thought we were."

It's my turn to glower at him. "Fuck off."

Whistle.

I push off, my legs screaming. My lungs need to catch a break, too. Too much talking and not enough deep breathing. Oliver skates out ahead of me, his movements quick despite his exhaustion. He leads the pack, and that's what makes him a good captain.

And yet, I have a feeling we're not stopping until he collapses.

Twenty minutes later, even I've puked twice.

Oliver stands straight and tall on the line, his chest heaving.

"Coach," someone calls. "You're killing us."

"Your captain will tell you when to quit," he replies.

The first words he's spoken since he put us on the line. An hour ago? Two?

"Sir," Oliver says. "I—"

Whistle.

"Fuck," I groan.

Our lap is pitiful.

"I won't go near her," Oliver gasps. "You made your point."

Coach hops over the boards and strides across the cut-up ice.

"I made my point?" He laughs. "No, I don't think I *made my point*. Because while you all have been living in the land of the fucking delusional, you've allowed my daughter to become a mockery of this school."

Silence.

"You think I give a shit that she gave plays to St. James?" He throws his hands up. "Not so much, gentlemen. What I would've expected was for you to play *better*. But no—you realized what happened and you all threw in the towel. It was a bloodbath you deserved."

Well, he does have a point.

"Instead, you blamed a girl who had nothing to do with the game. Not the SJU coach who authorized the use of it. Not the player who brought it to him in the first place." Disgust colors his tone. "You hold this grudge through to a new year, and you still blame my daughter for your past failures. Enough that a fucking gossip column writes about her almost daily."

"Coach—"

"QUIET," he roars. He points at the player who spoke. "If I want your opinion, Bradley, I would fucking ask for it." He pauses. Eyes us. Then asks, "Do you respect me?"

"Yes, Coach," comes the unanimous reply.

"And how is disrespecting my daughter respecting me?"

I press my lips together. My gaze slides to Oliver, who seems equally disheartened.

"If any of you want to skate for me again, you're going to do better." He meets each of our gazes one at a time. "To be perfectly clear: I am horribly disappointed in how you all have handled yourself. But your captain has set the tone. So the responsibility of making things right falls to him."

Oliver opens and closes his mouth.

Coach lifts his eyebrows, almost like he's expecting him to argue. When no words come out, Coach nods once and heads for the bench.

"Dismissed," he calls.

I blow out a slow breath. When everyone else moves, scurrying for the doorway to the locker rooms like Coach might change his mind and call us back, Oliver stays on the ice.

"What is it?" I'm dying to get out of these pads, but I'm not going to leave him out here alone.

"He wants me to make it right."

"Yeah."

"He doesn't know the full story." His gaze lifts. "I can't make it *right*, I just need to stay away."

I grimace. "Hate to break it to you, dude, but I don't think that's going to work. Walk her home and apologize again, then you can tell Coach you tried."

He grunts. His hand flexes on his stick, and he finally nods. Turns out, my scheming was unnecessary. Coach solved my problem for me.

fifty-four
sydney

Dylan didn't speak to me yesterday. We had the one class together, and she sat on the other side of the room. Which is fine—I kind of expected her to be completely furious with me. It hurt, but not as much as I was expecting.

In a way, I think I prefer that she's the type of anger that makes her want to avoid me. I don't know how I'd react to someone yelling in my face.

Today, I've got two classes with Brandon. I speak to each professor before class, apologizing for missing an entire week's worth of work. I even missed the Econ presentation I'd been stressing over, although they let me reschedule my presentation for the end of the lineup.

Crisis averted.

In my writing class, I talk to Professor Page in a low voice just outside the door. I don't really have any good excuse, but she seems to read between the lines anyway. She pats my shoulder and gives me an out.

The only class that doesn't is Crime Fiction. I take a zero on the paper that was due last Thursday, although if I somehow manage to hand it in before this Thursday, I can get some points for it and salvage my grade.

Brandon is in both my writing class and crime fiction. But

it isn't until we're walking out of the last class that he calls my name.

I stop in the hallway and slowly turn around.

"I'm sorry," he says.

My eyebrows hike. I wait, but he doesn't continue. "You're sorry? For what?"

"The mean text without asking if you're okay." He gulps. "I was caught up in Dylan's emotions, you know? She was mad, and I was focused on that instead of worrying about you."

Right.

"Thanks." I leave it at that. I don't know what else to say, other than... fuck off? I shake my head and turn my back on him. I just want to go home. Returning to campus has been exhausting, leaving me with no capacity for anything else. And it's only Tuesday.

"Sydney, wait—" He grabs my shoulder.

Immediately, he yelps.

I whirl around.

Oliver has his wrist at a funny angle, looming over Brandon. My friend's expression is pinched, clearly in pain—

"Oliver." I grab his arm. "Let go!"

His jaw clenches, but he finally does. One finger at a time, peeling off Brandon's wrist until he can snatch it back.

"Go," Oliver snaps at him.

Brandon's eyes round, but he doesn't waste any time. He scurries past, giving us both a wide berth.

I glare at Oliver. "What is your problem?"

He rubs the back of his neck. "I got carried away."

"Oh, really?" I force a laugh. "That's a change."

He winces.

"What are you doing up here?" This is the English wing, and I'm pretty sure most of the hockey guys avoid the writing-intensive classes on purpose.

"I came to see if I could walk you home." His expression is sheepish.

"No."

His eyebrows hike. "No?"

"Yeah." I shake my head and resume my trek to the exit. "You're capable of respecting a no, right?"

"Well..."

I pause.

"I'm sorry, Sydney, I'm going to follow you home either way. Just to make sure you're safe."

Great.

He's just doing this because he feels guilty.

The rest of the week follows a surprising monotony comprised solely of Oliver Ruiz. He seems to have taken over protection detail—minus sneaking in through my window and curling up beside me. Carter and Penn seem to have divided that responsibility up between them.

Which is what it's beginning to feel like: responsibility.

Carter confiscated the knife he gave me. I saw him pocket it one night, and my stomach twisted. He told me it would just be until I'm through this self-harm phase.

It's not like I can tell them I'm over it—they have no qualms with stripping me and checking.

Saturday morning, I wake up to Penn and Carter in my room. I hadn't heard either come in, which should be alarming. But I just inch closer to Carter, burying my face in his chest. Penn is on the foot of the bed, curled up more like a cat than boy.

"Couldn't decide?" I ask when Carter's fingers slide into my hair.

He laughs. It rumbles his chest, vibrating into my face. I like that I can feel his laugh as well as hear it.

"It was Penn's turn," he admits. "But I just wanted to wake up with you when we don't have anywhere to be."

"You do have somewhere to be." Penn uncurls and stretches. He crawls up over me, ignoring Carter entirely and dropping his weight onto me. He buries his face in my neck. "Mmm, you smell good. He's got a bus to catch, princess. But I'll be here until our game tonight."

"I have a presentation to finish at the library," I mumble.

Plus another mission: tracking down Dylan and Brandon and actually shoving my apology down both of their throats. The volleyball team is playing tonight, anyway, and I'm absolutely going to be there.

One of their hands—can't tell whose—slips between my body and Penn's. The fingers inch into my panties.

Penn grunts, making me think it's Carter's wandering hand. The long finger slides through my wetness. Penn rolls off me, his gaze dropping to where Carter's hand is between my legs. I was right, at least.

My legs fall open. He strokes me slowly, lazily. Dipping inside and then dragging my arousal up to my clit, which he rubs in tantalizingly soft circles.

We haven't talked about choosing in a while. I haven't voiced that I don't want to pick between them. They seem to be letting it go for now.

My alarm goes off.

Carter groans. On the outside of the bed, and therefore closest to my alarm, he rolls away to shut it off.

Quick as a whip, Penn yanks down my shorts and panties.

I let out a squeak, but Penn's already got his face buried between my legs.

Carter flips back over and lets out a hiss. "Not gonna lie," he says, his voice strangled. "That's hot."

Penn smirks and lowers down. My eyes flutter shut when he makes contact with my lips, his tongue perusing. He thrusts inside me, then drags back up to my clit. A similar pattern Carter's fingers followed. He sucks and nibbles until my hips jerk against him.

Carter pushes up my shirt and palms my breast. His lips close over the other nipple, and I gasp. He pinches the one, nips at the other, alternating attention and stimulation until I'm trembling. Penn seems to be of similar mind. He slides one finger inside me, curling and touching along my G-spot, then a second.

His lips never leave my clit.

"I'm going to—"

"Good." Carter kisses up my breast, over my collarbone, to my throat. He nips my skin, then soothes it with his tongue. Finally, his lips drift over my jaw and claim my lips.

Penn sucks harder, his tongue flicking against my clit, until my orgasm crests.

I gasp into Carter's mouth.

As soon as Penn moves away, Carter shifts. He edged his boxers down at some point, but now he thrusts into me with ease. My orgasm made sure of that. But after a minute of continuing to kiss me, he lifts. Then sits back on his heels.

He gathers my legs and hooks them on his shoulders, sliding back into me at a new angle. Deeper.

"Princess."

I turn and focus on Penn. He's standing by the bed, his cock pointing at me.

I open my mouth.

He slides across my tongue, going to the back of my mouth. He bumps deeper, and my gag reflex closes my throat around him. He grunts, gripping my headboard. His hips move, pushing him farther. I wrap my fingers around the base of him with one hand, my other going to his balls.

Carter's hands are everywhere else. Trailing across my torso, up to my breasts, then back down to between my legs.

"You going to come with his cock in your mouth, dream girl?" Carter asks.

I shiver and continue what I'm doing—stroking and sucking, cupping Penn's balls and trying to take him deeper. Even when I can't breathe, when he fills my throat and cuts off my air—

"She likes that," Carter tells him. "She clenches, *ooh*, fuck. Yeah, just like that."

My eyes roll back. I'm losing control, but it seems like it doesn't really matter anyway. Penn grasps my hair and holds my head still. He takes over, his hips driving his cock into my mouth. I keep open wide for him, while Carter stays even with the same tempo. Every stroke into me is hard and deep, but so fucking slow. The withdrawal leaves me trembling and gasping.

Empty.

Then it repeats.

They drive me higher and higher.

Carter breaks first. He stills and groans. The pressure on my clit increasing as he focuses all his attention on me. When I tip over a few seconds later, my cry is muffled by Penn's dick. The sounds seem to only work him up, and it triggers him like a domino effect.

I swallow what I can, but he pulls out and spills across my chin and throat, too.

"Fuck," Carter groans. He's still inside me, semi-hard, and he pumps a few more times. "I have no interest in touching dick, but..."

"Hot," Penn agrees. "Not that I like to watch her get fucked by someone else either."

They both pause.

I wipe at my mouth, my eyes closing again.

"It's time to get up." Carter kisses my cheek. His hand grips the back of my neck, his other across my back, and he forces me to sit up. "Shower with me."

"Or we could go back to sleep," I suggest.

He chuckles. "Penn's going to make coffee. Come on."

I sigh, but I let him help me out of bed and steer me into the bathroom. His cum seeps out of my pussy, smearing across my thighs. I run my fingers down my throat and collect Penn's. Most of it wound up in my mouth.

"Don't tell." Carter pushes me against the door and kisses me soundly. His tongue infiltrates my mouth, tasting all of me thoroughly. But then he moves lower, kissing my throat. Tasting—

I whimper. I cup the back of his neck as he licks and tastes more than just *me*.

When he hoists me up, I'm not even surprised that he's hard again. He thrusts back inside me. His motions are quick and frantic, a sudden, unexpected high he's forced to chase.

I just hold him. The back of his neck and his shoulder, my grip tight enough to be steady but not leave marks. My shoulders make a steady *thump* on the door. He comes with a gasp, his body shaking with the force of it.

Slowly, he withdraws and drops my feet back to the floor.

He clears his throat.

I smile at him. "It's okay."

It takes a minute for his gaze to come back to mine.

Suddenly, a fist hits the other side of the door. "You're supposed to be showering, not fucking and locking me out."

I smother my laugh.

Carter rolls his eyes. "Too late."

Penn grumbles.

I turn on the shower. We brush our teeth while we wait for the water to heat. When we're done, his gaze travels my body.

"No more incidents?"

I shake my head. My cheeks heat. "You guys haven't left me alone—"

"Don't give me that," he interrupts. "If you wanted to, you'd find time alone."

I spin in a slow circle. The cuts on my ankle are still ugly, but they're scabbing over. By some miracle, I've resisted picking at them. The ones under my watch—which sits on the counter—have progressed even farther.

"This week has been... better."

He waits.

"Hard to get out of bed sometimes," I admit. "And when I'm at school, all I want is to be back in bed. Peopling is hard. Doing my schoolwork is tiring. Remembering to do everything I have to—eat, go to bed on time, brush my teeth, wash my hair, laundry—is exhausting."

His gaze softens. "But you're still doing it."

"Mainly because of you guys."

I shed my shirt, my only remaining article of clothing, and drop it on the floor. The water is steaming, which I appreciate. I step into the water and wait for Carter to join me.

"You give us too much credit," he finally says. "You're stronger than you think."

fifty-five
sydney

Penn and I walk into the gymnasium. Purple-and-white-clad students line the bleachers, and I shrink in on myself. He squeezes my hand and leads me to a few open seats. I make myself busy unzipping my coat, fiddling with my hat...

"No one's looking at us," he says.

He finally told me about my dad's "practice" on Monday evening. "So if the hockey players are suddenly going out of their way to be nice, you'll know why," he added at the time.

I haven't experienced *that*, but it seems like they might be talking about me in a better light? Because not a damn person has glared at me since Monday. No one's purposefully not held a door or knocked their shoulder into mine.

I crane around. "Do you see them?"

My attempts to get Brandon or Dylan to talk to me has utterly failed. Maddy, however, was quick to sympathize. And after a strongly worded apology from both of us, we're good again.

I think.

"There's Maddy." Penn points to where more students are filtering into the gym. He waves frantically, even standing and bouncing up and down, until she spots him.

Then me.

She joins us, sitting on my other side, and smiles. "Glad you could make it."

"Yeah." I focus on breathing and not puking. "Did you tell Dylan or Brandon?"

She shakes her head. "I haven't seen either of them much. Dyl's been super busy with practices and her class schedule, and Brandon... playing the avoiding game."

"Love that." Penn squeezes my knee. "They're assholes."

"Eh." I shake my head. "They're just..."

"I told him he was an idiot," Penn continues. "And now he's just proving it."

Maddy smiles.

I... don't. Because my father is striding into the gym like he's on a mission, and it only takes him a minute to find me. I swallow hard, glancing at Penn. He's talking to Maddy now, going on about how my track record with friends is unfortunate.

"Dad," I blurt out when he gets even with our row. "What are you—?"

"Have you heard from your mother, Sydney?"

It takes a second for the words to filter. Heard from. Mother. Sydney?

I scramble for my phone, but there's nothing. Things on it have finally calmed down, and I didn't even have to change my number.

Maybe the hockey team had something to do with that, too.

"No," I finally respond. "Why? Did something happen?"

His expression stays stoic, even as he says, "She called me."

I jump up, but he holds out his hand.

"What did she say?" I ask.

"I need your cell phone, and I need you to stay here," he continues. "She didn't say anything—I missed the call."

But she's not dead.

"I can help find her." My voice is small.

"Sydney, please."

Maddy and Penn are both watching me. I slowly hand over my phone. He takes it and tucks it away. I give him the password—I don't really have anything to hide—and the question of *why* is on the tip of my tongue.

But he gives me the answer unprompted. "I've contacted the detective who's been looking into your mom's disappearance. He drove up from Emerald Cove, and I'm heading to meet him now."

"I should come—"

"You should stay," he interrupts. "It's okay, Syd, let me handle this."

His gaze turns imploring.

"Okay." I clear my throat. "Okay, well... let me know if you find anything."

"I will," he promises.

He leaves.

I sit.

"Are you okay?" Penn asks, leaning into me.

"Fine." I shake it off. "We're here for Dylan. Right? It's not about me."

Maddy snorts. "Sure. You really don't have to be here if he was asking—"

"Dad didn't want me to go with him," I interrupt. "I think it's fine, under the circumstances... What is he doing here?"

Oliver Ruiz climbs the steps toward us. His hazel eyes burn into mine, but he keeps going up. One more row anyway. I twist and track his movements. He glares at the group sitting just behind us, and soon they're all scooting down to make room for him.

"Hey, Ollie." Penn's voice is too cheerful. Nearly forced. "What brings you here?"

Oliver says nothing.

"School spirit," Maddy coughs. "Obviously."

I snicker.

We don't see any sign of Brandon, but the volleyball teams come out of the doors on the far side. It's not St. James, at least. The colors of this opposing team are dark green and gold. The girls are all tall and muscular, some more lean than others. I spot Dylan and smile.

What quickly becomes apparent, however, is that I know nothing about volleyball. Maddy and Penn don't seem to really know much either. All I know is that they have to get it over the net, stay within the lines...

Yeah, my knowledge is nonexistent.

Either way, I follow along with the FSU crowd and cheer when they do. I jump to my feet when Dylan dives for the ball and gets her hands under it, saving her team from ending the volley. Get it, *volley*ball? No?

Oliver doesn't seem to know much either. Whenever I glance back, he's squinting at the court like he's trying to puzzle it out. But I'm sure as hell not going to ask him anything about it.

When the game ends, our team comes out ahead.

Thank God.

"Do you want to go say hi?" Maddy asks me.

I force a nod.

We head down to the floor, and Maddy winds effortlessly through the crowd. I stick close behind her, and soon we're in front of Dylan and some other girls on the team.

"Hey," Maddy greets her. "You were awesome!"

Dylan thanks her, but her gaze is pulled to me. "You came."

"Yeah."

"Why?" Her tone isn't exactly warm.

"Because I wanted to see you," I say. "And if I was in any place to go last week, I would've. I'm sorry that I didn't make it."

Her brows furrow. "Brandon said you had some sort of episode."

"Dylan!" Maddy smacks her arm. "Seriously?"

"No, it's okay." I take a breath. "I didn't... I was in a bad headspace. I didn't leave my room most of the week. Not until my dad and stepmom came over and forced me into action."

Dylan grimaces. "My mom has depressive episodes that sound a lot like that. I'm sorry, Sydney, I just... I assumed when you didn't reply to our texts that you just needed some space. This semester has been a lot, but it still hurt."

I look away.

"Now we know," Maddy adds. "If you go AWOL, we'll just break into your apartment."

That brings a smile to my lips. "Thanks."

"Coming, Dyl?" one of her teammates calls.

Dylan glances back and waves, then faces us again. "Want to do dinner tomorrow?"

The invitation is aimed at me.

"Absolutely," I say.

Penn appears at my shoulder. "I've got to go."

"What? Where?"

His expression is pinched. "Some of the guys are planning on hitting up a St. James party. They won their game tonight, which probably means most of the players are going to be there. They want to make a scene... fight."

Carter. The fact that he goes to SJU parties doesn't even concern me. While we haven't had any sort of exclusive talk—how could we, when I'm technically dating two... three... guys—I trust that he's not doing anything stupid. But if he's there, he could easily get swept up in a fight.

Especially as captain. He wouldn't let his guys fight without him.

"I'm going with you—"

"No." Penn puts his hands on my shoulders. "Let me get

him out of this, okay? The fight's going to happen either way, but I can make sure he's not part of it."

A lump forms in my throat.

"Okay." I try to remember how to breathe. "Okay, go."

Penn kisses me. Too fast. "Ollie will take you home."

"Penn—"

He's gone. Disappearing through the crowd.

I'm left standing with Maddy and Dylan, feeling... lost. Worried.

More than a little nauseated.

I've seen Penn fight. And Oliver, too. But this seems like an intentional raid of a St. James party just to cause a fight. Players looking for blood. And it's not even following up a game either of them lost against the other.

"You okay?" Dylan asks. "You went pale."

They didn't hear.

I wave them off and scan for Oliver. He's still on the bleachers, high enough to keep eyes on me. Or at least, that's what I tell myself in my state of delusion.

It's dumb that I even care about him. That's what it is, right? That weird thump in my heart whenever I see or think about Oliver Ruiz. It feels different than how my body reacts to Penn or Carter.

Carter Masters has always felt like some version of home. Safety. Even when he's chasing me down in a parking garage or slicing my skin open with his knife, I trust him. The fling we had two years ago seems almost silly now. We were hot and heavy, from zero to one hundred. I secretly think it scared both of us, and that's why we ended.

But the trust wasn't broken... not until we set off the chain of events that landed me at Framingham State University.

How was I supposed to know those plays wouldn't remain anonymous? How was Carter supposed to know that word about them would spread like wildfire?

And Penn... I find comfort in the way he's never

demanded more from me than what I'm capable of giving. Even in the beginning, when he threw cash at me before he fucked me. When more money mysteriously appeared in my drawer with the rest of my cash, my stockpile seeming to grow after every nighttime visit.

His threats didn't curb my desire. The way he's always watching out for me makes me feel seen, more than anything. Plus, his kinks are unexpected. Toe-curling at times.

He makes me believe that he will protect me in whatever way I need. And Oliver...

I don't want to think about Oliver.

Oliver, who brought me to a rage room after terrifying me with a fake kidnapping, who stopped Bear from raping me, who then went on to... to simulate that very scenario again. But worse.

Oliver, who carefully laced up my skates for me. Who looks at me like he sees straight down into my soul. Who makes me think I'm not just broken pieces.

"Are we going out?" Maddy asks.

I shake my head slowly. The truth is, I'm so tired still. Always. I try to find Oliver again, but he's moved from where he was before. I catch the top of his head, the corner of his ear, and my lips quirk.

Recognizing him from just that?

"I'm going to head home." I hug her. Then Dylan, who's still lingered even though the rest of her teammates are filing back toward the locker room. "Good job, Dyl. Proud of you."

"Oh, stop it." She hugs me back, though. "Thanks for coming."

I make my way toward Oliver. He meets me halfway, his gaze dark. In all the times he's escorted me from my apartment to campus and back again, we haven't so much as spoken. I open my mouth to break that barrier, but nothing comes out.

I close my mouth again.

It's snowing. I zip up my coat and pull my winter hat from

my pocket. Oliver has a black beanie that he tugs on, then shoves his hands in his pockets. We walk side by side through campus and off of it. It's dark out, and the side streets are only lit by the intermittent lamps. The snow is more visible in their glow, fat flakes that float lazily to the ground.

The roads and sidewalks are coated in a thin layer of snow, with more piling on every minute.

I take a deep breath and pause at the top of my street. I tip my head back and close my eyes.

In the winter, especially when it snows, the sky doesn't get fully dark. It's like the night gets stuck at that sort of twilight hour, and it's like that now. It's enough to cast the world in shadow.

"Come on," Oliver says.

I crack an eye open. "Why? So you can go join your teammates fighting at the St. James party?"

He sighs. "No, because it's cold."

"I think it's quite nice."

"Nice if you like not having feeling in your toes."

"I prefer to be comfortably numb all over, thank you," I snip.

He doesn't have a response to that.

After another few drawn-out seconds, I lower my arms and continue on. He follows me to the steps of the brownstone.

I shouldn't invite him up.

But...

"You know what I've been craving?" I ask.

He raises an eyebrow.

"That hot chocolate you made." I bite my lip. "I have the milk, and, um, the brick of chocolate..."

He frowns. "Where did you get it?"

"Well..." I blush. "I asked Perri and she found it for me."

It was no big deal... it didn't feel like it, anyway.

But that was weeks ago. *Weeks* ago. And then everything

happened, and I shoved any thought of Oliver coming over right out of my head.

He nods, although he's still not smiling. I don't think I've seen him smile in forever.

"Okay," he agrees.

He comes upstairs with me, his breath even and as quiet as his footsteps behind me. I unlock the door and push it open, stepping inside.

I stop so suddenly, he bumps into me.

The light switch didn't work. But even then, in the gloom, it's easy to see that something isn't quite right. My apartment is in disarray—

"Sydney, *move*!" Oliver shoves me sideways. A second later, someone comes out of the shadows and tackles him.

I scream.

The door slams shut. Oliver and the intruder, wearing all black—including a ski mask—grapple on the floor. They twist, trading blows. It seems like Oliver is going to win. He comes out on top, straddling the intruder.

Movement across the apartment draws my attention.

I scream again as a second one charges forward. He picks up something from the counter. Belatedly, I catch the gleaming ceramic of the mug.

He smashes it over Oliver's head.

They shove at him, and Oliver scrambles backward. His gaze goes to me, frantic and wide-eyed.

"Sydney," he yells. "*Run!*"

There's two of them. Two huge men. They both advance on Oliver, who lurches to his feet. He's drawing them away from the door.

I pat my pockets frantically, belatedly remembering that I don't have my phone.

"Go!" he yells again.

One of them turns for me.

I rush to the door. Their fingers snag in my hair, my jacket hood. I'm yanked backward, and it takes me precious seconds to unzip my coat and slide free. My scalp burns, but I ignore it and shoot forward again.

The impact of flesh reaches my ears, but I can't look back.

Someone shouts. I'm halfway down the stairs when I risk a glance behind me. The second man hasn't followed—which means he stayed to help his buddy.

I get to the second floor and rush to an apartment, banging my fists on the door.

"Somebody help!" I scream. "Help me!"

No one answers, so I go to the second apartment.

"Please!" I beg. "My— I was attacked, there are intruders in my apartment!"

The door opens. A woman, older than college aged, steps aside and ushers me in. She closes and locks the door behind me.

"Do you have a phone? We need to call nine-one-one—"

"Here." She grabs her phone from her purse, dialing and pressing it to her ear. "Which apartment?"

"Three B. There are two men wearing ski masks. My friend is still up there, they were—"

"Yes. My name is Elle Thorpe," she says, her tone brisk as she talks to the dispatcher. "I need to report an intrusion in my building. An upstairs neighbor. Her friend was attacked..." She gives the operator her information, my apartment number. "No, sir, we are locked in my apartment."

I glance around the apartment. It's neat and tidy, if not a bit odd. There's a framed painting of a llama staring down at me from the closest wall. I can't tell if it's satirical or seriously her vibe. There are even little llama figurines surrounding one of those bowls that's for mail and whatever else.

Interesting.

Elle presses her eye to the peephole.

"The two are coming down the stairs now. Two men. Bigger guys. They're wearing ski masks. Okay. Thank you."

She hangs up, then faces me. "Police are on their way. And an ambulance."

I let out a shuddering breath. "They're gone? I need to get up there—"

"They don't advise it," she murmurs. "Just sit tight. You're safe here."

"He could need help." I move to the door, and she steps out of my way. I slip out, racing up the stairs. My door is open.

Inside, on the floor, is Oliver. And he's not moving.

fifty-six
sydney

The time between finding Oliver on the floor and now are blurry. I rushed to his side, dropping so hard the impact seemed to rattle up my spine. He was curled in the fetal position to protect himself, but there was already so much blood.

A wound on his head, across his eyebrow. Another on his jaw.

The paramedics showed up with the police, and after the apartment was cleared, they came up with a stretcher. He didn't wake up when they put a neck brace on and slid him onto the stretcher, and he still didn't after we got downstairs and was loaded into the ambulance.

The police take my statement before we leave. One breaks off to talk to Elle, my downstairs neighbor. The officer says a detective is going to meet us at the hospital to interview Oliver, too. But then I'm shuffled into the back of the ambulance and the doors close, effectively ending the conversation.

Now, I sit in the waiting room while a doctor examines Oliver. I have his phone and wallet, and that's it. My hands won't stop shaking. I double over and try to keep breathing, but my chin keeps wobbling. I sway between needing to throw up and wanting to pass out.

It would be easier if I could lose consciousness for a while.

I use his phone to call Penn. Then my dad. Both go to voicemail, which isn't terribly surprising. Dad was off on a mission to do with my mother, while Penn was busy trying to either save Carter or get fucked up in a brawl.

They're busy, which means it'll just be me...

I should call his parents.

With shaky hands, I find his mom's contact info. I hover over her name, debating... then do it. He seems close to his family. Maybe. I don't actually know—all I know is that his grandmother calls him Gabriel, and she seemed to love him fiercely. Even if, in her words, he didn't visit home enough.

"Hi, baby," his mom's warm voice greet me. "What are you up to?"

I clear my throat. "I'm so sorry, Mrs. Ruiz. My name is Sydney. Um, Oliver is in the hospital—"

"What? Is he okay?"

"Yeah." I pause. "Well, I think so. He... he's being looked at right now." A lump forms in my throat. "He was unconscious when paramedics brought him in."

"Which hospital?"

I tell her. She says she'll be there soon, and we hang up. I don't have any more information for her—I don't know that they'd give it to me anyway. We're not related. I'm not his family.

I slowly fold over again, that feeling of not doing or being enough intensifying.

"Sydney Windsor?"

I shoot upright, and white spots pop in front of my vision. "Yes?"

A nurse stops in front of me. "Oliver is awake, honey. He's asking for you."

"He's asking for me?"

"Yes. You can follow me." Her expression is entirely sympathetic. She leads me into the emergency department and down a hallway, to a curtained-off bed with a chair at its side.

Oliver lies shirtless, the blankets pooling around his waist. There are already deep black and blue bruises across his torso. His face is swollen, his cheekbone cut. He's got stitches closing a cut on his jaw and another on his eyebrow.

Tears flood my eyes, and I slap my hand over my mouth to cover an upcoming sob.

Don't lose it, I tell myself.

His eyes crack open. "Hey, *mi nena*."

The nurse closes me in. One blink and the tears spill over.

He lifts his hand. There's an IV attached to it, inserted into a vein on top of his hand and taped down. His normally warm, bronze skin tone seems too pale.

I step forward and grip his hand. His fingers are cold.

"I'm okay," he says on an exhale. "Just a few bumps and bruises."

I choke on a laugh. "You look *awful*."

"And you look worried."

"Because I am." I tighten my hold. "I am worried."

"Even seeing me?" He laughs but abruptly stops and groans. "Don't make me laugh. They say I have a fractured rib."

My knees go weak. I sink into the chair and lean forward, burying my face in the edge of the bed.

"You shouldn't have told me to run."

"Then you'd be in the bed next to me." He touches my hair. "And how would that make either of us feel, huh?"

The fact that I couldn't hold my own against someone like that... it doesn't really make me feel *good*. The opposite, in fact.

Oliver's phone buzzes in my coat pocket. I fish it out and scan the text from Penn.

"Penn and Carter are on their way," I tell him. "I told my dad, too. Left him a message anyway. And I talked to your mom."

"You talked to my mom?" *Shock.*

"I don't know if that was the right thing to do, and I'm sorry if that was overstepping. But I just wanted you to have family—why are you looking at me like that?"

His gaze is intense. Dropped into the middle of an inferno intense. "I just... thank you." He blinks, and his expression switches to contemplation. Moving on to the next piece of information to digest. "What was your dad talking to you about at the game?"

"He asked if Mom called me." I glance away. "She didn't."

"And he needed your phone?"

"I don't know. I wasn't really in a position to fight it. If it's going to help find her, then who am I to argue?"

"Okay." He shifts. "How about you climb up here with me while we wait for the cavalry to arrive?"

I stare at him.

He frowns. "Will you do it if I say it'll make me feel better? Or... if I say you seem utterly exhausted?"

I *am* exhausted. Maybe that's why I shed the coat and fold it over the back of the chair, carefully toe off my boots, and climb onto the narrow cot with him. He makes room for me, though, and barely grimaces when I settle my head on his chest.

"There," he breathes. "Much better."

I curl around him and breathe in his spiced cologne. It clings to him even now, penetrating through the cloying antiseptic smell all hospitals seem to have. But I'm not sure it's better for him—I've got to be hurting him like this. He doesn't say a word about it. His arm, coming around my back, rests on my shoulder.

Like I might move away? No chance of that happening.

I may as well be superglued here.

I fall asleep. I must, because when I resurface, there are voices drifting over me.

"She's sleeping," Oliver whispers. "Just leave her be."

"Is this the girl who you took to the rage room?" a woman asks. "Abuelita told me about her. She's pretty."

Oliver sighs.

"And you look like shit," a man says. Wait. Younger. Boy? "Did you go through a meat grinder?"

"There were two of them," Oliver replies. "I'd like to see you put your jiujitsu classes to the test."

The boy scoffs.

"Fractured ribs," the woman says. "Concussion. Contusions. You could've been seriously hurt."

"I know, Mom." His hand on my shoulder squeezes, although I can't tell if it's a reflex or he's trying to wake me up.

Either way, I stir. No use pretending to sleep any longer.

"You with me, Sydney?" Oliver asks in a low voice.

I open my eyes and blink up at him. I touch my mouth, suddenly afraid that I might've drooled on him. That would be peak embarrassment.

"How long was I out?" I clear my throat and start to sit up. What I need to do is get off this bed. But in my haste, I forget that his mother and... brother. Younger brother.

They're both staring at me.

I hop off the bed and straighten my shirt. My face heats.

"Mama, this is Sydney. Sydney, my mother and brother, Felix," Oliver says.

His mother is gorgeous. Light-brown hair, tanned skin, green eyes. He pulls some of his features from her, like his smile that she unleashes on me without warning. She stretches out her hand to shake mine. My gaze drops to it, and then the glint of gold on her wrist.

My heart stops.

I stare at the bracelet.

In the back of my head, I knew he said he gave it to her. Maybe, deep down, some part of me thought he was lying. That he didn't give it to her for her birthday, or... I don't know. It doesn't really matter what I thought.

The bracelet is right there, nearly smacking me in the face.

I shake her hand and tear my focus away from it.

"Nice to meet you," I manage. "Sorry it's under these circumstances."

"It's my pleasure, Sydney." She pats my hand with her free one. The damn bracelet shifts along her wrist.

Felix's handshake is a lot shorter. Not nearly as warm. Which is fine by me. I retract myself as soon as I can, stepping away inch by inch until my back is touching the curtain. I slide my shoes back on. My jacket is behind Felix, and it can stay there for all I care.

Oliver eyes me.

"I should find Carter and Penn," I blurt out. "See if they're..."

I don't bother finishing the sentence. I was just caught *sleeping* on him by his mother and kid brother. If that's not awkward enough, I want to rip his mother's jewelry off her wrist and sprint away.

It's better I run off without the robbery part.

In the waiting room they first sat me in, I find Carter and Penn and my father. All three stand, and for a split second, I'm torn on who to go to first.

My father wins out.

I'm kind of sad I went most of my teen years without his hugs. He envelops me, his arms banding across my back, and kisses the top of my head.

After I take a breath, I slowly extricate myself.

"Is he okay?" Penn demands. "What happened?"

"He's..." My attention is dragged to the doorway, where a man in a suit strides down the hall with a nurse. "Concussion and fractured ribs, and a lot of bruising. But otherwise... I mean, he's awake. There's no permanent damage."

Carter and Penn exchange a look.

"Did you see his mom and brother?" I ask them.

Dad shakes his head, but he moves toward the door. "I'm going to talk to the nurse. I'll be right back."

When it's just the three of us, they both crowd in close. I hug them both and, in a low voice, tell them exactly what happened. I glazed over it for the police, and I'm sure I'll answer for that later. I kept the details vague because I just—I didn't want to have to relive absolutely everything.

If I told them about Bear, then I'd have to explain how I got in that situation with Bear in the first place. And how Oliver hurt him at a fight, which would open that up for questioning.

No, we've been skating on thin ice for a while now.

Dad returns with news. "They're discharging him. He volunteered you three to stay with him and make sure he follows concussion protocol..."

He narrows his eyes at me.

I keep my eyes wide and innocent. "Um... we're on okay terms, Dad."

His gaze flicks to Carter. "And the captain of the Seawolves?"

Carter straightens. "Yes, sir. We've put our rivalry aside because we both care about your daughter."

"Uh-huh." Dad grimaces. He's no doubt recalling the spectacular practice interruption that happened not too long ago. "Fine. Oh, Sydney, here's your phone."

I take it from him. "Did it help with...?"

"Unfortunately not, kiddo." He sighs. "I shouldn't have said anything. I'm sorry for getting your hopes up."

"It's okay." I force a smile. "I'm kind of not expecting her to come back, you know?"

He pats my shoulder. But there aren't really words to answer me. Not without lying or agreeing—and neither option sounds particularly helpful. So he leaves it at that and heads out. I spot Oliver's mother and brother leave soon after.

Eventually, a nurse wheels Oliver out, and she motions for

us to join her. She hands me a pamphlet on things to watch out for with concussions, as well as a list of things not allowed.

Screens, in particular.

He has my coat on his lap. He hands it back, allowing me to shrug it on as we walk toward for the elevator.

We're all silent until Penn pulls his car around. Oliver slides into the front, while Carter and I pile into the back.

"Ollie's house, then?" Penn asks.

"Yeah," he grunts. "There's room for all of us."

As soon as we're on the road, I lean into Carter. He smells faintly of booze, which confirms he was at a party. However, there's no sign of bruising on his face.

"So, did Penn rescue you in time?" I ask him.

Penn chuckles.

Carter snorts. "Sure. If by rescue you mean he burst into the party, yelled my name on repeat until everyone was convinced he was going to punch me, and dragged me out."

"Sounds exciting." I smirk at him. "Maybe now they'll just think you two are dating."

He scoffs. "Yeah, right. He shoved me into the car—"

"He protested the whole way," Penn interjects.

"Just as the FSU hockey team arrived."

"Minus Ollie," Penn says. "Obviously."

"So eventually, I saw reason," Carter concludes. "But we stayed and watched the melee until the cops were called."

"Because who doesn't like to spectate?" Penn laughs. "It wasn't just me—you were watching, too."

"I'm not disagreeing."

"Fighting gets our blood hot."

I roll my eyes.

"And then we got your voicemail," Penn says. "That kind of killed the mood."

"Well, I'm glad you rode in to save the day," Carter mutters. "Although I'm sure I'll hear about it from the guys tomorrow. That I got a heads-up or bailed or... something along those lines."

I take his hand. "I'm glad you didn't get beat up."

He stares at me, then huffs. "I can hold my own, dream girl."

"Yeah, yeah." I glance at Penn. "You both can, but then I'd be dealing with two injured guys."

"And that would definitely steal my limelight," Oliver says.

Exactly.

Soon enough, we're pulling into Oliver's driveway. I hop out and hurry up the walkway, easily picking out the fake rock with the key in it. I unlock the door and turn around, only to find the three of them staring at me.

Oliver's smiling, but the others are just confused.

"Thief," Oliver teases.

Teases!

I nearly faint from shock. As it is, I don't want to be the center of attention. I just open the door and stand aside for them to maneuver Oliver in. Not that he really needs help walking... in fact, he seems to be more disgruntled that they're helping at all.

Or hovering.

I almost laugh to myself, but I refrain. He'll get used to them being insufferable soon enough. It's nice to have something to focus on other than myself.

We go into the living room, Penn and Carter claiming the individual chairs and leaving the couch for Oliver and me. I glance at him, then away. Because how fucking awkward is this?

"I don't have to stay," I blurt out.

Oliver lowers himself down, but his eyes bug out at my words. Not the pain.

Probably.

"You're staying," he bites out.

"I could go." I tip my head toward the door. "You know, if you don't want me here."

"Why wouldn't I want you here?"

Penn rises. "I'm going to get a drink. Carter?"

"Yeah," Carter mutters. "Right behind you."

I glance around the living room, mainly to avoid Oliver's glare. Why could I curl up next to him on a hospital bed, allow him to walk me to and from school every day, and balk at this? Sitting in his living room with him? Not even alone.

"I—"

"Shush," he groans. "Just stop. I don't know what you want me to say except sorry, *mi nena*. But I will apologize until I run out of breath if it just means you'll stay."

Oh.

"This isn't weird for you?" I confirm. "You're the one who wanted to walk away from me."

He laughs and grimaces, touching his ribcage, but the laugh keeps coming. "*Pinche mierda*. You know how to focus on the negative. I was ready to walk away because of how much pain I've put you through. I didn't want—I *don't* want to walk away from you."

I meet his gaze. "You don't?"

"No. You invited me up to make Mexican hot chocolate. You really can't get rid of me now."

I smile, and a weight lifts off my shoulders. Never mind that he's injured and I'm broken, and there are two other guys vying for my attention. I cross the room and carefully straddle him, barely letting my weight rest on his legs.

He grips my hips, though, and pulls me down.

I brush his hair back, careful to avoid the stitches, and lean in.

Our lips touch. It's better than expected. Like a release of pain from my bones. It all just evaporates, and it takes me a long moment to realize this is more healing than I could've anticipated.

Forgiveness.

I forgive him for scaring me. For acting how he did.

I kiss him and I tell him with my lips that I forgive him, and in return I ask for forgiveness back.

He cups the back of my head. It takes all of my willpower not to shift my hips and grind forward. I want to, as thrills of electricity wind through my body and spark between my legs. Instead, I run my tongue along the seam of his lips. When he opens for me, I take advantage. I slide my tongue into his mouth, tasting him. Exploring him like I don't actually know him.

In a lot of ways, this feels like a first kiss.

Tentative but entirely focused.

His tongue tangles with mine, gently pushing my tongue back into my mouth and joining. Feeling and tasting and exploring in all the ways I just did to him.

His teeth graze my lower lip, and I groan. His hands are on my hips, and his fingers dig into my skin like he's losing control of his willpower, too. I don't know where to touch him that won't hurt. My hands settle on his biceps, and I squeeze to keep myself from drifting.

Hurting him is the last thing I want.

And yet I can't tear myself away.

Our lips slide together, and it creates this symphony in my head. A sound so crazy and musical that I just want to live here in it for a while.

Penn and Carter bring my emotions back. They beat away the numbness.

But this... kissing Oliver makes me forget I was ever numb in the first place.

"Wow," Penn says.

We jerk apart. I keep my gaze locked on Oliver's face as soon as my eyes flutter open, and I catch the dazed, starstruck expression before he wipes it away.

I wish he wouldn't wipe it away. I want to see it again, to

take a picture and frame it, because I did that to him. And that causes me immeasurable pleasure—or maybe it's just that I don't know anyone else who's effected like that.

By *me*.

"We leave you for two minutes and you're making out like teenagers," he continues. He's got two beers in his hand, and he drops back into his seat. "But by all means, continue."

I smile and shake my head. "You ruined the moment."

"Did he?" Oliver asks, leaning forward and nipping my earlobe.

Another wash of fire hits me, traveling straight to my core.

"Maybe not," I allow.

Carter returns, glancing from us to Penn. His eyebrows hike. "Damn, what did I miss?"

"Obviously a make-out session," Penn says. His tone is sarcastic, but his eyes gleam. "We could ask them to recreate it if you're feeling left out."

"I don't think I've seen them go for heavy petting," Carter comments. "Would you mind repeating?"

My face flames. "Get out of here."

Oliver chuckles. He touches my chin, redirecting my attention back to him. His gaze drops to my lips, and I sway forward.

Before I know it, his lips are on mine again.

fifty-seven
sydney

A noise wakes me up.

My body tenses. I slowly open my eyes, trying to orient myself. The noise has stopped, which doesn't help me pinpoint what it was or how it woke me up.

We all slept in the living room. We put on a movie, and Oliver fell asleep shortly after. I suspect it had more to do with the painkillers Penn produced and less to do with the company. That's what I tell myself anyway.

Carter rearranged his legs, helping him lie fully on the couch and not slumped in his seat, while Penn went to find blankets.

He only has one couch—and even that isn't quite long enough to fit Oliver fully—and the two armchairs. But with no hesitation, Penn directed me toward the armchair he had been sitting in. I curled up on it while he put some folded blankets on the thick rug and sprawled out under me. Like a watchdog, almost.

Now, the bright morning sun burns my eyes, and I squint and blink, trying to adjust.

Oliver is gone from the couch, and so is Carter.

Penn moves into my line of sight, smiling faintly. "The cavalry arrived."

I frown. Oliver referred to his family the same way...

Oh, no.

"Oh, yes." He rocks back on his heels as I scramble to sit up. "Everyone got a look at your sleep face as they shuffled past. You're lucky his mom hasn't started vacuuming in here yet."

Now that he says it, the faint hum of a vacuum above us, maybe in one of the far corners of the house, reaches me.

I cover my mouth. "I don't even have a toothbrush, Penn!"

He snickers. "You can use mine, princess. In the bathroom upstairs."

I scramble up, leaving him kneeling in front of the empty armchair. I had one experience with his abuela and one with his mother and brother—and I'm pretty sure I made a fool of myself in front of all of them.

I make it to the bathroom without running into anyone else. There are not one or two toothbrushes, but three. I grit my teeth and pick one at random. A decent rinse and a healthy amount of toothpaste erases the fact that I'm using one of the guys'. And let's not even get started on the fact that Carter brought his own?

Somehow I missed that memo.

Anyway. A hair finger-comb later, and I emerge from the bathroom. It's a 'this is as good as it's gonna get' situation. But the silence that awaits me... The vacuuming has stopped.

"Sydney," a warm voice greets me.

I freeze and turn slowly.

His mother comes out of his bedroom, wheeling that damn vacuum.

"Nice to see you again, Mrs. Ruiz."

She waves me off. "Call me Jackie, please. Thank you for staying with Oliver overnight. And his friends. Although I don't think I could've imagined he'd be friends with the captain of the SJU hockey team."

I force a laugh. "No?"

Don't look at the bracelet. Don't look—

She's wearing it again. Maybe she never takes it off? Maybe it's a key piece to her daily ensemble? Maybe she only wears it around Oliver, because he gave it to her—

"Did this catch your eye?" She taps the gold. "Oliver gave it to me for my fiftieth birthday."

"Oh." My voice sounds hoarse to my own ears. "It's beautiful."

She unclasps it. Slips it off her wrist.

Holds it out to me.

My hands are shaking when I take it. I run my fingers over the designs, like I used to when I was scared and alone as a kid. It was the one precious thing that had history and sentiment attached to it. Everything else in our space was just... filler.

My throat closes, and I hand it back quickly. Otherwise I might be tempted to keep it, to clutch it to my chest and sprint out of the house without looking back.

This is what I came for all those months ago, and now it's in my hands.

"Beautiful," I manage.

She takes it back, eyeing me with concern. "You've gone pale. Are you okay?"

"Fine." I clear my throat. "Sorry. I just, uh, didn't sleep well."

"You were on the armchair all night?"

I shrug.

"And Penn slept on the floor." She tuts. "Come on, Sydney, let's get you something caffeinated. Tea? Coffee?"

She loops her arm in mine, leading me downstairs and into the kitchen. Everyone seems to be gathered there, his abuela, two teens—the brother and who I can only imagine is a sister —and another woman around his mom's age. Oliver, Penn, Carter.

The second woman more resembles Oliver's abuela than his mother.

"There she is," Penn says.

Everyone looks to us.

If I was pale before, I fear I'm trying to blend into a tomato vine now.

Oliver's mom, who still has ahold of my arm, makes introductions. Felix and his sister, Daniela. His abuela, Juana Ruiz. Her daughter and Oliver's aunt, Ana.

I don't think I've ever met a boy's family before.

Even Carter... Our fling didn't include parent introductions. Not that mine were around much. I kept him and everyone else at arm's distance. Mom didn't come visit. Dad was never around—my choice—to introduce.

Although, I suppose now all three of them have met him.

"We need to get Sydney some coffee," Oliver's mom says suddenly. "Poor girl slept on an armchair."

Oliver's abuela eyes me, but after a beat, she moves to the coffee pot and pours me a mug. I thank her quietly, taking it with both hands. A little cream and sugar from the fridge, and I take refuge between Carter and Penn.

"I charged your phone." Carter holds it out. "It was almost dead."

"Thanks," I whisper. I take it and scroll through the notifications. There aren't a ton, but... four from Dad stand out. "I've got to call my dad."

I slip out of the room, but it still doesn't feel like far enough. I shrug on my coat, hat, boots, and step out onto Oliver's front porch. We got snow overnight, although his walkway and driveway have all been cleared.

Wonder if that was Felix or someone else...

I brush snow off one of his porch chairs and sit, dialing Dad's number.

"Sydney," he says upon answering. "Where have you been?"

"Sleeping in Oliver's living room, accosted by his family…" I shake my head. "Sorry. Carter plugged my phone in and I didn't have an alarm set."

"I'm coming by," he says. "You sound like you could use an escape."

I pause. "Yeah, I could."

Five minutes later, Dad's truck rolls up to the front of Oliver's house. I stayed outside, and I'm not particularly inclined to go back in and make conversation. I'm just stepping off the porch when Carter comes out.

"Sydney," he calls. "Where are you going?"

"With my dad…"

"Hang on." He ducks back in the house.

A second later, he comes out with his jacket in his hand. He follows me to the car and hops in the back without preamble.

Dad twists around and glares at him.

"Good morning, sir," Carter says with a straight face. "I care about your daughter a lot. No amount of bag skating is going to change that for me. I'm sure you could talk my coach into it, though, if it makes you feel better."

They seem to have a staring contest, until Dad shakes his head with a noise of disgust. "Fine."

I smile.

"Where are we going?" Carter asks.

I buckle into the front seat and look to Dad expectantly.

He pinches the bridge of his nose. "The police station."

"What?" I sit up straighter. "Why?"

"Because you had a break-in, and… they need to talk to you about your mother."

A chill coasts down my back. "Why now? They haven't given a shit—"

"Sydney. Please." His expression is pained. "It's where I was before I got to the hospital. I hired you a lawyer—"

"What?" I screech. "Why?"

"The case was reassigned, and the detective from Emerald Cove seems to think she's not missing." He glances at me. "I don't know if he thinks she ran away or... Either way, he's liaising with the Framingham police station for now."

I shake my head. My throat closes. Ran away or *what*? Dead?

Not dead.

Why is he even searching up here? I was going to try and find her. I haven't had a chance to figure out where she went or— Or *anything*. And now this detective suddenly thinks she's dead?

"Dad," I choke out. "That's not..."

"I'm so sorry, Sydney. I gave them your phone because they don't have enough evidence to get a search warrant. I know you don't have anything to do with where she went, but they think..."

"They think I did something?" I cover my mouth. "Or know something?" My voice comes out muffled. "You can't be serious."

Too soon, we're turning into the precinct parking lot. I hop out fast, followed by Carter. He pulls me into a hug before I can bolt. Every part of me wants to sprint away and never come back.

Instead, I give all my fear to Carter. He absorbs it silently, his grip around my shoulders and back firm and unwavering.

"Here he is," Dad says.

I slowly peel away from Carter.

A tall man strides across the lot toward us. He screams... *expensive*. That's the only word that comes to mind.

"Caleb Asher," he introduces himself to me. "You're Sydney?"

"Yes."

He nods once. "Okay. Let me do the talking at first, when we get in there. See what kind of prejudice we're dealing with before you give them any information. I'll let you know what questions to answer or not."

I glance at Dad. "Information besides my phone, which they got last night."

Caleb Asher's lips quirk, but he seems to take it in stride because the next second, he's nodding. "Was there anything incriminating on it?"

"No."

"Any last messages from your mother? Did she ever threaten you?" He looks at me hard. "They're going to ask you these questions. I'm going to advise honesty, here, Sydney. They record everything. If you double back on what you say, they'll use it to make you seem guilty."

I swallow. "Right. She hasn't ever threatened me."

"Okay." He tips his head toward the doors. "Let's get this over with. We can end the interview at any time. They haven't arrested you, so this is just a courtesy."

Lovely.

fifty-eight
sydney

Dad and Carter follow us in, but not all the way. They both take seats in the lobby while Mr. Asher and I are escorted through the bullpen—a collection of desks, police officers swarming around the place—and into a small room. There's a camera in the top corner. A desk. Spots for four people to sit, if necessary.

I take a seat, and Mr. Asher takes the one beside me.

A few minutes later, a detective enters.

"Thank you for coming in, Ms. Windsor," he says. "I'm Detective Lassiter. You've had an exciting few months, haven't you?"

I glance at my lawyer.

Feels weird to have a lawyer at all...

"Exciting?" Mr. Asher frowns. "Poor choice of words, don't you think, Detective?"

Lassiter frowns. "Mom goes missing, you have to change schools, students can't seem to keep your name out of their mouths, now your apartment gets broken into and your friend hurt. Maybe not the good kind of exciting, sure."

There's a lump in my throat that won't go away.

"Now, Sydney. Can you take me back to the day your

mom went missing?" He opens a file. "Your report is a little scarce."

I lick my lips. "Because I don't really know much, sir."

Mr. Asher inclines his chin. I take that to mean, *you can keep talking*.

"I live in Framingham. I was staying here over the summer. Mom was back home in EC, although she stopped returning my messages. I'll be honest, that's not entirely unusual. But after a week, I got concerned and went home to check on her. Her home seemed abandoned, which is when I went to you."

The detective is eyeing me like I personally drove my mother off the side of the planet.

"But she has a history of leaving?"

"Yes." It comes out so faint, I have to repeat myself. "Yes, she has a history of going away and coming back."

"And this couldn't have been one of those times?"

"She wouldn't..." I glance at my lawyer. "I don't think she'd do that to me. Not for this long."

But really, anything is possible.

"It's different," I say instead. "She always comes back, and this time, she didn't. She still hasn't."

Detective Lassiter leans back in his chair. "What would cause her to leave?"

"Money." I suck my lower lip between my teeth, releasing it when he doesn't seem to take that answer as enough. "I think she had a boyfriend or something. She'd go for a day or two when I was a kid, then two or three days."

"How old were you when this started?"

"Six?"

He sighs and closes the file. "So how long did you wait to actually report her missing, Sydney?"

I don't answer.

I have a lot of excuses built up, but none of them seem sufficient.

She always came back.

. . .

"Mom?" I drop my bag and look around the trailer. It's been an eon since I've been here—at least, that's what it feels like. Old memories threaten to press in, which in and of itself is new.

That only happens when you've been gone a while. When it isn't home anymore. Otherwise, memories don't crowd to the forefront of your mind. You just exist in the space.

That thought gives me a chill, but what's worse is the silence. It's empty.

I flick the light switch, but nothing happens. There's no noise, not even the buzz of the fridge. Which means the electric bill didn't get paid.

I double-check the calendar she keeps taped to the fridge, making sure she's not at work. There's nothing written for today. Nothing for this week either.

Her bedroom, down the hall, is pristine. The bed is made, there's nothing in the hamper.

"Mom," I say when her voicemail clicks over. "Where are you? I'm seriously worried."

I hang up and throw my phone. She'd been so good, too. Drug-free, at least as far as I could tell. She hadn't disappeared in a long, long time.

Part of me wants to run back to Framingham. Maybe call up Carter Masters and get lost with him for a time.

But another part of me can't move without knowing what happened to her. The dread is starting to wind through me, icy-cold tendrils that I can't shake.

I sit on the couch and curl my legs up to my chest, and I wait.
I wait.
I wait.

And when I can wait any longer, I make two phone calls: one to the police to report her missing, and the second to my father.

Finally asking for help.

"I thought she'd come back," I repeat.

"You were probably furious," he says in a low voice, leaning forward. "Were you mad at her, too? Underneath all that worry, were you mad that she decided to pull the same stunt? Disappear when you need her? And before that, the bracelet she sold out from under you?"

I jerk. "I was upset that I couldn't find her, Detective…"

He taps his fingers on the table. "So what did you do when she came back without the money? When she walked in the door three, four, five days after walking out, and said, 'Sorry, Sydney, I lost it all. I blew it on drugs.'"

"She didn't—"

"Were you mad enough to kill her?"

"Don't answer that, Sydney," Mr. Asher snaps. "Detective. What is going on?"

He slides another folder out from under the first. I hadn't noticed it, or realized, but now he opens it and retrieves two photos. He shoves them toward me.

My chest seizes up.

The first is of her lying in the snow at an odd angle. There's blood around her head.

The second is a close-up of her face… her skin has a grayish pallor, her eyes are closed. She's lying on metal, her hair brushed back. Not the way she'd ever wear it.

She's dead.

There's absolutely no fucking question that she's dead. I don't think the horror could echo inside me any deeper. I grip the edge of the table and squeeze my eyes shut. If there was a way I could go back thirty seconds and erase those images from my mind, I would.

But when I open them, the photos are still in front of me. My stomach rolls, and saliva fills my mouth. I'm going to throw up.

In the back of my head, maybe I knew she wasn't coming back. But seeing her like that...

Mr. Asher moves suddenly, flipping the photos to face the table.

This detective—he thinks I did it? Is that why he showed those awful pictures to me?

"Where is this?" Mr. Asher asks. "And when?"

"She was found here. In Framingham, on the St. James side." His gaze sears into me. "Yesterday."

My chest hurts. But now I can't take in a deep breath, or any breath at all. I sit back and cover my face. Not that it matters. All I can see is her face behind my eyelids, permanently burned there. I think I'll be seeing her like this in my nightmares.

"We're leaving." Mr. Asher helps me up, his grip on my elbow firm and stabilizing.

I drop my hands and focus on my feet. Everything is blurry, but he navigates us through the door, past the bullpen, and into the lobby with little trouble. My breath is coming fast and shallow, but he shakes his head at my dad and Carter. He doesn't let me stop for them.

Not until we're outside and he bodily puts me into the backseat of Dad's truck.

Carter slides in behind me.

I let out a sob, *finally*, and fall into his embrace.

fifty-nine
carter

I get the story in bits and pieces.

Her mom isn't missing anymore—she was found dead in the woods early yesterday morning.

She had abandoned the trailer that Sydney was helping to cover rent on, and Sydney eventually let it go. That explains a lot about Sydney's financials... and her relationship with her mother.

I had assumed that Sydney was just bad with money, or at the very least tight with it. That the financial hardship had more to do with Scarlett picking an expensive apartment and forcing her to buy more clothes than necessary... I didn't think that she was trying to pay rent in two places, on top of school.

Oh, but the detective thinks Sydney has something to do with her mother's death. It's unclear if it was an accidental death or murder... or suicide.

Her dad's hired her a lawyer.

I guess we'll find out in the coming weeks what's happening. What comes with the investigation.

"He barely mentioned the break-in," Sydney whispers. "More to use it against me than anything."

Of course not.

"It's probably someone else handling that case," her dad says. "Where should I drop you off?"

"Oliver's," she mumbles into my coat. "But only if his family is gone."

I chuckle. "I got the all-clear from Penn. So we're good to go." I touch her chin, directing her to look at me. "I don't suppose I could convince you to come to my hockey game tonight?"

Her silver eyes stare into mine. It's almost eerie—there's nothing behind them, and then she blinks and seems to come back to life. The corner of her lips tip up.

"You want Oliver and Penn to come cheer you on, too?"

I smirk. "Only if they wear maroon."

Coach Windsor coughs. "Good luck with that one, Masters."

"Dad!" Sydney shakes her head. "We'll come."

It's weird to want to kiss her in front of her dad. I resist the urge. Barely. He drops us off in front of Oliver's giant fucking house, and we stand on the porch until he's gone. Only then do I give in. I grab her face and kiss her hard. Her lips are warm. The cold tip of her nose touches my cheek. I lean in, licking at her lips until she opens for me.

I just have the insane desire to climb into her skin sometimes. I know it's not normal. I know my kinks, if unleashed, would cause more harm than good right now. Especially because she's abusing herself with it. I want to slice into her skin and lap at her blood. I live for the tremble of pain and pleasure.

But not if it fuels the darkness that takes her away from me.

Us.

Fuck. Somewhere along the line, I seem to have given up the notion of winning her for myself. Fucking stupid, really, giving up the fight this early. But how can I take her away from

Penn? How would I ever make her pick? And, grudgingly, I add Oliver to that mental list.

Especially since seeing her make out with Oliver last night left me hard as a rock.

"Did you miss morning skate?" she asks me when we finally part.

"I told Coach I would." Although it feels like an eon ago that I had the conversation with him. "I told him my girlfriend's apartment was broken into."

He was understanding and pissed all at once.

She looks up at me, her eyes wide. In a way, they remind me of two perfect moons. And I'm just the ocean, unable to resist the magnetic force of her.

"Girlfriend, huh?"

"Yep." I kiss her again before she can argue.

The door opens, but I hold up my finger. The wait-a-goddamn-second finger. Because when I stop kissing her, she'll go in and explain to them what's going on with her mom. It's going to be a big fucking downer, and I just want—

I don't know. To kiss her without that for another moment.

They can be downers, and then I'll inform them that Sydney RSVP'd yes to my game tonight. Since they're not playing, it's fucking perfect. And this is the last home game St. James will have for a few weeks, at least.

May as well make it a good one.

sixty
sydney

Penn and Oliver don't put up much of a fuss about going to Carter's game. In their words: "It's an excuse to scope out our rivals."

Which doesn't really strike me as any better than what I did last year...

Whatever.

Oliver is without a phone. One of the concussion protocols is to avoid screens with blue light... so I guess the movie wasn't in his best interests last night. Either way, he turned it off and shoved it in his pocket for emergencies only.

He sits in the front, while Penn drives and Carter and I take the back.

Our first stop is Carter's apartment. Not his stalker apartment across the street from mine, but his *real* one. He assures us it should be empty, which it most certainly is not. His roommate, a d-man on his team, comes out of his room with barely any clothing on. As in, boxers only.

I can imagine what he's thinking: Vipers in a Seawolves apartment?

Laughable.

Penn covers my eyes before I can see anything else, and I shove him away with a roll of my eyes.

Carter slaps the boxers-only guy on the back and makes up some excuse about them losing a bet, but I don't know if his teammate buys it. He watches us, a mix of wary and skeptical, until Carter returns from his own bedroom with SJU sweatshirts for the guys and a long-sleeve shirt for me. It has Carter's last name and his jersey number—eight—on the back, and *St. James Hockey* on the front.

After a brief internal debate, I put it on.

Carter's smile alone is worth it.

Oliver and Penn both grumble. Oliver's is a zip-up, which helps with the sore ribs. I ease it over his shoulders, then slip in front of him and take over the zipper.

Completely unnecessary, but I like the way his eyes on me heat my skin.

This is all one major distraction from the shit going on in the back of my head. It seems like I've traded one trauma for another. But focusing on hockey lets me ignore the fact that my mother is dead.

Caleb Asher's parting words were that the medical examiner hasn't ruled anything conclusive yet. If it comes back to be a suicide or accidental death, then I have nothing to worry about.

Which is as shameful as it is relieving.

I hope she wasn't murdered. That would add more mystery onto my plate, more trauma that I don't want to handle.

Anyway. We pile back in the car, now fully clad in St. James attire, and head to the arena. Carter goes in the players' entrance. We've got another half hour or so before the doors will open for students.

I pull my legs up and rest my chin on my knee. "Truth or dare?"

Penn twists around. "Dare."

I smirk. "I dare you to post a picture of your outfit."

"Only if we're all in it," Penn counters. "Ollie?"

Oliver's slowly gotten paler since we left the house. "And tell whoever attacked us exactly where we are? No, thanks."

I exhale. "He's right."

"Okay, fine." Penn pauses. "Truth, then."

My stomach somersaults. "How would you feel about... me not picking?"

"Picking what?" He narrows his eyes. "Your seat?"

"Between the three of you."

It's a conversation Penn, Carter, and I have had before. In Michigan. But Oliver wasn't part of it, and now I watch for his reaction to my question.

Oliver laughs. Groans at the following pain. "*Mi nena*, you don't have to pick right now."

"That's the problem," I say before I can stop. "The more time I spend with all three of you, the less I want to pick at all. So what if I can't? Are two of you going to... leave?"

Oliver shifts so he can face me without twisting. His brows furrow. His eyes are more warm brown than green today, although when the light catches them, the inner circles are all green-gold.

"What are you saying, Sydney?"

Penn wets his lips. He looks equally interested in what I'm about to say.

"Do you think the four of us could be happy together?" I immediately bury my face in my legs. "Don't answer that if it's a no."

"I don't think either of us are going to say no to you, princess," Penn whispers. "Oliver?"

"I—" He cuts himself off. "Maybe."

Maybe is better than *no*.

My heart flutters, and I slowly peek up at them. "The thought of choosing makes me sick inside."

"Then don't," Penn advises. "Ollie. Truth or dare?"

Oliver frowns. "Dare."

"I dare you to call Carter some obnoxious nickname

during his first shift tonight. Something better than baby or sweetheart. Something that will make that man blush."

They're both so serious, staring at each other—I can't help the laugh that bubbles out of me. And then it's like a dam breaks, and I can't contain it anymore. I laugh until my eyes water and tears leak out of the corners. I laugh until my stomach hurts.

When I finally stop, I look at them through my blurred vision, blinking away the last of the tears and swiping them off my cheeks.

They're both staring.

"What?" My tone immediately shifts to defensive.

Oliver shakes his head.

"Just the most goddamn attractive girl on the face of the earth," Penn says under his breath.

Oh.

Oliver nods.

Oh.

My face flames.

I clear my throat and shove the car door open. "Time to go in."

Their laughter follows me.

ME

You've gone quiet.

L.

I was giving you space.

Seems like you might need more of it lately, with your entourage.

Don't do that. Please.

What? You've got, by my count, three guys drooling over you.

You sound jealous.

Maybe I am.

Maybe I just want you to figure out who I am.

That's not fair... I have tried.

You didn't try very hard when I broke into your room and fucked you.

Some part of you likes not knowing, hmm?

I don't know what to say to that.

Say it's the truth.

Or I'll just disappear.

Fuck you.

I don't know what's crawled up your ass, but I've been a little distracted lately. Sorry that I haven't texted you or—or whatever you expect from me.

Did you want me to take it up with the gossip column? Maybe I should dox your information, see how you like being inundated.

Why won't you just admit it?

Sydney.

There's a part of you that liked being taken by a stranger. By not seeing his face. MY face. I bent you over your desk and I left my cum in your ass, nice and plugged. Your guys probably found you wet and needy, hmm?

> They can thank me for that if you ever figure out who I am.

> I do want to know...

> Uh-huh. Should I give you another chance?

> Maybe you should.

> Where are you?

> At the SJU hockey game... second period just started.

> Keep your eyes peeled.

> The game of cat and mouse is one of my favorites.

I leave Penn and Oliver in their seats with five minutes left in the second period. They have strict instructions to come find me if I'm gone for more than ten because of what happened last time.

When I said that, though, guilt flashed over Oliver's face. He tried to get up and come with me, but I waved him off.

"Faster for me to jog up the stairs alone," I told him.

And now I'm in the women's bathroom—albeit a different one from the taping incident. I think. They all look mostly alike, but this one is smaller. Only four stalls, as we're on the backside of the arena. Carter apparently didn't want us sitting with the SJU crowd when he gave us tickets. We're far from the student section, which suits us just fine.

I don't need to see people I used to go to school with and drag up all those memories.

L.'s last words are imprinted in my mind, though. I can't shake the feeling that he's here, watching me or planning something nefarious. I finish my business in the empty bathroom and wash my hands.

Something catches my attention, and I frown.

The water isn't draining.

I turn off the tap and move to the next one down. There are only four sinks, and each one fills with water without draining. The last tap, on the sink all the way to the left, doesn't shut off. I step back and bump into something.

Someone.

My head snaps up, but I only catch a glimpse of the hooded figure behind me before his hand grips the back of my neck and shoves.

My face goes into the water.

His other hand grasps at my leggings, yanking them down. I grip the edge of the sink and try to propel myself up. I need air. My lungs scream. He gets my leggings to my knees and finally lessens his hold on my neck.

I jerk up and gasp a quick breath. "L.?"

His fingers squeeze once on my neck. I'm still too low to see in the mirror. My gaze is trapped on the sink, which is quickly filling with even more water. It sloshes up and over the edges, spilling across my hands and to the floor.

He slips his other hand between my legs, dragging two fingers down my center. Collecting my arousal. When I try to twist back and look at him, he shoves my head back into the water.

I managed to take a better breath, at least.

But then something else distracts me—something hard between my legs. When he thrusts into me, I groan. Bubbles escape my mouth and nose. He pulls me up again, and I focus on taking a breath and not looking at him.

Maybe he's right.

Maybe I like that I have no fucking idea who he is.

His grip changes, slipping from the back of my neck to fist my hair. I go back under. The cold water pushes at my face.

I'm horrified by how turned on I am, as he rocks his hips into me. His cock hits something inside me that makes my legs shake.

And suddenly I'm not just gripping the sink to try and lift myself, but to hold myself up, as well.

His movements are fast and jerky. His other hand reaches around me and strums my clit, rubbing harsh, almost painful circles.

I can't come while I'm underwater. I make a noise, something unintelligible, and water goes up my nose. My whole body heaves, trying to get rid of it.

He yanks me up and I cough, but he doesn't stop fucking me.

Who are you?

I cough and sputter. He keeps my face hovering just over the water, and my eyes roll back when my orgasm sneaks up on me.

The water kisses my lips and nose, my chin. He pushes me down as I come. My fingers flex, my muscles shake. It takes everything in me to keep holding my breath.

He stills inside me, his dick pulsing. My lungs cry for air, the burn somehow creating more fire along my skin where he's touching me.

And then he releases me entirely. He moves back, and I straighten. My hair around my face is soaked. My shirt. I lean on the sink and look at him in the mirror. But he's already turning away from me. The profile of his sweatshirt, the hood pulled low, obscures his face.

"Stop." My voice is raspy, and I have to slick water out of my eyes. "Just—stop."

He chuckles. Low. Harsh.

I yank up my panties and leggings, but by the time I've righted myself—he's gone.

sixty-one
sydney

It takes me an unfortunate amount of time to put myself back together. I pull my hair up into a long ponytail, ignoring the fact that it still looks wet around my face and past my ears. I took my shirt off and dried it as best I could under the hand dryer.

My jacket is back with the guys. So I just need to get it to a point where I can comfortably get back to them without drawing unwanted attention.

It's a good thing I didn't put makeup on today.

I shake my head at myself. I cleaned up the mess that L. left on my skin, and now I just feel caught between empty and fulfilled.

I proved him right. That shouldn't mean anything, though. I knew he was right from the beginning, as soon as he said I didn't want to know who he is. Knowing complicates things. I'm already struggling with three guys, how the hell could I add a fourth to the mix?

So, no.

Maybe this will convince L. to leave me alone altogether.

Not that I *want* that. But how long can I keep it up with him?

How much can we interact when it's all digital and secrets?

How close can I get to him when he tells me nothing?

My heart hammering, I head out. The period must've just ended, because people are flooding out of the tunnels through to the seating. I wait against the wall for an opening, then slip back through and down the steps to our seats.

I drop into my chair between them and blow out a breath.

They both look at me.

"What?" *Defensive.* I try not to wince or go back on it.

Oliver squints, but he shakes his head. "Nothing... You okay?"

"Perfectly fine," I grumble.

Penn chuckles. "You sure, princess? You seem..."

"I don't really want to talk about how I look," I say. "I just want to watch the rest of the game."

Which is only a slight problem, seeing as how we've got about twenty minutes until the next period starts. I sink lower in my seat and shrug on my jacket, zipping it up to my throat.

Oliver puts his hand on my thigh.

I look over at him, my eyes widening.

He glances at me with a small smirk. Especially when his hand inches higher.

I slap my hand over his, stopping his upward trek.

"This feels like a game of chicken," Penn comments. His palm touches my knee. "Ready, princess?"

He moves higher. Inch by inch. Until his pinky grazes where my upper thighs meet—

I stop him with a hand on his wrist.

His sweatshirt is damp.

I go still and stare at his arm. The black SJU sweatshirt Carter gave him... I grab at his sleeve, pulling it away from his skin.

No.

No, no, no.

When I meet Penn's gaze, there's an expectancy in his expression I was not ready for.

Penn is L.?

Penn has been L. this whole time?

I shoot to my feet, but he snags my hand and pulls me right back down.

"What did I miss?" Oliver asks.

I twist around. "Like you don't know?"

His brows furrow.

Okay, maybe he's innocent in this.

But *Penn*?

"How could you?" I face him again. "What the fuck is wrong with you?"

He doesn't seem perturbed by my reaction. If anything, he seems... amused?

I rip my hand out of his grasp and practically crawl over Oliver to get away from him. I shake out my limbs. Now he's got me rethinking every single conversation—both with Penn and L. They were the same. Are the same. But...

With shaking hands, I text Carter that I'm not staying. I don't know where to go that Penn won't follow, until Carter's reply comes in.

CARTER

Go to my apartment.

Please?

Okay.

I have no idea if I'll be able to get in or not—it doesn't really matter, I guess. Before I'm even out of the arena, I fall into a quicker pace. I run the whole way to Carter's apartment, thankful at least that the arena isn't too far from SJU territory.

I glance over my shoulder a few times, more worried about being followed by Penn than anyone else. He would follow me, I know that for sure. But I really don't know what else he would go to—the lines he would cross to get closer to me.

Why?

My throat closes. I make it onto Carter's street. It's all familiar in an aching way. Not like just a few hours ago, when we came here with him. Walking up to his apartment alone reminds me of before my world imploded.

When things were nice and easy.

Fuck that.

I get up to Carter's floor, to his apartment, and try the door.

Locked.

Sighing, I flip the welcome mat up. There's no spare key hidden there either.

Whatever.

Mentally done, I lean against the wall across from his door and slide down it. I curl my arms around my legs and tip my head back. Part of me wants to keep puzzling over it, but another part wants absolutely nothing to do with any of it.

Rightly so. My phone keeps buzzing with incoming notifications. As soon as I catch Penn's name on my screen, I turn it off. I drop my phone next to me and settle in to wait for Carter.

I don't know how much time passes when movement catches my eye.

A smile comes to my lips, and I turn to face Carter.

Except it's not Carter—it's Penn. Same black SJU sweatshirt with the hood pulled up. But it isn't just shadows hiding his face. He's wearing that stupid fucking clown mask.

I shove myself to my feet, scowling at him. "Seriously? Get the fuck out of here."

He doesn't say anything.

I point in his direction. "You don't just get to follow me around, Penn. It's fucking creepy. We haven't moved into the phase where the mask is funny."

Nothing. He walks toward me, slowly, and I narrow my eyes.

"Wait. Is this you pretending to be L.? Still hiding your face and identity like a coward?" I grimace. "Nice. So fucking nice."

He passes Carter's neighbor's door, and a chill sweeps down my spine. After a major fucking delayed reaction, something deep in me screams, *That's not Penn.*

"Oliver?" I try. I take a step back.

A low, rumbling laugh seeps out from under the mask.

On instinct, I spin around. There's another exit if I go the other way—

"*Oof.*" I smack into another body.

Another mask. This one not an exact replica, but a bloody clown mask all the same. And this body is bigger. Bigger and familiar in a way no one should be familiar with a body.

Ice grows along my limbs, freezing me in place. I stare into the eyeholes, at the dark-brown eyes that bore back at me. I can't move.

Can't fight.

He puts a bag over my head. There's a drawstring on the bottom of it, and they pull it so tight, it constricts around my throat. I can breathe, but just the sensation of it touching me sets my nerves on edge. I can't see through the fabric. I can't see anything, and it should panic me into movement. It only serves to bind my body tighter.

The other one secures my wrists behind me.

And then I'm picked up and tossed over a shoulder. I let out a wheezing breath and give a faint shudder.

Something pricks my upper thigh. Cold bleeds into me, that ice holding me hostage growing worse and worse. Until it travels up my spine and encases my brain.

Everything slows down after that. It's like my mind wants to follow but can't.

Down stairs, each thumping footstep driving a shoulder

into my stomach and abdomen. Dropped into something hard and dark. A door slamming.

Trunk, my tired thoughts finally produce.

I don't want to be here.

I don't want to do this.

I don't want...

I don't...

I...

sixty-two
oliver

There's no trace of Sydney. It takes cornering Carter outside the locker room—where he absolutely can't slip away from us —to realize that she texted him. He told her to go to his place, although he seems sheepish when he tells us his apartment door is locked.

So she's waiting for him outside it?

If she decided to wait at all.

"What's going on?" Carter asks. "She just mentioned…"

His gaze goes to Penn. I glance his way, too, although so far he's kept his mouth shut. Surprising for him, since he usually tells me everything. But now, with both of us glaring at him, he shudders.

He slowly pulls his phone out and goes to an app.

There's one conversation there, a long thread of texts back and forth.

Sydney.

I take it, going all the way up to the top. Where she asks him who he is, and he doesn't answer. When he finally settles on L. For Lucas, his fucking middle name. How he doesn't give her any more information about himself.

How they converse in lies.

My heart beats too fast for my liking, and I have to steel

myself against throwing his phone on the floor and stomping it to pieces.

Wordlessly, I hand it to Carter.

He throws it at Penn's chest—which I guess is better than smashing it. He shakes his head at Penn and brushes past us. We follow.

"Don't hate me," he says quietly, just to me. "I started talking to her when we still were supposed to hate her. I thought I would be digging up dirt on her or—I don't know. I don't know, okay? It went from being this fun game to... I looked forward to her texts. I know how insane that sounds, but then—"

"You could've told her," I growl. "You could've come clean any time. And she finds out... what did you do to her, Walker? When you went to the bathroom... you forget you're supposed to use the men's restroom and wind up with her instead?"

Carter whips around. "What?"

"I—"

"He's the one who put the plug in her ass," Carter suddenly says. "She was wearing it when I got there. I don't —" He shakes his head. "Damn, I'm a fucking idiot. I thought you put it in her then. But you fucked her ass, plugged her, left her there only to come back later."

"*Pinche cabrón*," I swear. *Fucking idiot*, is right. But not directed at Carter. No, the words are for my best friend, who I'm pretty sure I can't be more disappointed in.

They set me up that night—I don't regret that. It was hot. But the whole situation, the whole time, she thought there was another guy involved.

I don't have any more words.

We get in the car. It doesn't hurt to walk or remain upright, but lowering myself brings a grimace to my lips. Penn drives back to Carter's apartment, all of us silent. I'm not really sure what else I'm supposed to say to him besides fucking cursing.

Sydney is mine. No matter what she asked of us before the game. Her initials are carved into my skin, for fuck's sake. There's no way I'm going to let her go, not when it feels like she's finally starting to forgive me. Penn can screw up his own relationship with her—not mine.

Maybe she won't mind picking, in the end. The others will see themselves out on stupid fucking mistakes like this.

Either way, I'm going to be there for her. It took a minute —or a few weeks—to get it through my thick skull. But there's no denying that my feelings for her have been there for far longer. No matter how uncomfortable they are, or how confusing it is when I think about all we've done to each other.

To be fair—I've done far worse to her than she's ever done to me.

Carter throws the car into park.

"Stay," he barks at Penn.

I heave myself out without assistance, and I follow Carter up to his apartment. We round the corner from the stairs, and I expect Sydney to be waiting there for him.

But the hallway is empty.

He glances around, then unlocks the door and marches in.

Empty.

I glance around again, and my gaze lands on a phone on the floor. It's face-up, and the black screen nearly blended in with the dark carpet. It's been turned off. As soon as I power it up and it loads, though, the very familiar lock screen confirms that it's Sydney's.

"Carter," I holler. I press my hand to my ribs. That fucking hurt.

Who'd think yelling would be painful?

He reemerges, and I show him the phone.

"That's not good," he mutters. "And you shouldn't be looking at it in your state."

I roll my eyes. I've had a headache for the past twenty-four hours. Looking at a screen or two for ten minutes won't kill me.

"Call her dad," I suggest. "He'll probably answer if it's coming from her phone."

He nods and dials.

"Hey, Syd," Coach answers.

"Oh, hi Mr. Windsor," Carter says. "I found Sydney's phone. Do you know where she might be?"

"I thought she was going to your hockey game with Penn and Oliver." He pauses. "So maybe try them? Where did you find her phone?"

"I'll try them," Carter says, ignoring our coach's return question. "Thanks!"

He jams his finger on the end button and scowls. "Now what?"

"Now..."

"Guys!" Penn rounds the corner at a dead sprint, barely managing to stop from crashing into us. "She— I—"

"Breathe," I order. "You what?"

He holds out a mask.

I snatch it from him. It's the clown mask one of us wore. We both threw them out after scaring Sydney so bad. I flip it over.

My heart stops.

There's writing on the white plastic.

I wonder if she'll spill all your secrets before I spill all her blood...

"*Mierda*," I breathe. "Where did you find this?"

Penn tears it from my hand and shoves it at Carter. "I found it in the bushes out front. Did you have something to do with this?"

Carter blinks at us, then laughs. "Yeah, right. I'm in love with her. If I wanted to keep her away from you, I wouldn't have brought you here."

Penn scowls.

"Carter doing this wouldn't make sense," I say. "I..."

The pitch I gave to Bear comes back to me. I don't want to remember it. I was livid with Sydney for wearing Penn's sweatshirt around school. I hated that he played with her hair any chance he got, that he was able to talk to her and touch her. That he was fooled by her innocent act.

At any moment, she could give up information to Carter. To SJU. I was not about to be fucked over again.

Think of it this way, man. Penn's so delusional about her, he doesn't see that she's wearing a mask. So I say we grab her, we show her what a scary fucking mask is supposed to look like, and we prove to our teammate that she's not worth the dirt stuck to our boots.

When I recall it, the hungry gleam in Bear's gaze stands out. The way he seemed to light up when I laid out more of the plan. To buy masks, to grab her and toss her in the trunk, to generally terrify her with the threat of violence.

That plan obviously imploded when Penn found us and I left them alone.

I shudder.

Bear was someone I never should've involved. But he was my teammate, and I put misguided trust in him. He didn't deserve any of it.

And now he has her.

"We need to do something," I urge. "We need to find them."

My mind is already going back to how I found them. The rope around her throat, her wrists. The way she was gasping for air, her leggings pulled down—

I can only imagine what he'll do to her when no one is there to stop him.

sixty-three
sydney

I don't know when I lost consciousness, but I come back with a bolt of electricity. My body goes rigid, from sleep to pain. It arcs through me for another second, then stops.

I sag and slowly open my eyes. There's nothing to see, though. When I drag in a sharp breath, the fabric of the bag presses against my open mouth. My body aches. It takes me a minute to figure out where my limbs are.

My wrists are over my head. I'm vertical—barely. Most of my weight rests on my shoulders. My fingers are numb. I reach for the floor with my toes and just scrape it. I struggle for a minute before I can take some of my weight there.

Immediately, my shoulders burn with the release.

That same chuckle comes back to me.

A second later, I'm doused with cold water. I thrash, losing my footing. Dull pain radiates from my shoulders across my back and up my arms, ending at my wrists. Everything above it may as well be gone.

I bite the inside of my cheek to keep from crying out. Blood coats my tongue and grounds me to the present. Chains me here, really. I focus on the copper taste. Not my welling panic, which will overtake me at any moment. Not the bone-chilling cold now prickling at my skin.

Not the way my clothes are roughly stripped off my body.

I kick out. My bare foot connects with something soft, and a wheezing grunt reaches my ears.

Suddenly, the hood is whipped off my head, and the huge guy in the new clown mask looms in front of me.

Bear.

It's Bear. Whatever his fucking real name is—it flees my mind as pure terror takes over. I try to gain purchase on the floor, to back away from him, but my now-bare feet get no traction on the wet concrete.

He undoes his belt, his gloved fingers slipping it out of the loops too easily. It comes free with a snap, and I flinch. His eyes aren't blocked by this mask. He's so close that I catch his pupils dilating at my reaction.

Goosebumps rise on my skin. The horror of knowing what's coming curls in the pit of my stomach. He steps up closer, until the mask is almost touching my face.

He laughs.

With quick movements, he wraps the belt around my neck. He pulls it tight enough to cut off most of my air. I open and close my mouth, only able to draw in a whistling trickle of oxygen. He moves behind me, finicking with something. The belt gets tighter. My eyes bug out, and I thrash without warning.

It loosens a fraction.

When he comes back around, it dawns on me that he secured it at that tightness somehow.

He reaches around and flips the tail of the belt over my shoulder. "Like a little leash," he sneers. "What do you think?"

I open my mouth, but nothing comes out. The leather pushes at my throat, containing everything.

"It's a good look on her," another man says from behind me. "Did she think you were talking to her?"

Bear laughs. "She'll learn. Pets don't talk back."

If only looks could kill—he'd drop dead in an instant.

I choke on my own retort and struggle to bring myself back under control. Bear watches me behind the mask that will undoubtedly feature in new nightmares.

"She still has some spark in her," the man comments.

He moves into my line of vision. He, unlike Bear, isn't wearing a mask. He resembles him, though.

Brother.

Older. He's got a full beard, dark eyes, a cap obscuring the hair. He's not as tall as Bear—he's the one I confused for Penn. Or Oliver. Although watching him now, I have no idea how I could've made that mistake.

Where Penn and Oliver are lean, their muscles streamlined to be fast on the ice, Bear's brother is bulky. His shoulders are wide, his biceps straining against his long-sleeve t-shirt. He picks up a small black box. Attached to the top of it is a clamp with red rubber handles.

There's another one that isn't attached to anything.

I can't even fucking swallow. I stare at the brother. Bear moves out of the way, his arms crossing. The brother picks up the free clamp and reaches out.

In slow motion, he touches it to my stomach.

Instantly, agony arcs through me. I want to open my mouth and scream, but every muscle is rigid. My jaw clenches so hard, it's a wonder my teeth don't crack.

When he pulls away, I fall. My shoulders scream.

"Again?" he asks. He brushes my hair out of my face, then slaps my cheek. "I said—again?"

I shake my head.

He laughs. "Do you know why you're here?"

I shake my head again. Beyond the vague idea that Bear has some unfinished business with me—but is it really me, or is it Oliver and Penn who he has the issue with? They're the ones who stopped him after Oliver dangled me like bait.

"My brother will never play hockey again." He touches my rib with the metal clamp.

A high-pitched whine fills my ears. I know nothing but pain, like everything inside me is being ripped apart and set on fire. It's only when he removes the clamp and the noise continues that I realize it's me.

I press my tongue to the roof of my mouth. I can't catch my breath—it's like my lungs have vaporized, leaving nothing but blood. There's blood in my mouth, too.

"He just wanted a little taste." He reaches down and tugs at the hem of my panties. "And your boyfriends... you have a few, don't you? That's what Bear said. You're pretty enough to pull a few guys, but at the same time? You really must be a slut."

He sneers.

"Which is why it's even more pathetic that you can't open your legs for one more." He glances back and motions to Bear.

My gaze sticks on the former hockey player. He limps to a far wall in the nondescript room. I only now notice the higher-than-normal ceilings, the fluorescent tube lighting shining steadily above our heads. Up, up, up... my wrists are secured by chains which thread up and over a pipe on the ceiling, then down to where Bear now stands.

He undoes it, feeding the chain an inch, then two.

The balls of my feet touch the floor, then I'm flat-footed. My elbows bend slightly, my shoulders pulsing as they no longer strain to hold me up.

The brother tilts his head, watching me. "Do you know where we are?"

I frown. How the hell would I know that?"

"Bear," the brother says. "Show her."

Bear, now clearly reduced to being a lackey, goes to the only door in the room. He opens it wide, exposing the large, open warehouse floor.

There's even still a circle drawn in chalk in the center.

White spots flicker in the edges of my vision. If I don't

breathe calmly and slowly, I don't breathe at all. But it's hard to focus on that when the realization slips into me.

I'm bait once again.

"There's just one more thing," the brother whispers. There's a glimmer of a blade in his hand.

He kicks my legs apart.

No, no, no—

The fight bursts back into me, and I kick at him as hard as I can. He twists at the last second, letting my foot glance off his thigh.

He touches the clamp to my side. The pain is an overload. I can barely process outside of the million simultaneous stings.

It stops, and he backs away. I'm once again hanging by my wrists, but I have no energy to try and get my feet back under me.

"Insurance," he repeats.

Bear jerks, suddenly shoving the mask up to the top of his head. His wide eyes are locked on my body. "What did you do?"

"Nothing she doesn't deserve," his brother spits. "Now let's go."

He grabs him and hauls him out the door. They don't even bother closing it behind them. Their footsteps recede, although where they go, I have no idea.

Just breathe.

I take a shallow breath. The belt around my neck feels claustrophobic. It holds all my panic, which rises like an unstoppable tide and stops just short of exploding out of me.

Slowly, I push myself to my feet and take stock of the rest of me.

There's something wet between my thighs. Running down my left leg.

I look down and whimper.

Blood.

A lot of it.

sixty-four
penn

She's never going to forgive me.

I've kept this secret for far too long. In a way, it felt like a different life. She pulled me out of my head, out of everything, and made me be present with her. Through the phone. Through her candidness. As L., I had conversations with her that I don't think would've happened as Penn.

As me.

That hurts. It's been hurting for a while, a lingering bruise that I keep pressing on when I get bored or tired or comfortable. The ache, after some time, became soothing.

But the act of touching it, irritating it, over and over again? It meant it couldn't heal. It meant there was no way I could confess to her. Even when I spoke to her on the phone as L., my heart hammered. I spoke low, but I kept waiting for her to call me out.

For her to recognize me.

And in her room—the same thing. I pushed her against the desk and I fucked her, and I kept waiting for that moment of realization. The part where she was supposed to say, "Oh, I recognize this dick. Penn, you jokester!"

Probably would've worked better if she saw my dick instead of just felt it. The tattoo—a fucking spiral that I got drunk one night my freshman year, some stupid hazing shit on the hockey team—would be a dead giveaway.

Instead...

I took it too far.

I take everything too far.

As soon as I realized there was a way out of my small, nobody-leaves hometown, I leaned into it. Hockey was my escape. It had been an emotional escape for years prior, sure. But a physical escape? I went from practicing with the team to extra hours on the ice, a private goalie coach... anything and everything.

It's not like I thought I would get into the NHL. Goalies have a harder time than anyone, because teams only need two of them compared to the eighteen players across the other positions.

Competitive.

I am competitive. It's how I got into Framingham State U and became a Viper. I worked my ass off until recruits noticed me.

So it may or may not be a reasonable leap to want *Sydney* to notice me. Both as L. and Penn. Or any way possible.

It's just so stupid, it's not even fucking funny. And now she's hurting because it feels like a betrayal or some cruel joke. That's how she thought of it in the beginning.

Me, too.

It was just supposed to be... a game. A game where only one of us got exploited.

"Focus," Carter snaps at me.

I cringe. "I'm in it."

Oliver groans through his teeth. "Yeah, fucking right. *Vete a la chingada.*"

Oh, I know that one. *Fuck yourself.* Figures.

We're bouncing our way down a forgotten back road toward the mechanic's warehouse where we fight. Because that's where Bear and Oliver took Sydney the first time, and

Carter says it would be stupid for him to take her anywhere else.

The police still have the apartment under surveillance—her dad mentioned that at practice the other day, offhandedly. Like we wouldn't be upset by it, or shocked...

I don't know, maybe he meant it to just be a conversation piece. Or reassuring. "Don't worry, the police are still keeping an eye on her apartment." Not, "By the way, the police are watching her apartment, so don't do anything fucking dumb."

Whatever.

I cross my arms. My stomach is in knots over what we're going to find at the warehouse.

Bear seems to have gone into full psycho mode—judging by the unhinged mask with a note anyway. I've got nothing to base that assumption on besides that. But isn't that enough? If he took her...

"Should we call the police?" I ask, leaning forward between the seats.

"And what happens if they blame it on us?" Carter snaps. "The police already think she has something to do with her mom..."

Fuck. I pinch the bridge of my nose. "On top of all of this shit, I forgot about that."

"Of course you did," Oliver says in a low voice. "You only care about fucking Sydney."

He continues in Spanish and completely loses me, but I do catch *cullero*. Asshole.

Well, I'm not about to bare my soul to them when they're pissed at me. If I did that, they'd just have ammo to use against me later. I know how Oliver works... I can imagine Carter has the same mode of operation.

Most assholes pull from the same playbook.

So instead of letting the guilt over forgetting about her mom—temporarily, for fuck's sake—I say, "I happen to enjoy her body. And if it gets her mind off of things for a while, who am I to take that from her?"

"Her mind's not what's getting off," Carter mutters.

"All hail King Carter, the saint of the group," I snap. "Like you didn't rent an apartment across from her building to spy on her."

Oliver chokes. "What?"

"Oh, did he not tell you?" I cross my arms. "He's a stalker."

"I just wanted to keep an eye on her," Carter mumbles. The tips of his ears turn red.

"He copied her key," I add. "I at least break in the old-fashioned way."

Oliver's wheezing now. "Are you telling me you've both been breaking into her apartment...?"

Carter shrugs. "I mean... Penn's been fucking her while she sleeps, but I've just been watching her."

The wheezing stops. I lower myself in my seat, scowling at both of them. "She's fine with it, by the way. You could've added that."

"She didn't know—"

"She found out," I interrupt. "Focus—there's the warehouse."

Carter pulls slightly off the road and kills the engine. We're still a good distance away, which isn't too much of a problem. For me. And Carter. Oliver is another story entirely.

Actually...

He hoists himself out of the car, his face a mask of pain, and I frown. I can't be the one to suggest he stay behind, though, right? That would not fly.

I turn expectantly at Carter, who's eyeing Oliver with the same concern. He opens his mouth, but Oliver shoots him a look.

Carter shakes his head slowly.

Now they're having silent conversations?

What happened to me and Carter being pals?

"We can't go in there empty-handed," I say.

Carter nods. He moves to the trunk, popping it with a button on his key. He flips up the mat, unveiling a locked case. When *that* opens with a press of his thumb, it reveals a gun and two knives.

"Why do you have this?" Oliver asks in a low voice. "Are those even legal?"

"Um..." Carter makes a face. "My parents believe in the right to bear arms. So technically, yes, totally legal. For them. Well, for my uncle, who has a concealed carry license."

We stare at him.

"What?" He picks up the gun and does some mojo on it, sliding back the top and then clicking in a magazine from the bottom of the handle. "Every summer since I was old enough to walk, I'd be out hunting with my family. Gun knowledge is essential."

"Obeying the law, not so much." Oliver exhales. "How illegal is this?"

Carter shifts. "Let's just try not to shoot anybody."

"Great." I wipe my hand down my face. "Okay, clock's ticking. You keep the gun—"

I take a knife. It's not a folding one, like what Carter usually carries on him. This is a weapon. The blade itself is five, maybe six inches long, with a wicked curve at the top to a gleaming, sharp point.

"Here." Carter pushes a leather sheath into my chest. "So you don't cut your hand off. And hold it like this." He takes the knife from my hand and flips it the other way, so the blade isn't near my thumb, but my pinky.

"Great." I nod, then sheath it. I tuck it into the waistband of my jeans and shake out my limbs. "Ollie?"

Oliver moves slower, taking the last knife. He holds it as Carter instructed, seeming more comfortable with it than me. Maybe he spent time as a kid... carving?

Funny. Probably not, though.

As a trio, we head toward the warehouse. There's a car parked outside, the trunk open and empty. My blood chills, but I force myself to keep moving.

The zone I drop into is no different than when I step in front of the net. Clear head, focused. It's what Sydney needs.

We enter through a side door. This place was owned by Oliver's mom's uncle. He passed away a few years ago, but nothing with his estate—including this building—has been settled. Because of all the claims on it, it's been caught up in the courts ever since.

Which made it the perfect spot to use when we needed to get out of the public eye.

Now, I'm kind of regretting it. Definitely regretting ever bringing Bear.

I remember trying weed in here for the first time, the last hockey game of the season finished and a circle of my teammates on the floor. Playing a stupid game of pass the joint while we waited for girls to join us.

Bear was with us.

I remember hiding from my parents here, when my dad was on a rampage about something or another. I think it was when I crashed his car... Not on purpose, of course. It was an accident, but he took it to be intentional.

Carter lets me take the lead, sandwiching Oliver between us. I remove my knife slowly, holding it like he demonstrated.

The warehouse is split up into two main sections: the mechanic bay, where there are huge garage doors and car lifts, even abandoned toolboxes like Oliver's great-uncle's employees just suddenly walked out one day, and no one came back. Then there's the warehouse. It's all open, in a way, but the majority of the open space is there. What was once filling that space—pallets of supplies, parts, tires—all got pushed against the walls.

Then, of course, there's the old offices and storage room

444

for more delicate things. Oliver once said his uncle liked to be able to lock away the more expensive parts, the stuff that might be jacked more easily or whatever.

We used to play seven minutes in heaven in that storage room.

I inch along the raised lift of the mechanic's bay, using it to shield me.

Something in the distance clanks. Faintly, like chains.

"Oliver?" Sydney's voice floats out from a far corner of the warehouse.

I glance over my shoulder.

Oliver's eyebrows are raised. He's in a half-crouched position, his knife also out.

"Oliver?" she calls again.

"What do we do?" I ask Carter under my breath. "She sounds..."

"She sounds afraid," Oliver interjects. "She's calling for me—"

He moves past me without another word. I grab for his shirt and fucking miss. He straightens and strides out into the open, his knife at his side. I lunge to follow him, but Carter manages to stop me. His arms around my shoulders, dragging me back into the shadows.

"Oliver?" Her voice wobbles.

"Why does she keep calling for him?" I ask Carter. "She doesn't know we're here—"

BANG!

Carter and I both flinch down, but my gaze flies to my best friend.

Oliver wavers for a minute... and then he drops.

sixty-five
carter

I barely manage to hold Penn back. I get the urge to run for Oliver—I do, truly. But I don't see blood on him. And a minute later, their ex-teammate walks out from the opposite direction. His scary older brother, who resembles a bulldog, comes out behind him.

He's carrying a gun, but there's a very clear distinction: the green tip.

"He hit him with a bean bag," I breathe in Penn's ear. "He's alive. Okay? Come on."

I try to drag him back around the other way. We need to get to Sydney, wherever they're hiding her. In the middle of the room, Oliver groans and rolls onto his side. He heaves.

"Get up," Bear orders.

He's limping, too. Vicious thoughts of breaking his leg fills my vision. Just as a warm-up. An appetizer, so to speak.

Penn jerks free of my hold, but he doesn't rush out to save Oliver.

"Listen," I say, grabbing at Penn again. "You can either go be a martyr, or we can find Sydney."

"You find her," he says. "I'm going to save Ollie."

I groan, but he's already moving away from me. Bear and his brother are almost on top of Oliver when Penn steps out.

"Let's make it a fair fight, guys," he calls. The knife isn't in his hand anymore, and he spreads his arms out wide. "You don't think Ruiz came alone, do you?"

Bear laughs. It's fucking cold and goes straight through me. "I hoped there would be three of you. Save us some time chasing down the SJU rat."

I bristle. I force myself away from them, circling wide and creeping along the walls. There's only a row of lights on in the center of the warehouse, casting the rest in shadow. I'd guess Bear and his brother were going for some dramatic effect, but it works to my favor. I keep one eye on them. They're fully focused on a conversation with a rambling Penn, while trying not to make a sound otherwise.

I am good at this. I'm good at hunting, at stalking.

Maybe that's why I like acting it out with Sydney...

"Oliver?" her voice comes again. It seems to echo all around, the wobbling tone making my brows furrow.

There's something off about it. Because it sounds... the same.

Bear laughs. "You didn't fall for that, did you?"

Oliver pushes himself back to his feet, clutching his side. "What did you do?"

"Confronted her with the mask..." Bear tilts his head. "I must admit, I expected her to run immediately. Instead, she said—well, here. Listen."

"Seriously? Get the fuck out of here," Sydney's voice comes again. Stronger. Angrier. "You don't just get to follow me around, Penn. It's fucking creepy. We haven't moved into the phase where the mask is funny."

My heart climbs into my throat.

"Wait. Is this you pretending to be L.? Nice. So fucking nice." Then, "Oliver?"

They recorded her. Cut the audio...

Bear laughs. "She thought my brother was one of you two. Did you end up going through with my plan? Wear the mask and fuck her? She wasn't too happy... well, I'm sure you could tell. I thought it was fucking amusing. She turned and ran straight into me."

"You bastard," Penn curses.

Bear lifts one bulky shoulder. "Yeah? What of it, Walker? I was hoping she'd give us a good scream—I thought that might get you running, you know? Scare you a bit more. But she didn't. Not yet anyway."

I'm going to be sick.

I reach the offices and peek in through the window of the first. The room is empty unless she's lying directly under the window. Risking that she's not, I go on to the next. Then the storage room.

The door is open, but moving from my spot will leave me in the open.

I glance back at Bear and his brother.

"You assholes," Penn shouts. "So caught up in your vendetta that you'd terrorize an innocent girl?"

He steps forward, and Bear's brother hefts the gun up. Points it at him. Bean bag or not, it would suck to get hit with it. Penn stops, his hands going up.

"You think she's innocent?" Bear spits.

I will my steps to be silent as I sprint across the open space and practically dive into the storage room. If she's not in here, I'll be stuck—

But here she is.

Fuck.

Her arms are trapped above her head, her wrists wrapped in chains that hold her up. Her weight is fully on her wrists and shoulders. Her knees are bent, her legs not supporting her.

She lifts her head. There's a belt wrapped around her neck. She's also soaking wet. Naked except for her underwear. And there's a cut on her inner thigh. A steady stream of blood runs down her leg, puddling on the floor under her.

I rush to her and undo the belt first. It's so fucking tight, I don't know how she's still conscious. I have to physically swallow down my rage.

As soon as I loosen it, she sucks in a huge, gasping breath. Her chest heaves, and the blood flows faster from her leg.

Shit.

I shed my jacket, dropping it to the floor, then tear my shirt off and press it to the cut. They fucking made a nick in her artery—not big enough to bleed her out immediately. But if we hadn't come along, she'd surely be dead soon.

I wrap the belt around her thigh, cinching it to keep pressure on the wound.

Her gaze finds mine. Her expression is confused, her brows pulling down. "Real?" she mouths.

"I'm real. I've got you." I shake my head and examine the chains binding her wrists. It goes up and is looped over a pipe at the ceiling, then comes down to the far wall. "I'm getting you down."

I cross the room, gripping the chain and unwinding it from its anchor. I keep one eye on her and one on the door, conscious of the fact that any noise might alert them to my presence.

Carefully, I lower her to the floor. Her teeth chatter, and she curls onto her side in the puddle of blood and water. She brings her arms down, and I remove the chains from her wrists. I pick her up, although her hip and outer thigh are now coated in the blood that she lost.

"Hang on," I plead. "Stay with me, okay?"

She nods. I lean her against a wall. I wrap my jacket around her, then straighten. My attention snags on a car battery. One clamp of jumper cables is attached to it, the other on the floor. I stare at them, trying to figure out why...

It's fucking obvious why. *They tortured her.*

I wasn't going to resort to violence. I thought we might be able to save her and leave—but this is too far. God knows what else they did to her before leaving her like this?

A growl burns through my throat before I can stop it. I pull the gun and check it again, then slowly step out from the storage room. The handle fits comfortably in my hand. While Penn's uncle is apparently a private investigator, mine enjoys hunting... or just going out into the woods and shooting with a wide variety of firearms. It isn't quite what my parents would've approved of... my uncle is a bit of a black sheep in our family.

That's probably why I gravitated toward him. He taught me a lot, but mostly firearm safety and shooting accuracy. The proud smile on his face every time I shot a can off of a log was a hit of dopamine.

Fucking addicting.

Now, I keep my trigger finger straight along the barrel of the gun and creep toward the door. Sydney is silent behind me.

Bear and Penn are fighting. They both have knives. But as soon as Penn gets an upper hand, Bear's brother lifts his gun.

Not so fucking fast.

I raise mine. Aim.

Shoot.

The *crack* of my handgun going off, the jerk of the recoil, is familiar. Soothing, almost.

My aim is true. My bullet finds its mark. It buries in the brother's side, under his arm. Just like taking down a dear—well, different gun—the man staggers forward a few steps, shock coloring his expression.

And then he falls.

Bear roars. He's got a fucking limp, so I put away the gun. He charges at me at half-speed. I pull my trusty folded knife, flicking it open one-handed. Rage makes him move recklessly —my anger is more like ice. I avoid his blade and sink mine into his stomach, dragging it sideways. It rips at my hand, the blade snagging. I hold tight, taking it with me as I dance out of his long reach.

The pain hits him a second later. One hand presses to his stomach. Blood oozes through his fingers. His other, with the hold on his knife, tightens. Lifts. His gaze flickers from surprise to outrage.

Guys like him—asshole demons on the ice, who think they're superior and get off on causing injuries to their opponents—deserve all the shit that comes their way.

He rushes me again. He's faster than I anticipate, getting a shallow slice across my chest. I hopped back—just not enough. Penn shouts. I kick at Bear's knee, the one Oliver injured at the last fight. He lets out an ugly howl, going down fast.

"Grab him," I order Penn. "Before I fucking kill him."

It takes both of us to get Bear wrestled to the floor. Oliver appears with zip ties, and we secure his wrists and ankles. Then the two together.

Penn and I roll off him and stagger away. Bear is on his stomach, his wrists and ankles now all attached together, and he tests the strength of the zip ties immediately. It's almost comical, watching him struggle, but they hold fast.

"Where is she?" Oliver gasps.

Leaving Bear to struggle on his own, I lead them back to the storage room. Syd's head is leaned back against the wall, her eyes closed. There's a thick, dark-red ring around her neck where the belt was.

Oliver drops to the floor beside her, his hands seeming to worriedly flutter over her body before landing on her shoulder.

Her eyes crack open.

"Oh, thank fuck," he whispers.

"Oliver?" Her voice wavers. It sounds so much like that audio clip they played, my heart squeezes. "I—"

"We're here." Penn creeps closer on his knees, but he doesn't touch her. He seems wary to get too close. "You're okay."

"She's not okay," I cut in.

I show them the car battery. A discarded bucket on its side, with a shallow pool of water left in it. The pool of blood, with smears in it from how she'd lain in it and I'd picked her up, is impossible to miss. Seeing everything again makes it a hundred times more real.

Penn squeezes his eyes shut. It seems like he, too, is struggling to rein in his inner demons. His hands ball into fists and release, over and over again. Only Oliver seems to be keeping it together. He's on his knees next to her, the worry in his expression enough to break me again.

"I'm glad you didn't fucking kill him." Oliver strokes Sydney's wet hair out of her face. "He deserves to go to Hell and back."

I nod my agreement, but... "We can't send him to Hell at the moment. She needs to get to a hospital. She's lost so much blood."

Penn makes a noise of objection.

In quick sentences, I describe how I found her. Not that they really need it laid out for them, with all the evidence scattered around. Their eyes just get wider, but finally Oliver and Penn both nod. They trade another glance, having some wordless conversation, and then Penn leans forward and lifts Sydney into his arms.

She thrashes for a moment, almost tipping out of his grip. Her eyes are closed, have been closed, but her struggle seems instinctual. My stomach turns. I never want to see *that* much of her blood...

"It's just me, princess," he whispers in her ear. "It's okay, I've got you."

She stops fighting him. Or maybe she passes out, because the next second, she goes limp.

"You and Oliver take her to the hospital," I say. "I'll stay here with Bear."

Oliver's gaze darkens. "Save a piece of him for us."

Penn nods his agreement. Oliver lifts Sydney's head, tucking it into the crook of Penn's neck. Unconscious, maybe, but she hasn't stopped shivering. Even with my jacket around her shoulders. And yes, I'm fully fucking shirtless in the middle of winter—at this point, it barely registers. Not until Oliver strips off his zipped sweatshirt and tosses it at me.

"Thanks," I grunt. "Now get the fuck out of here."

I've got work to do.

sixty-six
sydney

I'm in the hospital.

At least, I think it's the hospital. There's a faint beeping of a monitor, and the smell of antiseptic sticks in my nose. I shift in the bed, wanting to wake up but being unable to drag myself out of the darkness.

I'm just so tired. At least it doesn't hurt anymore.

The last thing I remember is...

Oliver.

Penn.

I was so fucking mad at Penn. Terrified when my body went up, lifted into someone's arms. And yet, everything went calm as soon as I registered that it was him. The minute I heard his voice. I settled... and I don't know, something like peace swept through me.

Now, this.

Even though I'm still not convinced I'm not dying.

Would dying hurt?

Wait.

There's no pain. That means I'm dead, right? Because pain ends there. Shit, I don't want to be dead. There's a lot I have left to do—

"Why isn't she opening her eyes?"

Oliver.

The beeping increases in frequency. I will my eyes to open, to push away that repressive darkness, and—

There.

His face is the first thing I see, followed closely by Penn's.

Penn, who I should still be furious at, but somehow only feel grateful that he stuck around.

They got me away from Bear and his brother. They saved me. I have the vaguest memory of Carter picking me up, too. The painful pinch of something around my upper leg.

Did they call my dad?

I reach for them. Both hands. My muscles ache, and even that seems to take all my remaining effort. I'm going under again. They each take one, their hands warm and dry against my freezing fingers.

My vision dims, then darkens completely. My eyes close...

I don't know where I go.

Away.

sixty-seven
oliver

"Take it easy."

My words earn a glare from Sydney and her father. Calling him, telling him that his baby girl was in the hospital, was the worst phone call I could make. I almost pawned the job off on the nurse who's been in and out of Sydney's ICU room quite a bit.

Actually, calling it a room is laughable. They don't have rooms with doors in the intensive care unit—there are just partitions and an army of nurses and doctors ready to save lives. Which they do, on this unit. Constantly.

After two days, her doctors move her to a regular room for more observation. They ran countless tests, making sure the electrocution didn't fuck with her heart or any other number of organs. Since I couldn't say how many times or how long she was in contact with the car battery, they wanted to be on the safe side. Coupled with the potential for hypothermia—

It's been a long week, but she was finally given a clean bill of health.

The police came in and questioned her about her injuries, while I held my breath and Coach held her hand. But surprisingly, she said she didn't remember anything. Couldn't remember where, who, why...

A mugging, she mused.

My brilliant girl.

Not really mine.

Now, her dad and I are hovering as she climbs into the car.

When I do the same, sliding in behind her, I feel why they were glaring—it hurts me almost as much as it does her. So I guess I can eat my words about taking it easy.

We go to her apartment first.

The place has been transformed. My parents are still there, and they kiss me on the cheek when we walk in. Fixing it up from how Bear and his brother left it was truly a miracle enacted by my family. One call to my dad, and suddenly uncles and cousins showed up in arms. When it wasn't my turn to keep Sydney company at the hospital, I was here.

Or at the warehouse.

I watch her take it in. Her hand covers her mouth, although it doesn't really hide the way her chin wobbles. She goes over and hugs my mom. Then my dad. And finally, gingerly, she sinks into my embrace.

"Thank you," she whispers to me.

I can't keep the smile from my face. For this little slice of happiness before I pull her back, inevitably, into the darkness.

My parents leave. Her father hovers for a while, then he, too, retreats.

Penn arrives shortly after that. Sydney visibly stiffens from her position on the couch, where she's curled her legs up under her and pulled a blanket up to her chin. I move away, mumbling something about getting her water, and leave them alone.

Alone-*ish*. It's all open concept, not really any way to give them privacy unless I go lock myself in the bathroom or her room. Both things I'm not going to do.

"Can I..." Penn gestures to the couch.

I snort, and he glares at me.

"Sure," Sydney's faint reply comes.

He sits and faces her.

I lean on the counter. It's like a movie. A really bad movie. Actually, it could be the opening to a porno... "I'm sorry I pretended to be someone else, let's bang." Cut to a shot of Sydney choking on cock... I'd drop dead if those words left Penn's mouth, though.

You know what? It's best not to jinx it, otherwise the *cullero* might actually try to fuck her in this condition.

"Everything we talked about was true," he says. "I swear to you."

Her expression is closed off, but when her gaze drops to her lap, she says, "Tell me a lie."

"I'm in love with you."

I choke.

"If you want to run away from this fucked-up town, leave the trauma behind, I'll go with you. I'd follow you anywhere. If..." He pauses. "If you don't want to pick between us, I think I understand that, too. I would even accept it. For *you*. Because I fell in love with you between texts and actions, and I don't know what I'd do if you couldn't forgive me."

Wow.

He pulls something from his pocket. "I put this around your neck without asking. Carter took it off after I hurt you, betrayed you... but now, I hope that you'd do me the honor of choosing it."

That freaking necklace. The gold one with the pendant of the goalie mask and the snake. I admit, I didn't realize Carter was the one who'd removed it.

Sydney wipes at her cheeks, even though I don't think she's actually crying. She nods and leans forward, sweeping her hair aside for him to put it on. She continues to pick at the blanket on her lap, tugging a loose string.

"I love you, too," she whispers, when his head is bent next to hers.

The words do an odd thing to me.

458

Pain?

I'm moving before I can register doing so, slipping out the door without a word.

How did he get there with her? Seemingly so fast?

Against my better judgment, I walk home and retrieve my motorcycle from the garage. It's not supposed to snow until tomorrow, and the roads are dry. I tug on my leather jacket painfully slow. It hugs my ribcage when I zip it, and although it hurts initially, it actually kind of feels better. More support.

Helmet on, I ride out and head for the warehouse.

Carter is there, his car parked in front of one of the garage doors. I park beside him and enter through the side door. I stride through the empty, silent warehouse, and try not to marvel at the fact that so much good and horrifying things happened here. The good memories are layered under the bad, and nothing is left untainted.

There's a pool of blood soaked into the concrete where Bear's brother was shot, near where the fighting ring is still drawn in chalk. Parts of it have been worn away by feet and time, but no one has bothered to redraw it. I pass it and go to the offices, the only rooms in the warehouse that are heated to livable temperatures.

Which makes it all the more disgusting that they kept Sydney in the storage room. Without heat, without natural light.

I open the door and stroll inside.

Carter glances over his shoulder at me, frowning. He's got a computer in front of him, a split security feed on the screen. One shows the outside of the door I walked through moments ago, with a view of his car and my bike. The other shows Bear.

He's in the manager's office, handcuffed to the radiator. A bit of a nasty trick, seeing as how it gets hot as fuck when the heat kicks on. As an added bonus, he's got the mask he terrorized Sydney with duct taped to his face, wrapped around his head and over the eyeholes.

I think Penn came up with that one.

"Has he said anything?" I sit beside Carter, then stand again. The door to the manager's office is *right there*. We've been speaking in low tones in case our voices carry, and nothing is different now. "Has he... done anything?"

Carter drums his fingers on the desk. "Nope. Well, he whimpered for his mommy, but that's about it."

I grit my teeth.

"You look like a distressed ball of anxiety," he points out. "And I was counting on a few more hours before you got here, so...?"

Ugh.

"Penn told Syd he loves her."

Carter's eyes widen slightly. But then he nods and refocuses on the screen.

"She said it back," I add.

He exhales. "I mean, we saw it coming. You love her, too, don't you?"

I open and close my mouth.

Do I?

I mean...

"We're in the same boat, then. Hopelessly in love and unable to do anything about it. She's going to pick Penn. If she loves him, she'll pick him."

We didn't tell him about her question. And now, suddenly faced with the idea of letting him believe it's pointless or not, my stomach churns.

Who would've ever thought I'd be friends with the captain of the St. James hockey team? And not just friends, but... willing to share my girl with him? It's laughable.

And yet.

"She doesn't want to pick," I say. "She's been saying it."

"And you believe her?" His tone is hard. He's not focused on me, and it's out of character for him to give up.

I eye him. "You don't?"

He dusts off his thighs and stands. "As much as I'd love to believe in a happy ever foursome, I just... it seems unrealistic."

"So?" I laugh. "Who the fuck cares about unrealistic?

His expression changes into something... hesitant? I'll say it again: who the *fuck* thought I'd be having this conversation with Carter Masters?

"Get the girl," I continue. "Keep the girl. I'm the last person who wants to share her, asshole, but you're right—I fell in love with her. And I'd do anything to keep her *and* make her happy. And if she says she doesn't want to pick between us, if she wants it to work as some... foursome? I'll try it. I'd do anything for her."

It takes saying it out loud to realize it's true.

He considers it, then glances back at Bear.

"You got him?" he asks. "You... You said it, right? Get the girl, keep the girl. Shit. I've been here, barely spending any time with her in the hospital. I can't let her think—"

"Go," I urge.

He hurries past me. It isn't until the door closes with a soft *snick* behind me that I allow my expression to drop. Things are different for them. Penn and her overcame his deception. Carter... well, his only crime was stalking her from afar.

I broke her, which means there's no hope for us. For *me*.

If I was in his position, I'd be running to her, too. If there was a chance for us—but I destroyed it. And I have to live with the consequences.

sixty-eight
sydney

I don't think I've been warm in a week.

Between the ice bath bestowed upon me by Bear and his brother, the freezing room they kept me in, the blood loss, and then the blood-transfusion-driven fever and chills, I'm just... *done*. And ready to jump into a bonfire if it would mean getting warm.

When I drag myself out of the shower, later the same day I got home from the hospital, Carter waits for me. He's fully dressed, standing in my bathroom leaning against the back of the door like he's trying to keep himself from jumping on me.

It would make me feel normal, though...

"Hi," he whispers.

I haven't seen much of him in the past week. I think he came to the hospital, but I don't have solid memory of it. I just remember him holding my hand, drifting into consciousness to find to his head resting on the side of my bed as he, too, slept.

"Hey." I reach for a towel. "Long time no see."

He cracks a small smile. "Yeah."

"And intruding on my shower time..."

"Best place to catch you naked," he replies.

I nod carefully. "I got the all-clear. With the stitches..."

He stands straighter, a pained look crossing his face. "I, uh, heard about Penn's proclamation of love."

Ah.

"Yeah."

I keep the towel wrapped around me and use another one to dry my limbs. He watches me brush out my hair slowly, then blot out the excess moisture with the second towel. Penn saying he loved me—even with all the extra feelings about L. tied up in it—was overwhelming. In the best way possible, maybe?

But also, like something was missing.

Something that's now standing in front of me.

How can I tell Penn that I love him—*I do*—and yet still feel incomplete? One puzzle piece slotted into place. But there are more pieces. In the end, I didn't have to tell him. He knew. He preemptively accepted it.

"And you feel the same," Carter says.

I focus on him. "I... yeah."

I focus on the way his expression breaks, and how it breaks a little bit of me, too.

"But, Carter—I can't say I don't also feel the same for you, too. Because I do. We let each other go when it got scary. But I think I like scary from you. I've started to crave it." I inch toward him. There's nowhere for him to go—the door at his back, me at his front. "I can't pinpoint when I fell in love with you. I think I've been falling since you didn't let me disappear into FSU. You followed me. You saw me. And I see *you*."

He swallows.

"I love you," I repeat. "I'm *in* love with you."

I wait for him to leave. For him to brush me aside and hit the road because he won't be my *only*.

But he doesn't. His gaze seems to deepen and darken, and suddenly he's got my towel in his fingers, and he pulls it off my body in a quick jerk.

It drops to the floor, leaving me exposed. Bruises across my ribs, the stitches on the inside of my thigh, the ring of deep bruises around my neck—although, to be fair, those were visible even with the towel. There are burn marks where they touched me with the jumper cables, but those feel like nothing compared to the havoc they wreaked inside my body.

"Don't touch me like I'm broken," I beg him.

He exhales. Grasps my hips. Shifts me so my back is to the door. He braces his forearm against the wood next to my head and leans in real slow. I meet his storm-blue eyes, but my gaze flicks to his lips.

I close my eyes in anticipation.

The touch is sweeter than I remember. Soft, like a brush of sugar across my lips. Then away.

I open my eyes again.

His warm, throaty chuckle meets me. "I like that look, dream girl."

"What look?" I breathe.

"The one that says, *more*."

"Give me more, then."

"Yes, ma'am."

He kisses me again. Stronger. Sparks flood through me, and I grasp at his shirt. I use him and the wall to steady myself, to arch up into him.

More, I think, opening my mouth.

He tastes like strawberries. He scores my lower lip with his teeth, takes his fill of my mouth. He shifts forward, pinning me to the door with his hips. Showing me exactly what he thinks of *this*.

I tug at his shirt.

"Naughty," he says, barely pulling away. "You're not cleared to exert yourself."

"You can do the work," I say. "Please."

My hand travels down, palming him through his pants.

He groans. "You sorceress. Don't tell."

"Our little secret," I promise.

He moves my hands aside and shoves his pants down, unbuttoning his shirt and revealing his drool-worthy abdomen.

And a new addition—

"Is that a tattoo?"

He smirks, but—it says *dream girl's* along the left side of the V of his stomach. Like he's saying that *that* is—

"Like it?"

I wordlessly nod.

"Good." He hoists me up.

I let out a low noise when the tip of his cock slides through my center. He finds my entrance easily and slowly pushes into me.

I groan.

It's an odd combination of pain and pleasure. My body still aches. He's careful not to hit the stitches on my inner thigh, or even grip that leg and force it around him. But it means... I'm split open wider, and he goes deeper.

"You feel like my dream," he confesses, his lips at my temple. Running through my hair. "I'm going to wait to say it back to you, Sydney. But I hope you feel it."

It being... love.

I do. With every stroke, every kiss he peppers me with, it doesn't feel like he's making love to me—nothing so sappy as that. His thrusts are still hard enough to bump my spine against the door, to cause it to shake in its frame. I see stars. But I see everything he wants to give me, too.

I fall harder. Is that possible? I was already there—but I just sink deeper into it.

Into him.

He catches me.

When he makes me come, it hurts. It's like my brain rattles, everything vibrates. I cry out, and he comes a second later, spilling inside me. He keeps me full while I catch my breath and try to relate the pain into pleasure.

Not a hard task.

Eventually, he lowers my feet to the floor. His expression is still soft, and he tucks a lock of my wet hair behind my ear. "Get dressed. I need to show you something."

———

My stomach flips when we turn onto the driveway that leads to the warehouse. Each bump across the gravel hurts, but it's more of an emotional hurt. Like a stab in the chest, until I'm struggling to breathe.

Carter's hand lands on my thigh. "No one will hurt you."

I nod, although I'm not sure if I actually believe it. My lungs are tight.

We park next to Oliver's bike. What I think is his anyway. I narrow my eyes at it, then Carter. Oliver left Penn and I alone... Did he come straight here?

Is he fighting?

"Is he okay?" My voice is thick.

Carter inclines his chin, then gets out. He circles around and opens my door, offering his hand. I take it and let him help me out of the car. He keeps ahold of me as we approach the door. The wind whips at us, snatching pieces of my hair and the flap of my jacket. I wrap my free arm around my stomach.

I don't want to be here, but something tells me this is important.

We cross the warehouse. I pause at the bloodstain on the floor, my gut churning.

"Bear's brother," he says. "I shot him."

My brows pull together. I don't remember that. I don't remember any guns going off... I barely remember Carter getting me down from where I hung, and wrapping the belt from my neck around my thigh instead. It's all hazy, minus the sharp pinches of pain that kept me awake.

I lose track of events after that, though. Being carried... then nothing until the bright lights of the hospital emergency department.

My gaze jumps to the storage room. The door is closed, blocking my sight into the room where they held and... tortured me. I don't want to think about torture. The sharp pain of the jumper cables, the water... the inability to breathe.

We go into the offices, and I stop short.

Oliver is here. He sits in one of the desk chairs, tipped back with his booted feet propped up on a table. He drops them to the floor at our entrance and rises.

"Sydney."

I look between them. "What's going on?"

"She shouldn't be here," Oliver says to Carter.

Carter's expression darkens. "Shouldn't she?"

"We talked about this," Oliver hisses. "How she should be at home recovering, not—"

"Not what?" I interrupt.

They go quiet. I face Carter and glare at him until he relents, slowly nodding toward the computer on the desk. It's facing Oliver, so I release Carter's hand and move around to see it. It puts me in close proximity to Oliver.

Something I shouldn't mind.

I don't mind.

But my heart lurches, and our arms almost brush...

Damn it.

The missing piece.

I ignore the monitor and focus on his face. At the way his lips press into a thin line, seemingly waiting for me to rebuke him or push him away. At the heat in his hazel eyes—more green than brown today, I note—as his gaze tracks across my face.

I wind my arm through his, keeping him with me, and face the screen.

My knees almost give out. Only my hold on Oliver keeps me standing.

Fear lances through my body at the sight of Bear. I don't need to see his face—he wears that same, creepy mask, half obscured by duct tape around his head—to know it's him. He's wearing the same clothes. And even though he's hand-cuffed, too, it doesn't mean I'm safe from him.

"What is this?" I manage. "Why—"

There's another security camera pointed outside. I focus on the movement in it. Penn's car pulls up beside theirs, and he parks and climbs out without hesitation.

"You're not alone," Oliver says. "You're surrounded by guys who..."

I glance at him. "Guys who what?"

"Love you." He clears his throat. "Carter. Penn. Right?"

My chest is thundering, but I find myself nodding along anyway. Carter didn't say it, but he showed it. But... that means Oliver is out, right?

"And you?" Carter asks him. "You're included in that, too, right, Oliver?"

He doesn't answer.

I slowly pull away, just as Penn enters. I rush into his arms, and he catches me with an *oof*. His arms bind around my back, and I fit perfectly against him to bury my face in his chest. His chin comes down and rests on top of my head.

"Your hair is damp, princess," Penn rumbles.

Because I was too anxious to fully dry it before Carter and I left.

"What's got you upset?"

"Oliver won't admit that he loves her. We've got a bear in a cage..." Carter scoffs. "More the first thing than the second, I'd bet."

"Well." Penn leans back slightly. He runs his thumb along my cheek. "Let's deal with the bear in a cage first, then we can smack some sense into Ollie."

My chin wobbles. "What... what's the plan?"

"Reenact what he did to you on him," Oliver says. "Then kill him."

My jaw drops.

Carter slaps his hand to his forehead. "Tact. Where is your godforsaken tact?"

"Oh, sorry." Oliver sneers. "Let's go in and pour him some tea, ask him to pray for forgiveness, and then tell him to lie in the hole we dug out back."

"Jesus," Penn groans.

I... *smile*.

It's ridiculous. So ridiculous, in fact, that I can't help but let it play out in my mind. And the more it goes on, the more funny it seems. Until I'm silently laughing, my shoulders shaking with my need to contain it. I turn away from Penn, holding my stomach as it cramps with my uncontrolled laughter.

And when it finally passes, I face them. The sober reality of the situation falls on me.

"Okay," I finally say. I clear my throat. "Torture and murder. Let's do it."

sixty-nine
sydney

I'm not sure if there's supposed to be some sort of interrogation in here, but Oliver and I move out of the offices while Carter and Penn enter the room where Bear is kept. They hoist him up and wrestle him out, past us and into the storage room.

"It's okay," I say to Oliver in the wake of their movement.

He looks at me.

"That you don't, um, want to do this anymore." I touch my wrist. I forgot my watch, and the old, barely healed cuts ground me. Amongst all the other pain, that is controlled.

He just *looks* at me.

Until I glance away.

"I do," he says quietly. "I do want to do this. But I'm not going to give you my heart when you're..."

"Broken?" Bitterness fills my voice.

"Distracted. Penn and Carter both said it, didn't they? Or maybe Carter didn't, but I'm sure you had some sort of conversation." He touches my chin, turning my head back toward him. "Sorry, *mi nena*, but when I bleed my heart out for you, I want it to be the only thing on your mind. Not Bear, not being hurt, not how Penn did it or—"

"Okay." I wrap my fingers around his wrist. "Okay. I couldn't bear it if you... left."

"I'm not leaving," he assures me.

The storage room door opens, and Carter sticks his head out. He gives us a thumbs-up.

My stomach twists.

This is it, then?

I follow Oliver into the room, holding my breath. Much like how they had me strung up, Bear is in the center of the room with his arms over his head.

Like they had me, only the very tips of his toes touch the floor. He slides, trying and failing to get purchase. I grit my teeth and stare at the mask taped to his head. Strips of the gray tape cover the mask eyeholes. I don't want to know how they knew... or when Carter flicks open his knife and cuts Bear's shirt off him, that that's what they did to me.

Not until I find the scraps of my shirt in the corner of the room.

Oliver stands so close to me, his body heat radiates into me. We move around the room, until we're at the farthest corner of Bear's peripherals, with the profile of the mask clear in the low light. It takes me a second to notice the bucket of water. The jumper cables sit beside the car battery.

"What was first?" Penn glances at Carter. "Was it the water?"

Bear twists in his restraints.

"Yeah," Carter says. "Soaked him through. Even the hood over his face. Bit like waterboarding, don't you think?"

"We'll have to ask him," Penn replies. He picks up the bucket of water and dumps it, without warning, over Bear's head.

He makes a noise. It's muffled by something, but it would be a shout if he could speak.

Carter steps up and slices away the mask. The tape sticks

to the back of Bear's head, but the plastic mask falls away as soon as it's free, dropping to the floor.

Fresh blood trickles down his temple from Carter's knife, and a lone piece of tape covers his mouth. Before Bear can get his bearings—*no pun intended*—Penn delivers a hard punch to his gut.

The larger man contracts, his body jerking and shoulders stretching as his weight rests solely on them. He swings for a minute, his back to Oliver and me, until his toes scrape the floor and he brings himself to a stop.

Carter and Penn exchange a glance, and in one move, Penn rips the tape from Bear's mouth. He drops it, his lips flattening.

"You getting your licks in now, Walker?" Bear spits.

His voice brings goosebumps to the backs of my arms.

"Fucking cowards," he continues. "Resorting to stringing me up—"

"Oliver fought you," Penn interrupts. As he talks, he squats beside the car battery and attaches one of the clamps. "Beat you fair and fucking square. That didn't matter to you so much when you attacked him at Sydney's apartment. Two on fucking one with your brother."

"We weren't there for him," Bear growls.

Oliver frowns.

"Two guys to pick on one girl, then, huh?" Penn laughs. *Coldly.* "That doesn't make your case any fucking better."

He reaches out and clips the free cable clamp onto the waistband of Bear's pants, so one side of the metal is pressed to his skin. The reaction is instantaneous. He goes rigid, every muscle tensing and spasming, little tremors seeming to run through his legs. Electricity is always trying to find its way to the ground, after all.

That's why the prospect of them touching higher than my heart was what freaked out my doctors. They said the electrical pulse could've stopped it.

472

Should've... might've...

I breathe out slowly. I don't remember where they touched me with that clamp, just that it felt like I was being bit by an electric eel.

Penn and Carter seem content to watch him struggle. I move around, into Bear's line of sight. I go to the car battery and kick it. The battery goes tumbling away and the clamp disconnects.

He sags, the chains over his head clanking.

My guys regard me. Oliver moves behind Bear as I step closer. Like this, stretched to his maximum height, he towers over me. And Oliver, too. All of us. He's a beast of a guy.

The truth of the matter is that he didn't need his brother. He didn't need to bind me up and watch me struggle to breathe. He didn't need to fucking torture me. He's big enough, he's strong enough—he could've overpowered me the old-fashioned way.

But he didn't.

He chose to watch me choke. He chose to wear a mask for the terrorizing—not for the anonymity. Whatever twisted his brother up on the inside, it did even more damage to him.

"Henry Bernstein."

His real name. It deserves to be spoken now, right? Spoken into the quiet, forced out into the open. I break the silence with it. I smile when his eyes open and he flinches first, glares second.

"Henry. Bernstein." I inch closer, and Oliver mirrors me behind him. "What's your brother's name?"

He grits his teeth and looks down at me, then spits out, "Max."

"Well. *Max* is buried in the woods behind the warehouse."

He goes still. His muscles tense, like he's about to move—but Oliver is faster. He drops a looped cord over Bear's head and pulls it snug around his neck, stopping his idea of forward motion.

I shuffle backward. Bear roars, his body contorting and struggling. He kicks out, barely missing me, and Carter drags me farther away. While Oliver just—

"Is he going to kill him?"

Penn shakes his head. "Maybe."

When Bear stops fighting and goes slack, Oliver releases the rope. It hangs loose around Bear's neck—nothing compared to the prolonged trauma I endured.

"What else?" Penn asks me.

My gaze drops to the blood under Bear's feet. It's soaked into the concrete, dry little flakes of it sticking to his shoes. It's *my* blood. My trauma.

Carter nods and moves forward. He sinks the blade of his knife into Bear's stomach.

The guy comes awake violently again. His eyes are so fucking wide, and he stares down at the blade protruding from him. He passes out again.

I'm so fucking tired, and I can't tell if this revenge is making me feel better or worse.

"Is his brother buried in the woods?" I ask. I had guessed earlier.

They all exchange a glance, then shake their heads. "Not yet. He's in a barrel..." Carter frowns. "You look green. Do you want to go home?"

"Is he walking out of here?" I motion to Bear.

"No," they all say.

"Then, yeah, I want to go home."

I look to Oliver, whose skin tone has paled dramatically. I feel the same, my stomach twisting like I'm going to heave at any second. I can't take the smell of this room—the sweat, the blood. There's a wet spot between Bear's legs that grows by the second, the scent of urine overpowering everything else.

I cover my nose and mouth. "Take me, Oliver?"

seventy
sydney

Six Weeks Later

SJU and FSU rematch.

Oliver's first game back.

Am I worried?

I'd be fucking lying if I said no. I watched him wrap his ribs in the locker room—before my father came in and promptly kicked me out—and hovered outside. Even when Penn insisted that he was fine. That a doctor cleared him, that he's *fine*... Excuses.

I'm allowed to worry.

Most of my classes allowed me to make up assignments I missed while out. In the extreme, this meant I've been buried under the rubble of papers, presentations, and assignments since I went back to school.

We haven't talked about Bear or his brother. It's like he ceased to exist once we left that warehouse. I consider, from time to time, talking about it with the therapist I started seeing. I've told her in more vague terms about my trauma, but so far, our focus has been my mother.

Oliver drove me home and stayed with me, and, well, I

think Penn and Carter took care of Bear and his brother in a way I don't want to think about. Whether they buried him or dissolved him in a barrel of acid or cut him up into little pieces and dropped him in the lake...

I'm better off not knowing.

Which brings me to my mother.

Yesterday, the police concluded their investigation of her death. The coroner determined it was accidental, that she must've gotten high and wandered into the woods, gotten lost, and died from the elements.

We're also not considering how close she was to FSU... how close she was to coming back to me. She knew I was here. Even though she left Emerald Cove, she was found *here*. So close and so far away.

She was cremated, and my dad has her ashes at his house. We're going to hold some memorial over winter break, although I'm not sure anyone except immediate family will show up. And by that I mean me, Dad. Perri, and maybe the guys.

We didn't have anyone else.

"There you are!" Maddy drops into the seat next to me. "How long have you been sitting here?"

I shake my head. With her are Brandon and Dylan. Things haven't been the same between Brandon and me since my spiral and how he handled it. Maddy later admitted that she came and banged on my door, but it was locked and I never answered. It's unclear whether Brandon knew that, though, when he sent the nasty texts.

They sit on Maddy's other side.

Beyond them, Andi is on her way to a seat in the adjacent section. Her gaze meets mine for a moment, and she seems more visibly spooked than I've ever seen her. She turns and hurries away without a word.

The guys are already on the ice, warming up, and my

attention switches between Oliver and Penn on one side to Carter on the other.

Today, I wear neutral colors. A cream sweater and jeans, my black jacket over it. I'm purposefully not picking sides.

How could I?

"We've barely seen you," Dylan says. "Even in class, you're in and out."

I lean forward to see her past Maddy. "I've been trying to catch up on everything. It's been an avalanche of work."

Brandon doesn't say anything, and his silence is noted.

See? Awkward. Even after he apologized, it wasn't the same. It's not the same.

Maddy and I go get popcorn. By the time we return, the players have left the ice and the arena is darkening for the opening ceremonies. We stand through them, although it's a struggle not to wince when the kids they brought in to sing hit a sour note.

Then it's time for the first puck drop.

I watch through my fingers as one of the FSU players faces off against Carter. Carter wins it, shooting the puck between his legs toward one of his wingers. From there, it's a mess of back-and-forth action. As with this rivalry, nothing is ever easy. But the refs seem to have put their whistles away—well, never taken them out to begin with—because stupid, easily spotted calls are missed. A blatant slash, cross-checking in front of the crease.

The game goes from zero to a hundred as soon as SJU scores on Penn.

I leap to my feet, my heart in my throat. Penn knocks the puck out and reaches for the water bottle in the top of his net. Instead of drinking, he blasts himself in the face with the stream.

0-1

I'm not rooting for either team, I try to remind myself. But it's hard when I want to cheer and hide at every play. Not picking a team is worse than watching your favorite team perform badly.

Penn blocks the next six shots on goal, and finally a whistle is blown.

Tripping. An SJU d-man is tossed in the penalty box, and they set up to restart.

Oliver and Carter take the face-off, and Oliver flicks it back to his winger immediately. I go back to watching the game through my fingers.

Quick as a whip, Oliver gets the puck back—and scores.

The horn blows, the red lights behind the goal flash.

1-1

"How are you keeping calm?" Maddy asks, shaking my arm.

"It's not calm, it's dread!" I shout over the crowd.

She laughs.

The rest of the game progresses with minimal fighting, although the number of missed penalties is becoming absurd. Each team gets one power play—the first when Oliver scored, and then an SJU one for holding, where Carter comes *so close* to getting the puck past Penn.

As the seconds tick down on the third period, and the game is tied at four, it finally happens: a fight breaks out. One of the SJU forwards, on a breakaway, loses his edge and tumbles straight into Penn. The two go sailing into the net.

Immediately, though, another FSU d-man yanks the forward out. A little rough, sure. But then everyone is there, piling on and shoving each other.

The refs whistles blow, and they dive into the center of it. Pulling guys apart—

Oliver and Carter suddenly wade in. Not to fight, though. They do a better job of breaking it up and getting their guys to separate than the refs.

"Masters and Ruiz breaking up a fight instead of egging it on?" Brandon mutters. "That's a new one."

"Shut it, Moore," Dylan snaps.

I hide my smile. Truly, though, the guys have been getting along better. I've noticed that through my busyness, through my late nights at the library or spread out in the student center. There have been moments of not working—few and far between as they come. When Carter sneaks into my apartment, or Penn through my window, or sometimes both. When Oliver steals moments between class to kiss me breathless.

Truthfully, I'm ready for this semester to be over. I have one more final next week, on Monday, and then I can just... I don't know, relax? Perri and I are going to pick up a Christmas tree after it. She said it'll be an excuse to celebrate the start of winter break, maybe get me a new coat or boots...

Above all, I'm just trying not to think about the holidays without my mom. We never did anything major, but the few traditions we did have involved cutting down a tree—usually sneaking in through the back of the farm and stealing one of the smaller, undeveloped trees.

The refs finally restart the game, and I drag my thoughts away from the past.

With the score still tied, the final horn blows. Because they're in the same conference, it'll go into a five-minute overtime. The teams get organized and prepare to restart, and my anxiety creeps higher. Carter and Oliver are both on the ice. Penn looks ready in his crease.

"I can't watch." I jump up and slip past them, darting up the row before the game can restart.

In the hallway, I lean against a wall and close my eyes.

"Sydney?"

Of course... I can't have a moment of peace.

Scarlett is in front of me, just out of reach. Her brows are furrowed, a look of disdain painted on her features. I'm not sure how I ever... liked her. Got along with her.

My gaze moves past her, to her entourage. There are the familiar players. The girls she keeps close-but-not-too-close. I only don't recognize one. If I had to guess, Scarlett picked those clothes for her, much like she did for me. Same style and everything. Short dress, the hem of which she tries to subtly pull down her pale thigh, hair and makeup done almost over the top.

Almost.

A pang of disappointment rings through me. Not that I'm so easily replaced—there was never a question about my individuality within her friend group—but that she actually went and did it. She found someone who seems a lot like me, who probably didn't have a ton of friends, who will dress however she wants just to keep a friend.

"Leaving before the end of the game?" I ask.

"We're going to get the party ready," Scarlett says. "Are you hiding out here because you don't want to see FSU lose?"

I lift one shoulder.

"There's a rumor going around that you and Carter..." She looks me up and down. "There's no merit to that, right?"

"You don't think he'd date me?"

She coughs. Even that is delicate, behind her balled fist. Her tongue flicks out, wetting her cherry-red lips. "I don't think he'd have looked twice at you if not for me. And you broke up on such ugly terms..."

Did we?

"Ah, well. We'll see him tonight." She smiles. Nasty, cruel smile. "But not you. Because you're not welcome at any St. James parties."

"Don't worry, Lettie. I wouldn't go even if you paid me." I push off the wall and pass her.

I don't bother telling her that there's a great chance Carter will end up at my apartment tonight. And even if he didn't, I know he won't be with someone else. My newfound confidence straightens my spine and lets her nettling slip away.

480

I pause and eye my replacement. "Enjoy the ride, new girl. You'll probably end up in my shoes soon enough."

The roar of the crowd almost blocks my last word, and I smile to myself. I don't know who won, but it sounds like someone finally scored.

And I am ready to go home.

seventy-one
oliver

"Decide."

It comes from Penn, his arms folded over his chest. Carter's hands are in his pockets, leaning against the wall beside him. It comes off as supposedly less intimidating—and sure, it's not meant to be. But it fucking is.

I don't like being ganged up on. As the oldest sibling, I spent much of my childhood being outnumbered by Felix and Daniela. Which is why I let out a rough sigh and run my hand down my face.

"Decide," Carter says now. "It's not fair to her. She said she's not picking. She said she loves us. She loves you, too. Obviously."

"We can make it work," Penn agrees. "I've already seen you fuck her, dude. It was hot as shit."

After Sydney and I left the warehouse, I brought her to her dad's house. I made sure she was safe, settled, and I left again.

We killed Bear. Henry Bernstein. The thought should haunt me—it should make my soul turn black, right? It's not like letting out frustrations at the rage room. We stuffed him in a barrel, one of the oil ones from the mechanic's bay, and transported him to the dock. Carried it onto a boat.

Filled the barrel the rest of the way with rocks and water and pushed him in when we got to the center of the lake along with his brother.

For what they did to Sydney?

Worth it.

"Ollie." Penn steps closer. "Do you want to be with her?"

"Yeah." Of course I do.

"Then decide if we're worth it."

"Decide if she's worth it," Carter revises. "I, for one, haven't seen your dick. I've tasted your cum from her cunt, though..."

I glare at him.

He just fucking shrugs.

"We're basically brothers," Penn continues. "We took someone out together, you know? There's not much more that can bind us together."

Except love for a girl.

"Okay. Okay, I'm fucking in."

They exchange a look.

"What?" I demand.

"Grand gesture," they say at the same time.

"Why?"

"Because she thinks you still want her to pick," Penn says. "You don't join in our weekly group activities."

I scoff. "Group activities? There haven't been..."

Carter raises his eyebrows.

My jaw drops. "What the fuck, guys?"

"Grand gesture," Carter repeats. "It's the only way."

Great.

seventy-two
sydney

"How did it go?" Perri asks when I slip into her car.

"Pretty miserably. Dylan tried to help, but I don't think I really grasped it as much as I would've..." I shrug. "Ah, well. Hopefully I did enough to pass the class."

"That's the spirit." She pats my leg. "Are you hungry? Or shall we go straight to pick out a tree? Your father is going to meet us there, but we can easily divert him to that diner across from the lake."

"I can wait. I had a sandwich before the exam."

As in, Carter appeared at my library table with food an hour and a half earlier, saving the day because I hadn't made time to get myself food. Very thoughtful of him.

She smiles and nods, and we head to the tree farm on the edge of town. I haven't been to it—I just remember some kids at SJU talking about it last year. The ones who lived here full time or commuted from home. But apparently it also did a walk-through with lights and decorations, and that was a popular winter activity.

I don't know. I haven't heard of it, didn't bother looking into it. My holiday cheer is much lower this year than previous—for good reason. There's been a lot of shit going on.

But... I can do this. We'll go pick out a tree, take it back to Dad's house, decorate it.

Easy.

The farther out of town we get, the more pretty it gets. The snow clings to every tree branch, transforming the woods around us into a world of glistening ice.

Perri pulls into the tree farm. It's busy, even for the middle of the day, and she squeezes into a spot between two cars. There's a building with a low porch just in front of us, and a woodchip path to the left that goes under an arched fence opening. Through there are the trees.

"I got tickets online for if we want to do the walking portion after finding the tree." She shoots off a text. "And your dad is here, too. Perfect timing."

I bundle up and climb out of the car. Dad approaches from a few cars down, and he hugs me first, then kisses Perri. He shows us a hand saw and grins.

"Who's ready to cut down the perfect tree?" he asks.

I smile.

We enter and wind our way through the rows of trees. The ones up front have already been cut, but Dad just shakes his head and moves farther into the thick of it. Perri drops back, but Dad loops his arm through mine and leads me along.

"How're things with your boyfriends?" he asks.

I choke. "What?"

He side-eyes me. "Oliver, obviously. Penn... And Carter."

My stomach flips. "I don't know how to answer that."

He lifts a shoulder. "Convince Masters to transfer to FSU, sweetheart, and I'd be fine with you dating all three. *If* they make you happy. If not, we know where they'll end up."

On the ice, skating for their lives.

Dad being accepting of three... not something I ever could've predicted.

"Ah." He points. "What do you think about this one?"

We stop in front of a medium-sized tree. It seems full, with only a few extra long branches that could easily be trimmed. Good height... Who am I kidding? I have no idea how to pick out a tree.

"It looks perfect," I say.

He grins.

"Per!" He cranes around. "Can you go find her? I'll get to work cutting this down."

I leave him there and cut through the rows, but there's no sign of her. Her footprints are in the snow, though, clear as day. I'm assuming they're hers, anyway, so I keep going, glancing around. There are string lights wound around a cluster of trees ahead.

I hit a patch of woodchips without snow, losing her trail.

Brows furrowed, I head in the direction of the lights.

It forms a framed-in pathway of sorts.

Intrigued—and more than a little suspicious—I head down it. The path curves. I should call out her name, but something stops me.

When I round the corner, I almost think I'm intruding on something. Like a proposal in progress, or...

"Oliver?"

He's all dressed up. A light-gray peacoat covers a dress shirt and slacks, and his dark hair is combed out of his face.

And he smiles when he sees me.

"What are you doing here?" I blurt out.

He motions me closer, offering his hands to me. I take them and squeeze, appreciating the warmth and steadiness he brings.

"Sydney Windsor," he says softly. "I've never felt this way for anyone. You have such power over me... you rip my heart out with a single look. You put me back together with a touch."

The backs of my eyes burn.

"I've been cruel and you've been patient," he continues. "I was judgmental, where you were understanding. I told you a month ago that I wanted to be the only one on your mind when I give you my heart."

My breath catches.

"So..." He clears his throat. "I hope you forgive me for the delay, *mi nena*. Every day since then, I've forced myself to stay away. But I wasn't just hurting you, though. I was killing myself to prove a point—and I failed miserably."

He tilts his head. "Will you come with me?"

I find myself nodding. I take his hand, and he leads me farther down the path. The lights steer us off course at one point, and we cut between trees. Flickering lights catch my eye, and my brows raised. There's a blanket on the ground surrounded by candles. Pillows. Two more folded blankets and a Thermos nestled amongst them.

"Did you set this all up?"

Besides the candles, the little clearing is surrounded by those string lights that led me to Oliver. They give a warmth to the moodiness of the day, the clouds overhead storm gray and threatening to snow.

He squeezes my hand. "Sit with me?"

A lump forms in my throat, and I nod. I sit, and he arranges blankets on my lap. He sits close enough to scoot under them, too, and picks up the Thermos.

"You liked my hot chocolate, but I rushed you through the last cup."

"You did. I do." I laugh, my nerves making me uneasy.

He produces a mug and pours the spiced, Mexican hot chocolate into it. I cup my hands around the mug and lean over it, inhaling. The scents that mix with the chocolate are godly. Steam comes off the liquid, but I take a sip anyway.

I could easily drink it every day for the rest of my life.

I try not to audibly groan, but he nudges my side anyway. Grinning.

"You heard that?" My face is practically in the mug. There's no way he missed it.

He chuckles, and I lower the drink to my lap. I face him.

"I don't have any grand proclamation," I say. "I didn't plan anything—"

"You're not the one who has to," he says. "This... I just... it's not enough, is it? To make up for everything I've done."

I take his hands. "It doesn't matter. I mean—" I sigh. "It *does* matter. What you did to me in the past. But you've done more than enough to make up for it. And I realized along the way that I love you. We overcame it."

He leans in and kisses me. It's quick, just a brush of his lips on mine, but my heart skips all the same.

"Love doesn't cover it," he says without pulling away. "I want you to crawl under my skin just as surely as I want to be under yours. You live in my thoughts without fail. I truly think I carved out my heart and gave it to you, and you've been holding it safe ever since. It's the only way to explain how I feel with you and without you. That's to say, complete with you. And achingly empty without."

He touches my cheek.

"And," he continues, "I understand how interwoven your relationships are with Penn and Carter. I'm not asking you to choose. I'm just asking if you'll accept me, too."

Tears fill my eyes. "Of course I will."

"I have something for you." His voice comes out nearly hoarse, and he pulls something from his pocket.

A box.

Oh my God, is he going to propose?

I bite the inside of my cheek, fighting my emotions. We're still in college—

"It's not a ring," he says under his breath.

I exhale. "Not that I-I mean, one day—"

"Sydney."

I go still and take the box from his hands. Unlike a ring box, it's a bit flatter and bigger. I crack it open, catch a glimpse of gold, and immediately shut it again.

"You didn't."

He smiles. "Look."

I crack it open again. Slower.

My grandmother's bracelet sits nestled in black velvet, the inscription on the underside gleaming up at me.

It's better to have loved and lost than never loved at all.

Tears fill my eyes, and my hands tremble. "You took this from your mom?"

He chuckles. "I explained how I got it, but also where it came from. And she was more than happy to give it to me... for you."

He takes the box from me and lifts out the familiar bracelet. It's been cleaned, the gold shining in the string lights around us. I hold out my wrist and let him clasp it on. The metal is cold against my skin. The bruises and marks from the chains only recently completely faded, and I rotate my wrist to admire the bracelet.

"I love you," he says quietly.

I lean in toward Oliver and kiss him.

Cheers go up around us, and suddenly Penn and Carter burst out from behind two fuller trees. They dive on us—well, mostly on Oliver—and ruffle his hair. Penn smacks a kiss to his cheek.

Oliver groans and shoves them off us.

Carter crawls back up on my other side, lifting the blanket and sliding under it. "How was his grand gesture, Syd?"

I snicker. "Pretty good. How much did you hear?"

"All of it," Penn says. He sits across from us, leaning back on the blanket. "We're excellent eavesdroppers, but Ollie knows how to project."

"I was trying to be quiet," Oliver grumbles.

"A loud whisper," I allow, my smile widening. "It's okay. It happens."

Carter snorts. "Yeah, like premature ejaculation."

Oliver reaches over me and punches his arm. "Get fucking lost."

I lean against Oliver, resting my head on his chest. "Was Perri part of this? She disappeared..."

"Yeah, she's circled back to your dad by now. Nice of them to play along, huh, princess?" Penn grins. "Ollie's idea, of course. He went to your dad and made some dramatic speech about loving you."

I tilt my head back and stare. "Seriously?"

He shifts, his arm coming around me automatically. "Well, yeah. That was fun."

"I recorded it," Penn says. "Just, uh, for the record. We'll play it for you later."

"Can't wait," I whisper.

Because I can't.

In a way, this just feels... unreal. Insane. And a little bit like the happily ever after I never thought I'd get, with three guys I know I can't live without.

sydney

Five Months Later

Bracelet on. Necklace secured, the pendant in the hollow of my throat. Carter gifted me earrings not too long ago. They're little daggers with rubies in the hilt. A subtle acknowledgement of his kinks... and one of mine. Those are in my earlobes now.

To be fair, I wear all three pieces every day. They're armor, a safety blanket, a reminder.

It's been five months of seeing how things go. Of making it work as a unit of four.

But it's been slow. Inching progress instead of a sprint.

Of course, that's because there's been a lot happening. Just because some good things were happening in my life doesn't mean the trauma left me. I still have nightmares. I still occasionally flinch at random things, like the sound of chains or trunks slamming or even tall, bulky men coming at me on the sidewalk.

Holidays. Classes. Hockey.

Some weeks, it felt like I barely saw Carter. Being at a different school, on a different schedule and often playing away games in different cities meant too much time apart.

But now, FSU has made it to the Frozen Four championship game. In supreme irony, St. James was eliminated in the first round by a team from Minnesota.

Carter waits for me in my living room. I've barely spent time in my apartment, but I couldn't pull focus for Oliver, Penn, or my dad. Perri and I went to dinner a few nights, and Carter has been around more since his season ended.

It's been nice, but I'm still craving time with all three of them.

Together.

Today, Carter is wearing an FSU home jersey with Penn's name and number. The twenty on the sleeves and back, *Walker* across his shoulders.

"You look good in Framingham colors," I tell him.

His gaze drinks me in. "So do you."

I opted for black leggings and a long sleeve purple shirt, with an oversized jersey, emblazoned with the C on the chest, over it. For the record—I refused to wear his *actual* stinky jersey. This one, along with the one Carter wears, came from the merch table at a game.

He reels me in, hands on my hips, and places a kiss at the corner of my lips.

I smile.

"Ready?" He picks up a to-go coffee cup from my counter and hands it to me.

"Ready," I confirm.

We've got a four-hour drive to get to the game, and then we're staying overnight in the same hotel as the hockey team. Which means while Carter was in charge of supplying caffeine, I loaded up with snacks from the store near campus.

On the street, he opens the passenger door for me, waiting until I'm situated to close it gently and hurry around to the driver's side.

As passenger and partial navigator—I'm not really doing anything, since it's on the screen in the middle of the dash—

but I happily take the role of DJ. I scroll through his playlists and pick something we can sing along to, and it reminds me of before.

When things between us were light and fun.

My chest aches, and I find myself touching the bracelet. Grounding myself while I take a deep breath, then another, until my muscles loosen.

"You ever think about publishing your short stories?" Carter asks suddenly. "The girl with wings?"

I stare at him, but his gaze is fastened on the road. "Huh?"

"I mean, I kind of understood it was a connection to Icarus. At least, you were going along that same path. And the drawings..."

"Carter, I don't know what you're talking about."

His brows furrow. "Um, the journal you write and draw in. I snooped, I'll admit it, but then I got sucked in. Even if your handwriting was shit. I brought it with me."

"You—"

"Didn't think you'd notice," he says on a laugh. "And you didn't."

"I don't remember..." Well, that's not quite true. I have vague memories of writing in bed, furious scribbling to try and distract myself. Honest feelings in a fictional world.

But whether it's any good or not is up for debate.

He taps the center console, and I practically fall on it. I yank it open and withdraw my neglected journal.

I haven't opened it in six months, minimum. I run my hand over the cover, then flip it open. There's the one about being in love, there's the one about monsters and fragile things. I get to the last filled page and wince. The handwriting *is* rough.

I drew a girl with wings in the corner, practically sitting on the top line of words, her arms around her legs and feathered wings curled around her. I remember feeling like that.

She's on the next page, too, holding her stomach. Bleeding.

"I don't want to think about it right now," I murmur. My fingers have picked up remnants of charcoal. The cover of the journal, if not black, would probably show dark finger smudges. There are only about twenty pages left in the whole notebook.

"Okay," Carter agrees. "But I did type it up and submit some to an agent."

My jaw drops.

He shrugs. "You never know."

Great.

I mull that over. Carter leans forward and turns up the music—which is good, because I don't know what to think about his revelation.

Music in the club pulses through my body, urging me to move. I lean back on Penn, whose hands have been drifting since he stepped up behind me. His hips frame mine, and I allow a small smile.

Goalies have *moves*. I'm feeling warm, my body buzzing.

Oliver is surrounded by his teammates, but he's not far. They're celebrating a well-deserved win. They're champions this year.

Carter returns with drinks, a bottle of beer for Penn and him, a vodka and orange juice for me. Someone gave Penn a cardboard crown, like the kind the fast-food place would give out. Carter leans in and kisses me, and the vibration of Penn's groan in his chest travels through my back.

"We should get out of here," I breathe.

Carter's eyes light up, and he glances at Penn.

"Take our celebration more private?" Penn asks, his lips at my ear.

I nod.

"Get Ollie," Penn orders. He takes my hand and practically drags me to the exit. People know who he is, especially since the club is full of FSU students and fans that traveled to the game. I keep my drink in my hand, managing a sip when Penn gets held up by some guy wanting to shake his hand.

Which he does because you never know if there's professional representation. Imagine if he snubbed some guy in a club, only to find out they worked for the Colorado Titans?

Oliver and Carter meet us at the door.

As a unit, we head back to the hotel. We all get off on the same floor, but Carter stops at one door, while Oliver and Penn continue down.

"Where...?"

Carter glance over his shoulder and winks at me. A moment later, we're in the room and he's unlocking another. He opens it, revealing Penn.

My mouth drops. "You got us adjoining rooms?"

"You going to finish your drink, princess?" Penn asks, stepping through.

My gaze drops. I forgot I was holding it, which leaves me feeling a little guilty about stealing a glass from the club. I take a sip, then another.

"Hey, *mi nena*." Oliver draws my attention. He's already shed his shirt, his muscles gleaming in the low light. "Come here."

I go. He touches under my chin, tipping my head back, and leans down. My eyes flutter shut, just his fingers on my skin enough to undo me.

"You're wearing too many clothes," he says softly.

"You should solve that problem, then."

One of the others takes the glass from my hand. Oliver touches my waist, his fingers inching under the jersey. He lifts the fabric up, along with the shirt I wore under it, and pulls it off me. He drops it to the floor, his expression intensifying. My chest rises and falls, anticipation zipping through me.

I lick my lips, suddenly filled with the desire to taste him. I drop to my knees, my hands going to his pants. He makes a vague noise of protest, but then his cock is free, stiffening to point at me, and I take him in my mouth.

"Fuck," Carter groans. "That's hot."

Penn murmurs something too quiet to hear.

I look up at Oliver, my tongue stroking the underside of his shaft. His fingers slide into my hair. His expression is dark, his lips parted. He moves his hips a little, sliding deeper into my mouth. The tip of his cock hits the back of my throat.

I work him until he withdraws, stepping away. Penn and Carter lift me back to my feet. One unclips my bra, the other pulls my pants down. It's hard to keep track of who's touching where, until Oliver redirects my attention. His hand comes around the back of my neck, and he kisses me fast.

A finger slides inside me.

I groan into Oliver's mouth. His tongue strokes mine, the kiss—and other touches—burning me from the inside out.

We haven't all been together like this...

Honestly, it seemed like something I wasn't sure anyone would be cool with. But we're rolling with it now, and when I break away from Oliver's lips, Penn is right there, pulling my head to the side to have his turn.

"On the bed," Carter orders.

He slaps my ass, and I jump. I smirk at him, tossing my hair over my shoulder. The alcohol has lowered my reservations enough to even *wink* in the face of my sudden nerves.

I crawl on the bed and twist around, leaning against the row of pillows at the headboard.

My three guys—*that doesn't get old*—are all watching me with hungry expressions.

Good.

"Well?" I question. "How are we—"

"I'll watch. For now." Carter moves to the second bed and takes a seat.

Oliver and Penn exchange a glance. Penn sheds the cardboard crown, throwing it onto the desk, and climbs on the bed. He takes hold of my ankles and pulls me flat, then moves over me.

A chill travels down my spine. I part my legs for him, and he places a soft kiss on my throat. Then my jaw. The corner of my lips.

"Penn," I breathe.

"Are you nice and slick for me, princess?"

He shifts, running his finger along my core. I whimper when he pauses on my clit, and my hips automatically shift.

"Hmm."

"Stop teasing," Oliver murmurs behind him.

"Captain's orders, princess." Penn meets my eyes. He notches himself at my entrance and pushes, slowly thrusting into me.

The stretch is delicious. But I have a feeling this is just a drop in the bucket. He rocks into me faster, until he abruptly stops and rolls us. I gasp at the change—and how I now straddle him.

He smiles. "Give us a show."

I raise my eyebrows, but I'm not going to argue. My hands fall to his abdomen, keeping my balance as I rise up and lower back down.

"Oliver," Carter says. "Help her out."

The bed dips, and Oliver swings his leg over Penn's. His hands come around, cupping my breasts. He pinches my nipples. Penn makes a noise under me. He grips my thighs, but they drift toward my core.

"I want to feel you come on my cock," Penn tells me. "But I think I want to feel Ollie in your ass, first..."

Fuck.

I glance over my shoulder. Oliver smirks, then presses a

kiss to my shoulder. He releases my breasts and moves down, parting my ass cheeks.

"Lube," Carter interjects, tossing Oliver a small bottle.

I should really be better at getting the birth control shot...

I may have missed my last appointment.

The sudden stress is offset by Oliver's finger sliding down my ass crack and pressing inside me. He thrusts, almost lazily, for a minute.

No one is in a hurry, but I'm starting to burn up. Penn has gone still. Even his fingers on my clit aren't moving. Just a bit of pressure. He can probably feel the throb of it that's beginning to echo through my body.

Oliver removes his fingers. A hand on my spine urges me to lean forward. I touch Penn's cheek as Oliver slowly—*slowly*—pushes inside.

"Oh, fuck." Penn looks sideways at Carter. "How hot does this look?"

I glance over, too. Carter's expression is intense. He's got his cock out, and his hand is measuredly stroking it. I lick my lips, then open my mouth to say something—but then Oliver thrusts the rest of the way in, and my mind blanks.

"Ready?" Oliver asks.

Me, Penn—I don't know who he's talking to. I've never been this full. But Penn says *yes*, and suddenly they're both moving. Penn's fingers on my clit, the way he thrusts up into me. Oliver's purposeful, powerful thrusts that seem to match his teammate's. Every move feels compounded by the other.

"Fuck." Penn stares up at me, his pupils dilating.

And then I'm at the edge.

"More," Carter breathes.

Penn grabs the back of my neck, dragging me down and kissing me hard. His teeth score my lower lip. I give him my gasps of pleasure, and a minute later, I orgasm so hard everything goes white for a second. My vision, the sound in the room.

"Dream girl," Carter says suddenly.

I look sideways at him, blinking, and automatically open my mouth. His dick slides along my tongue, and I hum at the taste. There's too much sensation. I grip Penn's shoulder, trying to keep myself grounded. But on the heels of my climax, Penn's hands have drifted up to my breasts. And Carter's fingers thread through my hair. Oliver--

"I can't hold it," he groans. "The way you clench around me, *mi nena*. I'm—"

His pace quickens, then slams to a halt inside me.

I groan, sucking hard as Carter becomes more assertive. Every thrust into my mouth hits the back of my throat, then pushes deeper.

"You look so fucking hot, dream girl," Carter says. "Taking us at the same time like a good girl. Letting me take your throat."

Penn hisses out a breath, continuing to lift his hips and move slowly inside me from below. I think Oliver can feel it. His fingers at my hips tighten, then he carefully withdraws. Penn is the next to come. His cock pulses inside me, and my muscles tense around him again.

After a minute, Carter pulls out of my mouth and lifts me into his arms. He turns and pins me to the wall, sliding inside me where Penn was only moments ago. He kisses me fast and hard, matching the wicked pace he sets. My hand slips between us, rubbing my clit. I'm slick—a mixture of arousal and Penn's release—and I work myself toward another orgasm easily.

Because these three are it for me.

It's like their bodies were made for mine. Their minds, too.

I bite Carter's lip, and the taste of blood touches my tongue. He groans. It spurs him on, and I crest another climax right before him.

We come. Our mouths don't separate, not until he's done

thoroughly kissing me. My feet return to the floor, and his hands remain on my waist to keep me steady.

"That was worth the wait," I finally say, tucking my hair behind my ear.

"Good," Carter whispers. "I'm so in love with you, dream girl."

I stare into his eyes. Blue. Steady. Reassuring. It's easy to say, "I'm in love with you, too." And to tear my gaze away from his, to meet Penn's, then Oliver's. "I'm in love with all of you."

"Right back at you, princess." Penn's eyes gleam.

Oliver nudges Carter out of the way, until he's all I can see. He cups my cheek. "*Te amo, mi nena.*"

My heart swells.

Then Penn coughs. "Well, now that the mushy shit is out of the way, I'm going to order room service. We've got to fuel up so we can do that again."

And again, and again, and again...

THE END

acknowledgments

My readers made this story happen.

Okay, maybe not *literally*, since I wrote it. But without them saying they wanted all of the Hockey Gods, that they hated choosing between them (that's our favorite pastime, making readers pick their favorite book boyfriend, after all), the idea for this story wouldn't have been born.

Three dark hockey men focused on one girl.

I mean... I dig it. I hope you guys did, too.

There are a lot of people who've touched this story to help it take shape: my early readers with their invaluable feedback, my editor and proofreader, my wonderful cover designer. My Patreon, who has been reading along chapter by chapter for months now.

And you.

As I said, my readers made this happen, and you're one of them now. Sorry, no take backs. Just by reading this you've been inducted to the club (which has a physical form on Facebook: S. Massery Squad).

Thank you for your enthusiasm and support.

I appreciate you more than you know.

acknowledgments

about the author

S. Massery is a dark romance author who loves injecting a good dose of suspense into her stories. Originally from Massachusetts, she now lives in Southern California with her dog, Alice.

Before adventuring into the world of writing, she went to college in Boston and held a wide variety of jobs—including working on a dude ranch in Wyoming (a personal highlight). She has a love affair with coffee and chocolate. When S. Massery isn't writing, she can be found devouring books, playing outside with her dog, or trying to make people smile.

Join her newsletter to stay up to date on new releases: http://smassery.com/newsletter

also by s. massery

Hockey Gods

Brutal Obsession

Devious Obsession

Secret Obsession

Twisted Obsession

Fierce Obsession

Shadow Valley U (co-written with SJ Sylvis)

Sticks and Stones

SVU Book 2

Sterling Falls

#0 THRILL

#1 THIEF

#2 FIGHTER

#3 REBEL

#4 QUEEN

Sterling Falls Rogues

#0 TERROR

Fallen Royals

#1 Wicked Dreams

#2 Wicked Games

#3 Wicked Promises

#4 Cruel Abandon

#5 Wild Fury

DeSantis Mafia

#1 Ruthless Saint

#2 Savage Prince

#3 Stolen Crown

Broken Mercenaries

#1 Blood Sky

#2 Angel of Death

#3 Morning Star

More at http://smassery.com/ebooks

where to find sara

Thank you so much for coming along on these crazy boys' journeys with me.

If you like my stories, I'd highly encourage you to come join my Facebook group, S. Massery Squad. There's a lot of fun stuff happening in there, and they're who I go to for polls about future books (fun fact: some key details in this series is decided by their votes!), where I share teasers, etc!

My Patreon is also an awesome place to connect and get exclusive content! On release months, I do signed paperbacks. Plus, get ARCs, audiobooks, and artwork before the rest of the world. Find me here: http://patreon.com/smassery

And last but not least, here are some social media links for ya:

Facebook: Author S Massery
Instagram: @authorsmassery
Tiktok: @smassery
Goodreads: S. Massery
Bookbub: S. Massery

brutal obsession
(chapter sneak peek)

Greyson

The cash slides from my palm into the valet's. His fingers curl around the wad of bills as he pulls back, and he looks away.

Aw, he's embarrassed.

The girl on my arm giggles and leans into me.

Money and good looks will help people get away with just about anything. I learned that at the tender age of five from my father, thank you very much. He toted me around and flashed his smile or his wealth, and doors opened for us.

Sometimes literally.

Sometimes figuratively.

We were invincible.

Look at that sentence. Then read it again. *We. Were. Invincible.*

Back when I was a kid, my father and I wore gilded armor. He was a king, and I was a prince. We floated above the rest of society, and nothing was out of our reach.

I experienced the world through my father's view of getting everything he fucking wanted. It's only natural that I became him.

Look, I'm not saying it's right. I'm just saying this is how it works. People are sheep, all too eager to be sacrificed to the wolves. And the wolves... well, they only survived if they were willing to get a little dirty.

The girl releases me long enough to stumble around the hood of my car. She practically falls into the passenger seat, her dress shifting to give me—and the valet—an eyeful of her tits.

That right there is the only reason she's here.

Paparazzi cameras flash from across the street, and I turn on my brilliant smile. The one that worked on the girl at the bar. And the waitress. And the cop who pulled me over a few hours ago for speeding. He let me off with just a warning.

I raise my hand as someone calls my name. Trying to get me to make eye contact, to get the perfect photo. Everyone wants something but fuck them if they think they can *get* it. They get the bare minimum of my acknowledgement, and it probably gives them a hard-on.

The passenger door shuts. I take one more look at the valet, making sure he knows. I see him. I saw him put the cash into his pocket. I want him to know that the money doesn't buy speedy service—it buys his silence.

He nods once, then averts his eyes again.

I slip into my car and leave the restaurant parking lot with a screech of tires. The familiar, intoxicating smell of burning rubber follows me. I love it—it means I'm making an exit. One that people will notice—and remember.

The nameless girl leans over and licks my cheek. I'm undecided if it's hot or gross, so I ignore it. She whispers something that I also ignore, and I press my foot harder on the gas pedal. I don't care about her right now.

Only two more streets before we hit the highway, and I can push this baby to a hundred. She has a certain purr when she gets that quick. The steering wheel almost vibrates in my hands.

It's an adrenaline rush I never pass up.

Later, when the girl is sucking my cock and moaning my name, I might pretend to give a shit about her.

I shift her away and readjust my grip.

We skid around a corner, our light green. I hit the gas, and we fly down the darkened street. Ahead of me, the stretch of road is empty—until it isn't.

The car comes out of nowhere. My headlights illuminate the driver's pale face seconds before I smash into her vehicle.

My airbags explode, and only my seatbelt, which I don't remember putting on, keeps me from rocketing through the windshield. My passenger's head slams into her airbag, and she falls back against the seat. Blood drips down her face from her nose.

I struggle to inhale. The seatbelt is too fucking tight, and smoke fills my car.

I unbuckle and shove my door open, falling out.

Fuck.

The asphalt bites into my palms. Miraculously, though, I'm unhurt. I pat myself down just for the hell of it, but besides what I can imagine will be a pretty nasty bruise across my chest, I'm okay.

The girl in my car seems to be okay, too. She regains consciousness, blinking slowly and touching her upper lip.

I stumble around to the front of my car, which is currently smashed up against the other one. A silver compact car, one of those old ones from a decade ago. I hit the driver's side, but ahead of the seat. It almost appears like I was aiming for the front tire—in an effort to avoid her entirely, I guess, and I just miscalculated. That's how it could be argued, one way or another. *If* it's going to be argued.

"Help." Her voice is soft, hoarse. Like she screamed before impact, and her throat shredded.

I wince.

She has blood streaked down her face, and I can't tell if her eyes are open or not. Her airbags didn't deploy, but her window is broken. Glass cuts, then. And even though I didn't hit it, her door is dented inward.

The street is empty. No cars, no people. When does *that* ever happen in a city like this? A city that usually buzzes with nightlife—in fact, it *is* probably buzzing with people only a few blocks away.

I nod to myself, calculating. Always calculating.

Another gift from Daddy Dearest.

I go back to my car and open the passenger door. I pull the girl out and lead her around, sitting her in the driver's seat. I fold her into it, even as she stares at me. Confusion mars her face, turning it ugly.

Confusion is akin to stupidity. If you can't understand something, you're just not thinking about it hard enough.

"Where's your phone, baby?"

Bless her soul, she perks up when I call her that. It's not her fault she doesn't know it's my cover, because I don't have a clue what her name is. She points to the floor of the passenger seat. To her purse.

"You were driving," I tell her. I lean into her, cupping the back of her neck. "I need you to tell them that, okay?"

Her brow furrows. "Why?"

"Because I'll make sure your wildest dreams come true if you do this for me." I meet her eyes, my thumb rubbing a soft spot on her neck just under her ear. She leans into it, barely, and sucks her lower lip into her mouth. "You borrowed my car for the night. You were going to return it to me tomorrow."

"Tomorrow," she repeats.

I nod once and release her, closing her back into the door. I dial nine-one-one on her phone and hand it to her, then take a step back. Once I'm halfway down the block, I call my father.

I thought that would be the end of the story. He wouldn't blame me for leaving the scene. It isn't just about getting our way. It's about preserving his image. *Our* image.

512

Exactly as I predict, he doesn't say a word about my bad luck. Or who I was with. I send him the address of the house I'm sitting in front of, and he sends a car for me.

I arrive home thirty minutes later, and he doesn't ask what happened. He's like a lawyer, unwilling to incriminate himself in the fine print. If anything comes up, he'll expect me to smooth it over. If I can't, he will.

Two hours later, the cop cars come screaming into our driveway. I'm arrested on the spot.

Read it here: http://mybook.to/brutalobsession